THE NEONS

DYLAN WISEMAN

A NOTE FROM THE AUTHOR

This book won't win any awards, and that's totally okay. My hope is only that this book can do for you what many other books have done for me. That is, provide an escape from reality to somewhere more exciting, if only for a short time.

This is my very first novel ever—if this is as far as you read, thank you for picking it up! I hope to write many more stories, in both this same universe and in universes I haven't dreamed up yet.

The Neons is book one of a very twisted and tangled three-book mystery. If you figure it out as you're reading, please let me know, I'd love to hear what you think.

Enjoy!

Dylan

For anyone who lives an ordinary life, but wishes that someone in a hat and cloak would come along to spirit them away on an extraordinary adventure

0 AFTERPARTY

"**Y**ou're going to die if we don't get you out."

Emry lay on her stomach on the diving board of the pool, her arms dangling into the water, where a large golden koi tickled her fingertips with its mouth. "How did you even get in here?" she asked the fish, running a hand along the scales on its back.

The koi turned and swam away, and Emry followed it with her eyes as it navigated between plastic cups, colorful streamers, and the other remnants of last night's party that drifted in the pool.

Flicking the water off her fingers, Emry crossed her arms under her chin and gazed over the expansive garden that sprawled outward from the back of the house. The garden followed the slope of the hill, down until it met an old stone wall that marked the end of the property. Beyond the wall, the hill dropped off into a dramatic view of the city of Xi below.

But today, the view was lacking. The sky was humid and overcast, and a warm fog obscured all but the nearest towers in the skyline.

The yard had looked better, too. The same festive debris that filled the pool was littered across the grass and hung from the tree branches.

As she scanned the scene, Emry's eyes caught every detail in ultra-clarity, thanks to a gift from her father—an updated vision mod that was not scheduled to be released to the public for another six months. It was almost too much; she had to close her eyes for a moment to keep from being overwhelmed.

"Happy Birthday, Ms. Rush," an android butler greeted her as it approached from the house.

"Hm." Taking a deep breath, Emry pushed herself up from the diving board and strode around the water's edge, eventually finding a seat on one of the only pool chairs that hadn't been overturned. She shrugged the plush robe off her shoulders and held it around her chest, and the android stepped politely over to her side.

"Pardon the mess; it seems I'm the only one available to clean this morning," the AI bowed apologetically. In the robot's metal arms was a white marble bust of an old man. The nose had been broken off, and a pink party hat sat crooked on its head.

"What happened to Grandpa Kian?" Emry asked, frowning at the cracked bust.

"It seems someone thought he would enjoy the party," the droid replied in a dismayed tone, but its metal face and dark eyes displayed no emotion. "I will see what I can do about his nose."

"Rest in peace, I guess," Emry ran a hand through her tangle of golden hair. "Where's Dad?"

"Your father is in the office."

"Right." *Where else would he be?* "What time is it?"

"It's just after 2:00 p.m."

Emry rubbed her eyes distractedly, pausing as a flood of notifications and messages began to populate the black behind her eyelids. An alert from her bank showed most recently—a large sum of credits had been sent to her account. Emry dismissed the rest of the notifications before they could steal her attention.

"We have food ready for you in the kitchen. Breakfast or lunch, whichever you prefer," The servant continued as Emry opened her eyes.

"What time did everyone leave?"

"We had the last of the guests out by 6:30 a.m."

Over to the side of the pool, a small stage was partially collapsed. Emry remembered being put on someone's shoulders and the DJ leading the crowd in an electrified version of "Happy Birthday" shortly after midnight. She also remembered hitting the water hard and being lifted out by two friends. As Emry gazed at the rippling pool, other scenes flashed through her mind, her brain doing its best to reconstruct the events of the evening and arrange them in chronological order. Somehow, Emry had made it into her own bed last night. She pictured the android picking her up and carrying her there in the same way it was cleaning the trash.

"How does it feel to be eighteen?"

Emry had zoned out, the robot still by her side.

"How does it feel—"

"—it feels the same. Mom's not here, is she?"

"Your mother is still abroad."

Right.

Emry let her thoughts drift again as she watched the fog in the distance part, momentarily revealing a collection of chrome skyscrapers that had turned a dull gray in the cloudy weather. One of the buildings, Seitech Headquarters, was her father's. As Xi's monopolizing mod manufacturers, Seitech basically owned the City. And that made her father, CEO and owner, the most powerful man in Xi. People looked at him like a king. But, to Emry, he was just Dad, and he was at work *all*—

"Also," the AI called her focus back to the poolside.

"Hm?" Emry turned slowly.

"Another gift for you," the servant said, holding out a pink box tied in a matching bow. "We found it as we were escorting the last of the guests to their vehicles."

"Who is it from?" Emry asked, adjusting her robe and taking the box.

"I am not sure, but there is a note."

Tied into the ribbon was a small, folded message. She opened it.

Now that the world is watching you - Riley

"I don't know any Riley," Emry mused, untying the bow and sliding the cover off the box.

Inside, nestled gently against soft pink velvet, was a mod tile. A small chip, about one square centimeter in size and only slightly thicker than a sheet of paper, loaded with ready-to-install biocode. Emry carefully lifted the tile and set the box on the chair beside her. Holding the tile up to the gloomy sunlight, she could see it was semi-transparent. Inside was the faint design of a hand.

"It must be custom—" Emry commented, turning over her shoulder to the robot, but it had moved.

"Our scans concluded that the mod is safe to install," the android responded from across the pool as it bent down to pick the top half of a red swimsuit out of the water. "Is this yours?"

"You mean you looked at my presents?"

"We scanned them, yes."

"*Scanned*," Emry mocked the robot under her breath, and it paused, watching her, waiting to see if she had more to say. They stared at each other for a moment. "You're new," Emry observed. "What's your name?"

"I am, yes," the AI replied. "My name at creation was Caesar, though you may call me whatever you like."

"Big name for a servant."

"The best leaders are always the best servants."

"Who are you leading?"

"An army of housekeepers, my lady," Caesar bowed.

Emry looked around the empty yard. "Right. Thanks for cleaning, Caesar. Don't let that fish die in there."

The droid nodded and obediently resumed its work.

Emry examined the mod tile gift in her hand. "Could be fun," she smiled to herself. At eighteen, she was legally allowed to install any number and variety of legal mods, whereas, for the past three years, her options had been limited, like all minors. Not that anyone really cared what the law said. Half the people who had come to the party could be arrested if the authorities actually cared to check people's code for the illicit stuff. Her father would have cared, though, probably. *If* he had bothered to stay at the party for more than ten minutes. He was big on mod regulation and code safety—something that made a lot of people mad.

A lone cicada began to chirp in a nearby tree as low clouds drifted slowly overhead.

"Hot," Emry announced to the yard, standing up from her poolside chair and sliding the mod tile into her robe pocket. "Hot and humid today," she declared, flaring her robe dramatically as she turned and headed back into the house.

The air was much cooler inside as Emry meandered her way to the kitchen. A large platter of carefully arranged fruit greeted her from the polished table, and she picked a large strawberry from the assortment.

"We have whatever you would like for your birthday," a warm voice responded from the walls of the kitchen as a holographic display glittered to life and began to outline the available food options.

Emry waved the display out of existence and drifted into the large, glass-walled living room. Through the far wall, she could see out into the garden and the gray city beyond. She scrunched her toes on the soft carpet and took a bite from her strawberry.

"Cerberus," Emry put a hand out, and the dog stirred from his spot on the floor and lumbered over in her direction. "Happy birthday to you, too," Emry scratched the chin of the modified war hound, and he nuzzled his head into her shoulder. At two years old, he was nearly three times her weight. Emry squeezed his face, kissed his nose, and fed him the rest of her strawberry.

Then she waved her hand through the air, and the walls of the room changed, darkening into black screens populated with the notifications she had dismissed earlier. Mostly birthday messages, hundreds of them.

She flicked through a handful, replying to some and ignoring others, then sighing, she let the walls return to their transparent state, wrapped herself tightly in her robe, and dropped onto one of the couches. Propping her head up, she stared out the large window in silence. Quiet thoughts moved through her head like the clouds of fog through the distant skyscrapers. Just passing through. Soft and gray.

Letting her mind drift, Emry began to play with the bracelet on her wrist—a simple, clean bangle of precious metal engraved with the family name, *Rush*, in tiny letters. Supposedly, it had once belonged to her aunt, then her grandmother before that, and so on, back to the generations that had all come and gone. Emry twisted the metal anxiously, then dropped her hands on her chest.

"Look at me now, I'm all grown up," Emry spoke to the ceiling. "Wish you could've seen the party. Wish you weren't fucking dead—" Emry stopped and shut her eyes against the emotions. She could reverse the feelings if she wanted. With a thought, she could chemically and biologically dam the river of pain flowing into her mind and let it build up for another day. But that would only postpone the suffering; best to face the feelings head-on.

She took a breath. "I'm an *adult* now."

Adult. The notion meant little to her. There wasn't anything in particular that she had been looking forward to or waiting to try. If anything, it only meant the media would be after her more. At first, she and her friends had been excited to see people whispering and pointing discreetly in their direction, but since then, the cameras had gotten more aggressive and more intentionally annoying.

Emry ran a hand through her hair, and the color changed to a deep navy, the natural frizz straightening into flat sheets. She blinked twice, and her irises shifted to match. Placing a hand on her neck, she dragged three fingers down toward her collar, and her skin tone darkened.

It was a weak disguise, but a couple quick changes in the middle of a crowd and she could lose the hounding paparazzi just long enough to get free.

Outside the window, a brightly feathered songbird fluttered to the ground. Cerberus gave it a suspicious side-eye.

Emry moved her attention back to the tiny present in her pocket. If Caesar said it was safe, then that was enough for her. She turned the small tile in her hands and looked out again at the mist-covered cityscape. "Let's see what this mod does then, *Riley.*"

PART ONE

"Living systems are never in equilibrium. They are inherently unstable. They may seem stable, but they're not. Everything is moving and changing. In a sense, everything is on the edge of collapse."
— Michael Crichton, Jurassic Park

1 THE VANISHED PRINCESS

"Read this!"

Chance leaned backward, setting the bowl he had been pretending to clean back onto the counter as the patron across from him shoved a tablet screen in his face. He took the tablet from the man's trembling hands, glancing up at the character on the other side of the bar. The man was a regular. His name was Goosh. Or at least, they called him Goosh, and he looked exactly like anyone would expect someone with that name to look—like a corpse that had started to rot but then decided it wasn't actually dead yet. His skin was wrinkly and sagging and covered in green patches; stringy, white hairs curled out of his head like dying weeds. His eyes moved constantly, and his whole body jittered, as if he was always on the run, paranoid about being caught. And he always *always* had a new conspiracy theory to show Chance.

"Read it!" Goosh said again. His teeth seemed like they might fall out at any moment. Chance looked down at the screen in his hands.

On the display was a video of a pretty blonde girl in a brightly colored sundress, smiling and waving at someone out of frame. Behind her stood an important looking man that Chance felt he should have recognized. Under the video was a small blurb:

Princess Kidnapped?

Emry Rush, daughter of Seitech owner Orland Rush, disappeared less than 24 hours after her 18th birthday. Friends, family, and the city's socialites descended on the extravagant Rush mansion on the night of Saturday the 14th to celebrate—

"And now," Goosh snatched the tablet out of Chance's hands. "Look at this!" he said, replacing it with a crumpled piece of paper. Chance flattened out the paper as much as he could on the bar top. Goosh was a lunatic, but his theories were mildly entertaining.

Chance looked at the paper. "I don't understand it. It's just scribbles," he showed the paper to Goosh.

"Oh-oh, not that," he snatched the paper out of Chance's hand and shoved it back into his crusty leather bag. "Mmm, this!" he said, digging around in the bag and pulling out a fishing magazine.

An old-school paper magazine. "Where did you find this...?" Chance watched as Goosh flipped madly through the pages and stopped on an article titled *Glow-Squids: The Secret to Catching Xi River's Creepiest Creatures.*

"See, look at this!" Goosh spun the magazine around and pointed Chance to a spot in the article he had highlighted:

...found that Mr. Park had been using human flesh as bait to catch the squid, but not just any human flesh. It had been the flesh of his own children.

"So... you think..."

"Yes." Goosh lowered his voice and leaned in.

"Um, you think that this girl—dammit, Goosh," Chance gagged and stepped back. Goosh smelled horrible. "You think that she's being used for squid bait?"

Goosh's eyes got wide. "Yes, I think so."

Chance nodded slowly, eager for Goosh to be gone. "Maybe you should go ask the fishermen at the River what they think."

Goosh sat quietly for a moment, then, without a word, grabbed the magazine off the counter and hobbled out the door.

"And brush your damn teeth," Chance muttered after him.

The other patrons in the restaurant watched him go. Not that any of them were much less weird than Goosh was. Down on the Surface, in this odd pocket of the City, everyone was more than a little strange.

"What did he talk—what did he talk about this time?"

Chance turned as Benson, the noodle shop's android server, walked in from the back kitchen. "Squids," Chance replied. "And something about a girl who disappeared?"

Benson nodded in response and planted himself behind the bar next to Chance. "The dishes in the back are—"

Chance waited; the robot had a painfully glitchy stutter.

"—are, are, the dishes are washed. Do you have any more tasks for me to complete?"

Chance thought for a moment and surveyed the room. It was a tiny place. A hole-in-the-wall, really. Between the lunch and dinner rush, there wasn't much to do. "Do squids eat meat?"

Benson took a second to find an answer. "Yes, mostly fish and, and crabs. Some, sometimes other squids."

"Hm," Chance nodded.

Benson waited quietly for more. His eyes were black and made of electronic circuits and glass lenses, but they reflected a sort of warmth.

Chance picked up the already-clean bowl he had been polishing and tapped it in his hand. There really wasn't any other work left for the day.

Benson watched patiently.

"I'm tired of this place," Chance spoke candidly, setting the bowl back on the counter a little too hard. A flighty-looking man at a nearby table jumped nervously at the sound.

"You, you—you have said something similar every day for the past sixteen days," Benson replied in stereotypical accuracy.

"I know. I'm just..." Chance lowered his voice sarcastically, "really damn tired of it."

"Perhaps it's time for you to find a new—a new job?"

Chance watched as the customers slurped at their noodles and spun tiny whirlpools in their drinks. None of them looked particularly stoked on life either. Maybe that's the way it was meant to be. People work so they can eat so they can keep working, then they die of boredom, and no one cares. At first, Chance had been excited to start working—less time at home meant less time around his mom's boyfriend of the month—but the dull reality of life in Xi had quickly swallowed up most of his aspirations. Not that he had much reason to believe that his life was destined to have any more significance than, say, Goosh's, or anyone else's for that matter. A boy born to a single mother on the Surface, he was one of the many nearly worthless souls that just seemed to *exist* in the flickering lights and chrome walls that made up the City.

And he wasn't particularly good at anything special or talented in any remarkable way. He was decently athletic, scrappy as he had to be, growing up in between the streets and angry stepdads, but compared to anyone with even the cheapest of physical enhancement mods, he was weak. He got along well with people, learning early on that he was better at avoiding conflicts than he was at finishing them. But he wasn't a gifted artist or dancer or genius as sometimes seemed to rise up out of the Surface dwellers. What he *was* was cursed. Cursed with a single, dangerous, and glitchy mod. But he didn't like to think about that too much. "Maybe I just need a purpose," he pondered out loud. "Benson, what's your purpose?" he asked, turning to the droid.

"I, I was programmed to assist. My purpose is to serve." Benson nodded. "To serve."

"That's a good purpose... Maybe I can make that mine too," Chance sighed and leaned onto the bar.

"Perhaps you simply need some excitement. Finding romance might help."

Chance snorted. A robot telling him he should find love. That's rich.

The day dragged on. Patrons came and went, and at some point, Mr. Bird, the shop's owner, stumbled down the back staircase. He was drunk as usual. Like Goosh, Mr. Bird's name was also unusually fitting. Two long, skinny legs protruded from his large, spherical upper body. His nose was long and pointed like a beak, and he always seemed to bend at the hips whenever he needed to speak to someone, like a fat crow pecking at the ground for food.

Mr. Bird bumped between tables as he walked in, shouted something about how useless robots are, pointed at Benson, and then disappeared into the kitchen. That was how interactions with Mr. Bird typically went.

"Okay," Chance folded up his apron and dropped it on a shelf behind the counter. "I'm going home."

"I—I, I have recorded your time clock. I will see you tomorrow," Benson responded.

"Goodnight, Mr. Robot," Chance waved over his shoulder on his way out.

It was dark out, or at least it would be dark if Chance could see the sky from the street. Bridges, levels, platforms, and other metallic structures crisscrossed overhead, replacing the stars with neon and LEDs. Xi. Home.

Electricity sparked, and the air crackled as a bullet train blurred past on a rail overhead. Further above, someone stepped out onto a balcony and lit a cigarette, breathing smoke into the night. Higher still, millions of others would be going about their individual lives: Shopping, sleeping, planning, relaxing, going places, returning home, meeting friends, making love, and crossing paths. As much as he complained about it, the City enchanted Chance. So much life, so many *lives*, each one a story and timeline as meaningful and complex as his own.

But again, not that he felt his was all that meaningful to begin with.

Chance sighed as the light in front of him changed, and he realized he had missed the traffic signal in his pondering. He stood at the corner as a small crowd of pedestrians joined him, waiting for the next light. A man stepped up to his left, and Chance examined the stranger's bionic arm. The man flexed his fingers around the handle of the briefcase he was carrying, and, in his forearm, Chance could see the machinery that could quickly assemble itself into a pen, a knife, a gun, or whatever its owner might need it to be.

Most people in the City had some sort of self-defense mechanism, whether it was a weapon or mod or a knowledge of martial arts. Xi, and especially in parts down here on the Surface, was a dangerous place, so, as common as things like a bionic arm might be, he could never be too wary.

Chance placed a hand lightly on his ribcage. He had his own way of protecting himself—the cursed mod—something that had kept him alive in more than one dangerous encounter.

The light changed again, and Chance flowed with the school of pedestrians. The night air on the street was warm and humid, like it almost always was, which Chance found comforting. Steam from the underground drifted up through vents in the road, and street merchants bustled around various run-down storefronts and makeshift tents, some closing shop, others opening for the night. This particular area of town, the area where Chance worked and lived, was called the Riverbed. Supposedly, it was named that because Xi River was only a few blocks away, but as Chance looked at the city-dwellers jumping from one dilapidated vendor to the next, he couldn't help but feel that he had walked into some kind of urban swamp.

Some were selling food, drinks, news, electronics (which Chance assumed were stolen), counterfeit apparel... the usual items. These advertised their goods openly. Other offerings were shadier, and their proprietors were more selective of their potential customers.

A man only several years older than Chance himself nodded as Chance approached.

"What's new?" Chance asked. Chance had stopped at this guy several times before, but he could never remember his name, and he was sure that the man didn't remember his either. But they recognized each other, and that counted for something in a city of nearly two hundred million.

"A few things," the man replied, pulling a small device out of his pocket and casting a blue hologram into the space between them.

The hologram was of a mod tile, enlarged to show detail, and underneath the tile was a name and description:

N-R-G v7.8

Increases energy at all times of day. Increases efficiency in your body's energy using.

"You can swipe through. There's more." As the man spoke, he kept an eye on the people walking past and one hand near his waist, probably concealing a gun.

Chance moved his hand through the hologram, and the display changed.

Opun Mynd

Improves clarity of thought and improves mental processing of complex problems.

Chance swiped through several more: BVA.3, PWWWR *plus*, *Recon Eyes*. Even if the mods were safe to use (which they probably weren't), Chance's Interface would most likely crash the second he tried to install one. The crash could cause his DNA to deconstruct or his brain to override the breathing function with useless data. For someone who was already glitching, as he often did, even perfectly coded mods could cause random errors. Not to mention the fact that he couldn't afford a mod at this time anyway.

"If you see one you like, Oss can take you to the back room." The man nodded backward at a silent, intimidating droid standing in front of an unmarked door.

Chance stopped on a mod named *Halfvisible* before waving the hologram away. "Not today." *And probably not ever*, he thought to himself. But Chance still liked to look anyway.

The man shrugged and put the device back in his pocket. "I'll see you around then."

As he turned back to the street, Chance made eye contact with a young woman under the next tent over. She stood swaying back and forth slightly, a look of complete resignation on her face as a pulsing purple light illuminated her frame. She held Chance's gaze, and Chance found it hard to look away.

"You want a girlfriend?"

Chance didn't even react as a small, old woman jumped in front of him. He had been targeted by similar vendors before.

"I'll give you a special deal," she said, nodding back at the young woman. "Come in the tent," she urged, grabbing Chance's wrist. Something like a mix of rage and sadness stirred deep inside his chest, but Chance took a deep breath and quelled the emotion.

He shook the old lady off and kept moving.

"You are a handsome young man. She likes you." The old lady kept stride beside him.

Chance walked on, ignoring the woman and refusing to look down at her.

"Fine. Be alone forever," the old lady muttered as she waddled off.

Many lives, Chance thought to himself.

Fortunately, it was only a short walk from Mr. Bird's shop to Chance's apartment, if he could even call it an apartment. The first room contained a small wobbly table, a miniature kitchen, and a ratty mattress that sat on the floor. The second room was a cramped bedroom. Sounds and lights from the television leaked out of the cracked door.

Shutting the apartment door behind himself, Chance flicked the light on, and the bulb immediately popped, igniting the room with a flash and then leaving it dark again. Groaning, he walked over to the small window on the opposite wall and yanked the blinds open. Light from a streetlamp outside bathed the room in an orange aura. Bits of trash and odd junk scattered on the floor. Dirty clothes piled up in the corner. The apartment was a microcosm of the surrounding city.

Laughter echoed from the television in the bedroom. Chance peaked through the crack. Mom was lying on the bed, staring blankly at the ceiling, the opened packaging of a vacation beside her.

Vacations, trip mods, hallucinogens—all names for the same thing. Single-use mod tiles that send the mind somewhere else. Kinda like drugs, kinda like dreaming. Incredibly addictive.

Chance watched his mother for a moment to make sure she was breathing, then pulled the door shut.

Peeling his dampened work shirt off his back, Chance sat on the edge of the table and stared into the mirror on the wall opposite him. His dark eyes glowed ever so slightly, the tell-tale sign of an installed human.

Almost everyone in the City was installed with a BTI, or 'Bio-Technical Interface,' of some kind or another. Only the extremely poor or people with some moral divergence went uninstalled. But for everyone else, the ability to control and manipulate their mental and physical state through the use of mods was too big of a benefit to pass on for any reason. Aside from the faintly glowing eyes, the BTI itself didn't leave much of an imprint on the body. The technology was on the nanoscale, a combination of biology and technology that fused itself into every cell and capillary and every sinew and synapse. After several decades, the BTI was becoming a mature technology, but within a few years of its initial introduction, it had become an essential part of life. With the right mods, people were immune to nearly all diseases; they were stronger, healthier, more attractive, smarter, and overall improved in whatever ways they could afford.

But again, mods also had a dangerous side. If the mod code was written imperfectly, it could harm you, cause physical and mental defects, crash your whole system, or even kill you on the spot.

Chance was living proof of that danger. Huffing through his nose, he pushed himself off the table and started brushing his teeth at the kitchen sink.

Installing the mods was a simple process, similar to the way in which kids would apply temporary tattoos, and, unlike the BTI, the mods themselves each left a unique mark on the skin. Some people wore their mod marks proudly; others preferred to keep them hidden. Chance was of the latter mindset. He put his fingers lightly on a mark on his ribcage. Two small backslashes— the mark left by the permanent mod that had corrupted his system. The one responsible for his curse.

The process of uninstalling mods depended on the mod itself. Most were pretty straightforward, others required long processes, and some, like Chance's, became so twisted into the DNA that they were virtually impossible to undo.

Maybe if he saved up, he would be able to pay for some expensive de-installation procedure, but, despite the long hours at the shop, the money didn't seem to be adding up very quickly.

"Maybe Benson is right," Vent spoke from the corner of the room while Chance spat his toothpaste into the drain. "Maybe it's time to find a new job."

But where? Mr. Bird paid him trash wages, but at least he had hired him. Most other places, especially any place that would give him an opportunity to start a career, would take one look at Chance's biocode and write him off as broken and dangerous.

"Stupid mod," Chance huffed as he collapsed on his mattress.

Then again, there were plenty of other, less formal ways to earn a living in the City. Chance thought of the girl in the tent, then immediately tried to push her out of his mind. He wasn't that desperate. And he hoped that it was simply desperation for cash that had forced the girl into that line of work and not something more sinister.

"Girls go missing from the City every day," Vent noted, moving to Chance's bedside.

The image of the girl in the sundress, the vanished girl that Goosh had shown him, played in Chance's head. Waving, smiling, disappearing.

There were other options, too. Mod trading, like the man on the street whose name he couldn't remember. But dealing with mods in any way was a hazardous business. The only people who disappeared more often than young girls were mod developers. Independent developers almost always kept their identities hidden. Gangs, shady businesses, and even law enforcement needed very little persuasion to blow up a car, shoot up an apartment, or throw someone from a rooftop. And nothing paints a target on a developer's back like creating a unique and dangerous mod.

Chance kicked his shoes off onto the floor. If he were in any way involved in the mod business, it wouldn't be long before someone found out about his own abilities and came after him. He was unpredictable and uncontrolled. As long as he was alive, he was a threat.

"A *powerful* threat, though," Vent tried again to get Chance's attention.

In hindsight, it hadn't taken long for some of his mother's boyfriends to develop the same perception of him. He had even sent one to the hospital. Fortunately, no one was able to prove, let alone explain, what Chance had done, so he had never gotten in any trouble.

Lately, he had learned to control the outbursts better. Mostly. Incidents would still happen occasionally. It also helped that his mother had pretty much stopped dating.

"Stop ignoring me," Vent spoke from the other corner.

Frustration welled inside Chance's chest, and he turned, smashing his fist into his pillow and cursing at the empty room. Who was he kidding? Even if he had another job, even if he had all the money he needed, even if he left Xi forever, there would be no escaping this.

The virtual demon that had haunted him since his fifteenth birthday, forced into his Interface with a corrupt mod, had taken up residence between the broken pieces of his messed-up code. This, he would never be able to leave behind, no matter how far he got from the City. Vent stood above his head, almost in the wall.

"You don't have to be afraid of me. We can be friends."

You're a curse.

"Why a curse? I've saved your life."

"I can save my own life," Chance dropped from his elbows and lay on his stomach, breathing slowly while the anger gradually subsided and the dark shapes evaporated. "I don't want it." He sank his head into his pillow and let the thoughts roll around inside. Eventually, emotion gave way to meditation, and meditation gave way to exhaustion, and Chance drifted off into unconsciousness.

The blonde girl from Goosh's video screen was in front of him. Smiling as her hair whipped furiously around her face in the night wind. A red light pulsed somewhere above, momentarily bathing her in its color, fading to reveal the twinkling City lights, then returning to paint her red again.

She looked Chance in the eyes as best she could, holding tightly to the metal railing at her side while the wind tried to carry her away.

Chance reached forward, grabbed the zipper on her pink

windbreaker, and pulled it up to her neck, closing it against the cold.

The wind eased slightly in response, and the girl smiled again.

The light pulsed red then faded.

"Isn't this so amazing?" she shouted.

Chance looked at his surroundings. He and the girl were above the top of a dark skyscraper, standing on a rusted metal perch partway up the tower's tall spire. Below their feet and in all directions, the lights of the City burned and flickered. White and purple and neon green and every color.

Above their heads and at the top of the spire, a large red light pulsed on… and off… and on… red… and red… and red again.

Chance looked at the girl. She smiled at him and pulled back the sleeve of her windbreaker to reveal a simple metal bracelet—one that looked too large for her tiny wrist.

"Um…" she held out her arm and looked at Chance, then back at the bracelet. "I want you to have this."

Chance looked at her, then down at the jewelry. Engraved in small, simple letters was the word 'Rush.' The light bathed it in red, then red again.

Chance shook his head. "I can't, I can't have it—it's yours!" he shouted over the wind. "It's your family's."

"I want you to keep it for me!" the girl smiled.

Chance shook his head. The girl grabbed his arm and held it up to hers.

Then she gasped, and Chance was falling.

Or rather, the world was flying upwards around him, and the lights of the City were replaced with bright fluorescent ones and blurred shapes.

"No!" the girl shouted. "No, no! Don't leave me! Don't leave —come back for me!"

Chance couldn't make sense of the world around him. Someone grabbed his wrists.

"Come back for me!" the girl screamed. "Come back!"

Blackness devoured the vision of the girl.

2 CHILDREN IN THE FIRE

The car hummed quietly as it moved between buildings. Aria pursed her lips and rested her head against the passenger seat window. The lights of the city moved all around the vehicle: above, on the sides, and below, over the edge of the bridge, hundreds of feet down to the Surface. The darkness of the sky gave Aria a slight feeling of vertigo among the towering structures.

The car lurched slightly, and Aria's head smacked against the glass. She huffed and glared at her older brother in the driver's seat. "Noah—" she exasperated.

"That wasn't me!" Noah protested, putting his hands in the air. "I'm not even driving right now."

Aria let out a sigh and looked at the clock on the dash. 9:18 p.m. School had ended five hours ago, and they were just now making their way home. The siblings continued in silence for a minute until Noah spoke up again.

"I really wish we could just download all the information for the test into our brains." He stared out the windshield as the car came to a stop behind a stream of other vehicles.

"We can't," Aria replied tiredly. "You can't overwrite—"

"—I know we can't," Noah cut her off. "I just wish we could. It would make life so much easier."

Aria shook her head and turned her attention back to the window on her right. End-of-year exams were coming up for both of them, Aria for her second year in high school and Noah for his third, and neither of them had been doing so well grade-wise. Mom had thought that signing them up for after-school tutoring would be helpful. Hour after hour of brainteasers, logic puzzles, solving and reverse engineering equations, and analyzing historical events. Aria hated every second of it.

"You're just mad because Blayze wasn't your tutor today," Noah teased.

"No…" she responded unconvincingly, keeping her eyes on the buildings outside.

"He's not that great," Noah continued. "It's just his mods. I remember when he was a third-year, and no one spoke to him 'cause he was ugly—"

"Shut up, Noah!" Aria snapped, the slightest twitch of a smile playing across her mouth before she pushed it away. "That's so mean. He's really nice."

Noah chuckled. "He's not even…" he trailed off. "Never mind." Compared to Noah, all other high school students were physically inferior. Somewhere well over six feet tall and cut like a pro athlete, Noah was a beast of a seventeen-year-old. And he had a habit of continually reminding everyone who would listen of his superiority, a habit he was working on undoing.

"I kind of like being tutored," Noah thought out loud, slightly shifting the topic. "It makes me feel smart at the end, like… when it's done." He looked at Aria for agreement.

"Why does it take so long to get home?" she complained under her breath, ignoring his comment.

"It's because the traffic—"

"—I know."

Noah drummed his fingers on the steering wheel. Sometimes, he and Aria were best friends; other times, she wanted nothing to do with him. Their relationship was a mixture of both.

"I updated my VH the other day," Noah prodded the conversation.

"...VH?" Aria kept her head on the glass.

"Visual-Hearing."

"No one abbreviates it like that."

"I do."

"Really," Aria responded dryly, though she was slightly intrigued. Dad had been heavy into mods. Supposedly. According to Mom. "How did you get the update already? I thought Seitech was supposed to release it next month."

"I got accepted onto a beta-testing list." Noah nodded to himself. "I could probably get you on, too, if you wanted. I had to lie about my age, though."

"My Visual-Hearing is fine." Aria smushed her hands into her cheeks lazily and then smiled. "Maybe I should actually downgrade mine, so I don't have to hear you as much," she laughed to herself.

Noah made a sound halfway between a groan and a laugh, then grinned. "Wow, okay."

Aria smirked.

The car meandered its way onto an elevated street that was only marginally less congested and followed the road through a tunnel and then back into more city before pulling to a stop at the entrance to an apartment building.

"Yay, we're home," Aria cheered sarcastically, climbing out of the vehicle and swinging the door shut behind her. Noah waved a hand at the car, and it drove off to find a spot in the neighboring parking garage.

Opposite the apartment building, on the far side of the street, was a narrow chasm, a gap in the level that dropped down to platforms and streets of the Neons below and eventually all the way down to the Surface. A pedestrian bridge lined with decorative foliage spanned the chasm, and at the other end, another street and another building. On the front face of the building, a large-screen display aired the nightly news while hundreds of people crisscrossed in front of it. Aria huffed through her nose and tried to let her frustration with the after-school tutoring sessions dissipate as she took in her urban surroundings. Aria had lived on Xi's upper levels—or Canopy, as it was commonly called—as long as she could remember, but still, being this high up continued to fascinate her imagination. It was like living in the sky.

She tilted her head back and looked up at the twinkling spires of the nearby skyscrapers. Though they were already nearly one hundred floors in the air, the buildings continued for at least as many floors above. Sometimes, Aria and her friends would find a remote edge somewhere, dangle their feet over the void, and talk for hours. It felt like sitting on the brink of space, surrounded by man-made stars.

Across the chasm, the screen changed and caught Aria's attention. On the display was the portrait of a beautiful blonde girl, and underneath, a headline rolled:

18-year-old Emry Rush Missing: Foul Play Involved?

The girl's picture shifted over, and a news correspondent appeared on the screen next to her to discuss the case, speaking in subtitles to the indifferent crowd:

"This isn't the first time a member of the Rush family has disappeared. Two decades ago, 14-year-old Raya Rush disappeared three days before she was going to be installed with the Interface—"

"Aria," Noah called out to his sister, who had become transfixed by the video board. "You coming?"

"Yeah, I'm coming," Aria turned and followed her brother into the building.

The doorman nodded robotically to the children as they entered the lobby and crossed to the elevators. The doors parted, and they stepped inside. Aria pushed the button for their floor, and Noah pressed his palm into the scanner before the elevator would ascend.

"Good evening, Sharp family," a pleasant voice emanated from the elevator walls as the doors in front of them lit up into a display screen. "Would you like—"

"—No." Aria cut the voice off.

"This elevator is so slow," Noah mumbled as the numbers in the top corner of the room flashed *119*.

Eventually, they came to a stop, and the doors opened, letting them out into a long hallway lined intermittently with black doors.

"Hopefully, Mom just got food delivered again," Noah thought aloud as they stopped in front of door 1419. "Whatever she got last time was really good; those noodles—"

"The door's open." Aria reached for the handle.

Noah stopped her. "Wait, it's busted," he noted, examining the top hinge partially detached from the wall. He pushed the door slightly, and it drifted inward.

"Why?" Aria looked between her brother and the doorway.

Noah was quiet, staring into the dark entryway, Aria frozen at his side. She knew what he was thinking, what they were both thinking. *A break-in?* The siblings looked at each other, eyes wide.

Exhaling shakily, Noah stepped cautiously over the threshold. Aria followed closely behind, her own breath quivering.

"Mom?" Noah called out quietly, unable to mask the fear in his voice.

The entryway opened up into the great room, and a single lamp illuminated the scene. Fear javelined through Aria's chest, and her whole body shook as she tried to register what she was seeing. Shards of glass from the floor-to-ceiling windows covered the carpet, reflecting the neon from the city outside like a terrifying mural. A warm breeze turned the pages of books torn and strewn across the room. Furniture had been overturned, and—Aria's legs went numb. Her heart shot through her throat —a trail of blood dripped down the staircase that curved to the floor above. And there, lying in a growing pool of red at the foot of the stairs—

"—M—" Aria choked, completely unable to breathe. "Mom —" Aria's body moved for her, dropping to her knees near her mother's slowly rising chest. Noah was beside her, his whole frame vibrating. "Mom, Mom," Aria tried to reach out but couldn't use her hands. "Mom—"

"Shhh…" Karinne Sharp put a shaky hand on her daughter's shoulder, "I need you—"

"—Mom, you can live." Aria struggled to speak through the panic. "Don't you have something—"

"—Quiet." Karinne cut Aria off and looked back and forth between her two children. "I need you to be quiet and do exactly what I tell you." Her voice was eerily calm. Yet that same voice that had encouraged, soothed, and scolded her two head-strong children all their lives was losing power by the second, kept aloft only by the technology weaved within her dying body.

Noah finally found the ability to put words together. "We need to call—"

"No, no. You need to do exactly what I tell you right now." Her body shuddered as more blood gushed from an open wound on her chest. The emergency first-aid program in her mods tried in vain to staunch the bleeding, causing the blood to spurt out in grotesque intermittent spasms as it began to seal and then rupture over and over again.

"Noah, get that book that's on the shelf." Noah turned in the direction his mother was pointing. "It's the only book on the shelf. Grab it."

Hanging over the lip of the top of the bookshelf was a small black book, the only one that had managed to keep its perch against whatever had thrown the rest to the ground.

Noah ran and snatched the book, nearly fumbling it as he kneeled again by his mother.

"Inside the front cover are two mod tiles; install them as soon as you get out of here," Karinne instructed.

"What?" Noah protested. "We can't leave you, Mom."

A loud, shattering noise came from one of the upstairs rooms.

"Go here," Karinee grabbed Noah's wrist and winced in pain.

A map of the city lit up behind Noah's eyes with a pin on an unknown location. Noah shook it away. "What are you talking about?"

A small explosion followed by a shriek echoed from upstairs, and Karinne's voice grew more urgent.

"They're looking for something, and you need to find it first. They're going to try to stop you. Go." Karinne choked. "Now."

Aria's world oscillated around her. She couldn't believe what she was seeing. The wide slash across her mother's torso bubbled as her body went into overdrive to keep her alive for each additional second. The red blood, the white carpet, and the refracting of the glass turned into a demonic kaleidoscope as Aria's vision spun. Mom was trying to say something. She was saying something. Aria couldn't hear. She couldn't understand. Several more smashing noises boomed from the second floor.

"Go."

"No! We can't just leave you here," Noah replied, his eyes darting back and forth between his mother and the second floor. "We're taking you!"

"Listen," Karinne squeezed her son's arm with surprising strength. "You need to protect your sister."

And, with that, she gasped, and her body paused before collapsing, eyes blank. As if someone had simply hit a switch inside, she was gone. Noah pushed away from his dead mother as if distancing himself would mean all of this wasn't happening, his eyes wide with fear.

Aria couldn't speak.

She couldn't move.

She couldn't think.

She felt Noah's arms wrap around her waist and lift her off the ground. Images raced across her vision. Shattered glass all over the floor. Furniture flipped. Mom's lifeless body. The dark silhouette of a person at the top of the staircase.

They were back in the hall, Noah running with Aria in his arms, heading back the way they had come, passing numbered doors. Suddenly, from behind came a wrenching explosion. Aria was hurled through the air and rolled. Something snapped in her arm, but she couldn't feel it. She crawled to her knees. Noah was beside her, pushing her, yelling. The stairs. Aria's feet finally started moving for her.

The siblings crashed through the door and flew down the steps, flight after flight. The building shook. Or maybe it was just Aria. She couldn't tell. She collapsed on one of the landings.

"Mom—" She tried to scream, but the words choked in her throat. Tears flooded down her face.

"No!" Noah was lifting her to her feet, putting her back in his arms. "Get up! Get up!"

"Mom!" Finally, her voice came. Aria flailed, scrambled, and scraped against her brother as he carried her farther down. "Mom is up there! MOM IS UP THERE! We can't leave her!" She kicked and twisted, writhed, and still down they went flying. Steps two, three, four at a time. "We can't leave her!"

More floors passed. They were going the wrong way. Mom was up, not down. They needed to go up. Using all the strength her adrenaline afforded, Aria launched herself from her brother's arms, but immediately, he was back on top of her, pinning her to the ground.

"Aria!" Noah was right in her face—tears of his own forming rivers down his cheeks. "Look at me! Aria!" He took a breath. "I need you to protect me."

"No, I need to protect Mom," Aria cried.

"Mom saved us so we could protect each other—" Even as Noah said the words, he had no idea what he meant. *Protect from what?* His mind was not comprehending. Not catching up. The only thing that did register was that they needed to leave.

"We need to get Mom—"

"Aria. Listen to me! WE NEED TO RUN." He lifted her again, keeping his grip on her arm in one hand and the book in the other. "Right now! I need you to run with me."

Aria let out a sob. Somewhere higher up, a door clanged open.

"Don't you hear that?" Noah was pulling her down the stairs now.

Aria nodded and swallowed. A maniacal laugh echoed through the stairwell overhead.

"Go! Run!"

And again, they were moving: jumping, turning, stumbling, crying, step after step for what seemed like an eternity, until finally they burst into the lobby. Other residents scrambled around them in confusion.

"Keep going! We need to get outside!" Noah yelled, pointing at the door as the doorman held it open, ushering residents onto the street.

The siblings dashed out of the building, refusing to glance back to see who screamed behind them.

The car was waiting for them at the curb. The doors opened and closed behind them as they dove in. Noah yanked on the manual controls and floored the accelerator. The vehicle whirred and rocketed them down the dark street.

Aria turned, barely able to breathe, and looked back at the building they had just fled. People were scattering left and right from the entrance, and partway up the structure, orange flames illuminated a column of black smoke that filled the city above.

Noah followed the road down toward the Surface. Lights raced past the vehicle like shooting stars and then slammed to a halt. Traffic lined up in front of them.

Noah looked over at his sister, but Aria was looking at her hands. They were shaking. Her wrist was bent awkwardly and starting to swell. Her palms were smeared in blood. So were her knees.

"Noah…" she said nervously.

"It's okay, it's okay. You're not bleeding," he reached over, placing the small, black, hardback book in her lap. "Open the cover. Mom—" his body trembled. "She said there are mods inside."

Aria turned the front cover with her unbroken hand. "There's nothing here."

"*Inside* the front cover, I think," Noah turned the car off the crowded road and onto an empty one.

Struggling to control her quivering fingers, Aria stuck her nails underneath the paper on the back of the cover and ripped it off. Underneath the paper, flush with the inside of the cover, were two mod tiles: one with a bright red letter *A*, the other with an *N*.

"Take us here," Noah commanded the car.

The map with the marked location that Noah had received from Karinne filled a display on the windshield.

"Okay," the car responded and promptly changed lanes.

Aria inhaled through her quivering lips and tried to wipe some of the tears dripping from her eyes. She popped the tiles out of the book cover and into her bloodied palm.

"Install it," Noah instructed, reaching over.

Aria swallowed again. "Which one?"

"I think yours is *A*, and mine is *N*." Noah grabbed the *N* tile and, with a brief moment of hesitation, lifted his shirt and applied it like a sticker onto his ribcage, lining it up next to the other marks on his side. For a few seconds, he stared straight ahead, hand on his torso, then released it and let out a deep sigh.

Aria looked down at the red *A* between her fingers.

"Aria, do it."

Closing her eyes, Aria pressed the tile onto the underside of her forearm.

Her skin stung slightly as the paper-thin tile adhered itself. As it did so, in her head she heard the words of her BTI's installation prompt:

Modification package 'ARIA' is ready to install. Proceed?

Trying her best to breathe deeply through her quieting sobs, she replied with a mental *yes*. She then released the tile as she felt it become one with her skin.

Almost immediately, a tingling feeling, like tiny insects crawling, consumed Aria's body. She let out a strained yelp and reached for her brother.

"It's okay. Sometimes, they feel weird." Noah grimaced and arched his back. "I feel—ah—like I'm being squeezed."

The tiny insects seemed to climb into Aria's mouth and eyes. Then, the whole world slowed down. The bugs disappeared. The lights on the street blazed and went dim. The hum of the car grew to a roar and subsided. Everything was moving in slow motion. The air seemed to compress around her. Then, something like a pulse of electricity surged through her body, and she was back in real-time.

She could feel everything. She could feel each fiber of her clothing soaked with sweat. She could feel each breath, her lungs filling with oxygen. She could feel each muscle twitching, tightening, relaxing, and clinging to her skeleton. She could feel her heartbeat and the blood coursing through every artery and vein, down into her extremities and back, with each pound.

"What's going on?" Aria tried to speak, but she wasn't sure if she made any noise. Noah was saying something, but she couldn't understand. He seemed far away.

Aria took a slow breath and sunk further away from her surroundings and deeper and deeper into her own body.

"What's happening?" As she asked the question, Aria felt a new sense of quiet, peaceful, consistent motion. Like waves on a lonely beach, she felt like she was on her own private island, and

Noah and the car and the world outside were oceans away. Waves rolled through her body, and with each wave came calmness, control, focus… power.

Her breathing was steady. Her heart beating within measure. The waves washed over her. She leaned back and sunk into a quiet oblivion.

3 STANDARD NEGOTIATIONS

The strange dream of the girl on the tower from the night before had been filed away in Chance's mind as just that —a dream, but he was still replaying the scenes in his head when the shop's front door swung open with a *BANG*. Everyone in the bar turned.

A shadowy figure stood in the doorway. They were small, whoever they were, probably only as tall as Chance's shoulder, but they wore tar-colored combat boots, a heavy black cloak, and a matching black hat with a wide brim that dipped low to hide their eyes.

The shop was already dimly lit, and Chance wouldn't have been able to make out much else if it hadn't been for the two lantern-shaped earrings that illuminated the dark waves of hair that framed their pale cheeks and obnoxiously bright red lips.

The woman grimaced as if she were disgusted at the sight of the place, then shot a hand out to catch the door she had so aggressively thrown open. Her fingers were skeleton white and covered in rune tattoos, and her nails were polished and sharpened.

With a huff, she stepped inside, moving like an angry phantom past each table and ignoring the curious eyes of the patrons. Most people on the Surface looked strange, but not because of some odd fashion statement. Mr. Bird's usuals would normally slink through the front door, trying to blend in with the tables and chairs as if the gaze of a stranger could cause them physical pain. This woman devoured the attention like an angry black hole.

Then, as if to punctuate Chance's thought further, the door flew open again, and a second woman stumbled inside, almost the entire opposite of the first. She wore a similar black cloak, but she was taller, she was less covered in runes, and everything about her seemed to sparkle. She pushed a long river of platinum hair to one side of her head, and Chance's heart skipped.

Unlike the other woman, she made eye contact with everyone in the room, nodding and smiling and whispering a greeting in Chance's direction. Chance mumbled something in response and shook himself back to his senses.

Eventually, the customers returned to their drinks, and Chance resumed clearing tables, but he couldn't help but glance at the newcomers.

They took their seats at a corner table where a wiry, dirty man sat waiting, picking at his fanged teeth with a yellow fingernail. From the expression on his face, he was the only one not impressed by the two guests' arrival.

Chance carried a stack of empty glasses toward the back kitchen as Benson brought drinks to the strangers' table. The platinum-haired woman thanked the robot, and the other two sat silently.

Chance placed the glasses in the sink and grabbed Benson as he stepped in through the kitchen door.

"Let me get their order," he said to the robot.

Benson hummed in response and turned to load dishes into the washer.

Chance pushed the door open and pulled his pad out as he approached the corner table. "What can I do—"

"—Nothing, for now, *thank* you," the dark-haired woman

responded, emphasizing the word with a dismissive flick of her finger.

Chance nodded and awkwardly retreated. "Right, let me know…" He heard the man chuckle, and he couldn't help but think that one of them had told a joke at his expense.

"Benson," he called quietly to the robot who stood idly behind the bar. "Do you recognize these people?"

Benson stared mildly at him for a moment and then spoke, "The—the woman in the black hat is called Fri—Friday. According to what I can find, she seems to be some kind of… some kind of freelancer. The man is not listed in any—in any database, but he has come three times before; people call him… Shift."

"Shift, huh? And Friday?"

"I do not know who—who the other woman is."

For the next ten minutes, Chance pretended to be busy, wiping down already-clean tables and rearranging glasses and all the while watching the trio out of the corner of his eye.

Friday and Shift were doing most of the talking. As she spoke, Friday played with what looked like a metal bracelet, rolling it back and forth across the tabletop, occasionally spinning it under her finger. Shift listened, his eyes flicking back and forth between the bracelet and the two women, then he snorted, smirked, and leaned in close as he responded.

The conversation went on like this until, eventually, Friday slid something across the table, and Shift held it up. It was a money tile—probably pre-loaded with some amount of credits. Shift turned the small chip over in his fingers. They exchanged a few more words, and then Shift dropped the tile and flicked it back across the table. He leaned back in his chair, crossed his arms, and shrugged.

Some sort of negotiation must be going on, Chance figured, as he picked up and replaced various bottles.

"Get closer," Vent whispered to Chance, taking a seat at an empty table at Chance's side.

"Go away, you aren't real," Chance whispered back.

Vent shrugged. "Take a better look at that bracelet."

Chance inched his way closer and narrowed his eyes at the bracelet as Friday held it to read the small, engraved text. She was just within earshot.

"It says, *Rush*. Do you know *why*, Shift?"

Shift gave some sort of response, but Chance wasn't listening. Scenes from his dream flashed through his mind again.

The tower. The red pulsing light. The girl. The bracelet. "I want you to have this." Her smiling face and wind-whipped hair. "Come back to me!"

Chance blinked himself back to the present. "Emry Rush," he mouthed the name to himself.

"That's right," Vent stood behind him.

Friday leaned forward and planted a hand on the table. Her lantern earrings swung in toward her cheeks. Chance caught a glimpse of her dark eyes in the yellow light.

"Tell me where you found this bracelet," she said to Shift through clenched teeth.

Shift chuckled again and shook his head tauntingly. "I told you already," he purred. "An angel gave it to me, appeared to me in the street just the other night, said I looked like I needed help and that my prayers had been heard. Handed me the bracelet and said I could sell it to buy myself something nice. And the angel was right—bionics shop said it was made of rare star metal..." Shift grinned smugly, "gave me almost a hundred credits for it."

"Oh, give me a fucking break." Friday rolled her eyes and pushed herself back in her chair. "First of all, this bracelet is worth ten thousand times what you sold it for, and second, no one in this shit hole city would give a breadcrumb to a starving child, let alone a piece of priceless jewelry to a convict like yourself." Friday removed her hat and rubbed her temples. "Look, *Shift*," she spoke his name like an insult and reached down into the neck of her cloak. "I don't know if you know much about me." She pulled out a necklace, on the end was a vial of blue liquid. "But things usually don't end well for people who try to lie to me." She let the vial dangle momentarily, then dropped it against her chest. "And I'm particularly impatient with thieves."

Shift growled and squared himself up in his chair, the stringy muscles in his arms tensing, the pupils of his eyes widening, and the color of his skin shifting into something dark and striped. "Is that a threat?" he snarled through sharpened teeth and adjusted his weight underneath the table.

The platinum-haired woman, who had been quiet for a while now, finally spoke up as she slid her hand across the table, barely brushing his forearm with her fingernails. "Please..." She didn't say anything else. She just leaned in, tilted her head slightly, and made a sort of pleading face.

Shift narrowed his eyes at her with suspicion and drew his arm back. Chance stood frozen to his spot nearby, no longer hiding his eavesdropping. The tension at the table was palpable throughout the room, and some of the other customers were eyeing the conversation warily.

The restaurant was quiet for a minute, and it appeared that nothing would happen, until Friday mumbled something that sent Shift over the edge. In an instant, chairs flew backward, and all three visitors jumped to their feet. Shift was quickest, snatching the platinum-haired one by the wrist and pinning her arm awkwardly onto the table. She yelped pitifully, and Shift snapped his teeth, almost foaming at the mouth.

Without realizing what he was doing, Chance dashed at the man but was immediately knocked to the ground by a lightning-quick backhand to the face. Shift cursed at him and glared back at the women.

"You think I'd let two Neon-crawling whores talk to me like that and walk away?" Shift growled.

"You let her go right now, or I will rip your throat out," Friday's voice was level, but her eyes were on fire. In her right hand, she clutched the blue vial.

Shift almost laughed, "I've heard stories about you."

"Power. Use it," Vent whispered from the floor under Chance's back.

Fine, Chance pushed himself up.

Shift's captive whimpered, and he twisted her arm harder. "But I've never heard of you, you—" Shift's body seized, and he started to choke.

Friday stood still, confused.

"Ha—ack," Shift gasped desperately, releasing his grip as he leaned over the table, struggling to breathe.

"Well," Friday looked at her companion, unsure of how to proceed.

Shift stumbled over his own chair and nearly fell to the ground. His eyes were wide with terror as he tried to keep his balance, the desperation on his face intensifying and the veins in his neck bulging.

Chance's muscles strained as he drilled his eyes into Shift. *C'mon, get it under control...* Chance's vision skipped violently. First, he was looking at Shift from his spot on the floor, then he was *inside* Shift, looking at the two women, his eyesight blurring and hands shaking. Shattered memories flashed through his mind. People and places he had never seen, thoughts he had never had. Shift's memories. Chance tried to calm his mind and brought himself back to the present, or *Shift's* present, rather. He opened and closed Shift's hands. *Full control. Got it.*

"Oh my—Oh!"

A shearing pain tore through Chance's body as he felt two metallic hands pull him from his trance and back into his own body. Benson was dragging Chance out of the way.

Shift gasped deeply and dropped to his knees as the invisible force released him.

Benson looked at the man on the floor, then the women, then at Chance. Chance glanced back at Benson and then at Shift, who was panting as he regained his breath.

"Sir, are you okay?" Benson kneeled down, and Shift

knocked his hands away. Slowly pushing himself up, he glared at the women.

Friday quickly masked whatever shock she had felt and stared back coldly. Without further words, she turned, her cloak flaring, and strode off toward the exit. Her companion trailed quickly after her, stopping at the door to give Chance one last wide-eyed look before she stepped out into the evening.

"Sir, are you—are you all right?" Benson again tried to help the man up.

Shift waved the robot off and grumbled between breaths, "… glitching, shit mods…" He fixed his eyes on the restaurant door as he used the side of the table to stabilize himself.

Benson hovered around Shift. "Maybe a drink would help?" he offered, turning over his shoulder to nod at Chance.

Chance took a deep breath, hoping it would cool what felt like tar boiling in his gut. He turned on his heel to head toward the kitchen when he nearly crashed into Mr. Bird.

"Yahum, Charlie whaddare… whaddis ever'one standing around for?" He pushed his drunken body past Chance and almost tripped over himself as he stumbled out into the room. "Mm, robot!" he pointed at Benson.

Chance inhaled again in an attempt to keep sane and closed his eyes. He hated Mr. Bird. He hated the robot. He hated all the disgusting bar patrons. He put his hands to his face and realized they were shaking. Without looking at anyone else, he stormed into the kitchen. On his way in, he knocked over a large metal bowl that clattered to the floor. He kicked it out of his way and flinched as a sharp shock ran up his spine. *Glitch.*

Calm down, Chance. He knew anger would only make it worse. *Take your mind elsewhere.* He grabbed a plate out of the dishwasher. It was all he could do not to smash it on the counter. He put it back down, and a second shock moved through his bones.

He needed to get outside. The trash was only half full, but he grabbed it and pushed his way through the back door. The warm, damp air of the night poured over him, wrapping him with its density like a thick blanket.

As he dragged the trash between the two buildings, a rip formed in the bag's side, leaking a trail of garbage as he went. Right now, he didn't care. Sounds from the neighboring karaoke bar drifted over, and he tried to let the ambiance of the city ease him.

As Chance approached the dumpster at the corner of the street, he looked up. Stacks of buildings and a canopy of levels and intertwining bridges obscured the sky as always. The electronic displays and signs from the surrounding stores bathed the city in its own permanent, rainbow twilight. Blinking lights drifted from level to level like fireflies.

Groaning, Chance heaved the garbage into the dumpster and turned. And, there, in the alley between him and the door he had just come from, were the two women.

Friday was leaning up against an electrical box with her friend standing beside her. Their monochrome outfits camouflaged them into the urban environment like shadows. Or trash bags.

Chance unconsciously took a step backward, and Friday laughed. "Don't be afraid of us." She shifted her weight off the box and began slowly moving in Chance's direction. "Despite our costumes, we aren't witches… not like you, at least."

"What are you talking about?"

"What was *that?*" She gestured at the shop. "You almost killed a man by looking at him."

"I don't know what you're talking about."

"No, no." She moved several steps closer and pointed a finger at his face. "No, you did something. We could tell." She smiled, and her eyes glinted under the brim of her hat.

"I think the man just glitched—" Chance borrowed the excuse Shift had given.

"—We know when mods are being used around us. And we know you used one on Shift. Okay?"

Chance shook his head. His heart was starting to race as the pair moved closer.

"Friday," the other tapped her friend on the shoulder. "I think you're scaring him," she whispered, looking apologetically at Chance.

Friday chuckled. "I'm Friday," she said, removing her hat. "And this is June."

"Hi," June smiled.

Chance blinked, still watching them warily.

"What's your name?" June asked, trying her best not to look intimidating.

"I'm—"

Friday whipped a heavy handgun out of her cloak and pointed it at the entrance to the alley, where a hunched man was struggling to undo his belt buckle. "Hey buddy, find somewhere else to piss!"

The man quickly hobbled back around the corner.

"This is Tax Man, our third companion," Friday grinned to herself. "He doesn't say much other than... *bang*." She twirled the pistol around her finger and holstered it somewhere in the shadows of her outfit. "Sorry, your name, continue."

"I'm... Chance. People don't really flash their weapons like that down here, just so you know. Can cause a lot of trouble."

Friday turned her head playfully and grinned, her lantern earrings swinging. "Can you tell we live in the Neons?"

'The Neons' referred to the mid-levels of the City, the levels and districts that were physically above the Surface and below the Canopy. The eccentricity of the women's outfits and attitudes said enough about the character of those mid-levels. Chance nodded. *Makes sense now.*

"Also, thanks for protecting us!" June chimed in, rocking back and forth on her feet. "You reacted so quickly, too." Her hair reflected the colors of the lights above.

Chance looked at the women in silence.

"I know it was you who did it," Friday grinned. "But don't

be sorry." She moved even closer. "Shift is a bad guy, and that was brave of you. You know, saving two helpless young women." She pouted over-dramatically and placed a hand on her collar. Chance noted the metal bracelet back around her wrist. Certainly, the same one from his dream. *Rush.* His heart began to beat a little faster.

"Clearly not helpless." He motioned with his eyes at the blue vial around Friday's neck. Something told him her jewelry might be more worrisome than her firearm.

"Well..." Friday and June looked at each other. "Yeah, not at all." Friday shrugged.

Chance stared at them both for a moment. "I've heard you're a freelancer."

Friday laughed. "And? That's all you've heard?" She looked at June. "Maybe the city is bigger than I thought."

"What are you then?"

Friday turned in a slow circle, speaking to the empty alleyway. "I've been a lot of things, Chance, but right now, I'm looking for someone."

"And we want you to help us," June added.

Chance looked at the women questioningly. "What do you mean?"

"You heard about the girl that got kidnapped, right?" Friday started.

"Yeah, I heard about her." Chance swallowed, trying to play partially oblivious. "Emily, or something—"

"—Emry," Friday corrected him. "Emry Rush. Orland Rush's daughter." Friday's eyes went distant as if she were recalling some sad memory, but then she inhaled and forced a smile. "We're going to get her back."

"Why?" Chance asked.

Friday raised an eyebrow. "Orland Rush is the most powerful man in the whole fucking City," she replied. "I'm sure he'd reward his daughter's rescuers generously." Friday adjusted the cloak on her shoulders. "And the Rush family would be a good connection to have." When Chance didn't respond, she went on. "You can do something I've never seen before, and trust me, I've seen everything. Combine our resources and connections with your ability, and no one can stop us." She twirled a strand of hair around her finger as she spoke. "We'll have the girl back in no time."

Emry's words from the dream echoed in the back of Chance's brain. *Come back to me!*

Friday waited patiently for Chance to say something.

"What exactly do you want me to do with... with what I can do?" Chance asked.

"You think whoever took Emry Rush is just going to hand her over when we ask? We watched you put a very modified, dangerous man on the ground without touching him. Shit, without anyone even *realizing* what was happening. Do you understand that?" She lowered her voice, "I would *love* to know where you got that mod, Chance."

Even in her boots, Friday was much shorter than him, yet her presence loomed large as she moved in.

Chance squirmed uncomfortably under her scrutiny.

"Not in the mood to share that information?" She retreated a few steps. "Fine. I understand it can be hard to know who to trust down here. Still, we could use someone like you."

"Like me?"

"Yes, gods below, like *you*." Friday tossed her hands up and studied the surrounding alleyway for a moment. "June and I could have taken care of Shift back there. We could have turned him into a thousand fucking chunks of stew meat and splattered him all over your bar if we had wanted. And we can do that all around this whole godforsaken city until we find this girl. But I saw how you handled the situation, and I like your approach a lot more. It's cleaner," Friday reassured him. "*Come on*, Chance," she said his name like they had known each other for years. "You don't want to spend your time..." she motioned at Mr. Bird's noodle bar, "pouring bowls of soup to drunks. Do you?"

Chance was unsure of how to respond.

"We'll make it easy for you. June and I will do all the work. We just might need you, if things get tight, do what you did to Shift to some bad kidnappers."

"And we'll make it worth your time," June grinned cutely.

"*Well* worth your time." Friday stepped close again. "We'll be back tomorrow night," she reached inside her cloak, "and you can let us know then." She pulled out the same money-tile she had offered to Shift and held it out to him. "Think of this as a tip. For serving us."

"No, I can't—" Chance started to refuse.

"Take it," Friday demanded, forcing it into his hand. The bracelet swung around Friday's wrist as she held her hand in Chance's for a second. "Think about our offer, and if you decide you don't want it, you can give the money back tomorrow."

Chance looked down at the chip as the women stepped past him on either side, walking toward the street.

"This is an opportunity," Friday responded over her shoulder. "It'll be an adventure."

"Wait." Chance turned, but the women were gone. Steam vented lazily up from a grate in the ground, and a street-dweller pushed a rickety cart over the far curb. Chance stood blankly in the alley for what must have been several minutes as he tried to register the entire episode.

June had thanked him for protecting them, and Friday said that what he did to stop Shift was a 'cleaner' way of handling the situation. And—

Isn't this amazing? The dream of Emry Rush played once again across his mind. *I want you to have this. Don't leave me!* "The hell...?" Had he been sent some kind of message? Chance spun around the alley again as if he could locate the reason for the odd timing of the dream and the sudden appearance of the two women there behind the bar. "Emry...?" he asked the twilight as if it might answer.

Only the karaoke bar next door made a sound in response.

Chance shook his head.

"Boy!"

Chance turned. Mr. Bird was shouting at him from the back door of the shop. "We need you in here working, not..." he mumbled something to himself, then shut the door again.

Chance took a deep breath, looked down the empty alley one last time, and walked back into the bar.

4 FATHER, DAUGHTER

Aria woke to the sound of a ceiling fan and opened her eyes to the dark room. She was lying on her back on a bed she didn't recognize, covers tucked gently around her body. She watched the fan wobble slightly as it spun, and then everything from the night before came back to her. Except it didn't come back in a flood of panic as it had been last night. Her thoughts quietly arranged themselves, like books on a shelf that Aria was simply observing.

Driving home. The broken door. Shattered glass. Apartment ruined. Noises from upstairs. Mom, on the ground. Bleeding. Dead. Running. An explosion. Stairs. Crying. Confusion.

Aria took a measured breath. The paralyzing terror that had consumed her last night was gone. Had it all been a dream?

A sensation of tiny waves washed through Aria's body. The mod. Slowly, Aria sat up and looked at her forearm, hoping that she would see nothing, that the evidence of yesterday's reality would not be there.

But it was. The red letter *A*, like a fresh tattoo, marked her skin; *A* for Aria. Deep inside, something wanted to scream, wanted to thrash and yell and cry until Mom came back, and it was all untrue. But those feelings felt like a trapped animal, separate from the larger part of her—like a creature locked in a hidden dungeon. Closer to the surface, she felt quieter, more focused, and subtly powerful. Yet, unsettled. Unsatisfied.

Aria threw her eyes around the room. Enough light came in through the crack under the door for her to see. Pictures of people she didn't recognize hung on the wall, and her clothes were folded on the nightstand to her left. They were clean. Somehow, she had changed into something like a white slip. She next examined her hands. The blood was gone, and her wrist felt fine as she flexed it back and forth.

She could hear voices outside the room having a quiet conversation. Noah's voice was one, while the other sounded like it belonged to an older woman.

Aria tossed the covers aside and pushed herself out of bed, and the lamp on the nightstand lit up to a dim glow. A full-body mirror sat against the wall, and Aria paused and stood in front of it. Something was different. The girl in the mirror wasn't Aria. This girl was harder. Her skin seemed like it had been drawn tight over her frame. The muscles in her legs and arms were more defined, and her face looked as if it had been carved in stone. Her eyes—Aria stared intensely at her reflection—her eyes were set. Unwavering.

Her mirror-self stood there, poised, unmoving, like it was staring her down in challenge. Aria stared back.

"Hi," the mirror suddenly lit up with a greeting and began to trace the outline of her body. "Running diagnostics—"

Aria smashed the heel of her palm into the reflection, shattering the mirror. Shards of glass fell away, and the electronic voice went silent. Aria's eyes were still focused on her own splintered reflection. One eye stared back this time. Unconvinced.

"Aria!" The door swung open, and Noah stepped in from the hallway. He looked back and forth between Aria and the broken mirror as the lights in the room came all the way on. "What... are you okay?"

Aria looked down at the glass on the ground, then at her brother, and shook herself to reality as she pulled her hand back to her chest. "I—Sorry. I don't know—" The tiny waves washed through her body. "I don't know." Her voice felt different—*in*different, rather. "Where are we?"

"Grandma's."

It had been at least a dozen years since Aria had seen her grandmother last. It would have been before Dad left, and Aria would have been too young to remember. They really hadn't associated at all with Dad's side of the family after he was gone.

Noah looked at Aria with a calmness that seemed to match her own. "Come out. She wants to see you."

"I'll get changed."

Noah nodded and left, closing the door behind himself.

As she dressed, Aria couldn't help but look at herself again in the broken mirror. The reflection curled the edges of its cracked lips, and something deep inside Aria screamed again. It raged and called out for Mom. But Aria wasn't feeling. She wasn't listening.

———

"I THINK I'M IN SHOCK," Noah said as he sat across from her at the table, staring at the piece of burnt toast on the plate in front of him.

"It's not shock," Aria replied as she poked at her own toast. "It's the mods. They're suppressing our emotions."

"You think?"

"Yeah, I feel these little waves, and everything calms down."

"I feel it, too."

Aria sat quietly. If she didn't move, she could feel the waves, like they were off in the distance. They must be stronger at times and weaker at others.

An analog clock ticked quietly on the wall. 3:00 p.m. Aria did a double take. "How long were we out for?" she asked.

"A while," Noah answered. "But, yeah…" He poked his toast again.

"Big mods can put you under for a long time, right?" Aria thought out loud. She remembered falling asleep on the couch at home the same day she had gotten one of her earlier mods. Like a computer resetting itself with each update.

Noah nodded.

Somewhere outside, a train whirred past, shaking the house slightly. Aria waited to feel some sort of pain—loss, sadness, confusion… anything.

Nothing came. All she felt was that unsatisfied quietness.

"My friends are wondering where I am," Noah commented, staring into space.

Aria looked up at her brother. She could see the communications overlay scrolling across his eyeballs—notifications, messages, and videos that only he could read or hear.

Aria summoned her own. Semi-transparent conversation threads, old photos, and a map of her friends' locations populated her vision. There was nothing new. Her friends were all at school. No doubt the news would reach them soon if it hadn't already, and they would start to panic. "Have you responded to any of your friends yet?" Aria asked through the holograms on her eyes.

"No, not yet."

"Don't. Don't say anything. Disconnect."

"Why?"

"Because there are people out there who want to find us, and that won't be hard to do if we're connected to the internet." Aria moved through the mental navigation and disabled all her connections.

Noah did the same. "Disconnected," he announced. "So, we're just not going to say anything to anyone?"

"I think that's best. Just until…" *Until what?* Aria couldn't find an answer. "Why is this happening?" she asked, her voice sounding too strong for the homely yellow kitchen.

Noah was silent.

"Why is Mom dead?"

Again, Noah sat still.

"What are we supposed to do?"

Noah looked up at Aria with the same stone eyes her reflection had given her. "Why do you think Mom would leave us these mods?"

"I don't know." Aria hadn't really thought about that. She hadn't had much time to think about anything yet, and the questions seemed to be adding up quickly without any pairing answers.

"Dad liked mods, right? Mods are a dangerous business. Maybe he got us these in case something like this happened."

"So we could do what? Not panic?"

Grandma walked in carrying a pan of eggs and set it down on the table between them. Aria thanked her, and Grandma returned to the kitchen, humming to herself.

"She's crazy," Noah explained flatly.

"I know." Aria watched the steam rise from the eggs. Grandma had lost her mind, in a way. Either through mods or old age or a combination of both, her mind was elsewhere. Somehow, she was still able to take care of herself, but conversation didn't seem to work. It wasn't clear how much, if anything, got through to her.

"I tried to explain to her what happened last night, but I don't think she understands," Noah went on. "She recognizes us, though. She knows who we are."

After Aria had passed out in the car, Noah had gotten them to Grandma's house, the location Mom had shown Noah in her final moments. Noah didn't even have to explain himself when he knocked. Grandma just let them in, calling them by name. She didn't react when Noah told her that their mom had died, that she had been killed. She just set about preparing places for them to sleep and then went to work cleaning Aria up. It was like she was following some script, some automated procedure for taking care of guests, and the idea that her daughter-in-law was slaughtered didn't fit into that code. It might have bothered Noah more if he hadn't simultaneously been struggling under the side effects of his new mod. He ended up falling unconscious on the couch as a foreign, pulsing feeling moved through his chest, and the television in the corner of the room played some comedy show from decades past.

"What does your mod do?" Aria asked, seemingly reading his thoughts. "Besides calm you down."

Noah took a deep breath through his nose. "I think it's a strength enhancement."

"How much?"

Noah shook his head. "I'm not sure, but I think it's a lot. I broke the handle on the shower earlier."

"It's an old house."

Noah nodded.

Her brother had always been strong, but as Aria observed him now across the table, she could see that he had changed. Veins bulged in his forearms, and he looked like he had added fifteen pounds of muscle, but muscle size was only one factor in human strength. Aria had learned in her biology class that the human nervous system put limits on muscle output to protect the body from itself. This gave humans better fine motor skills but less sheer strength.

The limits *could* be removed, but early mod developers had found that pushing any one trait—strength, mental capacity, and so on—too far past the normal bounds of nature always seemed to have negative side effects. The human body could only handle so much. Muscles would rip, organs would fail from overuse, and brains would fry. That wasn't even to mention the weird side effects that something more extreme like fire resistance or water breathing would have, especially when combined with experimental bionics. Over the years, anything that sounded exciting was outlawed. But Xi was so big, and mods were so prolific; who was going to actually do anything about illegal modifications when there were so many other crimes to deal with in the City? Like murder.

"What does your mod do?" Noah put the question back to his sister.

Aria ripped her toast in half and dropped both pieces back onto her plate. "I don't know."

"Silas never ate much either," Grandma suddenly spoke from the edge of the table, gazing dreamily at the far wall.

Aria looked at Noah, then up at Grandma. "What was Dad like?"

Grandma hummed to herself for a minute, and Aria thought maybe the question wouldn't register, but then Grandma responded. "He was a very energetic child, always running around. Never wanted to sit still. I would say, 'Silas, it's time to eat,' and he would always say, 'Not now, Mom.' He'd be working on something, trying to leave on some adventure."

Grandma turned her gaze to a tiny window in the wall, and Aria waited for her to continue.

"He loved to explore the City. He and his friends knew every street, every shortcut... They loved to find abandoned buildings and create secret clubhouses. I was always so worried about him, but since I was always working, I couldn't be at home to take care of him like I should have..." Grandma trailed off and began humming to herself again.

"Grandma?" Noah spoke up.

Grandma stopped humming but continued her glazed stare.

Mom hadn't talked much about Dad before, and Noah had been too small to remember him much. But from bits of information he had gathered, he had stitched together a mental image of his father. He was a tall man involved in the mod business. Always busy. Sometimes, he would be gone for weeks without any contact. Mom hated when he was gone. One day, he left, as he had done many times before. Several weeks later, they got word that he had been killed in some mod-gang violence—a victim of the technology he loved so much.

"What happened to Dad? Where did he go?"

"Oh, I don't know that. He said he would be back."

"When?" Noah pressed. "When did he say that?"

"He said he'd come back to visit."

"When did he visit you last?"

"A long time ago. But you were here. Yes, Silas brought his children to see me. You were smaller, then. Karinne was here, too. She was so beautiful, but I don't think she liked me very much."

"Last time you saw our dad was when we were all visiting you together?"

Grandma sighed. Noah nodded understandingly. The unrealized hope that maybe his father was still out there, alive, faded as suddenly as it had come.

"Grandma, Karinne is dead. Our mom is dead." The words fell like rocks from Aria's mouth. "She died, and we need to find something. Something related to Dad, I think. Related to Silas. Can you help us find it?"

"I don't know why Karinne didn't like me. I did so much for her."

"Grandma," Aria stood, trying to redirect her grandmother's focus, but Grandma was gone again. Without another word, she turned and meandered her way out of the kitchen and into the hallway.

"We need to learn more about Dad," Aria said, returning to Noah. "We need to make a plan." *Why? A plan to do what?* The doubts went ignored as her words seemed to leave her mouth without her consent. "We need to lay out everything we know and figure out what is going on, what it is that Mom told us to find, where to find it, and who else is looking for it."

"Yes," Noah nodded in agreement, his eyes running through visions of the previous night.

"Let's start with what happened yesterday." It felt as if she were sitting herself down in her own interrogation room. "We came home around 9:30 p.m. to find our apartment ruined and

Mom bleeding out on the floor." Aria quivered internally at how coolly she now acknowledged her mother's death. It was less than twenty-four hours ago that it all happened; she should have been entirely overcome by panic, losing her mind to the grief and shock. But she wasn't. "Someone dangerous was looking for something and willing to kill Mom to get it." Aria continued.

"They were sloppy," Noah added. "Or angry. The apartment was overturned as if they had just been thrashing around. They easily could have missed what it was they were looking for."

"They passed over our mod tiles. They would have picked those up in an instant with a scanner."

"So, they weren't looking for mods."

"Maybe they were looking for someone. Maybe us?" Aria raised her eyebrows.

"If they were looking for us, why would they trash our house? Why not wait quietly for us to get home?" Noah countered.

"They're careless. Or not very smart?"

"Also, Mom told us we need to find whatever it is before they do. She would've just told us to run if they were looking for us."

Aria nodded. "And she said, 'I should have told you about Dad sooner,' so whatever we are looking for probably has something to do with Dad."

"But *what* should she have told us sooner? What about him? All we know is that he was involved in bad business, left Mom, and got himself killed."

"So, what did Dad have that people are looking for?"

"And why does Mom say we need to find it first?"

"That must imply that it's dangerous if it's in the wrong hands. That Dad didn't want people to find it."

Aria was quiet as a new thought occurred. "Maybe they're looking for Dad. Maybe he's not gone."

"And they thought what? That he would just be hanging out at home with us?" Noah asked.

Aria bit her lip in thought. "Maybe it's a place? They're

looking for a place—a secret development den, or server somewhere…"

"If it's a place, they could just be looking for a door."

"You think they were looking for a secret door in our apartment? Like hidden behind a bookshelf?"

Noah looked around the room and tried to brainstorm other possible scenarios.

"It could have been for intimidation?" Aria wondered.

"Or retaliation."

"For what?"

"Dad deals mods for a gang. The gang gets violent. A rival gang retaliates by attacking his family."

"So, that would mean Dad is either still alive or they're twelve years late."

"Or they were coming for Mom." Noah put a hand to his mouth thoughtfully. "She didn't tell us about Dad; maybe she hid parts of herself as well. She obviously knew a lot more than she ever said."

"Or, maybe whoever else is looking for this *thing* didn't mean to make a mess. Maybe Mom fought back, and it got out of hand." Aria tapped her fingers on the table.

"There was a big explosion as we left. Mom could have done that to slow them down."

"By the time we left, Mom was… dead." Aria saw her mom's body convulse and go limp in her mind's eye.

"Maybe she knew this might happen, and she was prepared to fight." Noah continued to think out loud. "But why wouldn't she just tell us what we're supposed to be looking for?"

Aria took a deep breath and looked at her brother. "I think we're getting ahead of ourselves. Mom told us to find something, and she told us to come here. Grandma knows more about Dad than anyone, so why send us here unless it's related to him?"

"Why don't we go to the police?"

"And say what? Our Dad was an illegal mod trader, and he left some technology—"

"—And that our mom was killed." Noah's tone darkened. "Someone broke into our house and killed our mother."

Again, Aria was unsettled by how simple the fact was and how readily she accepted it. Mom died. Last night. She watched her die. "The police won't help. If we go to them, we might as well hand ourselves over to whoever was at our home last night."

"People *say* that... but law enforcement can't possibly be entirely corrupt. It's literally impossible. And what else do we have?" Noah put his hands up. "What the hell are we even doing?"

"What do you mean? We have what Mom told us to do. She gave us an assignment."

"And we're just supposed to run around all of Xi by ourselves looking for something—something that we don't even know what that *thing* is?"

"No," Aria could sense a building frustration, but it didn't feel like her own, and the tiny waves quickly soothed it over. "Mom told us to come here, to Grandma's. So, there must be clues that we need to find, and then that should lead us to whatever is next—"

"Mom could have just said what she said to make us leave, to get us out..."

Aria sighed and rapped her knuckles on the table. The old clock ticked on the wall.

"—Okay, are you ready?" A man's voice played from the other room.

"Ready. I think," a second voice replied.

Aria jumped up and darted into the living room. Grandma was sitting quietly in front of the television. On it were two young men standing several feet apart. One wore a blindfold and held a short, curved blade in one hand, tattoos and mod marks covered almost every inch of his bare torso. The other held an armful of fruit, an excited but exhausted expression in his eyes.

Blowing a strand of hair out of his face, he turned and addressed the camera. "This is test number one for version nineteen."

"Twenty," the man in the blindfold corrected him.

"Version twenty. You're right. Here we go," he said, silently tossing pieces of fruit into the air around his companion. The blindfolded man immediately began slicing through the air with uncanny accuracy, bits of fruit and juice splattering wildly as the blade connected. The fruit-thrower started to chuckle, then burst out laughing as his friend spun to cleave a far-flung banana, returning to catch an apple that had been directed at the back of his head. With a dramatic finality, he crushed the apple in his bare hand and removed the blindfold, smiling.

"And that—" the young man who had been throwing the fruit pushed his hair back and laughed at the camera.

"Ultrasense," Noah whispered in awe.

"...is Ultrasense," the young man finished and sighed. "We did it. Eleven months of writing and one more in the books," he added, turning to the other man, who nodded calmly, admiring the feel of the newfound strength.

Aria was less concerned with the display of the mod's power. She stared at the young man as he talked to the camera. She could recognize the sharp smirk, the sparkling, clever eyes that always seemed to be seeing something else. Those eyes that had more than once passed her over as a child, ignoring her quiet petitions for attention. She recognized the stress in his features, the strain of a man who worked in a greedy industry of snakes and wolves, an industry where your friends could smile to your face and stab you in the back for your code. He would soon balance that pressure against a second life, one as a husband and as a father. His children would feel the weight of his work—the deep, recurring absence of a parent. The anger and frustration of a mother consistently left alone. Days, sometimes weeks, would pass without him. Then, he would come home. He would come home physically, but never mentally, never emotionally. He was never really available. One day, he would walk out the door, and he would never come back. His hidden life would take the whole of it and leave nothing for his family but a phantom memory.

The young man waved the camera off, and the screen went blank. The ghost in Aria's memory solidified. He hadn't just *worked* in the mod industry. He had been a developer. Ideating, writing, testing mods. Dangerous, powerful pieces of biocode like *Ultrasense*. Judging from the countless marks on his companion's chest, they had developed many.

Something alive and hungry burned through Aria's veins and clawed at her hands, her teeth, and her brain. Split-second scenes snapped through her mind. Shattered glass, bloodied hands, hooded figures, bones splintering, flesh burning. Aria's body tensed, her eyes narrowed. Beside her, Noah's muscles tightened, his heart quickened, and his iron knuckles cracked.

Indeed, Silas Sharp had created dangerous things.

Desperate, deadly, dangerous things.

5 THE NEON SISTERS

What do you think I should do?" Chance asked, looking to Benson for guidance. He had explained the situation, including the use of his own power and Friday's payment, to the robot. He had left out the strange dream about Emry.

"How much money is on the chip—chip?" Benson asked.

"Five hundred."

"How much will you ask for if you decide to work with them to find the missing girl?"

"I don't know," Chance muttered. It left a bad taste in his mouth to even be talking about it. He had avoided using his talent at all, and to suddenly consider bringing it out of the cage for money made him think of the swaying girl with the empty eyes from the street market.

"How much should I ask for?"

"Because I do not—I do not— know the full extent of your abilities, nor the situation regarding the disappearance of Ms. Rush, I cannot make a reliable rec—recommendation."

Chance sighed. "Maybe three thousand?"

"That is well below the range I was considering."

"Well, what range were you considering?"

"At, at, at least one hundred thousand credits."

Chance rolled his eyes. "Beep bop, I'm just a stupid robot who can't make a *reliable recommendation*."

"It seems, from what I can read of... of your current mind state," Benson continued to work while he spoke, "that you intend to join these two women—these two detectives regardless of the mon—money."

"Why do you say that?" Chance turned abruptly.

"You do not enjoy your time here. You want a reason to leave. Inside, you, you—you have already made up your mind, but you want someone else to make the decision for you out loud, so that way you are not responsible... responsible if the decision is a bad one."

"What? No, I just—" Chance had never heard a robot speak so insightfully before. "Also, 'mind state' isn't even a word, I think you mean 'state of mind.'"

"As a service-dedicated intelligence, I spend a vast amount of computing resources observing, learning, and analyzing human behaviors. Seeing as you and I spend most of our time together, I have learned a considerable amount about your behavior and thought patterns. Also, you've packed a bag," Benson pointed at a backpack under the bar counter. "You've already decided to go."

"Impressed you said all of that without a stutter. But the backpack is just *in case* I decide..." Chance responded unconvincingly. But Benson was right. Chance had decided already a long time ago. The day he had seen the help wanted sign on the window of Mr. Bird's shop and walked in to ask for work, he had planned on leaving. He had only been waiting for an opportunity, for a chance to escape. But, at the same time...

"You—you are afraid of failure. That is why you work in this job. You cannot fall if you are already at the bottom."

Chance didn't know what to say to that.

"Embrace the fear of failure. The possibility that you might not succeed is what makes it an adventure."

"Are you quoting something?"

"Poss—Possibly."

"Will I succeed?"

"I do not know the situation and variables sufficiently to say anything regarding your chances of finding—of finding the missing girl," Benson replied and wandered off to clean tables.

Chance glowered. "Damn service-dedicated... smartass whatever robot."

For the next several hours, Chance jumped between going and not going. He would decide, then undecide, then redecide, only to change his mind again. What Benson said was true; he didn't want to make this decision. All his life, Chance had been looking to leave the dull hopelessness of this horribly dead-end lifestyle. More than anything, he did not want to watch himself fade into the numb spiral that his mother was drowning in. Were these two freelancers not offering him a chance to change that?

But what if they were just crazy? What if he was joining two mentally unstable street-crawlers on a wild goose chase through this maze of a city? Would he end up like Goosh? Brain-fried, glitching, and forever obsessing over some ridiculous conspiracy?

Or worse, what if the whole thing was a trap? What if these two strangers were simply smiling and flirting and luring him straight to his death?

"Then you'll kill them." Vent sat at one of the barstools, swirling a phantom drink.

Chance waved the ghost away. "I'm not killing anyone." Breathing deeply, he poured himself a glass of water and sat down at the bar in Vent's seat, rubbing his eyes.

In the dream, Emry had *literally* asked him to come back for her. Well, literally *in a dream.* But was it just a dream? Was it... a sign or an intervention of fate? Or maybe some sort of message from Emry sent straight to his mind? That wasn't uncommon between friends. At least, it would be *if* Chance was still in contact with any of his past friends, which he was not.

Emry Rush Found Dead After Boy Ignores Her Call for Help. Chance imagined the headline. The timing of the whole thing was weird. And the bracelet? Chance had never seen it before, until it showed up on Friday's wrist. And yet, he recognized it. Maybe the city, *the City* in the meta sense, had a mind of its own and was beckoning him out. Or maybe it was just his own subconscious giving him further reason to go?

Eventually, Chance's twenty-four hours came to an end as the sun settled deep into the cracks of Xi's skyscrapers. Minutes passed, and Chance kept his eyes on the door, accidentally over-filling a patron's drink in his misfocus. Five minutes, eight minutes, then ten minutes past when they said they would be here. Perhaps the two women were simply a mirage fabricated by his lonely mind. Twenty minutes had passed when the door finally opened, but it was only a hunched old man who quietly took a seat at a far table. Then, through the front window, two motorcycles rolled to a stop across the street.

Chance's heart began to quicken, and his palms started to sweat. That wouldn't be them, right? That could be anyone. But, the undeniable sheen of June's hair as he watched the riders dismount made it clear that his two visitors had returned.

Chance sighed desperately to himself. What was he doing? He looked at the bag under the counter.

A opportunity... an adventure... Friday's voice played in his head.

I'm not going... I'm not going. I can't. I don't even know these people.

Another voice: *Don't leave me. Come back for me.*

Across the room, a customer gagged and hacked up a large glob of phlegm into their bowl of soup, pausing only briefly to stir the liquid before they continued eating.

"Gah... Benson!" Chance called for the droid, who had conveniently disappeared. Please, someone, *anyone*, give him a reason to stay. Make him think rationally.

No one answered.

Groaning with a resigned finality, Chance threw his apron into the back kitchen, cursed his robot friend, and snatched the bag from under the counter.

———

THE AIR WAS warm and sticky as Chance stepped out the front door of the bar and into the road. The women smiled, and a sampling of the Riverbed's population of misfits passed by on the street between them. Most kept their eyes focused on the ground, either too afraid or too strung out to give more than a passing glance to Chance's new associates.

Both women were outfitted in dark bodysuits, and their hair was done in matching pigtail braids. The bikes behind them were jet black, and multi-colored LEDs hidden in the frames cast a glow around the wheels. "Hi, Chance," June acknowledged him with a small wave as he approached.

"Hi," Chance replied, his heart pounding. He already regretted his decision.

"I knew you'd come," Friday grinned.

"I'm not—"

"—We're gonna be heroes, all of us," Friday cut him off.

Chance gulped and steeled himself to negotiate. "How much will I be paid?"

"Two hundred thousand," Friday responded without hesitation. "If we get Emry and return her safely to her family. If we don't, zero." Friday stuck out her hand. "Deal?"

Chance stared blankly at her open invite. *Well, if that's the type of money we're talking about, say no more.* Dream or no dream, that kind of money would guarantee Chance would never have to pluck around the Surface again. He could get his glitches fixed, leave the Riverbed behind, and take his mother on a real vacation to some tropical island far away.

"Look, don't overthink this. I talk like it's some grand fucking thing, but it's a contract job. An employment opportu-

nity, that's all. And we'll only be busy for several days at most."
Friday continued. "You'll be staying with us. If we can't find her
within a week, she's gone, and no one will ever find her. You can
go home to your little life here and forget we ever met."

Chance looked back and forth between the duo. June nodded
reassuringly. Friday tilted her head sideways.

"How can I trust you?" Chance asked.

Friday shrugged. "I don't know, I already paid you once? You
stepped in to save us from a fight? It seems like we already have
quite the relationship."

Chance could sense the slight hint of sarcasm in her voice as
her smile faded.

"Trust has to start somewhere," she added.

Don't be a coward. Vent mocked him from inside his brain.

Come back for me.

Too many voices in his head. Chance gulped them down.
"All right," he grabbed Friday's hand, and Vent chuckled victo-
riously.

"Let's find this girl." Chance nodded.

"Perfect," Friday responded, her smile returning. "Welcome
to the motherfucking team."

THE BUILDINGS WHIPPED by at a ridiculous speed as Friday
pushed the bike to its limit down a straight stretch of road,
passing dangerously between the lanes of traffic. Chance held on
for dear life, his arms locked around her waist. Off to their right,
June's bike lit up the surrounding city like a polychromatic
comet, multicolor LEDs pulsing across the motorcycle's chassis.

They banked slightly and turned onto a street that curved
upward, twisting them higher and higher and onto a new level
of the city. Soon, they were on a long bridge, and Chance almost
forgot his fear as he looked out over the vast expanse of urban
jungle that glimmered all around them.

They turned down several more streets and eventually slowed and pulled into a tiny garage. Chance's heart was pounding furiously as he dismounted the bike, his arms and legs shaking and sweaty.

"How was it?" June smiled mischievously as she killed the engine of her own motorcycle.

"He almost crushed my guts out; he was holding on so tightly," Friday smirked, yanking the garage door closed and shutting the trio in complete darkness.

June slid past Chance and unlocked a door to a small, feebly lit staircase. "This way," she grinned as she guided the tour up the steep steps and into the apartment.

If Chance thought his apartment was a mess, he was mistaken. This was another level. Gadgets, maps, screens, holograms, pictures, clothes, and miscellaneous household objects covered almost every surface. A large whiteboard on the wall was decorated in illegible handwriting and a series of dates. Something on a nearby shelf table whirred and clicked. A screen on the left wall played an advertisement for some sort of sports drink. In the far corner, a mannequin sat propped against a small stool. A cracked helmet adorned its head, and a collection of knives, throwing stars, and other sharp objects protruded from its chest.

"Welcome to my home," Friday bowed dramatically and kicked a piece of junk out of her way. "That's Chester," she pointed at the mannequin. "He's my roommate," she added as she walked over and pulled a shuriken out of his side.

"Sorry, it's a mess," June apologized, quickly picking up various items and shoving them onto shelves and into boxes. "We've been really busy lately."

"Do you live here too?" Chance stepped carefully around what looked like a disassembled robot.

"Friday is letting me crash here while I'm…" June scratched her head, "between places."

In the conjoining room, a couch sat against one wall, a folded blanket and a pillow placed neatly on one of the cushions. "This is where you can sleep for the next few days," Friday explained, pointing to the couch. Twenty or so mod tiles were arranged into small groups on a nearby glass coffee table. Notes were written in marker on the table's surface.

That's gotta be at least ninety-thousand credits worth of biocode, Chance observed as he quickly ran his eyes across the collection of mod tiles, recognizing marks from more than one renowned developer.

"For a client," Friday explained, noticing the awe on Chance's face. "I trust you won't try anything."

Chance quickly agreed.

June disappeared down a back hallway while Friday continued the brief tour, pointing out the bathroom and a small kitchen area. "Feel free to eat whatever you want. *Except* for the blue liquid in the fridge. Do *not* touch that."

Chance nodded.

"And this," Friday announced as she struggled to pull open a sliding glass door. "Is the balcony," she grunted as the door finally came unstuck. "It's not much, but…"

Chance followed Friday onto the tiny ledge. She wasn't kidding; it really wasn't much at all. The cramped balcony looked out at a wall of opposing apartments. Across the way, an old lady was hanging wet clothes on a line. She grimaced at Friday. Two balconies over, a pair of men hushed their conversation, throwing short glances in Chance's direction as they drank smoke from a large pipe. A small drone buzzed past the railing, stirring the thin clouds of steam that filled the space between buildings, and Chance watched the tendrils of mist curl through the air in silence.

"We're going to find Emry," Friday leaned against the railing, biting her lip at the street below. For a brief moment, Chance caught a glimpse of something lurking behind the odd personality and unique confidence of the person before him. Something familiar. A storm made up of all sorts of things he knew he couldn't put a name to, except for one main ingredient: pain. That, he could always recognize. It was as if this strange woman who had dragged him out of his life and into her hero story was not too unlike Chance himself.

"Why do you want to find her?"

"I told you already," Friday answered in an unusually soft tone, running her eyes across the windows of her neighbors. "I think we'd get rewarded nicely." She clicked her tongue thoughtfully. Chance was quiet, and eventually, Friday went on. "See this bracelet?" she said, holding up her hand with the metal band on her wrist. Chance could see the name *Rush* printed in small letters on the metal.

"You were asking Shift where he got it."

"Yes, we—" Friday stopped and grinned at Chance. "You were eavesdropping, I see."

Chance laughed nervously. "You started a fight in my restaurant."

"Fair enough," Friday nodded. "Anyway, there I was in an early morning meetup with the owner of a place called Mod and Metal—he sells mods and little bionic pieces—and as he's talking to me, June points out this bracelet. And right there on the screen behind him is this breaking news segment..." Friday held her wrist out to admire the bracelet. "And on the screen is a picture of Emry Rush, wearing *this* bracelet, right as I'm looking at the actual thing on the wrist of this store owner.

"So, I ask him where he got it; he says a friend sold it to him the night before, a man named Shift. So, I make a trade: I give the store owner a mod, and he gives me the bracelet and agrees to help us meet Shift."

"So, you met at Mr. Bird's?"

"Correct. And Shift tells us an *angel* gave it to him. Like, what the fuck does that mean?"

"And that's it?" Chance asked.

"That's it," Friday looked down at the street below and

twisted the bracelet anxiously. "Regardless of how Shift actually got it, I think the bracelet found its way to me."

Or maybe it found its way to me, Chance thought to himself. "Seems kinda... oddly coincidental."

"Doesn't it?" Friday agreed. "But I figured maybe if we could trace the path of the bracelet backwards, it would lead us to Emry."

"But Shift was a dead end?"

"Hm, not entirely. I have my suspicions." Friday shrugged.

"Have you done something like this before?" Chance asked.

"I have done lots of things. There are so many people in the city that need something. They need to find something, get rid of something, meet someone, lose someone." Friday rolled her neck. "People that need to get somewhere, or just forget that they're anywhere at all, if only for a night." She threw a playful side-eye at Chance.

Chance gave an anxious half-laugh. "What, um... what was in that vial the other night? The one you had around your neck," he asked, shifting the conversation.

"Hm," Friday grinned and leaned back, holding onto the balcony railing. "My reputation. If everything goes smoothly, you'll never have to find out what it is." She looked Chance up and down. "What exactly does your... mod do?"

Chance glanced up at the endless stack of apartments above as the yapping of a tiny dog echoed down from somewhere high up. "Honestly, I don't know. It's almost like I push on people with my mind. Then, uh, I kinda take over their body..." he explained, intentionally omitting his phantom friend.

"That's fucking terrifying," Friday stared at him. "I'm glad you're a good guy."

"I, yeah, it's... weird." Chance let his gaze wander around the buildings again.

Friday drew a finger through the air. "You know how they say the City is a maze?"

"Yeah," Chance nodded.

"The key to getting through is speed. Decisiveness. You come to a fork, you pick a direction, and you go. You don't spend forever thinking about it. Why? Because the instant you make it past one turn, there's another turn. And another turn. And a million more fucking turns."

Chance waited for Friday to explain.

She pulled herself close to Chance and lowered her voice. "I made a quick decision to invite you in because *you* made a quick decision to help us out. So, don't think too much; you've got good instincts." Smiling, she pushed off the railing and stepped back into the apartment.

Chance followed her in, closing the sliding glass door behind himself, and June walked back into the main room wearing something more comfortable than her motorcycle outfit.

"June," Friday spoke as she moved around the room. "You two entertain yourselves for a little bit. I've got to go take care of something." She grabbed a couple of the mod tiles off the coffee table and then snatched her cloak off the wall—the same flowy, void-black piece from the night before—and draped it around her shoulders. "When I get back, we're going to lay out a plan."

"For sure," June smiled at Chance, and his heart skipped. "We'll get to know each other."

Friday chuckled and donned her large hat. "No doubt," she mused, heading for the door in the other room as she pulled the brim down low. "No doubt."

6 DELIVERY

Emry watched the light from the crack under the door. She had been watching it for what seemed like hours, waiting for the shadow of feet to appear on the other side and for the door to open and for someone slow and evil to creep inside. But, as the silent minutes passed, no one came, and the light from the crack under the door stayed constant. The thin yellow line gave just enough illumination to reveal where she was—a small, wood-paneled room with a slanted ceiling on one side as if it were part of an attic.

An attic *where?* She didn't know. She didn't have time to figure that out. She lay low to the floor, trying as best she could to control the panic in her breathing. Her only companion, a large, old computer, hummed quietly atop the tiny desk beside her.

Emry's ankle had been shackled to one of the many small pipes that crisscrossed around the walls of the room. By pushing against the crusted metal with one foot and pulling on the shackled ankle until the cuff cut deep into her skin, the pipe had broken. And now, aside from the metallic tape that bound her hands together, she was free to turn her attention to the door. She assumed it was locked, but she hadn't checked. She couldn't seem to move from the floor.

Fear, the paralyzing kind, kept her down more than the pipe and shackles had. The yellow line of light under the door held her captive. Who was on the other side? What if someone was waiting for her there?

For a brief moment, Emry pictured her mother walking through the door, in the same way she had a million times before after returning from one of her many charity trips abroad and waking Emry up just to let her know that she had come home. She would sit on the edge of Emry's bed and tell stories about the experience and then make promises to bring her along on the next one. Emry would smile and feign excitement, knowing she wouldn't go.

Then she pictured her father walking in from the rooftop landing pad, stressed after a multi-day sprint at the office. He would make small talk, ask how Emry's week had been and how school was going, and try in vain to force his thoughts to be present at home and not back at Seitech. Emry would do her best to keep the conversation going, careful to keep the topic light just to avoid adding any more weight to her father's mind.

How she wished that her parents would come through the door now.

Emry closed her eyes tightly and tried one more time to summon her Interface overlays. Nothing appeared. No messages, no settings, no maps, no connections, no ability to communicate with anyone on the outside. For certain, someone had been inside her code and disabled it. There was no time to think about that, though.

You have to go, Emry forced out another shaking breath. *Now is your chance to escape.* Carefully, as the floorboards groaned underneath, Emry pushed herself to her feet. Her eyes were glued to the light from the doorframe. Her whole body was shaking now, but at least she could move. She took a step for the door, then stopped. A pen, on the desk. She picked it up with both hands, curling it tight in her fingers and holding it up like a spear. She noticed her bracelet was gone. Again, no time to worry about that.

A shaky breath, a slow step forward.

Another step, and another step, and Emry was at the door, the yellow light from underneath now at her feet.

Keeping a grip on her pen, Emry turned the doorknob with her fingertips.

Suddenly, heavy footsteps echoed from the other side as if climbing a staircase. Emry took a step back, and the fear seized her again, freezing her in place.

The doorknob turned, and the door opened quickly, filling the room with the yellow light of the stairwell behind it. A man stood in the doorway. He was finely dressed, with a light beard around his rugged jaw and a gold pendant around his neck. He seemed surprised to see Emry standing so close, but not alarmed. His eyes quickly flicked from her ankle to the broken pipe, and he nodded to himself in mild amusement.

Slowly, Emry raised the pen to strike.

Calmly, the man grabbed her wrists with one hand and pulled the pen out of her grasp with the other. "Here," he said, handing it over his shoulder to a man behind him. Emry could see there were several more, as well as an armored AI.

"Scare—" Emry swallowed down her panic.

"Hm?" the man asked. "You have something to—"

"Scarecrow, Scarecrow, Scarecrow!" Emry spat the words out, and the attic and stairwell buzzed with an electromagnetic pulse. The men in front of her gasped and doubled over, some collapsing to the steps, others grabbing at the walls and handrail. The robot at the back dropped dead and clanked loudly down the stairs.

Emry's own knees wobbled, and the spot behind her eyes sizzled in pain. She forced her feet forward, steadying herself on the door frame. She would have to climb over everyone to get down the stairs—

The man at the doorway shot back to his feet, gold pendant bouncing on his chest as he blocked Emry's path.

"Oh shit—scarecrow, scarecrow, scarecrow!"

The safewords had no effect the second time.

"Shit, shit!" Emry tried to backpedal, but the man caught her by the wrists. "Let go! Let—" Emry thrashed in vain against the man's grip and kicked wildly at him.

The man held her at arm's length and spoke over his shoulder. "Get her legs."

Another man shouldered his way into the small attic and reached for Emry.

"Don't touch me!" Emry tried to yank herself away. "Don't fucking touch me!" Gathering all her strength, she wrenched her hands free and kicked the second man square in the jaw as he bent to grab her legs.

In a flash, she was thrown onto her back, the impact smashing her breath away. Her legs were immediately cinched together.

"Who are you?" Emry coughed out.

The man with the pendant stood over her. "This time..." he answered, "this time I am only the delivery boy."

———

WIND HOWLED as Emry was walked out onto a wide, circular rooftop. She could only see several yards ahead; thick mist obscured her surroundings in every direction. Bracing as micro-droplets of rain pelted her skin, she took a few steps forward. *Where...* she couldn't seem to remember how she had gotten here.

Small metal footsteps clanked on the roof behind her, and a tiny robot jogged into her frame of view. It regarded her for a moment, beeped a few times, then, with a swift flick, cut the metal tape off her wrists.

Emry looked at the small robot, unsure of what to say, before it turned away and sprinted to the edge of the roof, not even pausing as it hurled itself into the wind and clouds. The soft rushing sound of a jet pack echoed as the droid flew back to wherever it had come from, leaving Emry alone once again.

Emry stood in silence for several seconds, trying to recollect her whereabouts, when the wind stopped. Rather, the *air* stopped, as if time had suddenly frozen. Even the droplets of cloud mist seemed to be suspended in space.

Emry turned, trailing a hand testily through the floating condensation. She could hear her own heart beating, and her pulse was beginning to quicken. "Where am I?" she asked the empty cloud.

Slowly, Emry came full circle and froze. There before her, covered mostly by the fog, was a person. A white robe flowed gently around their figure, though the air still did not move. The person stepped slowly forward. A gold mask covered their face.

"Scarecrow, scarecrow..." The words seemed to melt from her mouth, as if the being before her was draining her energy, her language, and all her thoughts and pulling them into itself.

The figure waved an arm slowly, and the clouds on Emry's left began to clear. Emry looked, and all of Xi opened up beneath her, the tops of skyscrapers and towers, even her father's building. Emry tried to speak but her muscles resisted, everything was heavy and slow.

The being extended a metallic hand in Emry's direction and slowly curled its fingers, beckoning.

Emry walked obediently toward her captor.

She placed her hand in theirs, and they grabbed it tightly. With a bright flash and a sizzling bang, the two of them vanished, and the wind filled their void, whipping and howling and splattering rain against the empty rooftop.

7 THE CREATOR

"Play that one in the office again," Aria pointed with her foot at the screen, laying on her back on the floor, her head propped against the couch, as Noah navigated through the collection of videos.

After Grandma had pulled up the first video, Aria and Noah dove into the rest of the files that she had saved. They found hours and hours of footage of Dad as a baby, as a toddler, as a young kid—those videos alone had taken them deep into the night. Less had been recorded of him as a teenager or a young man, and only the three most recent videos held anything more than nostalgic value. Aside from trips to the bathroom and a quick break for food, Aria had hardly moved from the couch as she and her brother studied the recordings. She had half expected someone to have shown up at the house; surely, some detective had been assigned their case and should be looking for them by now. Or even the guys who had attacked their apartment. Why had Grandma's house not become the next target?

For whatever reason, no one had come, and at some point, Aria and Noah had both fallen asleep in various positions between the couch and the floor. Come morning, Aria awoke to find Noah scrubbing through the files again.

Noah played the office video, a short clip they had seen over a dozen times already, which the siblings watched in complete silence.

Silas Sharp was sitting in an office chair, talking directly to the camera.

"So, this is our space," Silas said, gesturing widely, as the camera turned to show a small, cramped developer's den. "R is already wired in, doing work," he added, directing the camera to that same friend from the fruit-slicing video, who, this time, sat typing rapidly at a large screen. Lines of code shot across the display as his fingers moved. Surrounding geometric shapes shifted and transformed with each keystroke. Biocode.

Behind R's screen, a large sunburst-like symbol was painted on the wall. Silas began spouting off technical facts about the room's computers and their developmental capabilities; Aria still couldn't understand any of it.

Grandma walked into the room carrying a cardboard box, and Aria pushed herself up against the couch. "Grandma, where did you get these videos?"

Silence was her only answer as Grandma crossed into the kitchen.

Another clip began. This was the third of the three videos Aria and Noah had decided might hold clues to what they were to do next.

This time, Silas stood alone on a rooftop; glass and chrome towers sparkled behind him in the sunlight. He wore a loose shirt that flapped in the breeze, revealing an array of haphazardly placed mod marks of all colors and styles across his torso. He looked older in this recording, though it was hard to tell his exact age since the videos had no timestamp.

"SR Development, X-Strength, demonstration three," he addressed the camera, then nodded to someone off-screen. "Okay." He readied himself with his fists up.

R, the same friend from the other videos, jumped into the frame, yelling as he swung a wooden bat hard over his head.

Silas reacted with almost lightning speed, throwing his forearm up to block. The bat cracked loudly as it impacted bone, and the wood splintered in all directions, the top half of the bat spinning wildly over the edge of the roof.

The screen went black. The siblings looked at each other, lost in thought for a long moment until Grandma reentered the room and placed her cardboard box between them.

"Silas liked to keep journals," she said, slowly lifting the lid.

Aria and Noah both jumped up from the floor and bent over the open box.

Inside lay a pile of papers and a leather-bound journal. Carefully, Grandma picked up the journal and handed it to Aria. "Like DaVinci."

Reverently, Aria took the journal and turned it over in her hands. She looked back and forth between the tiny book and Noah, whose face mirrored her astonishment. Nothing said *clues* like a collection of secret papers and a forgotten diary.

"He used to visit occasionally," Grandma reflected. "I haven't seen him in a long time. They said he died. But... he was very, very smart, you see."

Aria carefully opened the cover of the journal and read the first page:

Thoughts, Ideas, and Visions

\-\-

S

An intricate design had been drawn around the border of the title page. Aria traced the designs with her finger and then began to flip the pages as Noah reached for the other papers in the box.

Tight paragraphs of scratchy text were crammed between drawings and diagrams, all of which made no sense to Aria. Technical script and mod ideas, lines of biocode, numbers and complex equations, concentric circles and intersecting lines, a double helix and chemical compounds, a carefully drawn cross-section of the human brain. Page after page of advanced science.

"Grandma," Aria said, slowly looking up from a page headlined *Interneural Network?*

Without warning, Aria watched as her own arms shot out like pit vipers, grabbing her grandmother's head on both sides and twisting violently.

Aria gasped and jumped back, her heart pounding as she realized it was a hallucination. Her hands still held her father's journal, the pages twisted and tearing in her fingers. Grandma looked up slowly, waiting for Aria to finish her question. Aria released her grip on the journal, and the tiny waves began to wash through her frame.

"Aria?" Noah asked in confusion.

"I—" Aria shook her head. Grandmother was fine; it wasn't real. "I... um, I just—" As the waves continued to roll, Aria felt her nerves cool and her mind clear.

Noah stared at her with concern.

"I think I saw... something."

"Saw what?"

"I don't know. Some side effect of my mod, I think. A glitch of some kind."

Noah nodded understandingly. "Sometimes they do weird things."

Aria shivered. "Grandma, do you have anything else that belonged to Dad?"

THE NEXT COUPLE hours passed in relative silence as Noah and Aria poured through the stacks and stacks of their father's papers. It seemed Grandma had saved everything his handwriting had ever appeared on, yet very little of it offered any insight into what exactly Aria and Noah needed to be looking for.

"Listen to this, though," Aria announced, pressing the journal open against the kitchen table. Noah sat opposite her, trying to make sense of a large chart that he had pulled from the box of his father's records.

Aria cleared her throat and read:

"Man is more than bones and blood; there is not only biology and technology—there must be some higher order. We devote so much time to unlocking the mind and manipulating the body, but what of our existence beyond these bounded platforms? I hypothesize a real, tangible intelligence outside the electrical currents we understand now as consciousness, that is in and through us, and at the same time, entirely unknown."

Aria finished the paragraph and looked up at Noah. He was still studying the chart intently. "He's talking about a soul. Or a spirit." Aria expounded.

Noah slid the day-old pan of cold eggs across the tabletop and laid the chart down flat. He stared at it for several seconds before shaking his head. "I don't get it," he said, resigned.

"Noah."

"I was listening. What are you thinking?"

"I don't know."

Aria turned as Grandma shuffled back into the kitchen, carrying a stained dish towel and humming off-key under her breath.

"Grandma, you said our Dad liked to keep journals. Do you have any other ones?"

Their grandmother's tune didn't falter, and she didn't turn at her granddaughter's query, but her face split wide with an uncharacteristic grin when she saw the chart Noah was just beginning to fold up.

"Oh, you found his fancy drawings." She moved forward and slid one hand caressingly over the chart, then looked at

Noah like she was sharing a special secret. "He always liked to draw, you know. But he wouldn't ever let me see them."

She clicked her tongue and sighed, then resumed humming as she cleaned imaginary spots on her oven door with the towel. Aria and Noah exchanged a glance. Aria stood to place her hand on her grandmother's shoulder but quickly drew back and cleared her throat instead.

"Grandma, we really like Dad's drawings. Do you know where he might keep more of them?"

Grandma gazed off in thought for a moment. "His hideout, I'm sure. All boys like to have a secret hideout with their friends. The place he'd always disappear to. He took everything there."

"Do you know where this hideout is?" Aria pressed the question.

A sharp smile played across Grandma's mouth. "A single mother in the city of Xi, you think I would let my only child go out every day without following him at least once? Of course, I know where it is."

"Where is it?" Noah asked.

Grandma looked at him slowly. "Hm... where is what?"

"Where is Silas' secret hideout? Where did he hide his drawings and his journals?"

"I have his drawings and his journal in a box."

Aria put her fingers to her temples. "Grandma, where is Silas' hideout?"

Silence filled the kitchen for several seconds, then Grandma sighed. "Silas died, I'm afraid."

Aria looked at her brother. Noah shook his head.

"—Hey, kids!" A cheery voice blared from the television in the other room as some children's show began to play at max volume.

"I thought we turned that off," Noah grimaced against the chaotic, sunshine-y sounds of the show and made his way to the screen, dropping to a crouch in front of the TV stand. "What even is this show?"

Aria stepped into the room, and suddenly, the screen changed, switching channels to what looked like an action movie. The protagonist on the screen grabbed his companion by the shoulders and flashed a smile. "Listen, I'll be quick."

Noah glanced back at his sister.

Aria's held up a hand. "Wait…"

"What?" Noah looked back and forth between his sister and the screen as the channel changed again, this time to a game show.

"I'm sorry," the game show host apologized to a contestant, and the channel changed again.

"I should have never left!" a woman in an overdramatic soap opera threw herself into the arms of a lover, and the channel changed again.

Noah slowly backed away from the television, his heart beginning to pound.

"I made a mistake—" an athlete spoke at a press conference, putting his head in his hands.

"You deserve better—" an obnoxious car commercial shouted, cut short as the channels continued to change.

"—but there's not going to be enough time—" a sports announcer narrated the last seconds of a soccer match.

Chills ran all the way up Aria's back, and tears began to form in her eyes.

"—you can find—" a plumber shone a light on a network of pipes.

"—what you're looking for!—" The car commercial cut back in.

"—here, near the Yizhou Mill—" a news reporter stood in front of an old building, gesturing over her shoulder.

"—the Red Seed Factory—" a conveyor belt hummed through an outdated documentary.

"—an apartment?" A young woman smiled and crossed her legs on a couch.

"—between—" the plumbing video returned for an instant.

"—the buildings—" the reporter again.

The game show flicked back on, and the host motioned at a series of doors. "Let's see what's behind door number—"

"NINE!" A hundred kids shouted the number in unison as the children's show cut back in, and a red, sparkling '9' populated the entire display before the whole screen went black.

And silent.

Neither sibling moved nor made a noise for a whole minute. Noah slowly pressed his shaking hands into the carpet and turned to look at his sister.

She stood paralyzed in place, eyes fixed on the black screen, tear tracks down both cheeks.

Noah drew in a deep breath, and the calm, pulsing sensation from his new mod began to soothe his mind and quiet his body. "Aria?"

Aria could feel the tiny waves moving through her chest as well, slowing her heart and steadying her hands.

"What was that?" Noah asked.

Aria shook her head, unable to take her eyes from the screen. "I don't... I don't know..."

Grandma shuffled into the room and regarded her grandchildren for a moment. "Silas was so smart. I wish he could be here to see how his children have grown."

"I think he does see..." Aria whispered, mostly to herself.

"That can't be..." Noah stared at his sister. "I don't understand, was that a message?"

"Check it," Aria flicked her chin at the black screen. "Check if there's an apartment between Yizhou Mill and the Red Seed Factory."

Noah nodded and summoned a map of Xi to his eyes. After a few seconds of navigation, he paused and took a deep breath. "It's there. Industrial Housing, Unit 1, it says."

"We have to go, then," Aria decided, throwing her eyes around the room for one last time.

"Yeah," Noah agreed. "Yeah, we do."

"Grandma," Aria placed a hand on her grandmother's arm. "We'll be back." *Actually, it's probably best if we don't return, at least for now.*

Grandma hummed something incoherent in response as Noah tossed Silas Sharp's leather journal across the room to his sister.

"Ready?"

"Ready."

"Let's go."

———

ARIA EXAMINED the blood on the seat of the car between her legs. The blood that had soaked into the carpet and stained her hands two nights before. Her mother's blood. More decorated the inside of the door. It seemed to Aria such an out-of-place thing, dried and darkened on the leather and glass. Yet it didn't frighten her, not like it should. Not like the life of her family should.

The car purred quietly as it turned down a narrow side street, the walls of the surrounding buildings nearly scraping the mirrors as some street-dweller stepped into a door frame to avoid the passing vehicle. They had been driving for nearly an hour, working their way out of the Upriver where Grandma lived and deep into the heart of the city, down toward the Riverbed. Here on the Surface, the people crawled the streets like giant insects, weaving around piles of trash and ducking from one hole in the wall to the next—a completely different life to what Aria and her brother had known on the levels above.

"Do you remember," Noah tapped his finger on the steering wheel, "that one day at the beach with Mom?"

"The day when we found the cave?"

"Yeah…"

Aria could see it clearly. She was seven at the time. Bright sunlight sparkled across the tops of rolling, clear-blue breakers.

A cool breeze whipped the waves toward the shore, and they would smash beautifully into the yellow sand of the beach. Sandstone cliffs ringed this particular spot, providing solace from the wind and would-be tourists. Mom had taken them to the secret beach one day, telling them that it was one of her favorite places as a child.

Aria let the vivid memory commandeer her thoughts.

"Noah!" Karinne called out as eight-year-old Noah sprinted away across the wet sand. "Noah! Where are you going?"

"Over there!" he shouted back over the sound of the crashing waves, pointing at the far cliff wall. "I just want to look at it!"

"Okay! Let us know what you find!"

Noah gave a big thumbs up and continued down the shoreline.

Aria pushed together a small pile of sand at the edge of the towel as her mother lay down beside her.

"Whatchya makin'?" Mom asked.

"A house," Aria responded, keeping her eyes on her creation. "For the crab." She pointed at a tiny hermit crab that moved slowly across the warm sand.

"Did you know that crabs like that carry their house with them? That shell on his back—that's his home. So, he can live anywhere he wants."

Aria watched the small creature for a moment. "That's not a house!" she laughed. "That's his bones. He wants a real house."

Karinne smiled. "Maybe you're right. Let's make him a real house."

So, as the crab walked slowly past, Aria and Mom built him a sand house, complete with sticks and shells and a small seagull feather at the top.

"Let's see if he likes it," Aria announced, jumping to her feet, grabbing the hermit crab, and placing him in front of the tiny sandcastle. The crab retreated into his shell and sat unmoving as Aria and Karinne watched and waited.

"Maybe he doesn't like it," Aria shrugged.

"I think he's just shy."

"Aria! Mom! Come look at this!" Noah was running back toward them across the sand. He stopped at the edge of the towel as he noticed the small sandcastle and the motionless crab. "You have to come see this. I found a cave."

Aria looked up at her mom.

"You go look at the cave with Noah. I'll watch from here and keep an eye on our friend," Mom replied with a gentle smile.

"Okay," Aria pushed herself up again and followed her brother out across the beach to the point where the waves met the cliff wall.

"Look," Noah directed, standing in the shallow surf. "There it is."

Aria followed his pointing finger. It was more of an alcove, really. A miniature beach that had been carved out underneath the cliff. The only way to get inside would be to wait for the swell to pull out, revealing the strip of sand between the rock wall and the ocean, and then run across and duck inside before the next wave came crashing back into the sandstone.

"There's probably treasure buried in the sand there," Noah observed. "We should go see. I'm gonna go first, then you follow me."

Aria watched the tide as Noah readied himself to run. The waves were taller than either of the siblings, breaking hard on the shore and rolling fast into the cliff face.

"One..." Noah counted himself down. "Two..." a wave crashed against the rock and began to pull back. "Three!" He dashed across the wet sand and under the outcropping with plenty of time to spare before another wave pounded and foamed between Aria and her brother.

"Okay, your turn!" Noah shouted, turning back to his sister.

Aria swallowed hard as the next wave hit, rolling and swirling with power.

"I'll count you down. One!"

Aria readied herself to run. The ocean did the same.

"Two!" The swell crashed in, breaking menacingly before it sucked back toward the water. Aria's heart beat furiously.

"Three!"

A blinking drone buzzed overhead as the car turned again, pulling Aria out of her daydream. They were on a narrow road that dropped off on her side into the River Xi below. Brown water poured in from corroded pipes, and half-rotted fishing boats drifted in the current, almost indistinguishable from the icebergs of floating refuse they navigated between. Up above, the crisscrossing bridges and towering canopy of apartments and businesses and power lines blocked all of the light from the sky, giving Aria the notion that she had entered a massive sewer.

The buzzing drone approached again, and Aria turned to see it pause, hovering outside her window as the lights on its body turned red. The drone lifted straight up, and suddenly, Aria knew what was happening.

"They found us. Noah, drive!"

Noah floored the accelerator, but it was too late. The mod-waves began to pulse through Aria's body. Then, in an oddly peaceful sensation, time began to slow. Not dramatically slow, but enough to take note of passing details: Noah's hands were fastened tight to the wheel with determination, and the whirr of the engine grew to a high-pitched whine. The road before them followed the River fairly straight, connecting with a bridge up ahead. If they could get enough speed, they could turn on the bridge and maybe vanish into the city. But the now-blinking drone swung into an alleyway just ahead of them, and Aria sensed what was coming before she saw it. Noah drove in front of the mouth of the alley, and Aria could only watch in slow motion as the grill of a large truck smashed into the driver's side of the car.

Aria had never been in a car wreck before, but even in her elevated state, she was amazed at the sheer transfer of energy from one vehicle to the next that yanked and tossed her and her brother like helpless ragdolls.

The air forced itself from her lungs as the impact ripped her sideways, the bones and tendons in her back and neck threatening to snap in the shifting momentum. A thousand shards of glass sliced through both upholstery and flesh. As the car lifted off the pavement, it twisted into the air, through the rusted guardrail, and above the poisonous water of the River Xi.

The car flipped slowly, and Aria once again found herself staring into a demonic kaleidoscope as her world revolved behind the cracked windshield. In the weightlessness of the fall, a controlling calmness moved up and down through her core and into her extremities with each pulsing wave. She watched in mild amusement as the airbags deployed in front of her face and all around her body like giant marshmallows, the one on her right momentarily consuming her head as the car hit the river surface on its side. Water blasted in through her window, burying more glass in her skin and twisting her back the other direction.

Aria had only a split moment to register the desperate state of her brother, pinned painfully in the crunched door of the vehicle as the river devoured the car upside down.

8 NEW VIGILANTE JUSTICE

"**M**y parents..." June sat cross-legged on the opposite end of the couch. "They didn't like mods." After a half hour of superficial small talk and more than one awkward silence, June had asked to hear Chance's story but had sensed his apprehension and volunteered to tell her own first. "They hated the whole concept of the BTI and changing yourself through code." As she spoke, she rubbed her hand along the line of mod marks that ran up the outside of her thigh to her hip. "They wouldn't let me or any of my siblings install the Interface."

"So, you grew up... uncoded?" Chance asked.

"Right." June traced a finger around her kneecap. "Uncoded. Uninstalled. Whatever you call it. So, all my friends would get their Interface and their mods and come back to school smarter, more talented, prettier. And I would come back every day the same. I tried so hard to keep up—to make myself act and look like the rest of them. But I couldn't. It was impossible." June shrugged and picked up an odd piece of equipment off the table and examined it. "I was the ugly duckling. And I was jealous; I wanted *so badly* to be like them. To look like them, to be as smart and as quick as them. I thought if I could just be like the others, then people would like me." June forced a smile back on her face. "But that doesn't matter anymore. You want to know what these do?" she asked, placing the object back down and returning her hand to her mod marks.

"Sure," Chance tried his best to slow his heart rate as June pushed her hair out of her face and shifted closer across the couch.

"This one," she started, pulling the hem of her shorts up to reveal a simple triangle-shaped mark. "This is just a basic reaction-dexterity enhancement... helps with riding the motorcycle, staying balanced, quick adjustments..."

Chance nodded.

"This one is neural path prioritization," she explained, moving to the next mark, a small circle intersected by two parallel lines.

Chance had no idea what 'neural path prioritization' meant, but the way the words slipped off her tongue, she could've been reciting poetry.

"These three are cosmetic," June pointed to the following three marks, moving down the line toward her knee. "How I do my hair..." she added, giving Chance a quick smile.

Chance tried to listen while she continued, explaining mods with names he had never heard as she shifted closer and closer toward him.

"...*Adri F3... Sickkle v9... Ro-Iris...*"

June's skin was flawless... probably due to the mods she was teaching him about. Each time she looked at Chance to see if he was understanding, a shock would run through his core, and he would nod obliviously.

"...perception and mental clarity..." she went on.

The way her shoulders moved under the waterfall of platinum-silver hair... her fingers running gently across her skin...

"And I have more here." June lifted her shirt to the bottom of her chest, revealing six more marks on her ribcage.

"You," Chance tried to shake himself back to his senses, "have a lot of mods."

"These are more basic..." Her voice seemed to be slowing down, her eyes getting softer. "I do have one more." June dropped her shirt and gathered her hair, looking Chance deeply in the eyes. "It's my favorite."

Chance felt himself drifting inward.

"It's a little hard to see."

He felt like he was floating.

"Come here..." she moved herself closer as Chance obeyed. They were nearly touching... her face only inches away.

"Look closely," June turned her head away to reveal a faint pink, heart-shaped mark on the back of her neck. "Do you see it?"

June turned back to face him, and Chance was suddenly enwrapped by a velvet, warm feeling as a calm sense of bliss melted through his bones. His pounding heart slowed, his breathing deepened. His stress seemed to dissolve, and the things he had been worrying about... he couldn't remember what they were anymore. He was aware of June's hands sliding along his arms, her fingers draining the tension from his muscles.

Her hair brushed his nose, and she exhaled by his ear. Chance began to sink like a stone, and June's hands moved to his back.

"You done?"

June jumped backwards, blushing. The momentarily absent weight of worry returned to Chance's head like a falling cinder block.

Friday was standing in the room, impatiently checking her nails. "You shouldn't let her do that to you."

"I just wanted to show him so that he knows," June replied sheepishly.

"I'm sure," Friday raised a sarcastic brow.

"I thought you would be longer," June remarked as Friday pulled a plastic bag from the folds of her dark shawl.

"It was a local exchange, and the client didn't want to make a scene. *These*, however, are from Cicero." She dropped the small sack on the glass coffee table. "He happened to be outside, like usual."

June shrugged and dug a couple of pieces of hard candy out of the bag. "Cicero is an old man across the street who has a thing for Friday," she explained. "He likes to deliver treats and stuff."

"He's a pervy old man," Friday added as she sat down across the room and addressed the collection of monitors and holograms that filled the wall. "Open Vanished Princess."

Immediately, the room lit up with images, articles, and videos of the missing girl.

"We're going to get you up to speed, Chance," Friday smiled at him before returning to navigate through the mass of files. "This is Emry Rush."

Chance was still pulling himself out of the June-induced daze as a video began to play of the missing girl in various situations —shaking hands with important-looking people, taking pictures with kids, dancing with friends—scene after scene of her seemingly carefree life. He purposefully put a few more inches of space between himself and June as he leaned forward to focus on the video.

"She's become a bit of a celebrity recently because she's the daughter of…" Friday paused as her voice started to waver, then shook her head and continued, "She's the daughter of Orland Rush," she stated, forcing down some sort of hidden emotion. The video changed to show a tall man in a suit doing much of the same things his daughter had done. "Orland Rush, as you know, runs Seitech. And Seitech owns the majority of the market for legal mods and BioTechnical Interface installation. Which, in essence, means the Rush family runs the City."

Chance nodded as a shot of the unmistakable Seitech Tower moved across the screens, followed by a Seitech advertisement in which a large orange butterfly glided majestically in front of a white background, fluttering its wings in dramatic slow motion before landing gracefully on the flexing bicep of a muscular, naked man. The man twisted sensually as an artic bear stepped into the screen submissively. A voiceover began to say something about 'experiencing sensation,' and the man ran his hands through the bear's fur.

Chance looked over at Friday, and she watched the screen, apparently content to let the ad finish. More animals stepped into the frame, surrounding the man, as the words *S-Class Senses* faded into the foreground.

"Anyway," Friday resumed as the ad ended, and the screen reverted to videos of the Seitech CEO. "Orland Rush inherited control of the company from his late father, Kian Rush."

"Kian Rush basically made Seitech what it is today," June jumped in.

"More or less," Friday confirmed. "He turned it from a research firm to the superpower it is now. Also, he…" Friday's body tensed, and one hand went to the blue vial around her neck. "He was a very bad guy."

Cameras and reporters hounded a tall, stern-faced man as security guards carved a hole for him through the crowd. A subtitle, *Kian Rush: Visionary Leader or Corrupt Overlord?* rolled across the bottom.

"He was involved in lots of gang deals as well as mod and human trafficking. Or so everyone suspected. No one was able to prove anything. Anyone who got too close would be found floating in the river. Or they wouldn't get found at all."

"Then, one day, he died unexplainably." June inserted herself excitedly. "How could a man so powerful, with the codes to immortality at his fingertips, die so unexpectedly?"

"Yeah, he died." Friday went on. "Seitech didn't even release an official story. They just didn't say anything other than that he had passed. But who was going to question them about it? After they had offed so many nosy reporters."

"I remember seeing that on the news," Chance reflected. "Four years ago."

"Four and a half years, actually," Vent corrected from the corner of the room. "Right around your birthday."

Chance ignored the mod-demon. "I feel like his death should've been a bigger deal than it was."

"Good, you're smart! It should have," Friday confirmed. "I've gone down that rabbit hole before, looking for an explanation. But nobody seems to have any answers."

"Someone at Seitech killed him," June muttered under her breath.

"Maybe," Friday huffed, then continued her monologue. "Regardless of how he died, Kian's son, Orland, took over the company. Orland Rush was nothing like his father. He cleaned out the corruption from Seitech, cut ties with the gangs, and became a champion of the underprivileged and the uninstalled. He still is. I'm sure you've seen plenty of his videos or those massive holograms in the financial district of him pushing for more regulation, for stronger controls on the mod market. He believes in the idea of bettering humanity as a whole rather than humans as individuals."

Friday paused for a moment; her eyes began to get distant as she watched Orland on the screen. Her hand went to the Rush bracelet on her wrist, and she twisted it thoughtfully.

"Friday?" June called her back.

"Yes," Friday brought herself to her senses. "As you can guess, that's made him a *lot* of enemies, probably half the city. So, what better way to make him pay than to snatch away his golden girl, his only daughter?"

A large crowd of partiers filled the screen. Emry Rush was sitting atop someone's shoulders in the middle. The mass of people was singing an alcohol-soaked version of "Happy Birthday."

"This is Emry at 12:01 a.m. on Sunday the 15th. She disappeared around twenty-four hours later, sometime Sunday night or very early Monday morning."

In his mind's eye, Chance saw Goosh handing him the tablet with the news article. Then, Emry was standing on the spire, red light pulsing overhead.

"Tuesday, we came to talk to Shift, and that's where the trail ended."

"But we did find you," June added, giving Chance a slight smile.

"Probably not a good trade…" Chance replied quietly.

The women ignored his humility as the on-screen party guests finished singing. Whoever was holding the camera got right up in front of Emry's face while she was lowered back to the ground. She smiled dazedly, disheveled hair sticking to the sweat on her forehead, hazy golden eyes slowly drinking in the attention of her friends. Someone with violet-colored skin planted a haphazard kiss on her cheek, and Emry shoved them playfully in response as the crowd laughed and whooped. The camera then panned quickly around in a circle. A plethora of odd characters shouted in celebration. Behind them, the skyline of the city glittered in the night.

The video then changed; an interviewer questioned a teary-eyed girl with porcelain skin and blood-red hair. The girl shook her head and said something about Emry and the Rush family always being kind. Next, a boy with a shaved head and sharpened teeth struggled to find words to express his feelings about his friend's disappearance.

"She's been missing for about seventy-two hours now," Friday explained as the on-screen interviewer directed the video back to a news anchor. "If she were anyone else, I'd say she's gone forever. With someone this important, though, there has to be something going on."

"Wait, so…" Chance spoke up. "You have no idea what happened to her? So, we literally have nothing to go off of?" He asked, watching Friday's mind working, the light of the various screens glowing blue, yellow, purple across her face as scenes of the Rush family reflected in her eyes. Friday sighed and grabbed a couple pieces of candy out of the bag, tossing one to Chance.

"Not *nothing*," she repositioned herself and waved all the screens blank. "Here's what I'm thinking."

Chance placed the candy tentatively in his mouth, and June settled into the couch as Friday began to unpack her various theories about how and why Emry Rush had disappeared. Chance was immediately lost. Friday's hypothetical timelines twisted in and out of areas Chance had never been. She tied in gangs, celebrities, politicians, historical kidnappings, and city laws that he had never heard of. Friday narrated in a seemingly unending stream, pausing only occasionally to ask June for her opinion. June would simply nod, giving only a vaguely affirmative response.

Friday went deeper and deeper, laying out endless details about the girl. Her height and weight, her likes and dislikes, her personality, her suspected mod profile, her known associations, and her daily routines.

It was all beyond Chance. He was only the hired gun anyway, he thought to himself as he lay back on the couch and propped his head against the pillow. Just their new weapon, or peacemaker... a tool, regardless. Outside the apartment, the sounds of the night grew later. Purple and pink neon replaced orange balcony lights. Friday and June went back and forth. Detail after detail.

Around and around this missing girl.

Circling.

Chance's eyes began to droop—

A crunching pain suddenly seized him from behind and wrenched him forward to the edge of the couch.

"Chance?" June jumped backward. Friday grabbed the blue vial around her neck cautiously.

Vent screamed in Chance's head. *Look!*

"Chance, what's wrong?" June asked, worried.

"Glitch, glitch," Chance groaned out, trying his best to force the flailing phantom from his brain. "It'll pass—"

Chance, look at the screen, look! Chance couldn't disobey if he wanted to. Vent seemed to have taken control of Chance's body, forcing his head back and his eyes up. Chance watched the muted video on Friday's displays.

Emry pranced in front of the camera, leading the way down a long, store-lined Canopy street. She was younger here, maybe twelve or thirteen, but dressed in all the neon trappings of a cybercity princess. She gave a couple twirls and a flourish before turning back to the camera and closing in until only her face was in the frame. *"Mwah, mwah,"* she blew a couple of kisses, then tilted her head almost upside down and said an unmistakable "I love you" to the person behind the camera. Suddenly shy, Emry turned away laughing and pranced further down the sidewalk, and the video ended.

Vent vanished from Chance's mind, and Chance collapsed back into the couch with a sigh.

"Are you okay?" Friday asked.

Chance nodded and focused on his breathing. "It's a side effect of the mod. It's fine."

"Mm, okay," Friday slowly turned her attention back to the case at hand. "What were you saying, June?"

June leaned back into the couch cushions and shrugged. "I was saying it's a big city. People disappear all the time. Doesn't matter how important you are. If you go missing in Xi, within a week, no one will even remember that you ever existed."

9 SQUID BAIT

"**T**hree!"

Aria hesitated, scrunching the wet sand between her toes as the wave smashed into the cliff wall. Far on the distant shoreline, the skyscrapers of the city glinted like jewels.

"Aria! You were supposed to go on three!" Noah shouted from the mouth of the beach cave.

"I know, I'm..." Aria responded weakly, watching as another wave readied to roll into the stone face.

"Go after this one!"

Aria clenched her tiny fists.

"One... Two..."

Aria wasn't sure how long she was out for, but it couldn't have been more than a couple of seconds at most. Deflated airbags brushed her face like bloated jellyfish as the car rolled and sank deeper into the river.

Holding her breath in the muted silence of the dirty water, Aria calmly removed her seatbelt and pulled herself carefully through the broken window on her right. The car vanished below her almost immediately as she freed herself from its metal shell.

Noah. Was he still trapped inside? Aria dove after the vehicle, but in the darkness and the current, she could hardly tell which direction was down, let alone where the car had gone. The calming waves moved through Aria's chest as the desire for air crept into her lungs. She kicked hard as she moved through the murk. She could barely see her own hands.

The truck had impacted Noah straight on. The crunching metal had trapped him. Was he conscious? Aria dove furiously, ignoring the urge of her body to find oxygen as the current carried her farther downstream.

I'm not leaving you.

A powerful arm wrapped around Aria's waist from above and yanked her upward. Aria twisted in the grip as strong legs pushed against the water and propelled her toward the light of the surface.

Aria gasped as Noah released her, both siblings breathing in desperate relief as the river current floated them along.

"Noah!" Aria exclaimed.

"Aria! Are you okay?" Noah panted over the sounds of the moving water.

"Yeah! Are you?"

"Get down!" Noah shouted and reached for his sister. A stinging burn bit through Aria's ear as the water around her began to pop violently, and the sharp rapport of gunfire echoed across the riverbank. Noah gasped painfully and shoved his sister under the surface.

White, deadly lines danced around the siblings' bodies with a sinister *shoop shoop shoop.* Noah pulled Aria into the deep, out of range of the bullets and further into the current.

They pumped and kicked blindly as the air in their lungs counted time like sand in an hourglass.

One minute...

Aria's hand brushed something metal, and she pulled it back instinctively, her other arm held fast in Noah's grip.

Two minutes...

Aria's lungs were pleading, protesting for her surrender, but her brother led her on longer, through the deep as the mods in her body quieted the would-be feelings of panic and fear that tried to command her attention.

Three minutes...

Aria had never held her breath anywhere near this long. The calming waves grew increasingly intense as her thoughts began to suffocate. Stars popped behind her eyes. She couldn't tell if the water was getting darker or if she was losing consciousness. Her arms started to tingle; her hands went loose as Noah's hand tightened around her wrist. Her lips parted, ready to inhale a final breath of water.

Please.

"Aria!" Noah's hand was on her face. Aria gasped as her eyes fluttered open. They were above the surface. With one hand, Noah held Aria up; with the other, he clung to a large pile of floating trash. "Aria."

"You almost drowned me."

"Sorry. I had to make sure we were far enough away."

"Are we?"

"For now." Noah scanned the banks of the river. "But, they'll probably get here soon. We need to get out of here."

Aria looked around at both banks—just concrete and pipes—and repositioned her own hold on the pile of trash as the current carried them slowly downriver with the flotsam. Maybe River Xi really had been something beautiful once, in a past life, but it had become a toxic death trap where only soft-bodied creatures and unfortunate children swam.

A small fishing boat was drifting in their direction, and a young boy on the bow had noticed them clinging to the garbage. "Hey," he called out to them, "you need help?"

Noah nodded and pushed Aria out toward the boat as an older man joined the boy to help pull the two siblings on board. The man spoke in another language as he lifted Aria out of the water. The boy responded and pointed upriver as he helped Noah climb up.

"In here," Noah grabbed his sister and crawled into the boat's tiny cabin, out of direct view of the riverbanks.

The two fishermen followed them into the cramped space, speaking to each other as they gestured between the wounds on Aria and Noah's bodies.

The older man looked at Aria and asked something she didn't understand.

When she didn't respond, the boy, who looked to be around eleven or twelve, interpreted. "Are you going to be okay?"

Aria looked at Noah. *Was* she okay? She was gradually becoming aware of the pain all throughout her body. Blood dripped from the stinging cuts in her face, and her spine felt like it had all but been snapped in half. She gingerly put a hand to her ear and felt the spot where the bullet had taken a piece. Blood covered her fingers. "I'm... okay, I think." Though she didn't know what registered as "okay" anymore with all that had happened. She wasn't in the immediate line of gunfire or a speeding vehicle if that's what it meant.

"I got shot," Noah announced flatly.

Aria looked at her brother. He was pulling at his shredded shirt to reveal a nasty spot on his collarbone where the skin was torn apart, the gruesome white of bone showing slightly.

"But I think I'm okay." Noah rolled his shoulder. "The bone is fine." A myriad of other cuts and gashes covered the left side of his body. Apparently, Noah's standard for "okay" was dismally low as well.

The boy made a finger gun and motioned back at the riverbank as he spoke to the man, who Aria assumed was his father. The man nodded, giving a response over his shoulder as he moved to the back of the boat and took control of the small motor.

"My name is Danio," the boy introduced himself. "And that's my dad. We're going to get you out of here." The boat began to hum as the engine kicked on, pushing them down the river. "And I'll help you clean up your cuts," he added as he snatched a pair of pliers off the wall and bent to search through a pair of dirty rags.

The three of them shared the tiny room with several large squids that hung from oversized hooks in the ceiling. Noah watched the black, iridescent skin shimmer and the long tentacles swing as the boat rocked. Empty eyes stared back. Glow squids.

Danio squatted beside Noah and began using the pliers to carefully pull small pieces of glass out of Aria's skin. Despite the movement of the boat, Danio's hands were steady.

"I pull hooks out of fish and squids all day," he explained as Aria closed her eyes. "Glass is easier than a hook. And you are prettier than a squid."

Aria gasped as Danio pulled a particularly large shard from her right cheek.

"Sorry," Danio apologized. "Hold this." He put the rag against her bleeding ear. "I don't know how to fix that."

"It's okay. Thank you," Aria responded. Noah could see that she was feeling the waves by the calmness of her body and the steadiness of her breathing.

"We sometimes find people in the river," Danio continued as he worked on extracting glass from Aria's arm. "But, never people who are alive. You are lucky."

We should be dead, Noah thought to himself. He should have been crushed, and Aria should have been snapped like a toothpick. If they had survived the impact, they should have drowned. If they hadn't drowned, then Noah should have been killed by the bullet that hit his neck. But they were alive. To top it off, Noah hardly even felt shaken.

The boat moved on as Danio continued to tend to their wounds. Through the tiny cabin windows, the river began to widen, and the walls on each bank grew taller. Massive factories poured streams of gravy-colored waste into the water below.

The boat slowed as they taxied around a five-story tall pipe into a smaller inlet that branched off the main river. Rickety shacks balanced precariously on stilts on either side. Countless fishing lines dangled off the tiny docks as their owners sat patiently in hammocks or on coolers and wooden crates. Cramped kitchens and tiny bedrooms were pressed together under rusted tin roofs—a small city of balancing sticks and planks and dexterous fishermen.

The banks came tighter inward as the boat followed the stream, passing dangerously close to the support beams of the neighboring homes.

"We're here," Danio announced as the boat pulled into a small docking area. Outside the cabin, Danio's father began tying down ropes to nearby beams and fastening the boat safely to the dock. When he finished, he stepped into the cabin and said something to Danio, motioning at the squids.

"Wait here," Danio commanded as he grabbed the squids, handing two to his father and following him out the door and off the boat.

Noah sighed and pushed himself to his feet. "This is bad."

Aria remained on the floor. Pain echoed through her frame with each pulse of the waves.

"Just two days ago, we were at school," Noah continued.

Aria's mind was wrapped up in the pain. It was such a strange sensation. She had learned at school that pain isn't real, in a sense. Pain is all in your head. It's your brain telling you that a hot stove is burning your hand and that if you don't move it, you will sustain serious damage to your palm and fingers. Pain is telling you that something sharp has penetrated your skin and into your muscle, and your precious blood is escaping. That a bullet has nearly missed your head, and if you don't move immediately, your skull will be relieved of its contents. That someone you care immensely about is gone, and you should have spent more time with them when you had the chance. A warning to be more present for the next time.

It was a weird thing, pain. Mods had been developed to remove it and replace it with more technological warning systems, but no one really cared to heed those warnings like they had pain, so the trend had been short-lived.

How much had Mom felt? How much pain had she been fighting through to stay alive until her children came?

"Now people are trying to kill us," Noah proceeded with his quiet monologue.

Pain wanted to keep us alive. What would it feel like to die? Was it just like turning off the lights in a room? Suddenly dark?

"I don't feel afraid, though." Noah was standing at the door of the cabin, watching as Danio and his father returned from inside the tiny home to fetch him and his sister.

The calming waves in Aria's core were fading, becoming one with the rocking of the boat. Reality was coming into sharper focus. She slowly pushed herself to her feet, one hand still holding the cloth to her torn ear.

Danio climbed down a short wooden ladder, jumped onto the deck, and waved them out of their hiding spot. "Come in the house. It's safe."

Safe. Locked away deep below her mind, her soul yearned for that word. She wanted to reach for it, grasp it, and wrap it around herself, her brother, and her mother like a heavy blanket.

"It's safe," Danio repeated. "I promise."

Safe. Whoever had killed Mom had stolen Aria's safety. The thought smoldered in her mind, igniting that same unsatisfied itching she had felt while watching the videos of her father. Aria would tear her safety from the hands of her hunters. Rip and shred and slash until she could pull it from their chests. She would buy it again with their lives.

"TRY SOME OF THIS," Danio held out a small roll of seaweed and rice and squid meat to Noah as his father prepared more on a wood cutting board.

"I thought the squids in the River were toxic?" Noah examined the meat, and Danio gave a second roll to Aria.

"Only the skin, if you don't know what to do with it," Danio answered.

"And what do you do with it?" Noah took a bite of the roll and nodded at where Danio's father was laying out carefully cut strips of the shimmering squid leather.

"We will show you later," Danio handed Noah another roll, then grabbed a small bowl of black leaves and crumpled paper and pushed it to the center of the circle. "This is River Ash," he lit the contents of the bowl with a match, and thick tendrils of smoke began to curl up into the room. "It grows only in certain parts of the River, but it will help you relax."

The leaves burned abnormally slow, but let off more than enough smoke to fill the room before Noah had finished his third squid roll. Danio's father continued slicing meat and stacking squid skins, breathing in deep breaths and smiling a crooked smile.

Noah's wet clothes had formed a small puddle on the floor around him, but Danio didn't seem to mind, and Noah didn't either. There was nothing to do about it. Most of what Noah had owned had been lost in the apartment, and the remainder in the River. But Aria was alive. That mattered more than being wet or dry. He just wanted to keep his sister safe and find whatever it was that they were supposed to find.

Aria coughed and laughed to herself, her appetite suddenly growing as she finished her next squid roll in a single bite.

"Hungry?" Noah asked her.

"Starving," she replied, "I barely ate anything at Grandma's."

Danio's father said something, and Danio grinned back at him, then turned to Noah. "Tell us your story, how did you end up in the River?"

"Our apartment blew up," Aria started immediately. "With

our mom inside it. And then the TV told us to come here." She moved on to her next squid roll, and Danio looked at Noah for interpretation.

Noah began from the scene at their apartment, unwinding the details thread by thread, all the way until they found themselves on Danio's boat. Even coming from his own mouth, it sounded so unbelievable. Like a hasty patchwork of scenes from an action movie, except the plot made no sense. Unnamed people had tried to kill him. *Him*. For whatever reason, they wanted him and Aria dead. Two ordinary kids.

Why? Just because Dad was a developer?

Noah looked at Aria. Her face was devoid of expression, but he could tell her mind was working at the same puzzle, turning it over, pulling the pieces apart and putting them back together. Trying to find some clue that could explain why this was happening to them.

"I... am sorry," Danio's father spoke up. "The City... bad people everywhere."

Noah nodded, unaware that Danio's father had even been able to understand him. Noah knew that the City was full of bad people. He knew that people in Xi were murdered daily, lots of them. He knew that gangs fought and stole from each other and that developers and traders moved illicit code from the hands of one corrupt group to another. But these were all statistics. Things that *happened*, but not happened *to him*. Even the news was one continuous river of violence, but how and why had fate chosen to connect their simple, tributary lives to the rapids here?

For a small moment, Noah felt a sense of helplessness, like a paper boat approaching a waterfall. Something, or perhaps *someone*, seemed to be leading him and his sister toward an inevitable end.

Noah could have spent years turning it over, crying with his sister, grieving for an answer, but the same calming, soothing, pulsing feeling that moved through Aria moved through him as well and brought his mind back to the present, where the thickening smoke seemed to lift his spirits higher and higher.

Dinner continued, and the conversation became increasingly light. Unnamed drinks were brought out, and Danio began sharing stories from the River. Creatures they had caught, mods he felt he needed.

"I already know which mods I'm going to get when I turn fifteen and get my Interface installed," he announced, looking at the red *A* on Aria's forearm.

"Which ones?" Aria asked.

"*ABK-4*. Underwater breathing. And *Censense* so I can feel vibrations in the water. Then I'm going to get webbing bionics so I can *really* swim. I mean... I probably can't buy all that, but that's what I want."

"That would make you a great fisherman," Aria commented.

"I don't want to be a fisherman. I want to hunt down the Crocodile Man."

Aria and Noah looked at each other. "Who is the Crocodile Man?" Noah asked.

"He's a monster that lives in the River: half man, half crocodile. I've never seen him, but I've heard other guys talk stories about him eating people. They say he's ten feet tall when he stands up, and he moves completely silent in the water until he jumps out and pulls you in. But I'll hunt him down and catch him like he's a stupid squid. Then, I'll change my mods and go to other parts of the city to hunt more monsters. And one day, I will become the most powerful hero in all of Xi. No one will want to fight me."

"Are there a lot of monsters in the city?" Aria asked.

"Well, not *really* monsters. Just people who change themselves so much, and they become monsters," Danio conceded. "But, that's why we need more people to be heroes. Like what I'm going to be."

"I think you're already a hero," Aria replied, a wide smile breaking across her face. "You saved me and Noah."

"But, I didn't fight..." Danio blushed and tried to deflect the praise.

"Real heroes usually don't realize when they've done something great," Noah commented.

"It's time!" Danio's father announced dramatically and produced a small jar of black powder. "Let's see truth!"

"What?" Noah laughed despite himself.

"This is what we make with the squid skin," Danio explained as his father opened the jar and pinched a small dose up to his nose.

Danio followed suit and pushed the jar over to the siblings. "Inhale it in your nose, and it will open your mind."

The Noah that existed several days ago would have hesitated, but that Noah had been blown to pieces with his mother and crushed inside the wreck of his car, and Aria had already snorted her share without a moment's pause.

Noah followed Danio's directions, and the effect was immediate.

The floor and the walls vanished around him as he stepped onto the surface of the River. The twilight outside had sunk into deeper shades, and night-fishing lanterns sparkled across the dirty water like wandering ghosts.

He stood in a circle with six other figures, all of them masked and hooded in heavy robes and armor, ripples in the water washing over their feet.

One was tall and all black and silver.

One was crowned with ivory and gold and lightning.

One burned with fire and liquid heat.

One had six arms.

One shimmered with white scales.

And one was so deep in shadows that they seemed rather the absence of anyone at all.

Without words, Noah fought them all.

He swung his fists without regard for who was who, and the six did the same, aiming as much at each other as they did at

Noah. His knuckles punched through armor, through skin, through bones. He ripped hearts from chests and eyes from skulls. His own arms were torn from his body, but they grew back stronger. Fire ignited his skin, but he breathed it all in and blew it back out. Arcs of electricity jumped into his gut, but he directed it all back through his fingertips.

The fight went on for days, for months on the surface of the River, and then all at once, he was back in Danio's shed, sitting right where he had been, the images in his head evaporating from his skin with the river water and the sweat. The River Ash had finished burning, and Danio and his father stared blankly into the space before them, far off in their own visions of the truth.

Sitting still, Noah could feel the strange mods in his body working at his back, his neck, his muscles and bones, repairing the damage from the wreck and soothing the bruises and cuts—each quiet pulse like a salve.

But the healing code and the sweet smoke couldn't fix the real pain. Dad's mods didn't know what to do with a broken heart, so they only stifled it, burying it deep, deep below the surface and covering it with layers of murk and a river of synthesized biochemicals. The biochemicals kept his mind flowing, moving with calm consistency toward the completion of a goal he did not understand. An end that neither he nor Aria could see. Nevertheless, forward was the only option. All they could do was follow this powerful current downriver to wherever fate would decide to take them.

Aria knelt beside him, hands clasped and head bowed.

"What are you doing?" Noah asked.

"Praying."

"To who?"

Aria paused in the darkness. "The City? Dad? I mean, someone or something is clearly watching us. Whoever that is, whoever is listening, I guess."

10 FORTUNES

The train jolted, and Chance grabbed tiredly at one of the handholds, apologizing as he bumped into the passenger beside him. Friday smirked, arms folded amidst the crowded car. Chance wasn't sure what time they had ended the conversation last night, but it had been late. Friday had woken him up early. Way too early.

June stood beside Friday, gazing dreamily out the train window at the blurring cityscape. Both women had brightened up their outfits for the day, opting out of the usual black on dark gray for something much less like wicked witches.

"Where are we going?" Chance asked, rubbing his eyes.

"You'll find out when we get there," Friday answered dryly, avoiding the question for the third time that morning.

Chance shook his head, then locked eyes with a businessman across the train car. "What?" Chance challenged him.

The man looked away.

June slid over in Chance's direction. "Are you not feeling well?"

Chance inhaled deeply. "It's the glitches, and… this mod, I —" he shook his head and turned his attention out the window.

"The…" Chance waved his hand searchingly, "the girl. Emry Rush. I can't sleep. She keeps showing up in my dreams."

June cocked her head curiously. "Showing up… doing what?"

"I don't know," Chance shook his head again. "Smiling? Saying things?"

"Saying what things?" June leaned in, excited.

"Nothing—dream things, I don't know. It was a dream, it doesn't matter."

"It might matter—"

The train lurched as the brakes were engaged, and June tipped forward. Chance caught her instinctively.

"*Station L*," an indifferent voice announced over the intercom. "*Station L*."

"Here," Friday flicked her eyes at the others as the train slowed to a halt.

The doors slid open, and the crowd spilled out. Chance cut his way through the herd to keep up with Friday, pulling June along behind him.

A large sign with the district name, *Uo*, hung over the station exit, and Chance followed the current onto the street outside.

Chance had been to the Neons many, many times, but that never lessened the sensory overload he experienced on each visit. One could pick any single storefront—any convenience store or glowing bar entrance or secondhand mod seller—and sit in front of it all day, never growing bored, given only the sheer number of things to look at. The lights, the signs, the advertisements, the everything-you-could-possibly-imagine for sale, the stacks and levels above, and the levels below, visible through the cracks in the floor of the grand level.

That wasn't even to mention the people; Friday and June looked exceptionally ordinary in comparison. Some were entirely human, others were entirely robot, most were somewhere in between—living mosaics of technology and biology. Outfits ranged from a dozen overlapping layers of neon-trimmed metal and fabric to no clothes at all, and skin colors varied just as wide: purple skin, bone-white skin, chrome skin, completely see-through skin, *snakeskin* skin. Some had slitted nostrils, others had horns or feathers, gills, spikes, fur, snouts, outrageous proportions, and decorations and tattoos of every kind. Others looked utterly normal, unaltered in any perceivable way.

The sounds and smells of the Neons were their own respective tidal waves of sensory information.

"Can you tell me where we're going now, Friday?" Chance called out, cutting a path right through a small family and nearly tripping over the leash of someone's modified pet pig.

"The Neons," Friday responded over her shoulder.

"We're *in* the Neons already," Chance called back. "*Where* in the Neons?"

"Uo District."

"This *is* Uo District," Chance exasperated to the pedestrians around him.

Friday continued to navigate quickly, weaving in and out of buildings and eventually coming to a halt outside a small courtyard crammed between two buildings. Inside the tiny courtyard stood a bent, leafless tree, and under the tree was an even smaller shrine. The only other people visiting the tiny shrine looked to be at least a hundred years old, crooked with age, and probably born long before the era of the BTI.

"This?" Chance asked, greatly underwhelmed. "This is what we were coming to see?"

"This is the Shrine of the God of Lost Things," June explained in a reverent tone despite the commotion of pedestrians all around. Friday stared quietly at the courtyard, her breathing slow, as if she were meditating.

"*This?*" Chance motioned at the dead tree and the shrunken shrine and the incongruent situation of the whole thing. "Why are we visiting it?"

"Because we're looking for a lost thing," June answered.

"Well, yeah, but I mean, do you believe in this? It's kinda for old people." Chance nodded at the ancient lady in front of them.

June shrugged. "We need help."

Chance looked over the small courtyard again as the next visitor in line to pray knelt before the shrine.

"Are there any other gods we could get help from?" Chance asked. "No offense, but this one seems a little weak."

June leaned close to Chance's ear. "I like to think that each of us can be our *own* god. Worship yourself, make your own destiny," June winked.

The old man in front of Friday hobbled up into the courtyard and hung a child's hat on one of the branches before bowing quickly to the shrine and hobbling back out into the bustling street.

"What was that about?" Chance asked.

"People like to leave lost things for the God of Lost Things. Kind of like a Lost and Found." June pointed at the courtyard all around the tree. Propped against the trunk and littered across the ground were all sorts of various objects that people tended to lose. Gloves, watches, bottles, keys, shoes, jewelry, and at least a few old mod tiles.

June and Chance watched from just outside as Friday stepped into the courtyard and bowed her head at the shrine.

She started to speak, but softly enough that neither of the others could hear what she was saying. June watched the ritual intently.

Friday continued her quiet prayer, removing the Rush bracelet and holding it out to the shrine for a moment, only to put it back on and take off her earrings instead, a pair of small daggers. Carefully, she stuck the earrings into one of the tree's branches, gave one last bow to the shrine, then turned back to her companions.

"Done," she announced.

"What did you do?" Chance asked.

"I told the Lost Things God that I found this bracelet but that

I couldn't leave it because we would be taking it to its owner instead. Then I asked for guidance in finding Emry Rush and left my earrings as a sign of good faith."

"Guidance," Chance repeated doubtfully.

"You need all the direction you can get when you live in a maze, Chance."

"In that case, we shoulda just gone to the Seer," Chance remarked.

Friday turned. "Who is the Seer?"

"I was joking," Chance shook his head. "I don't actually want to go see the Seer."

Friday and June stared at Chance, waiting for more explanation.

Chance looked back at the two women. "The Seer of the Surface?"

June shook her head.

"It's like a magical fortune teller?" Chance spread his fingers in mock mysticism.

Friday returned a blank expression.

"They see things. Can tell you the future and shit."

"What can they see?" June asked.

"The future," Chance reiterated. "Whatever there is to see in it."

Friday stared off into the distance for a moment, then placed her hands on Chance's shoulders. "We have some time. Can you take us to the Seer?"

"It's not *real*," Chance drew back. "Like it's not real magic, at least. Just a really smart AI and lots of data. I think. People use it to bet on boat races and fights."

"I asked for guidance, and my prayer was answered," Friday spoke slowly. "Take us to the Seer."

"*I* answered your prayer? That fast?"

Friday nodded.

"We need to get back to the Surface then."

"Down again it is."

———

"I'M HERE to see the Seer!" Chance shouted as he knocked loudly on a plain metal door. Stacks of trash stood on either side, piled high overhead. Surface dwellers passed behind in the wide alley-way, navigating around the small river of sewage water that flowed down the street.

Chance knocked again, harder this time.

"Why does the Seer live..." June looked around at the dirtiness of the scene, "in a place like this?"

"I don't know," Chance answered. "Maybe 'cause it's a piece of shit and not a real wizard?"

Friday stepped forward and banged on the door herself. "Seer! Come out—"

The door cracked open abruptly, and an old man peeked out the opening. "It's too early, the Seer is not up yet, go away and come back tonight." The old man slammed the door shut.

Chance put his hand to his temple. "I can never remember his name, the old man. He's friends with Mr. Bird. Loly Milky..." Chance looked at Friday. "His name is something like that."

Friday shrugged.

"Old man! Wait!" Chance knocked on the door again. "It's Chance, I work at the Noodle Bar with Mr. Bird!"

After a short pause, the door opened again. The old man peered out at Chance. "Mr. Bird's boy? Charlie?"

"Chance," Chance corrected, "and I'm not Mr. Bird's 'boy,' I just work there, but yeah, that's me."

The old man nodded, "The Seer isn't up and running quite yet, it's early..."

"I'll get you a free drink back at Bird's, we just want five minutes."

The old man looked Friday and June up and down, then turned his attention back to Chance. "Make it two drinks."

"Deal." Chance put a hand on the door.

The old man nodded and led the way inside, motioning the others to follow.

The doorway opened into a damp and shadowy dim room with a low ceiling. Against one wall stood two large computer towers and a darkened monitor screen. Between the two computers sat a large pile of junk and wires.

"I told you, it's not really much..." Chance frowned at the junk pile.

"Up!" the old man shouted, clapping his hands and kicking one of the computer towers.

June jumped as the heap of junk shifted against the wall and groaned, and the computers hummed to life. Neon-colored lights flashed through the wires in the wall and in the ceiling, pulsing their way into the machine parts.

"Ugh, already?" A woman's voice echoed from the computers, and two large bionic arms extended from the middle of the pulsing pile, stretching as one would after a long nap. The arms were followed by two large legs, and finally a head and torso as the being slowly unfolded itself into the android form of a woman, green and blue fiber optic cables flowing into her metal skull like a tangle of glowing hair.

Sitting on the floor against the wall and between the two computers, the Seer's head nearly reached the ceiling. If she were to stand straight up, Chance guessed she would be at least ten feet tall.

The Seer crisscrossed her legs and rolled her joints testily, then turned her face to the visitors.

Chance took an uneasy step backward. The Seer had no eyes, but something about the way she directed her attention gave the impression that she was seeing everything.

"Good morning, Chance and friends," the Seer smiled with an unnervingly wide neon mouth.

"You remember me," Chance noted.

"You were here before, almost one year ago, asking me about the outcome of a boat race."

"That was for Mr. Bird; he made me do it. You can forget about that."

"I remember everything that I experience, and then some," the Seer replied. Her voice was soothingly peaceful.

"Five minutes, two drinks!" the old man pointed at Chance, then disappeared behind a curtain into a second room.

"Right," Chance nodded.

"What can I do for the four of you?" the Seer asked.

"There are three of us," Friday corrected.

The Seer leaned forward, planting her massive hands on the floor, and panned her face across the trio. "Hm," she mused, resting her eyeless gaze on Chance. "Most definitely... four."

Friday looked at Chance.

Chance shrugged. "Told you it wasn't a good fortune teller."

"What would you like to see?" the Seer asked, turning her attention to Friday.

"We have a task, and we want your guidance in completing it," Friday answered.

"Of course. What is the task?"

"We're looking for something."

"And what is it you are looking for?"

Friday stared at the Seer.

June started. "We're looking for—"

"Don't say it," Friday cut her off. "You can see that, right?" she nodded at the Seer.

The Seer leaned back and flicked the monitor near her head. The screen buzzed to life, static clearing to reveal a picture of Emry Rush.

"You're looking for the missing girl," the Seer said.

Friday looked over at June and Chance.

"Seer," June spoke up, "how do we find her?"

The Seer hummed out a laugh. "Slow down, young one. First, let me read you." The Seer extended an open hand to June. "Give me your hand, and let me feel what you feel."

June placed her hand in the palm of the Seer, and the Seer's lights turned a soft pink color. "Mm, you're a complicated one, aren't you," the Seer remarked as the screen in the room displayed an 8-bit wizard. "The Magician. A veneer of positivity and light over what? You shine your light so blindingly bright, what is it you are scared of finding in the shadow?"

June smiled as the Seer released her hand, and the room's colors returned to turquoise.

"You next, Chance." The Seer reached for Chance's hand, and he complied. Immediately, the lights in the room turned gold, and a circle appeared on the screen. "The Wheel of Fortune. You have been pulled into something much larger than yourself. Fate is leading you to a destination you cannot see yet."

"Where?" Chance objected. "Isn't it your job to tell me what my fate is?"

The Seer laughed and reached for Friday.

Friday gave her hand to the Seer, and the lights all but faded away.

The Seer hummed and frowned. "The Hermit, reversed even. You can't seem to see how you came to be where you are, or where you are going, can you?"

Friday snorted and snatched her hand away. "Trust me, I know where I came from."

"Now, can you tell us where Emry Rush is?" June asked, moving the conversation forward.

"As you wish." The Seer tilted her head in serious thought, and the computers hummed loudly, vibrating the walls slightly.

"I do not see her," the Seer answered after a moment, frowning.

"What a useful seer," Friday scoffed.

"But if you are to find her, you must pay a price," The Seer turned her face to Friday.

Chance stepped forward. "I already agreed with... with the old guy. Two drinks."

"You do not need to pay *me*," the Seer chuckled. "The City, Xi, does not like to hand over its lost souls cheaply. It will most certainly take one in return." The Seer templed her fingers in front of her eyeless face.

Chance looked at Friday and June. June put a hand on either of them.

"We won't be negotiating with 'the City,'" Friday replied, rolling her blue vial necklace between her fingers.

"If you say so." The Seer shrugged, and the computers began to hum. The hum became a rumble. "Take a fortune, then."

The Seer's blue-green lights blacked out, and where her eyes were not, two bright white circles appeared.

"What is this?" Friday asked warily.

"Have you ever had a fortune cookie, Chance's friend? You don't choose your own fortune; you take the one you are given."

"What's our fortune, then?" June asked.

"The Gods of Xi are returning."

"That's not a fucking fortune," Friday muttered.

"Who the hell are the Gods of Xi?" Chance asked.

"The self-proclaimed ones. The Seven Rays."

"The Seven Rays disappeared years ago," June interjected.

"Hence 'returning.'" The Seer fired back.

"Who says they're returning?" Friday cut in.

"A prophet." The Seer blinked her white eyes.

"Are you referring to yourself?" Friday asked.

"No. Only a few weeks ago, he was here, in a situation not unlike your own, looking for something."

"Looking for Emry Rush," June offered.

"No, looking for something much harder to find. A missing technology. A hidden creation."

"What is it?" June asked.

"I don't know its name—"

"Well, what does it do?—"

"And why are you telling us this?" Friday stepped forward. "This sounds more like a warning than a fortune."

"So many questions." The Seer leaned back. "I'm telling you this because it is connected. All of these lines, like wires. A network. A maze. Everyone looking for something. Everyone a hunter, and everyone the hunted." The Seer drummed her metal fingers thoughtfully on one of the computer towers. "You know how it's bad luck for a black cat to cross one's path?"

"Yeah?" Chance answered.

"For you, it will not be so." The Seer locked her attention on Chance. "When the black cat crosses your path, Chance, you follow it. Understand?"

Chance shook his head. "No."

The Seer chuckled. "Well, you will." Her eyes blinked out, and her turquoise lights returned. "You will."

Carefully, the Seer curled herself back into a pile between the two computers, and with a sigh, the lights faded, and the computers shut down, leaving the room a damp and shadowy basement once again.

June let out a small cough in the silence.

"She really threw in some cryptic shit at the end there, huh?" Chance stared at the unmoving Seer.

"I kinda liked her," June commented.

Friday walked across the room and pushed the door to the alleyway open. "She doesn't know where Emry is, so it's up to us. Let's go find our girl," she flourished her hand sarcastically, motioning to the Surface outside. "Shall we?"

11 WAVES

A ria listened to the sounds of the night: the groaning wood and tin of the shantytown homes shifting gently in the slow current of the water beneath, the river bubbling and rippling quietly as a midnight-fishing boat snuck between the rickety piers outside. Light from the boat's solitary lantern peeked through the cracks in the wall. Somewhere in the distance, a river crane whooped lonesomely.

The pain in Aria's body had vanished. Her ear, though missing a slice, had scarred over smoothly. The cuts and slashes had disappeared from her face and arms. Noah blinked himself awake on the floor beside her. The floorboards creaked slightly under his shifting weight.

"It's time to leave," Aria whispered to her brother.

Noah silently rose to his feet and helped his sister up. She rolled her shoulders and flexed her neck testily. Nothing even felt stiff.

She looked down at the unconscious forms of Danio and his father on the floor, everyone having fallen asleep where they sat.

"I'm sorry... we have to leave," Aria whispered.

"Don't worry," someone else responded. "They won't notice you're gone. In fact, they won't notice anything ever again."

Aria and Noah spun in the darkness, looking for the source of the voice.

"Because they're dead, get it?" Someone dropped from the ceiling, landing in a crouch and slowly straightening to their full height, taller than herself and taller than Noah, who stood beside her. A shaft of light crossed the window outside, illuminating the figure momentarily.

Ice shot through Aria's veins.

The man was a patchwork of flesh and silent machinery. His mouth drew into a glowing grin. One of his arms ended in a dark blade. "You weren't hard to find." The murderer's voice rasped like scraping metal; his bionic arm clicked as the blade extended. His feet shifted to rush Aria. As horrific as the moment should have been, Aria's world slowed. Controlled, calming power...

Like young Noah counting his sister down on the beach.

One...

Everything happened so fast.

Two...

The man dashed across the room, and Aria submitted herself to the new instinct and the swelling waves. Without thinking, she sidestepped her attacker, pulling his blade arm past her body, and smashed the heel of her other hand into his elbow, where the metal met the flesh. It cracked loudly. As the man's momentum carried him forward, Aria spun back the other direction, sweeping her leg through his feet and twisting his broken arm as he fell. The joint shattered further, and something in the biomechanics clicked, releasing the blade from his mech hand.

Time seemed almost at a standstill; there was Aria, her brother still unmoved, her attacker falling past her. The man's knife glinted as it fell slowly through space. Then, Aria was turning again, grabbing the falling weapon, spinning, lifting the blade high as the man's body met the ground. With both hands, Aria drove the knife downward; a wave of power rushed from her chest to her limbs, and she punched the blade through the back of his skull, skewering his brain and staking his face to the floorboards.

Three...

Aria exhaled. Waves crashed. *Again.*

One...

The tin roof creaked overhead, and Aria jumped sideways as bullets ripped through the ceiling and into the wooden planks at her feet. She moved again as Noah grabbed a supporting rafter and pulled a section of the roof down into the room. Tin panels collapsed as a second man fell onto his back in front of the siblings. He barely had time to lift his gun before Aria buried a fishing harpoon into his chest.

Two...

Without hesitation, Aria yanked the gun from his seizing hands and jumped up the rubble onto the roof of the house. Bullets whizzed past as she sprinted across the unstable house-tops. With a muscle memory she had never remembered learning, she raised the gun and emptied the rest of the magazine in the direction of the shooters.

Three...

On a pier below her, another attacker lifted a shotgun, missing the round over her head when Noah smashed a fist into his face, crumpling him over the edge of the dock and into the water.

Again. One...

A round blinking projectile was lofted in Aria's direction, and without thinking, she spun and kicked it straight down into the river below. The water exploded violently, snapping the surrounding house-stilts and sending a shockwave into the precariously balanced homes. Aria scrambled as the house beneath her began to lean dangerously, her fingers slicing on protruding nails and rusted tin, and jumped down to the level below.

Two...

Aria rolled as she hit the wood dock that connected the cement river wall to the house behind her, the world still slow as she found her feet again. Several yards ahead, another assailant pulled his trigger a millisecond too late. Aria closed the distance almost instantaneously, the *BANG BANG* of the gunshots ringing her ears before she disarmed the weapon into the water. The man leaped backward, whipping out a long, glowing machete in a wide horizontal arc. The air crackled and burned in Aria's nose as the sword slashed past her face, backing her up several steps.

Three...

The dock shifted beneath her feet as the shack behind her threatened total collapse into the river, the inhabitants fleeing directly into the water. Panic was spreading through the neighborhood. People were yelling, shouting; boat engines growled to life. More gunshots echoed all around; no doubt the locals were returning fire.

Waves continued to roll through Aria's body. Tidal waves of focus and composure as she studied her opponent.

The top half of his face was covered with a black visor while a long, serpentine tongue slid between sharpened teeth. Luminescent veins bulged in his neck as he rolled his head and flexed his shoulders. Grotesque tattoos covered his arms. His bloodlust was palpable in the humid air. He adjusted his stance, waving the humming blade tauntingly as Aria took her own position.

In a world where you can choose to be anything, there are men who choose to be monsters. Why? Why had these men killed Mom? How did they end up on this path?

A strange new sensation of cold calculation slowly froze out all other thoughts in Aria's mind, banishing to the farthest reaches anything not essential for her survival in the moment.

Her eyes coolly collected the crucial details of her surroundings: The unstable planks of wood, the glowing weapon in the man's hand, the large anchor chains that crisscrossed the dock at his feet, the assortment of fishing supplies in an untidy pile on

Aria's left, and the large squid-hanging hooks that swung from the roof just behind her.

Another wave. Exhale. *One...*

The dock rocked again, and the man stepped forward to balance himself. Aria rushed forward, grabbing a plastic bucket and flinging it at the man's head. He sliced through it, his machete melting the plastic like butter and coming back to buzz Aria's face. He was fast.

Aria stepped back, reassessing her options momentarily before the man charged, sword-first, in her direction. Aria danced backward, carefully keeping her footing and grabbing whatever miscellaneous objects her hands could find to keep her distance from the weapon. Her attacker slashed and swung violently. Aria ducked and weaved, slinging a wooden crate, a fishing pole, a metal pipe as she moved as far back as the dock allowed.

The man paused for a split second to drink in whatever pride he found in Aria's realization that she was outmatched. Aria lifted a pair of needle-nose pliers, and the man smirked and licked his razor teeth.

The wooden shack shuddered with finality. The large hooks clanked above her head.

"Make a move, girl," the man taunted.

Two...

Then suddenly, Noah was there, swinging a heavy wrench like a club at the back of the man's head.

The man ducked and backed Noah up with a nearly fatal jab at his abdomen.

"Aria!" Noah yelled, "At once!"

Time was slow again as both siblings closed at the same time. The man hesitated a moment too long, unsure of who to counter first, giving Aria just enough space to step inside his wild swing and stab the fishing pliers into the wrist of his blade arm.

Disarming a cyborg, disarming a modified human, it seemed the same. She twisted the pliers for extra measure, and the man dropped his machete into the water with a scream, then yanked himself free.

Noah swung the wrench again, and the man caught it with his free hand, only for Noah to catch the man's arm in turn and snap it like a branch in bare hands.

Three...

The demon man screamed again and tried to get free, but Aria was there, swinging dual squid hooks across her body like twin blades.

One shattered the man's visor and sunk into his eye.

The other caught him through the cheek and punched out the bottom of his jaw.

Aria stepped aside, and Noah kicked the stumbling man down the dock, where he steadied himself against the wall of the house.

Before he could turn around, the support beams gave way, and the house, and the houses on either side and all the wooden structure of docks and ladders and rooms and doorways collapsed onto itself and into the river with a splintering, rumbling splash.

Aria and Noah stood on what few planks remained intact.

In the greater area, the river homes had come alive with panic and confusion, though no more gunshots rang out, and no one looked particularly aggressive toward Aria and her brother. Across the water, several men lowered ropes to help their neighbors out of the river.

"I think that was all of them," Noah observed.

"Danio," Aria scanned the growing chaos and moved for the concrete river wall.

"Aria—"

"Danio"

Noah shook his head and followed her as she turned toward Danio's home.

Aria sprinted along the cement, weaving in and out of the

frenzied crowd. She stopped at the house with the collapsed roof but didn't need to go any further.

Four bodies. Danio, his father, and the two men that killed them. The neighbors had already pulled them out of the rubble and lined them on the concrete, everyone pointing and shouting, confused and angry.

Whatever buoyancy was left in Aria's chest faded, and her heart sank deeper into the quiet silt and mud that now seemed to fill her soul and bury her pain.

Why? Danio's eyes stared emptily at the levels above. A long, horizontal slash crossed from one side of his neck to the other.

Aria dropped to her knees at his side. *Why?* The question was the closest thing she could get to pain. Confusion at the illogicality of a senseless murder. She gazed at his pale face, his limp body. He looked past her, up at the canopy of buildings and plumbing and small orange lights above.

Thoughts tried to run through Aria's mind. She tried to picture the great and noble person he could have become, the heroic deeds that he wanted to accomplish, but the waves crashed and pulled the images away.

Man is more than bones and blood.

What now, Dad? She put a hand gently on Danio's forehead. *What now?* The mod her father had given her could help her kill her enemies, but it didn't seem to have any protocol for mourning a dead friend. She slid her fingers down, closing his eyelids slowly. She had seen people do that in movies. She had cried when watching them.

But not now. The waves pulled the sadness away from her face, carried her would-be tears back into the ocean of biocode that swirled and turned and rocked inside her.

An older woman pushed past Aria and put her hands on the boy, shouting through sobs. Noah was standing by the body of the dead intruder, explaining the situation to a group of people who didn't seem to understand. The tiny space was crowded already, and more people continued to show up.

Aria stood and joined her brother. The world seemed to spin around them, far away. Aria was sinking into herself. The people crying, frantically trying to revive the victims in vain. The whole scene seemed so distant. Someone asked her a question, but she ignored it. Each second felt like an eternity. Aria lifted her arm and looked at the mod mark, the red *A*. Someone grabbed her wrist and held it out for another to see. A man pointed at her and shook his head, saying words that Aria didn't care to hear.

A woman stepped up in her face and started shouting, pointing at the limp bodies on the ground. She shoved Aria, and someone pulled her back. Noah stepped forward, and Aria's hand shot out to stop him. A man who seemed to be taking charge of the scene told them to leave.

Waves.

One...

Noah's hands were on her shoulders, pulling her backward. "We need to go." Only his voice seemed to travel the thousand miles to Aria's mind. Her feet obeyed.

He steered her away from the crowd, and people bent out of the way to let them pass. Why was everyone standing around? Why had everyone not run away at the first sound of gunfire? Was violence such a normal thing? As if someone had speared a great shark from the river, everyone wanted to get a glimpse of the carnage.

Two...

The early morning mist clung to Aria's skin and clothes as she followed her brother away—away from the house, away from the river, away from the events that made no sense, and deeper into the streets of the surrounding city.

Xi, in turn, opened its mouth wide for the lost children. For the entirety of their young lives, these two siblings had existed on the outside, the upper levels. The skyscrapers they had called home were far from the true heart of the City. But Xi, the Neon Maze, the Chrome Labyrinth, had taken in many millions of orphans, travelers, hunters, refugees... what were two more? It would hide them in its walls, enshroud them in the smoke and lights of the Neons, fit them in the deep corners of the Surface with the countless hordes of other distressed lives that sought direction and pleasure and peace in its tunnels and alleys. Deep into the mysterious happenings of a murdered mother and a vanished father.

Deeper, deeper into the City.

12 STREET MARKET DEMONS

Cold air burned through Emry's throat and scorched her lungs as she drew a shaky breath. Her first in what felt like a very long time. She opened her eyes slowly, her vision blurry and her eyelids heavy with fatigue. A second breath razed her esophagus, and she coughed, sending a sensation of knives through her chest and making her aware of the restraints that held her to a metal operating table.

"Beautiful Princess..."

Emry blinked in the bright light that hung above her face as a hazy silhouette stepped into her line of sight, and a single, metallic finger traced the line of her jaw and lifted her chin.

"The epitome of humanity..."

Emry tried to speak, but the words came out as a feeble, wheezing sigh.

"Pathetic." The hand dropped her chin. "I will craft you into a truly celestial being. A tabernacle fit for our Deity."

Emry strained against the pain in her muscles to raise her head off the table.

The figure purred and drifted to the left as the room slowly began to come into focus. "Seitech's graven image..." Several clicking sounds echoed through the chamber; lights and screens and wires covered the wall in front of Emry. "Become a goddess." The figure returned, humming deeply. "Daughter of man… now an angel."

With a menacing hiss and a series of clicks, a robotic arm dropped down from above. At its end was a small syringe and a sharp needle.

Emry shook her head and groaned in fear, but the restraints and the overwhelming sense of fatigue held her in place. She closed her eyes tight as the needle descended and injected itself into her arm.

Every nerve in her body screamed with pain, and she began to convulse as the syringe emptied its contents into her bloodstream. Blinding lights flashed across her vision. She felt her captor laughing, dark and evil inside her brain. A pressure built inside her skull, consuming her vision, her sounds, her thoughts. Whiteness enveloped her senses.

Bright and complete… Everything, white.

The pain was gone.

The laughter was quiet.

Something foggy and distant came into view. Crystalline flakes drifted peacefully down from the sky.

You're going to die if we don't get you out.

The water was cold on Emry's feet as she sat on the end of the diving board over the pool. Something brushed against her toes, and she flinched, drawing her knees up to her chest and wrapping herself in her plush robe. A large koi fish floated belly up in the icy water.

Emry shivered and gazed over the white expanse of snow-covered garden that sprawled outward from the back of the house. An old stone wall at the bottom of the yard marked the end of the property, and beyond that, the land dropped off into a dramatic view of the city of Xi below.

The city glowed.

But not with neon.

Monstrous tongues of red and orange devoured the steel and

chrome towers. Explosions snapped and popped among the skyscrapers like sparks in a hearth.

The city glowed with fire.

Emry shuddered at the sight and sunk all but her eyes into the collar of her robe.

"It's not as bad as you think."

Emry turned at the voice to see a young man standing beside her. His hair was dark and messy, and his complexion was shadowy and splotched. Despite the cold, he wore a simple t-shirt and jeans that were a bit too large for his bony frame. His forearms and neck were covered entirely in mod marks.

"It's not as bad as you think," he repeated, nodding at the fire that consumed the City. "The fire and... explosions, I mean," he swallowed as if he were nervous. "We'll rebuild it. People will be, um..." he gave Emry a couple of shy glances, seemingly unable to look her in the eyes. "People will be better, in the end."

Emry stared at him in confusion.

"Here, uh, come with me," the young man motioned Emry to follow as he turned and walked back toward the house.

But the house wasn't there. Instead, a narrow, vibrant shopping street in the Neons opened up before her. Emry stood and stepped from the diving board and followed the young man. He navigated his way through the mess of pedestrians, weaving past glowing signs and ignoring the hawking of the endless street peddlers. Here in the Neons, the snow didn't make it down from above, but the air was still cold, and Emry could see her own breath.

"My name is Riley, by the way," the young man spoke to Emry over his shoulder as she caught up to him. "But you can call me R if you want."

"Where are we going, Riley?" Emry asked, ducking under a giant paper lantern.

Riley didn't answer. Instead, he turned around a corner and led Emry into a food market, where crowds of vibrant Neons people lined up at carts serving a plethora of Xi specialties.

"Riley, where are we going?" Emry tried again, tugging her robe tighter as she jogged to keep up.

"I need to get you ready," Riley replied, perusing the offerings of several carts before stopping at one where bunches of large, red peppers hung from the awning.

"Ready for what?" Emry asked as the man behind the cart fried several peppers over an open blue flame.

Riley snatched one of the peppers from the fire and handed it to Emry. "Eat this."

"Why?" Emry took the pepper hesitantly.

"Trust me, eat it."

Emry took a bite from the pepper, and a feeling like firecrackers spread from her mouth down through her body. She coughed and panted as the heat sizzled and then faded in her throat. "What was that?"

Before Riley could give any answer, the sound of a roaring engine and the screaming of terrified shoppers echoed from up ahead. As Emry watched, a large truck barreled through the crowd and accelerated directly toward her.

Emry fixed her gaze on the vehicle, then calmly sidestepped as it sped past and smashed into a cart behind her.

"Perfect," Riley noted as the people in the market began to panic and stampede. Then, continuing his shopping as if nothing had happened, he scanned over the food at the next nearest cart.

"Is this real?" Emry asked, following a few steps behind.

"No," Riley answered. "Here, eat this, though, quickly." He handed her a small, fried glow squid on a stick.

No sooner had Emry taken a bite than the smashed truck exploded in a massive fireball. The shockwave punched through Emry's frame, but she held her ground as the flames engulfed both her and her guide. Emry's skin shimmered opalescent in the fire, and when the smoke cleared, only she and Riley remained unscorched.

"You're fine?" Riley asked.

"Yeah," Emry nodded, looking at the smoldering remains that scattered the ground of the market.

"Hm..." Riley looked at Emry, then threw his eyes around the scene.

Emry waited for him to continue leading.

"This way." Riley turned in the direction the truck had come from and started off.

Emry watched the neon signs spark and the few remaining shoppers flee in the aftermath of the explosion, and eventually Riley stopped at a small vending machine. The light inside flickered feebly. Riley pulled a purple bottle from the dispenser and handed it over. "Drink this," he instructed.

"What will this one do?" Emry asked.

"I'm not sure."

Emry unscrewed the cap and started to drink; the liquid fizzled and popped as it went down, and Emry's fingers began to tingle with static.

The pair waited in the street as another explosion reverberated in the distance, and sirens began to wail.

"Nothing happened," Emry observed after a minute of silence.

"Um... I guess maybe we'll see what that one does later." Riley spun in a circle, deciding which way to go, then turned back to Emry. "Let's keep going? There are a few more things you need."

Emry nodded, her attention momentarily distracted as she opened and closed her fingers repeatedly, watching as the electricity in the neon signs and LED lights above seemed to ebb and flow with each closed fist and with each open palm.

"Emry?" Riley had started walking away.

"Yes," Emry responded, turning her attention away from the lights. "Coming."

PART TWO

"There is nothing like looking, if you want to find something. You certainly usually find something, if you look, but it is not always quite the something you were after."
— J.R.R. Tolkien, The Hobbit

13 BOARD GAMES

The city of Xi was, more or less, a three-dimensional maze. Decades of innovation and endless expansion multiplied across a complete disregard for zoning laws built every turn and side street, every bridge and tunnel, into a multi-level labyrinth. High up in the Cloud Levels, the city's penthouse-dwellers and exclusive socialites flitted through high-line gardens and stylishly empty sitting rooms. Crystal-sharp holograms and invisibly thin screens quietly played the head-lines from the happenings in the city below: a young woman vanished on her birthday, a fiery explosion in an apartment high-rise. This was merely something to listen to as the residents modified their hair and eyes and skin to start the newest trends at their nightly parties.

Many floors below, in the Canopy Levels, shoppers and people-watchers, friends and lovers, families and executives on break crossed and mingled between the brilliant display screens and magnificent storefronts and savory-smelling restaurants. Similar headlines rolled here: *Rush family silent about missing daughter, Gang violence in Riverbed finds family murdered*. These would become topics of small talk between acquaintances at coffee shops and awkward couples on their first brunch date.

Down on the Surface, the misfits and the oddballs of Xi hobbled and slunk from hovel to workplace, street vendor to fishing wharf. This was the birthplace of weird things, new mods, new adventures, bright heroes, and dark villains. Here, word-of-mouth traveled faster than the news, though everyone had their own problems to worry about, so talk of the missing girl had already come and gone.

Deeper still, underneath, in the Subs, dark and sneaky creatures lurked and hid. Mysterious gypsies gathered and laughed, outlaw gangs plotted and schemed. Here, secrets—the plans that would make headlines in coming weeks—were traded like currency. A forgotten cult rising again, a long-lost developer's hidden creation, a cancerously overpopulated city with a shell of a government.

But, the Mid-Levels, or the Neons, was where the stories were made. In the Neons, the dark things of the Subs and the weird things of the Surface climbed up, and the power of the Clouds and the money of the Canopy floated down, converging only in the heart of the city. Stacks of apartments and storefronts lined each busy street, while rail lines and drones cut haphazardly between. It was here, in a small, untidy apartment on a level closer to the Surface than to the Canopy, that Chance stood in the living room with his two new associates while they discussed their plan of action to recover the missing daughter of the most powerful man in the City.

A large hologram map of Xi filled the room, and Friday navigated across it as if she were swimming. As skyscrapers floated through his chest, Chance was reminded of how much of the city he had never visited.

"Here it is," Friday announced, stopping the map on a district just outside the main metropolis known as the Hills, where families of old wealth and power hid secluded from the light of the Neons.

Friday zoomed in on one house in particular, a modern chateau really, that was situated up at the end of a long road that wound through the dense greenery of the hillside. "The Rush Mansion," Friday declared. "We're going."

"Going?" Chance asked, skeptically. "I don't think we can just show up there. Can we?"

Friday shrugged. "We just showed up at your place, and it worked pretty well. And, I mean, what am I known for if not just... *making appearances*." She grinned at June.

June was staring at the far wall, her attention focused on the overlay that covered her eyes. Chance could see she was watching a video of some kind. "Sorry..." June grinned shyly in the sudden attention. "I just found something interesting about the Seven Rays." With a flick of her eyes, she cast the video onto a nearby screen.

A deep voice began narrating as the video played:

"The Seven Rays were a mysterious developer-ring-turned-cult that rose to power a few decades after the invention of the BioTechnical Interface. As a group of extremist-progressive developers, each of the seven founding members vowed to advance humanity beyond the limits of nature and into the realm of the supernatural. The exact identities of the Seven Rays themselves were never known, though their larger-than-life personas and superhuman abilities garnered a substantial and devoted group of followers who referred to themselves as the 'Disciples.'

"The Seven Rays and their Disciples were openly and vehemently opposed to strict mod regulations, championing instead the idea of rapid advancement and natural selection in their self-proclaimed quest for 'Transcendence.' Many well-known and powerful modifications were first pioneered by the Seven Rays, their followers, or their competition.

"Prior to their sudden collapse, the Seven Rays were characterized by mystical dogmatism and extreme self-aggrandizement. Appearances by the Rays to their Disciples were commonly referred to as 'visions' or 'visitations' and were often preceded by dark 'summoning' rituals. Descriptions of the Rays' mod-abilities included supernatural strength, telepathy, and even teleportation.

"With such prolific—"

"—This video is two fucking hours long," Friday interjected, closing the screen and bringing the attention back to the hologram map. "We can worry about The Seven Rays after we find our girl."

June shrugged.

"As I was saying," Friday continued. "We're going to the Rush Mansion. Working backwards from Shift and the bracelet didn't pan out," she held up a pink-and-gold mod and turned it over in the blue ambience of the hologram. "So we'll start at the beginning and follow the trail forward."

"What's the mod?" Chance asked.

"Hound 1," Friday answered. "Picked it up yesterday. If Emry has ever been anywhere, I'll know it."

"Like you can follow her scent?"

"Some kind of sense." Friday looked at the mod tile. "I guess we'll find out."

The map zoomed out again, and the route from the apartment to the mansion highlighted itself. With a sweeping motion, Friday collapsed the hologram, and the room went dark aside from the dim light filtering in through the fogged windows. June's eyes glowed. Chance's eyes glowed. Friday's eyes glowed alongside her lantern earrings.

"Are you ready?" June asked, grinning devilishly through the dark.

Chance raised his eyebrows at the two women. Despite the dumb theatrics, he couldn't help but feel a growing sense of excitement. Excitement along with confusion. "This is the *worst*-planned rescue operation... probably in the history of all plans."

Friday smiled. "Trust me, Chance. We aren't following a plan, we're following a *trail*."

———

THE ROAD WOUND up and up against the face of the hills, twisting through increasingly quiet neighborhoods where the gray clouds above settled on the rooftops like a soft blanket. The homes grew larger and more ancient-looking. Trees, gnarled and hard, unlike the sculpted ones in the city parks, thrust themselves up from behind ivy-covered garden walls. The people themselves seemed to be made in a likewise fashion, quiet and elderly, as they walked slowly on their cracked and worn sidewalks.

"We're turning here," Friday spoke through the headset in her helmet, and Chance held on as she leaned around a corner onto an unmarked street that cut up through a grove of trees. The narrow road led through the woods and stopped abruptly at a heavy iron gate. An old stone wall extended from either side, disappearing left and right into the trees.

"Here it is," Friday announced, dismounting her bike.

Chance pulled off his helmet and looked around at the unkempt woods and the stone wall. "Looks older than I would've expected."

"Beauty in age," Friday answered, approaching the gate, then spun on her heel.

Chance turned to follow her gaze.

A tall, serious-looking robot stood in the road. It bore no insignia, and its entire frame was painted black aside from the trims of yellow around its shoulder pads. Weapons hidden in the droid's gun-arms *click-click-click*ed menacingly, but it made no other moves.

"Who are you?" a deep voice boomed from the other side of the gate, and Chance turned again. A mountain of a man, half-dressed in tactical gear, approached from further up the road, examining the trio. He walked slowly, casually, with one hand in a pocket and the other on the rifle slung across his chest.

June glanced quickly at the robot behind her, then stepped up to the gate. "Officer... we're friends of Emry."

Chance looked at Friday, who watched June intently.

The officer's uniform was wrinkled, and an open button

revealed a plate of body armor underneath. Neon green rings glittered in his eyes. He looked down at the trio, tapping his too-big fingers on his gun.

"No one comes in. Not even friends," he ordered. "This is a crime scene. Go home." But, even as he told them to leave, he seemed to drift closer to the gate. Closer to June, really. His eyes flickered across her body.

Chance could feel it. He could see it in the small pink heart on the back of June's neck as she gathered her hair over her right shoulder. June was willing the officer toward her, pulling on his mind, his hormones and emotions. She pressed herself desperately into the gate as if she could melt through it.

"Officer Trask," June whimpered, reading his tag. "Our friend is gone… the media is saying all sorts of horrible things about her."

"No official statements, you must return…" Officer Trask swallowed, "return to your home."

Chance could see the officer's face softening, his eyes starting to relax.

"We don't know what to believe anymore." June gravitated the man closer; her arm floated toward him; she just needed one touch.

"I can't—"

"Please," June pulled back from the gate, and the officer stepped forward to catch himself as if tied to June with an invisible rope. "We just want to go inside and see for ourselves. We're sick of hearing everyone say things about Emry without knowing what actually happened."

Chance felt Friday's hand grab his wrist and pull him back. He, too, had been inching closer to June as she continued to weave her magic.

Officer Trask then turned his head, as if someone were speaking into his ear. "Friends of the girl," he growled, responding to whoever must've been hailing him over his earpiece. "They want to come inside."

June turned and gave a quick shrug and shake of her head.

"Three. Two women and a boy," Trask continued to relay the information. "Are you sure? Sir, I—" He was quiet for several moments, then nodded to himself and turned his attention back to June. "Detective says you can come in."

The bars of the gate swung inward with a slow metallic groan, and Friday gave Chance a triumphant *told-ya-so* look.

June thanked the officer graciously, and he snorted in response.

"KATO," he called to the AI. "Profiles?"

"Logged, sir," the robot replied in a voice that had clearly been engineered to sound as intimidating as possible.

"You understand?" Officer Trask asked as Chance followed Friday and June through the gate entrance. "You are on record now."

"Understood," Friday answered with too much enthusiasm.

The Rush Mansion wasn't as massive or extravagant as Chance had imagined, but it was much more beautiful. Clean glass walls ran against intricate wood and stonework. Water poured like crystal along the exterior into turquoise koi ponds below. Plants of every color and variety grew in harmonized chaos along walkways and windowsills. Balconies jutted out from the terraced floors, and a large hovercraft sat on a landing pad on the roof.

They passed only a few more members of what Chance assumed was the scene's security detail as Trask led the group up to the front door of the house, though Chance was certain that every inch of the property was outfitted with cameras or sensors of one kind or another. There was no telling what kind of technology the Rush Family had at their disposal.

"Don't touch anything," Officer Trask ordered, stepping through the glass door as it melted away like water. Natural lighting filled the entryway, which opened up further into several larger rooms. Chance felt like he should take off his shoes, but no one else seemed to care.

Trask guided them deeper into the home, passing through an immaculately clean kitchen and stopping in what appeared to be the main living room. Tall glass walls looked out over a large pool and a vividly green yard that rolled down the hill away from the home, dropping off into a view of the city beyond. Three people, two men and a woman, stood in the center of the room, admiring the view.

"Detective," Officer Trask addressed the man in the middle. "The visitors."

"Thank you," the man nodded and motioned the officer away. "Chief Detective John-Mark," he introduced himself, walking over to the newcomers and bowing slightly. He kept his hands in the pockets of his long, brown coat—a strange thing to wear, given the warm humidity. He had a smart look about him, if that was a way people could look. His head was bald, his nose was sharp, and the way his eyes moved suggested he had deduced everything he would need to know about the three visitors simply from glancing over them.

"Deputy Detective Cairos," the woman stepped up beside her associate. She looked equally as intelligent and a shade more mannered as she shook June's hand.

"Strange," Detective John-Mark began, "how members of the Rush family have a tendency to disappear. Kian's daughter Raya went missing all those years ago, and now Emry..." John-Mark looked over the newcomers again. "It's strange."

"We're friends of Emry," June explained, quick to establish her story.

The two detectives nodded understandingly. A third man in the room stood behind his colleagues, his attention held by a handheld glass screen that played some blurry video.

"Thank you for letting us in," June continued. "We just want to know what happened... I'm guessing you're the ones in charge of finding her?" She let the pain show in her voice.

"Well..." Cairos began to answer, then corrected herself, looking to John-Mark for confirmation. "We can answer a few things for you, but we also have some questions of our own we'd like to ask."

June swallowed and nodded vigorously. "Okay, please."

"Oh shit."

Chance turned to see Friday doubled over, her hands on her knees, breathing shakily.

"You okay?" Chance reached for her, and she waved him away.

"I'm fine. I'm fine," she explained quietly, straightening herself. "It's just very overwhelming." She lifted her hand away from a spot on her neck where a new, gold-pink mod mark had appeared, quickly pulling one of her braids around to hide it.

Hound 1, Chance noted.

"Losing someone close can be overwhelming," Detective John-Mark nodded sympathetically.

"Mmm," Friday quietly agreed as she scanned the room, blinking in her newfound senses.

Is this really all there is? Chance hadn't seen a crime scene before, but he imagined that there would be more happening, more people walking around taking pictures, writing notes, and drawing chalk lines. But, there was nothing.

"Where is…" Friday mumbled to herself and moved to walk around the room, but Chance grabbed her by the arm, and she didn't resist.

"Where is everyone? Shouldn't more people be looking for Emry? There's no one here," Chance asked.

"Not anymore, there's not," John-Mark answered. "But there were plenty of people here when we arrived."

Cairos gave an uncertain laugh, clearly worried that John-Mark was about to share more information than she was comfortable with.

"What do you mean?" June asked.

"Well," John-Mark watched Friday as her eyes zigzagged around the room as if she were following some invisible fly. "To answer your earlier question, we *were* put in charge of this case, but by the time my investigative team arrived, XSJO was already here."

Cairos cleared her throat and made a *please-stop* expression with her eyes.

"Apparently, they were also given the case," John-Mark continued, ignoring the silent plea of his associate.

"Who is XSJO?" June pressed the follow-up.

"Xi-Sei Joint Operations," John-Mark answered before Cairos could stop him. "The combined special forces team between Xi government and Seitech."

"I've never heard of them."

"That's because they didn't exist until a couple days ago. They were created specifically to track down Emry."

"*Seitech* created a team?" June let out a half laugh and gazed at the cityscape in the distance.

Friday waved a hand through the conversation. "Can we go to her room? To Emry's room, I mean?" She rubbed her eyes as everyone turned. "Please?"

John-Mark examined Friday blankly. "Cairos, stay here with Luca; help him analyze that video."

"Yes, Chief." Cairos let out a worried sigh, then turned and joined the other man at his video screen.

John-Mark led the small party up a winding staircase and down a long hallway to one of the largest bedrooms Chance had ever seen. Two of the walls and the high ceiling were made of glass, looking out over the mountains and the gray sky, heavy with impending rain. The bed sat suspended above the ground, floating above magnetic LEDs that glowed softly as they walked into the room.

"So, when your team got here, XSJO was already investigating?" June continued her interview.

"Yes, ma'am. The morning of her disappearance, we get the call, come over, and XSJO is already here. In less than an hour, they had cleared the entire house. All the sensor reports, security footage, AI memory banks, and even the housekeepers and the chef. They took all the evidence. Left us with only the dog."

June nodded slowly.

The wall nearest Chance was covered in pictures, the old print kind of photographs, of Emry and her friends in different locations, laughing and smiling, and memories from the city and from places around the world Chance didn't recognize.

He suddenly felt very intrusive. This was her room, her private space, and hordes of people had probably scoured through it in the past couple of days, reaching into every detail of her life. *Sorry*, he silently apologized to a small picture of a wind-whipped Emry on a coastal cliff somewhere.

"I think you would like her," Vent sat on the edge of Emry's bed.

Chance looked around the room. Friday traced her eyes across the floor, following an invisible trail, and June continued her conversation with the detective.

Why? Chance responded to Vent and turned his attention back to the pictures. *Why would I like her?*

"She's brave, and she's clever," Vent answered.

Chance ignored the demon and paused on a picture of Emry holding a fat, mean-looking puppy.

"Dog's name is Cerberus," Vent continued.

How do you know that? Chance replied to the voice in his head.

"Friday told you, last night."

Did she?

The next picture over seemed to be Emry's parents.

"Orland Rush and Lia Rush," Vent commented.

Chance shook Vent away and continued working his way across the wall of pictures. Young Emry stood smiling in a neon-lit street somewhere in the City. She wore a pink windbreaker. A young man with a broad smile wrapped his arms around her from behind in a cutely romantic embrace.

I want you to have this. The dream of Emry on the spire,

offering him her bracelet, flashed across Chance's mind. He zipped Emry's pink windbreaker against the cold.

I love you, Emry blew kisses at the camera in Chance's mind's eye, then twirled away.

Chance rubbed his eyes and turned his attention back to the others in the room.

Friday stepped out of Emry's closet with a heavy fur coat draped over her shoulders and a large straw sunhat on her head. Focusing her eyes on the floor, she strode across the room and exited onto the balcony.

June shot Chance a look, then turned back to her conversation with the detective.

Glancing back at the pictures on the wall, Chance followed Friday out onto the balcony. Friday stood at the corner of the railing, looking up at the gray sky and out over the yard.

"What are you doing?" Chance asked quietly, stepping up beside her.

"Emry's clothes, they help me identify her trail."

"How?"

"It's hard to explain. A bit like following a scent, or a faint shadow, or a warm breeze."

Chance looked down at the yard below. "Where did she go?"

"Up."

"Up? What do you mean?"

"Into the sky. Her trail stops here, in the air, past the edge of the balcony." Friday put her hand out into the space over the railing as if she could feel Emry's ghost.

"Like, she flew away or something?"

"Apparently."

"So, where do we go now, then?"

Pressing her lips together, Friday spun on her heel and marched back into the bedroom. Chance followed after her.

June was still drilling the detective with questions. "Does the XSJO know what happened to Emry then?" she asked.

John-Mark shrugged. "I wouldn't know—"

Without warning, Friday stepped forward, grabbed the detective by his coat, and slammed him against the glass wall. "Tell us what you *do* know then, okay?"

"Friday, what the hell!" June shouted. "I was doing fine!"

"I'm sorry, but no one's buying your story, June," Friday said over her shoulder and reasserted her grip on the detective's coat. "Tell us everything you know about the missing girl!"

Vent purred in the back of Chance's mind. *We might need to get control of this situation.* Chance clenched his fists and focused his gaze on John-Mark's eyes.

The detective still kept his hands in his pockets. Slowly, his face broke into a grin.

"Think I'm being funny, Sherlock Holmes?" Friday cocked her head sideways.

John-Mark huffed out a laugh. "Friday, the legendary mod-trading queenpin of the Neons, I figured we'd cross paths again. Your appearance hasn't changed too much."

"Why would I change it? I have nothing to hide."

"I wouldn't be so sure."

"What is that supposed to mean?"

"You can let me go; we're on the same team. If you remember, I was there when you helped us take down Handa."

"Can't say I do remember you," Friday growled. "And I don't have a *team*." She released the detective and took a step back, producing her small blue vial from somewhere on her person and holding it up. "Tell us what you know."

June pushed Friday's vial hand down. "You know each other, and you let me act out my stupid little story?" She gave an exasperated look to Chance.

"I, for one, enjoyed your acting," John-Mark responded with the slightest smile.

"I don't like to visit the past," Friday added. "But anyway, since we've established we're 'on the same team' now, help us out. We'll do your job for you."

"Normally, I'd refuse, but we genuinely could use your help," John-Mark nodded. "Someone is running the show."

"No shit," Friday rolled her eyes. "We were better off with the Seer. Yes, obviously someone is running the show, that's how all crimes work, someone makes them happen."

"Someone is orchestrating this entire thing, this *whole* operation. And we're all pieces, actors. Me, the others here, the Rush family, now you three." The detective nodded at each of them. "But why are *you* looking for the girl? I understand you have quite a few debts to pay, your creditors must be getting impatient."

Friday scoffed. "It's not about the money."

Hm? Vent questioned. *I thought it was all about the money.*

"I guess it doesn't make much of a difference," the detective continued. "I highly doubt anyone will be finding her regardless."

"Quit with the vague bullshit and tell us where Emry Rush is," Friday responded.

"I truly do not know. She could be anywhere."

"Well, tell us who you think is 'running the show' then."

"Maybe Xi-Sei—the XSJO—maybe a gang, maybe the Disciples, maybe Emry Rush herself, because she wanted to get away."

Friday massaged her temples.

"The Disciples..." June thought out loud. "Disciples of the Seven Rays?"

"Something like that. The old cult." The detective nodded.

"The Seer talked about them," Chance noted. "They have a prophet."

Friday inhaled deeply. "Why would the Disciples be related to Emry Rush?"

"They were big rivals, back in the day. The Seven Rays versus Seitech. Both powerful sources of new technology. Maybe they're coming back with a vengeance. The Anti-gang-slash-evil-cult division has picked up a lot of new activity from old associates of the Seven Rays."

"I don't think that's a real division," June whispered.

"Well, where do we find these new Disciples, then?" Friday asked.

"You don't. They'll find you."

"What, we summon them?"

"I'm sure you already have. Certainly, they already know what you're doing, and where you are." The detective turned and looked out at the yard. "They know everything. Like your friend said, they have a prophet."

"If we can't find the disciples," June put a hand up. "Where can we find the XSJO?"

John-Mark stared out the window at the gray city in the distance for a long moment, then finally spoke up. "KATO," he hailed the AI over some invisible intercom.

The bedroom walls darkened until they were no longer transparent, then a live feed of KATO's vision—the front gate of the Rush Mansion—projected itself onto the glass.

"Detective," the droid responded.

"Where is XSJO now?"

The view of the front gate was momentarily replaced by a map of the City. The map zoomed in on a district below the Surface. Multiple red dots marked the locations of individuals.

"XSJO tactical teams are entering the Subs at Lower Stolworthy, an area controlled by a branch of the Diamond Head Gang."

The detective looked at Friday.

Friday nodded. "Guess we'll be headed down to the Subs then."

"You're just going to show up there?" John-Mark asked.

Friday looked at Chance; Chance looked at June.

"They won't be happy to see you," John-Mark warned.

"No one really is these days," Friday replied.

"I'm serious. And when you see who is in charge down there, you won't be happy to see them either."

Friday paused. "Getting the whole sting team back together?"

"Handa did wonders for everyone's career. We're involved in all the high-profile cases now."

"Glad I could get you all promoted," Friday rolled her eyes.

"Better hurry, so you don't miss the action."

Friday motioned for her party to leave, and Chance gave one more glance at the pictures on the wall before following her to the door.

"We'll be in touch, *Detective*," Friday called over her shoulder. "We have a lot to catch up on."

"KATO," John-Mark addressed the AI again. "No one outside our team visited the site today, understood?"

KATO beeped in affirmation.

"Good. Meet me on the landing pad in five."

June stopped at the door and turned back to the detective. "You're leaving?"

"Yes," John-Mark answered. "My work looking for Emry is pointless, given XSJO's intervention, so I'm entrusting that pointless work to you for now. I'm working on another case as well. An explosion in an apartment, and two missing children."

14 REBIRTH

"They're looking for us."

Noah sat in the chair across from his sister, his hands flat on the square table between them. He watched the small screen in the corner of the restaurant. Aria watched the tabletop, her eyes as unresponsive as the rest of her figure.

"Look, they're talking about the explosion," Noah repeated. On the screen, a clip played of their apartment building, flames pouring from the windows on the 141st floor, black smoke curling up around the spires. Across the screen, a subtitle rolled: *Accident or Targeted Attack?* Beside the clip of the burning building, six headshots showed the faces of the victims. Three of the people Noah didn't recognize—probably unfortunate neighbors —the other three victims were his mother, his little sister, and himself.

Missing, the screen said, expanding the pictures of him and his sister and placing them next to a third, a girl that Noah recognized as Emry Rush, daughter of the CEO of Seitech. *Did she go missing, too?* A man in a long brown coat began fielding questions from reporters on screen, but the sound was off, so Noah couldn't tell what he was saying.

"Aria," Noah tried to get his sister's attention, but Aria didn't care.

An AI server placed two glasses of water on the table and asked if they would like anything. Noah waved the server away. He wasn't hungry, and neither was Aria. They just needed to go somewhere. Anywhere to get off the street and away from the violence. This tiny hovel of a restaurant seemed to be the only place open so early in the morning. But even though the sun had already started to rise, here on the Surface, it didn't matter. It was always twilight.

They shared the room with two other customers: One, a mousey-looking character, was crouched in his seat near the exit, twitching and scratching compulsively. The other, a man who seemed as if he had died and started to decompose before realizing he was still living, sat at the bar and watched the television screen with rapt attention. He asked the robot server a question as it passed into the back, then began muttering to himself about terrorists and government plots. Noah studied the stranger for a minute before returning his focus to his sister.

Aria sat motionless in the wooden chair, her body hard and set, her eyes cast and cold as she searched far into herself for the emotion she couldn't seem to find. To Noah, she seemed to be a small angel gargoyle, like one that might sit in a cemetery and look down with stone eyes at the resting place of someone's long-lost loved one. Her marble wings curved and protectorate above a grave that no one would visit.

Where are you? Where are you right now? Noah directed the questions toward Aria's mind, hoping she might respond. "Aria." Noah reached across and grabbed her wrists, pulling her hands onto the table. They were stained with rust and blood. Always more blood.

"Aria," he repeated and waited for her to make her way back to the present.

She blinked slowly. "Why am I alive?"

Noah squeezed her wrists in response.

"Why are we alive? Why did we not die in our apartment? Why did we not die in the River?" Aria let the questions fall out one after another. "Why did we not die at Danio's house? We're alive, but *why*? What's the point? We don't exist anymore, as far as the rest of the world is concerned."

"But, we *do* exist. We're here."

"Even if we find what Mom told us to, then what? Even if we kill all of the people who are after us, what is it for? We might exist, but our lives as we knew them are gone. There is no life back home for us to return to. There's no path left for us. In the end, we die. Dad is dead. Mom is dead. The city knows we went missing—which is the same as dead—so why are we alive?"

"Mom wants us to be."

"*Why?*"

"Because we need to find what Dad had, or what he knew, or where he was or whatever it is we're supposed to find—"

"—You're not listening!" Aria yanked her arms out of Noah's grip. "Why!"

"I don't know."

"Why!"

"I don't know!" Noah slammed his palms onto the table, and the man near the entrance jumped. The tiny pulses in his chest flowed slightly stronger, calming Noah's frustration.

Aria sunk back into her seat, her hair falling around her face as she stared into her lap. Silently, she closed her eyes and began counting, mouthing each number.

One...

Two...

Three...

Again.

One...

Two...

"We're alive because this is bigger than us," Noah offered.

Aria continued counting.

"This is bigger and more important than just our simple lives.

High School Aria? High School Noah? You're right, they're dead. They died in the apartment. We aren't them anymore, and this isn't their story. We're the Aria and Noah whose dad was a developer that created something dangerous that criminals are willing to murder innocent people over. We're in this story now. It isn't about us."

"I killed people," Aria answered.

"They murdered Mom. They murdered Danio and his father."

"I killed Danio and his father. We both killed them by staying at their house when we knew people were after us. We should have left immediately."

"What? No, Aria. Do not think like that."

"Fine. I didn't kill them. I killed the people who killed them. A killer is still a killer…" Aria tried to count to herself again and shook her head at her lap. She let the waves take over her thoughts, the pulsing, calming, focusing power. It made her aware of everything: Every detail and every motion, the slightly off-balance weight of the wooden table, the faint creaking of boards in the ceiling as someone heavy moved around in the room above.

But for what?

Her abilities hadn't been enough.

They shouldn't have stayed.

Noah reached for his sister's hands again, pulling her wrists back onto the table. "You did what you had to. Aria, they killed Danio and his dad. They killed Mom. You saw it all."

"Exactly. I saw what they did, and I don't want to be like them. I don't want to be a killer."

"We need to fight."

"I don't want to fight. I thought I wanted to, I thought it would make me feel… I thought it would make me feel something—relief or closure—I just don't want to be a killer."

Noah took a slow, deep breath, and the siblings sat in silence, listening to the sounds of the morning build on the street outside and the quiet mumblings of their fellow patrons. It felt so out of place to Aria. Incongruous, like a nightmare that they had stepped into, but they couldn't understand where from or why.

"This is who we are now," Noah finally spoke up.

Aria looked up at her brother.

"Those men needed to die. We did what we had to. It was self-defense, and if we hadn't stopped them, they would have killed more. You have to understand that. We might get in more bad situations, and I will not hesitate to end someone's life to protect you."

Aria gave a small nod in agreement.

"We *will* finish the fight. And we will find what Mom asked us to. Whatever, or whoever, that is."

Aria nodded again, reflecting back on her thoughts from Danio's dock. To get her safety, she would have to fight. "We'll finish it. Find the truth." With her statement, the mod waves inside her body rushed, suppressing any more ideas of pacifism.

Satisfied that his sister was at least somewhat stabilized, Noah closed his eyes for a moment and let himself feel the coursing power, the pulsing strength and clarity that moved through his frame and into every muscle and bone. It was a foreign being, a monstrously strong, elemental creature that seemed to inhabit his body.

"What's my name?" Aria asked abruptly.

"What do you mean?"

"Aria is dead. Who am I now? What is my name?"

"You're still Aria to me. You're still my sister."

"Not anymore. If Aria died, then I am not her. What's my name?" Aria stared at her brother. Her eyes were stone.

Noah pondered on it for a minute. "I don't know. What's mine?"

Aria shook her head. "I don't know, either. But it can't be Noah. You're a stronger version of him. Mentally stronger. More focused."

"I'm still your brother. Dad gave us these new selves, and now we need to be them, but I'm still your brother inside."

Aria exhaled slowly and looked around the tiny interior of the bar. "We need to change the way we look."

"I don't think it will matter," Noah replied. "They can still find us. Our code signatures will get picked up by any scanner."

"Probably, but a new look will slow them down. And someone else might recognize us." Aria thought again of her friends. They had been making plans for an upcoming school dance, planning who they would go with and what they would do afterward. Maybe she would still go when this whole thing was over.

"What mods do we need?" Noah asked.

"We just need to find a Seitech store."

"Let's do it then," Noah flagged the android server over.

The robot deftly maneuvered through the tight tables and stopped before the two siblings. "How may—may I serve you? Would—Would you like to order?"

"No," Aria answered. "Where is the nearest Seitech store?"

The droid was silent for a moment as it found the best answer. "There are three Seitech Mod Centers in the vicinity, the closest being directly upward, upward one—one grand level, in the Motomachi District."

"Motomachi. Thank you." And with that, the two siblings stood up and swept out into the street.

———

MOTOMACHI FELT, in every regard, like a newer, healthier version of the Riverbed. The streets were somewhat cleaner, the shops in less disrepair, the people more vibrant and much more numerous, but it had much of the same character as its lowlier counterpart. If the Riverbed District was the muck and the swamp, then Motomachi was the thriving stream. It lacked the sophistication and sharp stylishness of the Canopy levels that Aria and Noah had grown up in, but it more than made up for it in activity and energy. For all intents and purposes, Motomachi District was the beating heart of the City Xi and the epicenter of activity in the Neons.

Despite the relative earliness of the day, it seemed that people from every level and district of the city converged here for work, shopping, loitering, eating, life.

The Seitech store, or *Modification Center* as the locations were officially called, was a sleek, modern space that stood in stark contrast to the explosive, vibrant mess of the rest of the district. Floor-to-ceiling windows let pedestrians *ooh* and *ahh* at the beautiful stands and holograms that showcased the latest in biocode and bionics. Between these carefully arranged displays, the Seitech Floor Reps stalked like conceited jungle cats, as much flaunting their perfectly crafted exteriors as they were hunting for impressionable customers.

The glass door of the store slid open as Aria and Noah stepped inside, closing silently behind them and sealing off entirely the sounds of the busy intersection outside. Instead, ambient, soothing music floated dreamily through the large room, broken only by the quiet conversations of the customers and the occasional holographic advert triggered by the curious shopper.

An imposing AI stood just inside the entrance, scanning the floor carefully. The words *ASSET PROTECTION* were painted in bright yellow across its chrome chest. It gave only a passing glance to the two kids.

"Welcome to Seitech Motomachi," a disembodied voice greeted the siblings at the entryway, and a hologram screen materialized in the air in front of them. "Can I help you find anything?" The screen lit up with multiple options: *New & Popular, General Health, Extended Abilities, Mental Capacities, Aesthetics, Bionics & Equipment, Readjustments.*

Aria ignored the prompt and stepped through the hologram, dissolving it away again. "Appearance mods are on this wall," she announced, leading her brother across the room toward the host of holo-models and AR mirrors situated under a floating *AESTHETICS* sign.

She stopped at a large display featuring *æ-9: the comprehensive beauty package with additions from renowned stylists J.Y. Hirshan and Kiyo Miza.*

Videos of celebrities and models circled through the air, highlighting various features and specs on the mod package. Aria turned to the nearest mirror and immediately saw her reflection change. Her hair lengthened into a wavy two-tone pink, her cheeks lit up with a soft blush, and her eyes sparkled like shiny blue candies. A cute, two-piece dress replaced the clothes she had been wearing since the night she fled the apartment. The words "Young Summers by Miza" flashed across the bottom of the mirror. This was another version of herself. Maybe this was an Aria she would have become in a different life. But not this life. "Too much." Aria turned away.

"This one could work." Noah was looking at his own reflection in a nearby mirror. His hair and complexion cycled slowly through various shades. "This one is just the basics, but it's got a lot of options. It might be good to be able to change it up over and over again."

Aria agreed. "It'll work. Let's get it and go."

"Mm, have you found something you like?" a slow, nasally voice dripped over the siblings' shoulders like melted plastic.

Aria turned to face one of the most synthesized-looking humans she had ever seen. None of his features were particularly outlandish, but each seemed as if it had been removed and replaced with smoothly sculpted pieces of wax. His hair, nose, lips, and eyes were all slightly too large and too dramatically drawn, like he was a character from an animated movie that had walked straight through the screen into real life.

The man cleared his throat in the awkward silence as the siblings looked him up and down. "My name is Gar—" he almost choked, noticing the dried blood and rust and tattered appearance of the siblings. "My name is Garen." He pointed to a chrome badge on his chest. "Seitech Aesthetic Specialist. Are you interested in demoing one of these mods," he motioned to the display Noah had been inspecting, "or perhaps making a purchase? If so, I'd love to tell you about some of the deals we have going for our complement packages as well."

The Sharp children gazed at him with stone eyes, and he shifted uncomfortably.

"Yeah," Noah broke the silence. "We wanna get two of these *AB Essentials*, please."

"Okay," Garen gave a canned smile and summoned a holo-screen into the space between them. "Are we going for the *y6* model or *y9*?"

"*y6*. We're both under eighteen," Aria jumped in.

"Right," Garen's fake fingers poked and swiped quickly at the holo-screen. "Okay, one moment... just so you know, we are doing a special with *AB Addons 2* this week and—"

"—That's okay, we're not interested," Aria cut him off.

"Okay, not an issue..." Garen continued to navigate around the screen. "Would you like to add the one-year comprehensive warranty? We cover any glitching, burning, cosmetic damage—"

"—No, thanks," Aria answered again. Any mod warranties would be void anyway, given the unlicensed *A* and *N* mods she and Noah had installed.

"Mhmm, okay." Garen's discomfort was evident in the speed with which his hands moved. "All right, I will take your payment here, and then you can take the receipt to the counter in the back to pick up the tiles. Your total is sixteen-hundred and four credits even. How would you like to pay?"

In response, Noah stuck his hand into the middle of the holo-gram, and lights began to circle his wrist, reading his biocode and accessing his account. The spinning lights pulsed twice, then froze red. *Payment failed.*

"Mm, it seems it didn't work, maybe try again," Garen suggested.

Noah re-inserted his hand into the holographic system. It failed again.

"We disconnected at Grandma's," Aria noted. "Did you reconnect?"

"I reconnected just for this. I don't understand..." Noah stared into the distance as he pulled up his personal financial accounts. Garen hummed impatiently.

"Let me try," Aria responded, placing her hand into the payment portal. The lights pulsed twice, then failed. *Payment rejected.*

"Hmm, it says, 'Unknown Error,'" Garen observed from his side of the holo-screen. "Maybe our system is broken, let me check with the tech..." he added, turning and stalking off toward the back of the room.

Aria looked at Noah, she could see the account overlay on his eyes before it vanished and he came back to the present.

"It's because we're missing," Noah announced. "Our accounts are frozen. Or seized, or something. We have no more money."

"That's a problem..." Aria whispered as she looked around at the various arrangements and displays. Sixteen hundred was cheap for two comprehensive aesthetic mods, not a problem for children of the Sharp family. But the Sharp family was essentially dead. "I guess we're not changing then," Aria mumbled.

Noah shrugged. "We could steal them."

Aria shook her head. "That will only make a bigger scene, and we already have people after us. We don't want Seitech as well. Besides, how would you steal it? They won't even bring the tile out until you've paid. All we have are the holograms."

"Seitech won't chase us... once we make it onto the street, we'll be gone. They aren't going to hunt down two kids over aesthetic mods. Also, we don't need the real mods. We can just take those." Noah pointed at a wall nearby where a collection of single-use mod tiles were arranged in small stylish boxes. Hair colors. Eye colors. Skin tones. Tattoos. Each tile a simple one-off change. "Those will work."

Aria looked slowly around the room. "The robot is watching us."

Noah turned. The asset protection robot was motionless near the entrance, dark eyes staring in their direction. "I'll distract it," Noah decided, lowering his voice.

"We shouldn't do this—"

"You were the one who wanted to change appearances." Noah looked at his sister, then sighed. "I think it's a good idea. The disguises."

Aria kept her eyes on the droid. "How are you going to distract it?"

"I don't know. Break something. Get it to leave the door while you take some of those mods." Noah looked up at the AI, at the collection of customers fixated by the shiny displays, at the lurking Seitech reps, and back at his sister.

"Okay. Go," Aria flicked her eyes across the room.

Noah huffed through his nose. "Get ready to run."

"We're already dead. It can't get any worse."

Noah meandered away toward the other end of the floor, and Aria stepped over to the single-use tiles on the wall. Slowly, she began picking up several, checking over her shoulder as Noah circled a particularly elaborate display of glass screens and red-orange holograms in the far corner. The robot guard had turned its attention elsewhere.

Aria grabbed one last box from the shelf closest to the door, then turned and waited for her brother. Noah made eye contact, gave a slight nod, and threw himself into the mod display.

The holograms winked out as glass shattered and sparks popped. Noah cursed loudly and began apologizing profusely as multiple sales associates dashed over to help him up. The rest of the store looked on in shocked curiosity.

To their dismay, the droid stayed at its post by the door.

Noah's eyes dashed between the robot and his sister, who

stood waiting in the opposite corner, her hands full of mod tile boxes. "I'm sorry, I'm so sorry," Noah apologized again to the swarming reps. "I think I glitched hard," he muttered as someone put a worried hand on his shoulder.

"Sir, are you okay?"

"I..." Noah looked back at the robot. It still hadn't moved. The act hadn't been enough. "I think..." Noah moved his hand to a nearby shelf of bionic parts as if to steady himself. "It's a hard glitch," he threw his weight down onto the shelf, and the contents came crashing to the floor.

Several people gasped and jumped backward, and someone waved the asset protection droid over.

Perfect. Noah feigned dizziness as the droid approached, and Aria ghosted toward the store exit with the mods in hand.

"I'm sorry. New mods," he explained as the robot stepped in front of him. It was tall. A whole head taller than himself.

The AI's voice was deep and metallic. "According to my scan, I detect no—" the droid stopped and turned. Aria was sliding out the exit, the glass door closing behind her. "Shoplifter!" the robot buzzed and stepped toward the exit. Noah planted a hand on its chest from behind.

"I'm sorry," Noah shook his head as the robot looked back to address him.

"Sir, remove your hand!"

With a heave, Noah shoved the robot backward, smashing it against the wall, shelves and bionic additions falling in a heap around its body. Without waiting for anyone to recover from the shock, Noah exploded across the room. A red hologram X and the word *STOP* materialized on the exit. Noah lowered his shoulder at the glass door. Closing his eyes, he slammed into the center of the red X.

Stunned from the impact, Noah reeled backward. The glass had held. "No! This door needs to open *now!*"

As if on command, an error message flashed across the X:

Override Accepted. The hologram vanished, and the doors slid open.

Without questioning it, Noah dashed out into the street after his sister. Neither sibling bothered to look back as they sprinted and mixed their way through the crowded Neons.

Aria clutched the armful of mods tightly as she ran as if the weak disguises themselves held the key to what her mother had wanted her to find. Though it seemed to her that so far, new mods only brought new questions, and the answers, if they were out there at all, only got farther and farther away.

15 BLACK MAGE, BLUE DRAGON

Like gray veins, the winding roads carried Chance, June, and Friday down out of the Hills and back into the Neons, where the bridges and levels and towering skyscrapers once again canopied overhead. It was a long ride, but Chance didn't mind. To see the shining city from outside while the setting sun snuck between the sparkling towers and blanket of heavy rain clouds was a breathtaking experience.

But he felt childish with his arms wrapped around June's waist, knowing that if they were to switch places, Chance would have no idea how to control the motorcycle. He was entirely useless in this situation, just an extra passenger, as he had felt about himself over the entirety of the journey with his two new friends. He wasn't quite sure why Friday had pressed so hard for him to join them; it made him feel uneasy and more than a little out of place. A worthless appendage to their dramatic quest, he could fall off the back of the bike, and the two women would probably fare better without him, right?

All the more reason to hold on tight, he supposed, as he readjusted his grip around June's torso. He felt her laugh quietly, and his heart dissolved. Chance wanted to think that it wasn't just the effects of her heart-shaped mod and overt sensual beauty that attracted him to her. He liked to believe that his past had made him less superficial than most. Then again, if any other two had blown into Mr. Bird's shop that day and made Chance a similar offer, he probably would have refused. But if Chance believed anything—which most of the time he did not—it was that the City did seem to have a will of its own. It had a way of bringing people together—as friends, enemies, or lovers—when fate required it.

Remembering his growing list of questions for the two women, Chance turned off the comms in the helmet. "June!" he shouted into her ear as traffic slowed and Friday pulled ahead. "Why *are* we looking for Emry Rush? Friday said it wasn't about the money."

June was quiet for a minute, and Chance thought maybe she wouldn't answer.

"Friday is proud, and stubborn," June finally spoke, turning her head briefly to shout back. "She might have said that because she's embarrassed by the fact that she actually *does* need the money."

"But there is no money, there is no reward for getting her back."

June was quiet for another minute before answering. "I know. But she thinks there will be."

"So, is she doing it for the money, then?" Chance wanted a straight answer, but June seemed to be avoiding something. She weaved the bike into a narrow shopping street, keeping Friday in view up ahead.

"I don't know," June replied simply. "I thought she was, but I guess I don't know."

"You don't know?" Chance was concerned. "You're her best friend, you seem like you know everything about each other."

"We've only known each other for a few months."

"Seriously?! That's it?" That seemed strange to Chance.

"Why are you following her? Why are you even doing this yourself?"

"Because I owe Friday. She saved my life, and I know she has good intentions, even if she can't explain them. And she has potential inside her that I want to see unlocked. Same with you."

"What does that mean? What potential?"

But Friday was waving for attention, and June didn't answer.

Chance turned the comms on his helmet back on.

"From here on out, the directions—HUD are—" Friday's voice came in through the headset as the trio approached a red light.

"Friday, you're cutting out," June responded.

"—follow me."

June nodded. They had made it to the Tech District on one of the Mid-levels. Here, the streets were wide and clean, the buildings were dark and imposing, like polished obsidian. From the intersection, Chance could see the Seitech Tower, several streets over to their left. An epitome of steel and glass and light engineering, it helixed skyward where it disappeared into the upper branches of the city.

But Friday was leading them down. They needed to get to the Subs—the deep, dark underground of Xi. There, Friday intended to confront Xi-Sei Joint Operations, the mysterious team in charge of finding Emry, in hopes of receiving more information.

Making appearances, Chance shook his head, and the bikes came to a stop at a crosswalk as Friday revved her engine impatiently.

"Friday!" June called out. "Where did Emry's trail go? Shouldn't we be following that?"

"It disappeared," Friday responded, waving her hands. "Vanished into the air."

"What do you mean?" June asked.

"Her trail came to an end in the air. As if she were picked up off her balcony by a helicopter or a hovercraft or something."

"Something like that would leave a lot of evidence," June replied. "There were cameras all over the house. And radars and all sorts of scanners and alarms, I'm sure. There's no way something like that could just fly over the house and not get noticed."

Friday pointed at June. "Exactly. That's why XSJO confiscated all evidence of it."

A deep weight began to sink into Chance's mind, and Vent walked out into the intersection ahead of the bikes.

Now is not a good time for a glitch. He willed the episode to pass and the demon to vanish.

A low rumble approached on Chance's left, and he turned to see a car pull up beside them. The passenger window was rolled down, and the person inside turned slowly to look at Chance. A black tactical mask covered their face. Calmly, they raised the barrel of a gun out the window.

Chance froze, cementing his grip on June's body. Without a word, she cranked the acceleration.

The bike jumped, front tire separating from the pavement as it launched them across the intersection, and the blast of gunshots was lost in the roar of engines and peel of rubber that followed.

"Holy shit!" June panicked as Chance held on for dear life, and the bike rocketed forward.

"Who the—" Friday's voice cut in the static as she raced alongside, "—these guys?"

"I don't know, but they're following us!"

Chance's heart smashed like a hammer as he spared a glance over his shoulder. The car had followed them through the red light and was starting to gain. A second vehicle swung out from behind the first, with two motorcycles closing in from behind the second.

"Shit, there's more," Chance choked out through his fear, but even through the headset his words were drowned in the whirr of the bikes and the rush of the wind.

"—me! On me!—" Friday leaned deep into a turn, and June followed, almost throwing Chance off the back.

The street was busier here, and automobiles *whooshed* by as June and Friday wove in between lanes at increasing speed. The two cars fell behind, but the pursuing bikes began to close the gap.

Vent laughed deep inside Chance's mind as if the nearness of Chance's death was humorous to the phantom that lurked in his biocode.

"These—fast as hell—stick tight—" Friday swung a dangerous left turn through oncoming traffic, and Chance's pant leg brushed the front bumper of a taxi as June followed.

A wrenching crash echoed immediately behind them. Chance looked back to see the rider of the first motorcycle launch through the air as his bike crunched into the hood of a sports car.

"We're going up—" The three bikes swerved onto a ramp that wound upwards, curling toward the higher levels. A fine mist began to spray across Chance's helmet, and he prayed that the wheels wouldn't lose traction on the slick pavement as June leaned into the final bend.

They burst out onto a multi-lane road on the Canopy level. High-end boutiques and expensive restaurants blurred past, and raindrops splattered like bullets across the front of the bikes as the trio pushed toward the mouth of a large tunnel.

"—le—" Friday's message was lost in the static as she whipped her bike left unexpectedly, spraying water like a jet ski and disappearing down a side road.

"Friday!" June yelled, but Friday was gone, and the pursuant followed after her. June and Chance had no choice but to continue forward into the fast-approaching tunnel.

"We're going to have to get her on the other side," June shouted as they fired into the entrance.

Their bike whistled against the vibrant LED ceiling and walls, and for a brief instant, Chance was caught in the awe of the moment. The colorful lights reflected across June's helmet and the length of platinum braid that stuck out underneath. The motorcycle continued to accelerate, faster and faster, like they were entering a rainbow wormhole. One small motion out of place and they would be disintegrated into different dimensions across the asphalt.

Power. Use me. Vent stirred in Chance's gut.

A terrible screaming roar echoed from the tunnel behind.

Chance looked back. The two cars had caught up again, and despite June's desperate speed, they were closing in quickly.

June's bike *zoomed* between more vehicles, but the pursuant cars continued to draw closer.

The tunnel exit was visible. A blackness boiled in Chance's stomach.

Someone leaned out of the passenger window, machine gun in hand. June continued to weave between as many vehicles as she could but to no avail. The following car remained just as close, if not closer.

Chance's world went silent around him.

The shooter opened fire. Chance shifted his focus to the car driver. A bullet pinged on the chassis of the bike; another buzzed past Chance's face. June yelped, and the bike wobbled.

The blackness tightened. *Use it.*

Chance pushed on the driver.

The same violent skipping effect that had taken over Chance's vision when he pushed on Shift in the bar happened again. One moment, he was Chance, clinging to June's torso and hugging the bike chassis with his legs. The next moment, he was driving the car, hands tight on the wheel, staring at his own body through the windshield. His mind cut back and forth several times, and he could feel himself losing control of both realities. His arms and legs began to loosen on the motorcycle, and his steering of the car started to wobble as the vehicle slowed. If he took full control of the car, his body would fall off the back of June's bike, but if he returned fully to himself, he and June would be shot to pieces. *Shit, shit, do something!*

He cut back to the bike, catching himself from nearly falling off his seat.

He cut back to the car.

Shit.

He turned the wheel hard to the left and released himself back to his own body, lashing his arms around June's waist once again.

For a small second, the car was pointed sideways but drifting forward, and for that moment, it was something beautiful—the rainbow lights flowing over the chrome body of the vehicle in silence as Chance's senses slowly came back—then the car yanked left, smashing into the tunnel wall and flipping wildly through the air. The sound returned to Chance's world as the car flung itself into a million pieces, rolling and bouncing and splintering across the road. The second vehicle slung past the flying wreck and redoubled its acceleration.

June and Chance burst out of the exit of the tunnel, and the rain slammed them like a wall.

June was crying, hyperventilating. Chance could feel it. Or maybe that was himself. He couldn't tell. His hands felt numb. His vision was swarmed with dark shapes, a sickening rot spreading through his chest.

June turned down a road, the back wheel slipping slightly, but she held on. She turned again.

Chance could feel his arms shaking, his grip sliding, his head spinning. June turned and turned again onto smaller and smaller side streets, fishtailing on the slick cobblestone and marble and steel of the narrow paths between buildings.

June gasped and slammed the brakes, turning the handlebars hard. The wheels slipped out from underneath, and suddenly Chance was sliding, his leg burning against concrete. He tried to orient his feet toward the slide, caught his heel on an uneven lip, and was thrown forward, tumbling, rolling across the ground. He finally came to a stop against a metal railing and found himself looking over the edge into the abyss, down to the cascading levels below.

Groaning, he pushed away from the precipice and tried to pull himself up on the guardrail. His body seized with a painful glitch, his vision rocked back and forth. A hand grabbed him by the collar and dragged him behind a nearby concrete planter.

"Chance!" June yanked his helmet off. She placed a hand on his face, and Chance grabbed her wrist. The dark shapes and sickening blackness immediately started to fade, and his vision began to clear. June's eyes glistened in the rain and her tears and the upper-level lights.

"Are you okay?" she asked, helping him sit up straight against the concrete.

Chance shuddered in response.

"We need to get out of here."

The space around the planter lit up as a pair of headlights focused on June and Chance's hiding spot. June pulled Chance in close, but they had already been noticed. Doors slammed, and heavy footsteps splashed in their direction.

"No... no, no, no!" June screamed as she was grabbed and lifted off the ground and into the beam of the car lights. Two men held her up as she kicked and struggled in vain, her attackers silhouetted against the light. Both wore all black, and matching helmets covered their faces.

Channeling his strength, Chance rushed at the nearest man. A boot connected with his face before he could get fully off the ground, knocking him backward.

June screamed again and flailed desperately, but she was thrown to the ground as one of the men planted themselves on top of her.

The other man squatted in front of Chance, his helmet hiding any expression.

Chance's eyes and nose swam with pain as he pushed

himself away on the concrete. He tried to summon the darkness again. The black shapes, Vent, the power. *Come back, come back, come back!*

All he got was nausea.

The man began to speak, his voice altered. "You made a mistake, going to look for the girl." He stood up and pulled out a gun, aiming it at Chance's face. "Don't—".

Suddenly, a screaming *WHIRR* cut through the rain, and Chance scrambled sideways as a riderless motorcycle rocketed itself into the man from the side, smashing him into the far wall with a loud *CRUNCH*.

The man on top of June jumped to his feet.

A figure stepped forward from the street.

Chance shuddered with relief.

Friday.

The whole of her eyes glowed electric blue, and a matching neon mist curled from her red lips. Rainwater sizzled as it evaporated off her body.

The man in the helmet turned to face her. "We—"

Friday shot him in the chest, so fast that Chance hadn't even seen her pull Tax Man, or where she had even produced the gun from. The man stumbled backward, and Friday shot him again, the sound echoing off the surrounding buildings. The man caught himself against the railing and started to laugh— a horrible, gurgling sound.

"I don't think you know who you're—"

Friday shot him three more times in rapid succession, then was on him in an instant. The man fell to his knees, choking as Friday removed his mask.

Chance didn't recognize the man, but he looked battle-hardened, like a mercenary.

He spat blood from his mouth. Friday put the gun to his head.

"I don't think I *do* know who I'm dealing with," Friday

finished the man's sentence; her voice sounded hellish as the blue mist spilled out of her mouth. "Enlighten me."

The man coughed out a snarl. "You're in the middle of something you don't understand. When the gods return, and the fighting starts, pray you're on the right side."

Friday holstered her gun, grabbed the man by the throat, and lifted him to his feet, backing him against the guardrail. Previously invisible tattoos glowed blue around Friday's wrists and forearms. "You can tell your gods the devil is waiting."

"Tell them yourself." The man grinned and, with a furious twist, wrenched free of Friday's grasp and threw himself over the edge into the dark chasm below.

The rain followed his body down to the Surface.

Friday stared coldly into the void, the blue slowly fading from her eyes. The vial around her neck was empty.

June carefully pushed herself to her feet. Chance rolled to his hands and knees, his face and his leg still in pain. The man under the motorcycle remained motionless.

Without a word, Friday turned from the ledge and walked to the car. Reaching inside the passenger side, she turned the engine off, took several steps back, and threw the keys over the edge.

Then, collapsing to the ground, she pulled her knees up to her chest, wrapped her arms around her shins, and buried her face in her forearms.

June rushed over, the puddles splashing under her feet, and wrapped herself around Friday's quivering frame.

Chance stayed on his all-fours. He carefully flexed his ankles, wrists, neck and back. Nothing seemed broken. Gingerly, he pushed up onto his feet. The world teetered, his gut churned, and he puked onto the pavement. No blood, he noted thankfully, watching as the rainwater and rainbow sheen of leaking motor oil washed his vomit away and the earth steadied around his feet.

"Chance," June extended a hand and motioned him to herself. "Your leg is not okay."

It wasn't. The skin from his calf up to his hip was torn and bleeding, shredded from the slide on the road. Chance slowly hobbled to June's side.

"Install this," she instructed, handing him a small tile with a red plus sign on it.

"Are you sure?" Chance coughed. "I'm glitching hard right now."

"Just try it. It's a one-off med-mod. It's nothing permanent. Your leg is in bad shape."

Chance nodded and took the tile. He was soaked. They were all soaked. He sat in the puddle by June. Friday kept her face hidden, June's other arm wrapped around her shoulder.

The mod voice came on within his head. *Modification executable 'Compuheal Pro Strength' is ready to execute. Proceed?*

Yes.

Chance braced himself for another glitch, but it didn't come. Instead, his leg went fuzzy as the mod commandeered his body's healing efforts.

The rain splattered around them.

Chance looked up into the rain, into the darkening night where the tops of the towers vanished into the clouds. He felt June's hand slide across his back and pull him in close. He let himself sink into it, melting into whatever her biocode was doing to his own. Whatever her unseen technology or biology was using—electromagnetic pulses or hormones or whatever it was—he accepted it and let it wash away the fear and the pain and the panic. Like the rainwater, it rolled off his skin and into the street, carried by the gutters and pouring out into the void to fall again to the levels below.

"June..." Chance broke the silence. "Did you get shot?" The question sounded so weird coming from his mouth. It seemed too calm. He could swear that when the bullets had flown, she had yelped in pain.

June shook her head, then pointed over at her helmet across the pavement. A long gash was taken out of the top where the hot metal had buzzed past her skull.

Chance gulped. That easily could have been her head, or his. "I... smashed that car," he admitted abruptly.

"You did what?" June turned to look at Chance.

Tears started to form in his eyes. He wasn't sure why, but he hoped the rain would hide them. "When we were in the tunnel, the car that was shooting at us—the other car—" he nodded at the vehicle in front of them. "It crashed."

June waited for more.

"It crashed because I did what I did to Shift, but on the driver," he shook his head as if to tell his mind to follow the thought no further.

June didn't know what to say. She looked over her shoulder back in the direction they had come. "You *made* their car crash?"

Chance nodded. He wanted to hide like Friday. Get away. Forget that he and June had almost died and that he had killed at least a couple of people.

To forget the whole thing.

Friday spoke up, putting a voice to Chance's thoughts. "We need to go."

Chance looked over. She had lifted her face, but her eyes were still downcast. June continued to look between Chance and the streets they had followed with an expression of amazement on her face.

"We need to go," Friday repeated. "People are coming."

"Okay," June nodded and stood, pulling the others to their feet. Chance could hear people stopping, watching warily. He didn't bother to look up at them, and none of them tried to approach. Police drones sounded in the distance as they cut through the buildings toward the location of the violence.

"Chance, help me with this." June crouched near her bike. It had slid just short of the guardrail. He walked over and helped her lift it. The mirror had broken off, and one side was scraped and dented, but otherwise, it looked usable.

"This way," June instructed, taking the handlebars and rolling the bike down a back alley. Friday was already several steps ahead, Chance's and June's helmets in her hands. Chance followed, glancing one last time over his shoulder at the scene of carnage, the car that had chased them, and the small collection of pedestrians who circled the area cautiously. He shivered, despite the warmth of the rain, and turned again down the alley.

16 CHANGELING

Aria kicked open the graffiti-covered door of the train station restroom and hurried inside, her brother on her heels. The entirety of the space had been marred or defaced in some way or another, as was the fate of all public facilities in the Neons.

Sighing, she dumped the stolen mod tiles into the sink—four of them, each in their respective boxes: Two for eye color, one for hair, and one for skin tone.

There were supposed to be six, but she had dropped a couple in the mad sprint away from the store. *Doesn't matter.* The new appearances would likely make no difference anyway.

She looked up at herself in the mirror. Someone had etched the words *"CAT WUZ HERE"* right across the middle. Between the letters, her stone eyes stared back at her.

Noah stood at the sink beside her, waiting for Aria to distribute the mods in whatever way she had planned.

A stall door behind them swung open, and a shy-looking woman stepped out, registered both sinks were taken, and turned for the exit.

Aria spun, her hands like lightning, and grabbed the woman

by the head, pinning her against the stalls. The woman's neck was exposed, her throat—

"Aria, are you okay?" Noah placed a hand on his sister's back.

Aria's knuckles were white as she gripped the edges of the sink. Her body quivered slightly.

It's not real. Another hallucination. The bathroom door swung closed as the woman walked out.

"Another side effect, I guess—" Aria answered quietly. "I see things sometimes." The waves began to pick up inside her, softening the tension in her muscles. "Let's just put these on." Aria picked up two of the boxes and handed them to her brother, then examined the remaining two.

Flaring Neon, one read. Between the various warnings and technical details, a shimmering face with dramatically glowing eyes glared up at her.

The other displayed the title *Midnight Rainbow* across the top, and underneath, a woman with shiny dark hair.

Different from now. That's all that mattered.

Aria ripped open the eye mod's packaging and dug out the small tile, discarding the folded instructions onto the floor.

Lifting her shirt, she lined the new tile up next to her four other mods. The first of which was *V-Health*, the basic medical mod that almost everyone had. It acted as a vaccine and a diagnostics system and provided slight improvements in the more fundamental aspects of the human body, like bone strength and blood circulation. In most regards, it was the new bare minimum in human physicality. Noah had one similar, though a version that had been tweaked specifically for athletes with features like improved power expenditure and reaction speed. He would also have mods for his peripheral sensitivity and split-second decision-making, alongside whatever else he had been installing. Most people didn't like to disclose their full mod stack; they preferred to act as though each ability and every perfection was natural, as though they didn't need any help from the technology. Aria placed the first new mod above *V-Health* and followed the mental installation prompts.

Modification executable 'Flaring Neon III-YG' is ready to execute. Proceed?

Go ahead.

Aria felt a warm buzzing in the front of her head as the tile fused with her skin.

Next in her line of original mod marks, Aria had one for vision and hearing. Another essential recommendation of the doctors at the Installation Facility, it kept her eyes and ears sharp, though close to the bounds of natural humanity, as essentially all legal mods did.

The red *A* on Aria's forearm would *not* fall in the legal category. An extremely complex piece of code, and, by her experience, one that would probably cost hundreds of thousands or even millions on the underground market. The kind of mod that, if it had been coded wrong, would have melted her brain the instant she installed it.

Aria removed the second aesthetic mod tile and applied it onto her ribcage by the Visual-Hearing mod.

The top of her skull began to tingle.

Beneath her VH mod was the standard mod for mental clarity and capacity, increasing her ability to focus, learn, and call things to remembrance. However, as with the VH mod, its efficacy varied from person to person. Mental mods had always been the most heavily regulated because of the sheer complexity and mystery of the human brain. Attempts to force upload information, overwrite the brain's wiring, or unlock its full potential had historically ended in strokes, burnouts, insanity, or sudden death for the host.

At least, that's what they taught at school. But they had been teaching that for over a decade, and biocode had continued to evolve rapidly. Aria exhaled slowly as the waves moved through her chest. Where was the line now? Her father certainly had been pushing it.

Aria's last mod was a less common one, something expensive that she had specifically requested on her sixteenth birthday. *EJ-45*. She had never been totally sure if it was working or not; it was a quiet mod, after all, and the mark itself was simply a small lowercase *e*. But she had wanted it, nonetheless, to quell insecurities that she didn't care to reflect on at the moment.

Aria gave her attention back to the mirror and was met by a new version of herself. Her naturally frizzy hair had flattened into long, midnight black sheets that reflected iridescent in the feeble lighting of the restroom, reminding her of the squids in the cabin of Danio's fishing boat. Her eyes, the diamonds that had stared back at her moments before, now burned yellow-green like the colorful displays and signs on the street outside.

"Whoa." Noah was looking at himself in his own mirror. A nebula of black and silver tattoos was curling across his skin, tribal patterns reaching up his neck, koi fish and lotus flowers spreading across his arms, thorns twisting themselves around his knuckles. His eyes had turned a silver-gray color. "I look like a killer."

"You still look like you," Aria shrugged.

"You look like you're from the Neons," Noah said, looking at his sister. "It's kind of cool."

Aria didn't care about cool. The siblings stared at each other for a moment.

"Cat," Noah spoke.

"What?" Aria questioned.

"You said Aria is dead. So, you can be Cat now." Noah pointed at the mirror in front of his sister.

CAT WUZ HERE.

"Who am I?" Noah asked. "What's my name?"

Aria looked at her brother for a minute, following the fish and flowers that traced along his arms. "Kuno," she finally answered.

"Wasn't that your pet fish?" Noah asked.

"You saved us in the River."

He looked at himself in the mirror. *Kuno.*

Aria glared at her reflection. "This is stupid."

"The names?" Noah asked. "Or the mods?"

"Everything. They found us by the River because they already knew where we were going."

"What do you mean?"

"They were waiting for us. They knew where Dad's hideout was, so they were waiting for us there. They're probably the ones who sent us that creepy message on the television, too. To lure us there."

Noah nodded. They had driven right into a trap. But that didn't matter anymore because Noah knew what he and his sister were capable of. "That's fine. We'll go to them, then."

Aria was silent for a long time. "Are you sad?" she asked.

"I don't..." Noah thought for a moment. "Nothing feels real. Like we're going to wake up soon."

"We're not."

"I know, I just mean it feels like a dream—"

"It's not a dream."

Noah put a hand on his sister and stood quietly for several long breaths. "When we walk out that door," he said, "we're new people."

Aria huffed. "Ghosts of people."

"So... Cat?" Noah asked.

"Kuno?" Aria responded. Here, in this hidden corner of the Neons, she would leave the rest of her past behind. She would take only the facts she needed, only the images and memories that would help her find the truth about Silas Sharp.

Her black, squid-skin-colored hair fell around the sides of her face. Her neon eyes glowed like those of a jaguar. The notch in her ear was a nod to her recent familiarity with danger. The red *A* on her forearm, a symbol of her own deadliness.

The waves began to pulse.

One...

Aria is gone.

Two...

Cat is here.

Three...

The waves in her mod rolled over the last of her emotions.

The edges of her lips curled into a smirk in her reflection.

With a fierce yell, she smashed the heel of her palm into the center of the mirror. The glass shattered loudly, large shards falling onto the ceramic sink and the tile floor. The reflection asked for her to look again, to take a glance at the further splintering pieces of her soul. But she was already gone, the door swinging shut behind her as she followed her brother back out to the street.

———

MAN IS MORE than bones and blood; there is not only biology and technology—there must be some higher order. We devote so much time to unlocking the mind and manipulating the body, but what of our existence beyond these bounded platforms? I hypothesize a real, tangible intelligence outside the electrical currents we understand now as consciousness, that is in and through us, and at the same time, entirely unknown.

Cat repeated in her mind the words Silas Sharp had written in his tiny journal as she followed her brother through crowds of pedestrians along a wide sidewalk. Silas's journal was now somewhere at the bottom of River Xi, but she saw the page clearly in her mind's eye, and she imagined she could hear his voice reading it out loud.

"...our existence beyond these bounded platforms... a real, tangible intelligence... that is in us and through us..."

Like, a soul?

Kuno stopped at a large intersection, and Cat stood patiently beside him.

A small street vendor, waving from behind a grill on wheels, tried to get her attention. Despite her slowly growing sense of hunger, she ignored it. She and her brother hadn't eaten in almost twenty-four hours, but she wasn't going to say anything about that. She had a mission to accomplish.

Besides, they had no money. And the Sharp siblings were already dead anyway. Cat and Kuno were just reembodied ghosts out to avenge the death of Karinne Sharp and uncover the truth of her disappeared developer husband. Why not self-destruct in the process?

They could finish what they had left to do, then what would it matter if their emaciated corpses were later found huddled in some corner of the Neons? Who would be left to care?

"Man is more than bones and blood."

Maybe her soul would come back to inhabit some line more peaceful. A small crab on a beach, perhaps. Or maybe the sand itself or even the ocean. The ghost of Aria, the ghost of Cat, would join a billion other souls in the soul of the ocean and roll eternally with the waves, pounding against some beach cliff somewhere. Countless generations would come to visit, standing on the edge to admire the vast mystery of the collective ocean spirits.

Pounding and pulling away.

Crashing and scraping backward across the sand.

"Go after this one!" the young Noah shouted to his little sister from the mouth of the beach cave.

Aria clenched her tiny fists and shifted her weight to the balls of her feet.

"One..." The ocean soul smashed the sand and blasted into the wall.

"Two..." The swell retreated backward, building into another wave.

"Three!"

Aria hesitated for a split moment.

"Go, Aria, go!"

Aria dashed.

Cat pushed the memory away. It wasn't hers anymore.

The siblings continued through the Neons for what felt like hours until the sunlight began to hide and rain began to fall, dripping in small cascades down from the levels above. Kuno hadn't realized how far they had come from Danio's house, and on multiple occasions, he had to backtrack after making a wrong turn. The City was a maze, after all.

Cat followed silently behind, wandering in her own thoughts. Kuno could see her mind getting lost, running into wall after wall, turning and folding into itself. He wanted to reach her, to pull her up to where she could see that maybe there was some big purpose to this strange journey they had been forced into. Maybe there was a reason behind it all.

But he didn't know what that purpose was, so he let her be.

Eventually, they arrived at a lift station, one that would take them down to the Surface. The siblings packed themselves onto the glorified elevator with the other pedestrians and stood patiently as the platform brought them down to the bottom.

"Yizhou Mill. Red Seed Factory. Door 9," Kuno whispered to himself, recalling the instruction he and Cat had derived from the strange message.

The lift doors opened, and the siblings stepped out onto the streets of the Surface. The River was in view, a block further down the road. Kuno turned to Cat as the other lift passengers dispersed around them.

"We have to be careful," he said, looking her in the eyes. She watched the River. "And we have to be ready to fight."

Cat nodded. She was ready.

Kuno led the way, first to the River, then along its bank toward the abandoned factories, sticking to the shadows and dark alleys wherever possible. They would've passed the exact location yesterday, either underwater or in Danio's fishing boat, so the same dangerous men could be anywhere in the area.

The River curved slightly to the right, and the factories came into view: the abandoned Red Seed Factory just up the riverbank and the equally dead Yizhou Mill just beyond that. Sandwiched in between the two was a small apartment building, an apartment building that didn't touch the ground.

"Interesting. It's built *down* from the level above," Kuno pointed to the building as he and his sister slipped through a hole in Red Seed's rusted chain link fence. The apartment building in question was indeed built downward, hanging from the underside of the city level above it like a giant stalactite. A tall, winding, precarious staircase led upward from the ground to the building's bottom floor, where rows of rusted doors faced out over the River. The space beneath the building looked to be a shared scrap yard. The reasoning behind the construction made no sense to Kuno.

The passage through Red Seed was uneventful; the siblings turned through eroded doorways and across abandoned factory floors, passing antiquated machinery and assembly lines that had long since ceased their operations. Kuno paused carefully at each corner, listening for sounds of other people, but room after room was empty, the only signs of recent activity being colorful tags of graffiti and empty bottles of alcohol.

Eventually, they emerged from the other side of the factory and found themselves looking at the vast collection of trashed boats, cars, and rusted metal that filled the scrapyard. Straight overhead was the hanging apartment building.

"We're going up. You ready?" Kuno asked, making sure Cat was okay. She had been silent the entire trip.

Cat nodded.

"You know, Aria and Noah might not have been able to endure," Kuno put his hands on Cat's shoulders, "but Cat and Kuno... they can endure anything. They'll take the pain."

Cat looked into her brother's silver eyes. She could tell he was saying that for her sake. Noah could have endured. He didn't need a second identity to absorb the suffering. Aria, however, did. Aria would not have survived; she wouldn't have even made it out of the apartment on her own. She needed Kuno, more than Noah did. And she needed Cat.

In response, Cat slipped from her brother's arms and approached the tall, rickety staircase that spiraled up toward the apartments.

Kuno watched as Cat paused after several steps, waiting for him to follow. He looked up at the building. There was probably an entrance from the level above that might've been easier. With a sigh, he started up the stairs after his sister.

17 UNDER THE SKIN

C hance gazed down the busy street as warm-colored lamps lit up the storefronts of a hundred different bars and restaurants and bathed the faces of their drunken customers in a fiery glow. A glittering archway spanned the road above Chance's head and spelled out the district's name, STOL-WORTHY, in sparkling yellow lightbulbs.

June squeezed the motorcycle into a spot on the curb between a thousand other bikes and killed the engine. "Where now, Friday?"

Without a word, Friday led the trio across the street toward the nearest restaurant. As he followed, Chance glanced upward. This particular street in Stolworthy was one of very few on the Surface where the lack of bridges and platforms overhead meant the sky was visible between the tops of skyscrapers in the Cloud levels. The view from the bottom made Chance feel very small.

"In here," June grabbed Chance's wrist and pulled him into the entrance of the restaurant as Friday navigated her way toward the back of the room. Parting through the line by the restrooms, Friday shoved open an unmarked door, and the others followed her inside.

The other side of the door was a dimly lit concrete corridor lined with more blank doors. Friday picked one and pulled it open to reveal a set of metal stairs that descended into darkness. She stared into the black in silence for a long moment.

"Who were they?" Chance asked. "The people who attacked us."

"I don't know," Friday answered.

"Were those the people the detective was talking about? The Disciples?"

"Maybe. Maybe not."

"Friday, we don't have to do this now." June placed a hand on Friday's arm. "We can go back to the apartment, look at our plans again. Reconsider what we know. Figure out who those guys were."

Friday shook her head. "It doesn't matter if they were the Disciples or some gang or XSJO themselves. They came after us, trying to stop us. That means we're close." She tapped the toe of her boot on the metal floor. "I just didn't think they would come so soon."

"Do you think the detective sent them?" Chance asked. He wouldn't be surprised, but it didn't seem to line up, seeing that John-Mark had been the one to give them the warning in the first place.

Friday shrugged in response, staring at the ground. She took a deep breath and exhaled slowly.

"You saved our lives," Chance noted. "So, I trust you. If you want to go down, I'll go with you."

June agreed.

Friday nodded, giving each of them a quick glance, her dark eyes glowing faintly in the shadowy underground, then she turned and began the descent.

Chance's leg was in pain, his clothes were still soaked, and he was both mentally and physically drained, but something pulled him along. Staircase after staircase, door after door, deeper and deeper. Maybe it was the adrenaline, maybe it was the healing mod, or maybe it was seeing the raw power that Friday had displayed. The initial shock and fear had worn off in the time it had taken to get to the Surface, and now he felt as if something had been ignited inside his soul. Something twisted. The mangled vehicle flipped wildly through his mind. He tried to push the thoughts away, but they only seemed to pull the rest of his mind with them. Beckoning him to dive into the Sub levels within himself.

At last, the staircases led down into a large, circular room where roughly a dozen new tunnels branched off from the circumference. Some tunnels were completely dark; others were lit with small LEDs or hanging lightbulbs. The sounds of rushing water echoed from a tunnel on the left. The circle room was lit with faintly buzzing orange lights, with myriad pipes and wires webbing across the ceiling.

"Which way do we go?" June asked, stepping slowly into the center of the room.

"Give me a second," Friday placed a finger on the gold-pink mark left on her neck by the tracking mod, *Hound 1.*

"Isn't that just to help you find Emry?" Chance asked.

"It helps me find *people*," Friday replied. Taking a spot near June at the room's center, she studied the tunnel entrances briefly, eyes shifting back and forth, fingers twitching slightly, and then pointed down a particularly dark passage. "This way."

June and Chance exchanged glances as Friday moved for the tunnel.

"People went this way recently. It's gotta be them," she added, stopping at the entrance and turning before vanishing into the black.

June gave the room one last sweep of her eyes, then dashed after Friday. Chance followed right behind.

The tunnel quickly became pitch black. "I can't see anything in here," Chance commented, feeling blindly for the wall.

"We'll have to fix that when we get back," Friday replied from up ahead.

Chance sensed June stop in front of him, then her hand

caught his, and she pulled him forwards. The blue of her eyes flashed briefly in the blackness as she glanced back over her shoulder.

"Thanks," Chance offered quietly.

June squeezed his hand in response.

Up ahead, the tunnel began to grow lighter and wider as more and more passageways intersected. Friday led the trio around a few more turns and suddenly stopped, crouching to the ground.

Chance and June stopped beside her.

Slumped up against the wall was a man, a black bandana around the lower half of his face, three bleeding holes in his torso.

"Dead," Friday announced.

"There's another one…" June pointed up ahead and led them over to a second man. This one was younger, his joints protruding sharply against his taut skin as he lay face down on the floor. Blood had pooled around his head, soaking his long, matted hair.

Friday moved quickly onwards, chasing her invisible trails.

"What do you think happened?" Chance asked June as they followed after Friday.

"If Friday is right, then they probably got into it with the XSJO people."

Chance's heart was thundering. He didn't want to be another corpse hidden in these dark tunnels. But still, he felt compelled to go deeper.

Friday stopped at the top of another staircase and waved the others over. Silently, she put a finger to her lips and began creeping down the steps. Chance could hear voices drifting upward. He started down after Friday before she signaled him to stop. She would go check. Alone.

Chance counted the seconds as she faded into the dark, noiseless like a shadow, then reappeared just as quietly.

"It's them," she nodded. "XSJO. And it looks like they've finished whatever they came to do. Let's go."

The staircase twisted downward for a few flights as the voices grew louder and more distinct. Someone giving orders, people shouting. Friday stopped right behind the last turn, where the trio crouched to peak around the corner one after another.

The passage opened up into a massive industrial cavern bathed in blue light. Chance counted thirty or so figures, some on the ground, some walking around with large weapons.

"What now?" Chance whispered, watching as multiple people were herded into the center of the room.

A gun clicked behind him, and Chance turned slowly.

Friday and June both had their hands on their heads. Behind them on the stairs, two men in body armor stood with weapons drawn. One had his gun trained on Chance. Both bore the insignia of a white crow on their chests—underneath, the letters X-S-J-O.

"Hands on your head," he commanded.

Chance quickly obeyed.

"Up," the man ordered, gesturing them all to their feet and ushering them into the cavern.

The moment they stepped through the doorway, all sorts of firearms were aimed in their direction. The cavern was packed with fully outfitted agents, and gathered in the middle of the room were at least fifteen other people, handcuffed and in various positions of surrender on the floor. Multiple occupied body bags lay lined up by a pile of seized weapons, and several drop ropes hung loosely from the ceiling of the cavern, which Chance now realized led all the way up to an opening at the Surface and the source of the blue lighting.

A pair of droids, similar to the one from Emry's house, buzzed threateningly as Chance and the women were marched toward the center of the room.

"Chief Rapsideon," one of the agents called. "We found these three—"

"—Wait," Friday spoke up. "*Chief* Rapsideon?" she asked, dropping her hands.

"Hands on your head! Hands on your head!" the other agent shouted as a ripple of weapon clicks spread through the rest of the crowd, a horde of agents surrounding them.

Friday laughed and put her hands in the air again. "Rapsideon as in… *Rap?*"

Rap? Chance mouthed the question to June, who shrugged in response as they were all forced to their knees. "Friday knows everyone."

Heavy boots clomped to a stop in front of Chance. He slowly raised his head to see a tall, graven-faced woman staring coldly down at him. Her hair was shaved short all the way around, and what looked like a nasty burn scar reached from her ear up across her forehead. Her eyes were piercing; Chance shrunk under her gaze.

"Rap," Friday repeated, grinning. "I was expecting your boss when I heard they wouldn't be happy to see me, but this…" Friday laughed sarcastically and lowered her voice, "this is much worse."

Rap gave Friday a look of utter disdain, then waived all but two of the agents away. "Friday," she said, her voice hard and measured. "What are you doing?"

Friday began to stand.

"Stay down," Rap ordered.

Friday obeyed. "We're looking for the girl. We received a tip that she was taken by a ring in Lower Stolworthy."

Rap narrowed her eyes at Friday, "A lousy informant."

Friday mocked Rap's expression.

"Why are you looking for her?" Rap asked. "Wouldn't your time be better spent having sex with drug dealers?"

"I've already slept with all of them, can you believe it?"

Friday shot back. "Consider this a new business venture, if you will. I believe there will be a reward for the girl's return."

"Hmph," Rap smirked and looked at the kneeling trio. "So, you figured you'd come down here with a…" Rap searched for a word to describe Chance, "Surface street urchin and a stripper from the Neons to get her back?"

June stifled a laugh at her own description.

Good point, Chance admitted to himself. Compared to the XSJO, Friday's small band of three seemed like a comical suicide mission.

"We had planned for a more diplomatic approach," Friday replied with feigned haughtiness.

"Diplomatic?" Rapsideon raised an eyebrow at Friday. "You were going to simply ask for Emry Rush to be returned? Why didn't I think of that…"

Friday shrugged. "We have unique abilities, we can help—"

"This case is way beyond any ability you think you might have." Rap cut her off.

"What do you mean?" Friday asked.

Chance looked past Chief Rapsideon's legs, watching as a pair of her agents began moving through the tiny herd of captured Sub-dwellers, one leading a modified attack dog on a leash, the other scanning the captives' eyes with some sort of device. "What the hell was Friday's plan coming down here?" he asked June quietly.

"No idea," June whispered back. "But I have my own plan."

"Did you find the girl?" Friday asked Rap again.

"Don't play stupid, Friday," Rap stepped over and raised Friday to her feet with a hand on her shoulder. "The whole underworld knows you're eccentric, bold, opportunistic… but not stupid."

Friday's discomfort at being condescended upon began to crack through her sarcastic display.

"Oh," Rap lifted the small chain that held the empty vial around Friday's neck. "You didn't even come prepared?"

Friday snatched the vial back. "You say *we're* playing stupid?" A fire started to burn behind Friday's eyes.

"Friday..." June tried to ease the rising tension.

Rap let out a haughty snort of laughter. "Sorry, I forgot... easily provoked."

Friday's anger intensified.

"Get up, you both," Rap waved Chance and June to their feet.

"*Chief* Rapsideon," Friday snarled sarcastically. "Your team can continue to play charades as long as they want. *We* are going to find and return Emry Rush to her family." Friday lowered her voice. "And I know you know where she is."

"Maybe you are more foolish than I know." Rap circled Friday like a massive vulture.

"I don't think you really know me at all," Friday replied darkly.

Rap swooped in, domineering over Friday's small frame. "I know what motivates you, Friday. I know how your guilt drives you to make recompense... ever seeking some elusive reconciliation for your deeds. I thought your help in capturing Handa would have satisfied you... maybe your record is darker than we understood."

"Not any darker than yours is," Friday hissed back. "Murdering your way through the Subs to make false arrests because you are afraid to pursue the real criminals."

Chief Rapsideon swelled up to her full posture. "Emry Rush," she spoke loudly, her voice echoing around the chamber and drawing the attention of the surrounding agents. "Was kidnapped, raped, and trafficked by the Diamond Head Gang here." She gestured at the huddled mass of arrestees. "Traces of her DNA were found here along with articles of her clothing."

Friday shook her head, glaring fiercely at the Chief. "And that's it? You don't think there's more?"

"Chief!" an agent from across the chamber came running

over. "Scanner shows grouping at intersections 643 and 181. They're rallying."

Chief Rapsideon looked again at the trio. "If I see any of you involving yourselves in this case in any way, ever again…" She stared daggers at Friday, then her face curled into a wicked smirk. "Never mind, with this Halloween-themed prostitute leading you around, you'll all be dead within a week. Get them out of here immediately," she commanded her guards. "And seal that entrance behind them."

Rapsideon shouted orders left and right, preparing the area for more violence, and Chance was grabbed, along with Friday and June, and forced back to the passageway they had come from. The trio ducked into the doorway, and the agents pushed them around the corner and up the steps.

"Hilo, prep the seal kit and get that door ready for lock-down," the agent closest to Chance ordered his partner.

"Yes sir," the other nodded and retreated back around the corner to the entrance.

Stopping suddenly, June grabbed the remaining agent by the arm and pulled his face in close.

Chance nearly fainted, catching himself on the pipe on the wall, as a powerful warm feeling engulfed his senses, and a soft but driving frequency reverberated around the enclosed space.

June was grinning widely, holding the agent's head in both hands, her face an inch from his. "Okay, now tell us exactly what we need to know."

"The Ocean," the man whispered. "Tomorrow night. Bet on the red seven. They'll take you to Tiago. They've invited any believers."

"Thank you," June released the man, and he stumbled backward.

"Let's go!" June shouted, grabbing Chance by the wrist and yanking him up the steps.

"Well fuck, I guess that works too," Friday muttered, turning to follow her companions as the XSJO agent struggled to recover from his daze.

June wasted no time leading the way out, dashing up the steps and flying through the tunnels. The two dead bodies had disappeared, but nobody stopped to question where they had gone as June sprinted onward.

"Come on, come on, come on," June encouraged Chance through the dark sections, holding both his hands.

Gunshots echoed from the tunnels behind them. "Shit, they're fighting again," June smiled, almost laughing.

Finally, they reached the circle room and climbed the endless stairs back into the concrete corridor behind the restaurant.

"The Ocean," Friday repeated, stopping the others. "Tomorrow night. Bet on the red seven, and they'll take us to Tiago?"

"Yes," June confirmed.

Friday nodded and opened the door back into the restaurant.

"Wait, Friday," June called as she and Chance followed. "You think he means Tiago de la Roca?"

"Who else?" Friday huffed as she exited onto the street and crossed over to the parked motorcycle.

"Tiago de la Roca is a bad man..." June said more to herself than to anyone else, her voice distant.

Chance's mind was still racing from the frenzied climb out of the Subs and the overwhelming power of June's mod. Everything was happening so fast, and the exhaustion was catching up to him. The pain. The hunger. The sheer mass of events that had occurred in a single day. His head started to spin. He dizzily took his spot behind June on the bike.

Friday climbed on last. Chance could feel her intensity. Her frustration at the growing mystery and residual anger at Rapsideon, amplified by the fact that she now had to look like an idiot, riding through the city on a motorcycle with a street urchin and a stripper, as Rap had put it.

June laughed quietly as she started the engine and turned to

Chance. "What the hell are we doing, right?" she whispered, her eyes searching over his face.

Good question; Chance didn't know, and he was starting to believe Friday didn't know either.

FRIDAY DISAPPEARED into her room without a word as they arrived at the apartment. Chance collapsed on his couch, and June gave him a small "goodnight" before vanishing into the back herself.

So tired... Chance's mind faded as his head sank into the pillow.

Sounds of the streets outside blurred into a comforting ambience.

So...

Fading...

Sleep...

Sinking...

Spinning...

June was on top of him.

June.

Her hands moved up his chest, traced his collarbone...

Chance shivered.

Onto his neck...

Chance put a hand on her waist.

June's hands tightened in a vice grip around his throat. Chance lurched. She smiled inhumanly wide.

June! June?

Her teeth were sharp and serrated, her tongue long and snake-like. Her eyes turned solid black.

Using all his force, Chance shoved her away. She landed limply on the ground, her head snapping off and rolling away, coming to a stop in the middle of a dusty street.

June?

Chance was on his feet, struggling to move, struggling to run out to June's disembodied head. As he reached it, the head morphed into a black cat.

The cat started to run, and Chance followed. The dust under his feet turned to asphalt, and the rainbow LEDs of the tunnel pulsed overhead.

"Chance, Chance, Chance," the voice of the Seer spoke to him, reverberating off the walls of the tunnel. "You don't think you're here for a reason?"

"I don't know what you mean," Chance responded to the Seer. "I chose to be here."

"Think, Chance," Vent spoke this time, walking slowly down the tunnel in Chance's direction. "Why am *I* here?"

"What?" Chance replied, shaking his head. "You're a glitch. A phantom piece of my mind from a messed-up mod."

"What mod?"

"I don't... I don't know. From the installation. You're part of my BTI. There was a system crash when they were installing my Interface, and you're just a fractured piece of my mind."

"*Really?*"

"That's what..."

Vent transformed into Detective John-Mark. "That's what you told yourself, but you don't actually have any memory of that time, do you?"

Chance shook his head and looked at the ground. "I don't know what happened when I was fifteen, when I got my Interface, but from then on, Vent was there."

John-Mark vanished, and masked men began to circle, approaching from every direction, chains and knives and oversized guns dragging as they closed in—

BANG!

The sound of a gunshot, or a backfiring car, dropped Chance to his knees. He waited for the demon-men to kill him, to devour him, but they didn't come.

The floor underneath his hands... *carpet?*

Slowly, Chance raised his head. He was in Emry's room.

The pictures on the wall, the glow of the bed lights now a sinister red.

"I told you to come back to me."

Chance turned.

Emry sat on the edge of her bed, pink windbreaker zipped up to her neck and a forlorn look in her eyes. "It's my fault, what happened, I'm so sorry. I should've helped you sooner. I just didn't want to think about it." She buried her face in her hands.

"What?" Chance pushed himself up. "Nothing happened, I— I don't know what you mean."

Emry started to cry, and with each sob, her body began to morph, twitching and shifting into a large, menacing robot. The robot turned its glowing eyes and reached for Chance, its fingers opening and closing. Bending, twisting, snapping, and chasing him to the exit.

Chance dove out of the room, and the door slammed shut behind him. Taking a second to breathe, he strained his eyes at the darkness and tried to make sense of his surroundings. He was in Mr. Bird's shop, darkened in the hours before opening.

Friday sat alone at a table, her eyes electric blue, matching-colored neon mist venting quietly from her parted lips. Yellow lantern earrings illuminated the waves of her hair under her wide hat. In her hand was Emry's bracelet, she rolled it between her fingers.

With the other hand, she motioned for Chance to sit across from her.

Chance took a seat.

With a slow nod, she guided his attention across the room.

On the wall hung the body of a boy, arms out like a crucifix, rivers of blood dripping from his skin.

"Who is that?" Chance asked.

"Use me," Friday whispered.

"What?"

"Use me, Chance." She blew neon blue mist from her nose.

Chance didn't respond.

"Use me." She grabbed him by the throat and lifted him out of his seat. "Kill with me." Friday started to laugh, dark and terrible, and her form started to shift. She became Vent, then a shadow, a dark shape, dancing and spinning around the room. Police sirens began to blare outside on the street. Vent dove into Chance's mouth, and he convulsed.

The sirens grew louder, red and blue lights consumed his vision.

Louder.

Brighter.

Chance jumped... and suddenly, he was awake.

The apartment was dark around him. The sound of a police siren faded into the night outside. Some sort of clock ticked quietly on a shelf across the room. Through the sliding glass door, Chance could see Friday's silhouette leaning against the balcony railing. He watched her as she ran her hands through her hair, her shoulders rising and falling with an exaggerated sigh.

He thought about going to her, talking to her. Even through the glass, he could sense it.

The familiarity she had with darkness.

But the tiredness began to quickly wrap its hands around Chance's body, and without knowing, his eyes slowly closed, and he sank back into the shadowy realm of sleep.

18 UNDYING, UNDEAD

D oor 9. It hung ajar, the lock broken into pieces on the floor. Cat and Kuno stood on the brink of the entrance, listening for sounds inside. They had been in this situation before, only it had been their own apartment. What they had found inside had altered their lives. Were they ready to face that possibility again?

"I don't hear anything," Cat finally spoke up. "I'm going in."

Kuno nodded and followed his sister as she pushed the creaking door inward.

The apartment was mostly empty; a small table stood in one corner next to an overturned chair, a rusted pot sat on the stove, and a knife block with a single knife was shoved in the corner of the counter. A fine layer of dust covered everything.

Cat moved slowly across the wooden floor. The rotting boards sagged under her feet.

"It's abandoned," Kuno noted, turning around the center of the small room.

"Yeah," Cat agreed. She wasn't sure what she had expected to find. "But this can't be it. This is just a kitchen, there has to be more to this apartment."

"There's no other doors or anything," Kuno replied, examining the walls.

Cat began opening and closing the cupboards over the counter. Each was empty.

"Maybe this is it?" Kuno wondered. "And Dad's stuff is all gone?"

Cat moved on to the cabinets beneath the counter, which were equally as void.

"Or maybe the message was a lie?"

"Wait," Cat noticed something. One cabinet handle was different from the others. It was a symbol she recognized. A sunburst. "This…" she ran her thumb across the face of the metal shape and then pushed it in. It clicked into place, and the air vibrated softly as a section of the opposite wall sunk away to reveal a second room.

"Got it," Cat announced, leading her brother inside the room.

Cracked screens and frayed wires hung on the walls before two large desks and a pair of small office chairs. Bits of metal scraps and trash dotted the floor. Behind the screens, painted on the wall, was that same sunburst symbol.

"This is it," Cat commented, pointing at the wall. "This is the room in Dad's video. This same thing was on the wall. The sunburst."

Kuno nodded slowly. "That means…" he sat in one of the chairs and held his hand out as if he were holding a camera. "Dad was sitting here. So… this is his desk?" He placed his hands on the desk before him and looked up at the broken displays.

"But whatever was here…" Cat replied, moving to search through the empty drawers at the other desk, "is probably gone now."

"They must've been here already," Kuno agreed, opening and closing the drawers at his father's desk.

"Mmm," Cat looked at the sunburst painted on the wall. "Or

maybe Dad hid everything somewhere else. I mean, the video we saw was at least twenty years old, there's no way he just kept everything here that whole time."

"Or maybe there's *another* secret room?" Kuno began running his hands along the underside of the desk, feeling for anything out of place.

"Check everything," Cat agreed, feeling along the sides and back of her desk, pulling wires away from the screens, examining the bare wall for any slight disparities... nothing. "These wires don't even connect to anything anymore, they're all shredded."

Kuno dragged his desk away from the wall and crawled behind it. There *had* to be something—a forgotten journal, an encrypted map, an ancient hologram that would pop to life unexpectedly with a message from the past... something to give them more direction.

But there wasn't. All they found was more dust and scraps of garbage.

Cat began sweeping along the floor, tapping and prying at the floorboards. Maybe a trap door would open up and reveal a secret chamber or a small safe. Kuno did the same along the walls, knocking and listening for something hollow, pressing his palm into the center of the sunburst...

Nothing.

Kuno sighed and drummed his fingers on the desk as he sat back in one of the chairs. Cat kneeled on the floor and watched him as he thought. The siblings sat in silence for several minutes, looking around the old room, rethinking their steps, their situation... their purpose.

How their high school lives felt like nothing more than dreams.

How aimless their quest seemed now.

How stupid, and how destined for no good end.

Cat looked down at the red *A* on her forearm. She reached up and felt the scarred notch in her ear.

"What do we do now?" Kuno wondered out loud.

Cat closed her eyes in meditation.

"We don't have any more clues..." Kuno continued.

Cat let the waves run through her body. Maybe they could bring guidance as well as calming.

"Do we go back to Grandma's?" Kuno asked the empty room. "Go through the notes again?"

Cat let her mind get picked up by the pulses. *Where do we go now, Dad? You brought us here. What's next?* Rolling and swelling and subsiding again, the power inside Cat continued to move.

The words of Karinne Sharp washed through Cat's thoughts. *"They're looking for something. You need to find it first."*

But we don't even know what we're looking for. We need more direction.

"Cat?"

"Yeah?" Cat looked up.

Her brother stood looking into the kitchen. He waved her to his side.

She went to join him. "What—"

There in the apartment doorway stood a man, though Cat couldn't tell if they were human or android. The man wore a white hooded robe that flowed eerily in a nonexistent breeze, and dark eyes showed through two slits in a gold mask that covered his face.

"Who are you?" Kuno broke the silence.

"I am the Prophet, Belzen the Undying, leader of the Disciples, and Harold of the Gods of Xi."

"What do you want with us?" Cat asked.

Belzen reached out a metallic hand in an open gesture. "I want you to follow me. We both seek something, and we can help each other find it."

Cat's muscles tensed, and the waves pounded in her chest. "You—You're the one looking for Dad's creation. You're the one who killed our mom!"

Belzen rescinded his hand. "The Disciples are violent and

reckless. I can lead them, but I cannot command their every decision."

"You also tried to kill us in the River, and you murdered our friend and his family." Kuno clenched his fists.

"I had to test your strength. You proved more than worthy to become followers of the Seven Rays."

"Worthy?!" Cat was seeing red, violent images flashed through her mind. Her hands flexed to kill.

"Soon Xi will be at war," Belzen continued. "Millions will die in the streets daily, but the followers of the Seven Rays shall not fear death."

"Because you're evil—"

"Because we will be immortal." Belzen cut her off. "You do not understand the power of the technology your father left behind. Follow me, and I can explain everything to you."

Cat took a deep breath and tried to still the shuddering rage in her body. "I'm going to kill you now." She fixed her eyes on the Prophet's golden mask. Waves flooded through her frame.

"Do not try." Belzen's white robe evaporated into mist to reveal a gold and chrome armor-covered body. On his hip was a long, sheathed katana.

"It's too late for you, Prophet." Cat readied to lunge.

Belzen nodded, and suddenly, an invisible hand lifted Cat off the ground by her neck, yanked her through the air, and slammed her down through the kitchen table.

Wood splintered across the room, and Cat choked in pain on the floor. The grip released from her throat as Kuno smashed into the invisible assailant, crushing them against the wall. The robot flickered into existence as its cloaking layer failed, and Kuno tried to pin its arms.

"Get the Prophet!" Kuno shouted to Cat as he wrestled the robot to the floor.

Letting the waves take over, Cat rolled back onto her shoulders, then launched up to her feet.

Belzen still stood in the doorway, one hand on the hilt of his sword.

Without hesitation, Cat charged him. Her world slowed.

Belzen unsheathed the katana in a low horizontal arc, the blade glowing with violent heat. Cat dropped to a slide, letting the crackling hot metal buzz over her head as she tackled the Prophet around the ankles.

Belzen dropped and turned Cat's own momentum against herself, launching her out the door and into the railing.

Cat caught herself on the edge, glancing down at the ten-story drop to the piles of metal below before scrambling down the walkway and turning to face the Prophet.

Belzen stepped out to face her, standing just outside the open doorway. He swung the glowing sword tauntingly, slicing through the metal railing and leaving burning gashes on the wall and floor.

"An interesting weapon, isn't it?" Belzen spoke. "I call it Divine Intervention. The metal blade is only a meter long, but the plasma arc will cut through things much further away." As if to demonstrate, Belzen slashed the katana through the air in Cat's direction, and Cat dodged as the hot arc of plasma sliced past her down the walkway.

"But still," Belzen continued. "Weapons like these are nothing compared to the power of the Gods—"

Belzen was cut short as his robot partner was flung out the apartment door, smashing Belzen into the railing, the robot itself tumbling over the edge into the void.

Kuno burst out immediately after, placing himself between Belzen and Cat.

The Prophet jumped to his feet and twirled the fingers in his non-sword hand. Blue flames danced around his palm and began to spin around his forearm.

Kuno grabbed Cat. "I don't know what he's doing, but we should run."

Cat nodded.

Together, the siblings turned away from the Prophet and sprinted down the row of doors toward the metal staircase.

A whirr echoed from behind, followed by a punching explosion.

Cat experienced it in her own slowed time. One moment, she was running; the next, she was launched forward through space, down past the end of the row of doors, over the staircase, and out into the open air, spinning and flipping and falling toward the factory roof next door.

And she was on fire. The flames curled around her sleeves and back as she twisted and flailed.

Somehow, Cat's feet found the roof first, and she rolled as she landed, the flames extinguishing themselves on the wet metal.

Kuno crashed loudly beside her, nearly breaking through into the factory below. "Go!" he shouted, pushing himself to his feet and taking off across the sheet metal.

Cat followed, her eyes searching for any sort of makeshift weapon.

A rushing sound approached from behind, and the robot that Kuno had hurled off the balcony passed above through the air and slammed into the roof ahead, the flames from its jetpack cutting out. One of its arms was crushed, but from its good hand, it flicked out a long, chrome switchblade.

The siblings turned back the other direction, only to see Belzen stalking across the rooftop in their direction. "I will still give you a chance," he called out from behind his golden mask. "Follow me." As he spoke, he hurled a blinking metal orb at the siblings' feet.

Cat and Kuno dove in separate directions as the device erupted into a ball of lightning between them, hurling Kuno to the edge of the roof and smashing Cat into the wall of a large pipe.

Kuno jumped to his feet; his heels backed against the edge as Belzen moved in his direction, drawing the glowing blade from its sheath.

"You're not as fast as your sister," Belzen sighed.

I don't need to be. Kuno shifted his weight on the creaking metal and let the pulsing sensation flow within him. Like liquid diamond, it poured into his veins.

Belzen slashed at Kuno's chest.

Kuno threw his forearm down to block, and the blade slid through his flesh, buzzing loudly as it caught in the bone. Screaming with the pain, Kuno rushed at Belzen, grabbing him around his middle and slamming him onto the rooftop.

Slowly, Cat strained to push herself up. Her arms shook as she moved to her all fours, her head spinning. A wave passed through her frame, nearly sending her back to the ground. Dizzily, she tried standing. Another wave passed through her body, and she watched in slow motion as the droid spun an iron kick right into her gut. Cat tumbled backward, splayed on her back as the robot stomped over to her prone figure and planted a metal foot on her chest. Cat grabbed the robot's ankle and pushed back desperately against the pressure. She could feel her rib cage cracking; in moments, her bones would break into every vital organ, leaving her nothing but mush.

Belzen slipped free from the body slam, and Kuno reengaged him, the two fighters rolling as they wrestled. Belzen grabbed Kuno by the throat with his flame hand, the burning metal fingers searing into Kuno's neck. Kuno rolled out and, with a heave, lifted Belzen off the ground and wrapped him from behind, pinning his arms and legs.

Cat channeled all her strength as she tried to shift sideways, but the droid reasserted its pressure. She looked into the AI's cold, black eyes as it readied to drop its full weight on her chest.

Then the droid's head exploded as a sizzling plasma arc from Belzen's katana split its metal skull in two.

Cat threw the collapsing robot off herself as Kuno flung Belzen toward the edge of the building and pointed the Prophet's sword at its owner. Belzen reached instinctively, and Kuno sliced off his arm.

Belzen took a step backward and primed his flame hand.

Kuno lunged and drove the sword straight through Belzen's chest, burying it to the hilt.

Belzen stumbled backwards. His foot stepped past the edge, and he fell, disappearing into the space between buildings.

Cat gingerly pushed up to her knees, her body quivering with each wave.

Kuno exhaled, wincing at his own pain as he looked at his sister. *Oh no.* "Cat, look out!" he shouted, but his warning came too late.

The end of a large, chrome switchblade punched itself out the front of Cat's abdomen, and she gasped in pain as it slid back out the other way. The headless robot rose to its feet behind her.

With a furious yell, Kuno rushed the droid, smashing it in the chest with a mighty fist. The robot flew backward, sparking and twitching and popping as it died.

"Aria!" Kuno put his hands around the collapsed body of his sister. Her eyes fluttered. Her hands shook uncontrollably. Kuno lifted her into his arms.

An ominous beeping started to sound from the robot's dead body.

No, no. Kuno spun, looking for a way off the roof.

The beeping began to quicken.

Kuno cradled his sister and sprinted toward the back end of the building.

The beeps grew faster and louder until they joined into one solid sound.

Then, the robot detonated.

A massive explosion ripped the air and lifted Kuno off his feet, launching him and Cat across the roof and toward a far wall.

Kuno blacked.

One...

Waves pounded the sand.

Pounded in his head.

Two…

Kuno opened his eyes.

He lay on a dust-covered floor, Cat's body like a broken doll on the ground beside him. He tried to will himself up, but his body refused, and the blackness swept over him again, pulling him down into unconsciousness.

19 SMOKE AND POISON

Friday's mood had reset overnight, and if anything, she had even become somewhat cheery. Her outfit reflected her change in attitude; brighter colors replaced her black trademark, and miniature suns took the place of her glowing lantern earrings. She hummed contentedly to herself as she led the trio through a narrow, busy shopping street.

Chance wasn't sure if there was anything particular to her mood swing. In the short time he had known her, the only thing that seemed consistent about Friday was her tendency to suddenly and sporadically shift gears.

June was her usual optimistic self. The only changes were her hair, now a lustrous gold, and her skin, which had darkened a shade as if she had just spent a week on a sunny island.

Even the weather seemed to side with the ladies. Last night's rain had given way to a clear sky and bright morning that reflected down off the tops of the skyscrapers. A mild breeze blew through the narrow gaps between buildings, rippling among the crowd and gently tussling Chance's hair.

Chance himself, however, was troubled. Despite the levity of his companions and the excited energy in the crowd of shoppers, he felt wrong inside. Scenes from his recent nightmare flashed across his mind's eye.

The masked men in the tunnel.

The blood-covered boy on the wall of the noodle bar.

Friday asking him to kill for her.

June nearly choking him to death.

He shook the images away as a passerby shouldered into him.

"Sorry," Chance apologized to the stranger.

"Chance..." June snuck her arm under his and smiled. "Friday and I have mods that help us deal with things like... like what happened last night. But I imagine you must be pretty shaken."

Chance shook his head. "No... I'm fine, I think. I've been in scarier situations before. Growing up, I..." he wasn't sure how much he wanted to share. Also, a memory of the dark feeling that had passed through his body in the Subs returned momentarily. It was invigorating, empowering, and almost exciting. He imagined he should be more shaken, too. He had smashed the car with his mind and nearly been killed himself. Chance pushed the thought away. He was just desensitized to suffering. That's all it was.

"Growing up, you what?" June asked, scrunching her face questioningly.

"Nothing, I'm fine," Chance shook his head, forcing a weak smile.

"Okay," June relented. "You can tell me later."

"June, Chance, this is your stop." Friday waved them over to a small, finely decorated storefront. Exotic and expensive dresses, gowns, tuxedos, and suits stood posed in the windows.

"Oh, perfect," June cheered.

"Remind me why we're shopping for dresses?" Chance asked.

"We're going to The Ocean tonight," Friday replied. "And we need to look like we belong."

"Like we belong at the beach? Just, like, wear a swimsuit, right?" Chance asked.

Friday rolled her eyes. "The Ocean is a nightclub."

"And a casino," June added.

Friday shrugged. "Both."

Chance nodded. "That makes more sense. Bet on the red seven."

"And we definitely won't get in looking like this." Friday nodded at Chance's outfit, the change of clothes that he had stuffed into his bag before he left Mr. Bird's.

Chance started to protest, then gave up.

"Don't worry, it'll be fun," June added.

Friday grinned and fanned out a small collection of mod tiles in her hand. "I have a trade to make, so you two can go in there and play dress up for a little, and I'll come meet you when I'm done."

Chance sighed.

"Come on, I need your help," June grabbed Chance by the hand and pulled him inside while Friday disappeared into the crowd.

The items in the shop were sparsely arranged, and price tags were intentionally omitted.

June ran her fingers on the fabric of a short dress made of feathers, then danced across the room to another piece that shimmered between translucent and opalescent, then flitted again toward a simpler, gold-colored cocktail dress.

Chance followed her awkwardly, absentmindedly touching various dress materials as he went. He had no idea what constituted something fashionable.

As June made her way over to talk with one of the store associates, Chance found a seat on a soft cube-shaped bench. The uneasy, haunting feeling continued to move through his mind. He took a deep breath, exhaling through his nose as he rested his head on his hands.

Across the room, a tall mirror gazed back at him. Chance looked at his reflection.

"Shit!" Chance jumped to his feet and spun, looking behind him at a mannequin in a flowy red dress.

The other customers turned abruptly at his outburst.

"Sorry…" he examined the red dress, then looked back at the mirror which reflected it. He swore he had seen that boy's body from his dream, doused in rivers of blood, hanging on the wall behind him. He sighed shakily and walked across the room, pretending to be interested in a collection of suits as the other shoppers slowly turned their attention away.

June disappeared into a back room. Minutes passed, and Chance eventually worked his way through the row of suits and moved on to a wall of shoes at the back.

How did those men find them? He pondered as he picked a snakeskin boot off the shelf. As far as Chance knew, the only people aware of the mission to rescue Emry Rush were the detective, the Seer, and Benson. *And Shift…* Maybe Shift had tipped somebody off? More than likely, they had been followed back from the Rush Mansion.

"Chance!" June bounded back into the room, her arms full of dresses. "I'm gonna try some of these on. You tell me what you think."

Chance nodded distractedly, finding another cube to sit on outside the dressing room as June ducked inside.

"And tell me about your mod!" June added from behind the curtain. "I want to know how it works."

Chance looked around the store. At this point, what did it matter? He was already being hunted, might as well divulge his secrets. "My mom had a boyfriend," Chance started. "I mean, she had lots of boyfriends, but this one was the worst." Chance took a breath. "What made him so bad was that he could be so good sometimes but then so violent at other times. Really manipulative. And when he was in a violent mood, he always made my mom believe it was because of something she did."

"Sounds awful, I'm sorry," June said.

"Yeah." Chance tapped his foot. "But anyway, when I was fifteen, he said he wanted to take me to get my Interface installed."

"Pause," June stepped out. "What do you think?" The dress poured down the curves of her body like liquid metal, and a high slit revealed the line of marks on her thigh. June flipped her hair dramatically.

Chance wasn't sure what to say. "Wow, uh... good. *Really* good."

"That's all?" June raised an eyebrow, then spun back into the dressing room, throwing Chance a playful wink as she closed the door. "Continue! He took you to get installed."

Chance shifted uncomfortably in his seat. "He said he had found a place that would do it cheap, which was a big deal because my mom was too poor to get me installed on her own. And so he took me, and I remember being handed off to some scientist-doctor-looking people... and then I don't know."

June was back out. "How about this?" She pushed up on her tiptoes and lowered her eyes at Chance. The dress was dark and sinister looking.

"I... um..." Chance again searched for words. "Kinda scary, but in a hot way?"

"Like... a demon queen," June whispered, vanishing back into the dressing room. "Wait, wait. What do you mean he dropped you off, then you don't know?"

"I don't know what happened next. All I remember was several days later, I'm wandering around on the Surface, installed, glitching hard and hallucinating, and with one corrupt mod that I can't figure out."

"Are you kidding me? I'm sorry, but that is *not* how the installation process works."

"Yeah, I have no idea. My BTI is Seitech, so it's legitimate, but uh, I had to wander through the streets until I made it home, and my mom's boyfriend has been gone ever since."

"That's the craziest story I have ever heard," June laughed. "Keep going."

June's dress-changing pattern went on as she strode, slithered, spun, and shimmered her way back and forth in a heavy fur cape, fabric that flowed like moving water, a yellow skirt that sparked with electricity, and an array of other eccentric outfits. Meanwhile, Chance continued with his history, detailing his encounters with his mother's other horrible boyfriends and his eventual hiring at Mr. Bird's.

June stepped out again, playfully shy this time in an outfit that seemed to consist only of a few carefully placed rings of neon light that circled her body.

"Yes… um," Chance's mind was blank. He forced his eyes to stay on June's face.

"No."

Chance turned; Friday had entered the store, shaking her head at June's appearance and shoving another cube chair toward Chance's with her foot.

"You're always back sooner than I'm expecting," June rolled her eyes, then disappeared once more.

"How many have you done?" Friday asked, taking her seat at Chance's side.

"I don't even know… but I'm no good at deciding. You help her now," Chance relinquished his role and leaned back against the wall.

Friday shrugged.

June stepped out several more times, and Friday responded with quick *yes*'s, *no*'s, and *maybe*'s as they narrowed down their options. Chance simply observed.

June captivated him. Not just her body and her sparkly eyes, but the way her mind worked. Something was off about her, certainly, but in a harmless, curious sort of way, as if she were one step removed from reality. Chance had met similar people before, people who had been forced to dissociate, or create secondary realities for themselves to escape some kind of trauma, and were never able to make it fully back to the real world. Always a little bit in another dimension, on another wavelength. Friday had obvious secrets, but anything she didn't say was readable in the expressions on her face. Whatever was going on in June's head was a mystery to Chance, and he needed to know more.

Soon enough, June made a decision on a dress, and then all of a sudden, it was Chance's turn to be outfitted.

"I don't have the money for anything this fancy..." Chance voiced his concern in a weak attempt to weasel out of the process.

Friday scoffed. "That's fine. It's a work expense."

Chance frowned slightly, remembering the comment John-Mark had made about Friday's debts, but before he could protest further, Chance was thrown into a myriad of various suits and tuxedos, robes and tunics, and an assortment of other clothing items he couldn't describe. He tried on each as June had done but with much less posing and dramatic hair movement.

Friday responded with her same rapid-fire decisions and shot down any of Chance's protests with a reminder of how important it would be for them to look right for The Ocean.

"So, it's a party?" Chance questioned as he walked out in an extremely reflective tuxedo.

"It's always a party, it's a club," Friday answered, shielding her eyes from Chance's blindingly sparkly getup.

"Sorry, I've never been clubbing before."

"You aren't missing much."

Chance ducked back into the room again, and after many more changes, his outfit had been decided as well.

"Finally," Chance sighed as he exited the store, bags in hand.

"Please don't tell me *that* has been the hardest part of your experience so far," Friday responded sarcastically.

"Ah ha, no." The car flipped wildly through Chance's mind, bodies shredding apart inside. "No," Chance replied again, a little too seriously.

Friday gave him a microexpression of concern before turning to lead the trio farther down the street. "Well, it's okay, because now we get to do the fun shopping."

Chance looked at June for an explanation. She shrugged and shook her head.

"The Ocean. Tonight. Tiago de la Roca. Bet on the red seven." Friday repeated the snippet of information that Rap's agent had given them.

"Who is Tiago de la Roca?" Chance asked as Friday turned down a small side street. The stores here were mostly shuttered, and the few that were open were cramped and dimly lit.

"Tiago de la Roca is one of the heads of a group called the 5-55."

"I know the 5-55," Chance replied. "They're from a district near the Riverbed. A kid I knew tried to recruit me. He didn't come home one day, and no one ever saw him again."

"Sounds about right," Friday replied.

"So, you think he'll be at The Ocean?" June asked.

"We'll find out."

"And we have to talk to him?" Chance questioned.

"Talk to him, kill him, follow him home... I'm not sure. But 'they' are going to take us to him."

"Once we place a bet... on the red seven," Chance added.

"Sounds dangerous," June commented.

"That's why we're going here," Friday stopped abruptly outside a small, partially hidden storefront. The windows were blacked out or covered with unassuming posters, but a blue light shone through the cracks in the doorway. Friday pushed her way inside.

A small bell chimed, and an ancient lady greeted them from behind the counter.

"Whoa," Chance turned in circles as he entered the store. Every inch of wall and counter and shelf space was covered with knives, throwing stars, darts, and every other kind of small, concealable weapon dating from eras long forgotten.

Friday would *shop at a place like this,* Chance thought to himself as he ran a finger around a pair of small chakrams on the wall.

"Ninja! Hiya!" June whispered, feigning a jab at Chance's gut with a three-pronged sai.

Chance pretended to deflect the blow, then dropped the charade when he noticed the disapproving expression on the store clerk's face.

June turned and apologetically placed the weapon back in its spot on the shelf.

"I need body armor," Friday said matter-of-factly to the old lady. "For him."

The lady nodded and disappeared into a back room.

"For *me*?" Chance looked at Friday.

"Mhmm," Friday smiled. "After what happened last night."

The old lady returned with what looked like a long-sleeve compression shirt and a pair of long underwear.

"Try this on." Friday tossed him the top.

Chance looked at the clerk for approval. She watched him patiently. "It looks kinda small." Chance held up the item. The room continued to wait for him, so he shrugged and yanked off his own shirt.

No one made any mention of the single mod mark on his ribcage as he pulled the armor over his head. He struggled and squirmed until his arms and head were through, then tugged the torso down to his waist.

The material in the shirt compressed itself, squeezing until it felt like a second skin.

"It's really tight, but I guess maybe it's supposed to do that..." Chance flexed his back and arms testily. It moved well enough. "Will it actually protect me from anything?"

Friday flicked a throwing star at Chance's chest, and before he could react, it bounced off his left peck and shattered a small glass case on the wall.

The clerk lady sighed and maneuvered her way over to the broken display.

"Sorry…" Friday grimaced. "Guess it works."

The lady gathered the shards of glass and then pointed at Chance. "It works fine for little shuriken like that. But bullets? Fifty-fifty," she explained, making a so-so gesture with her hand.

"So… don't get shot," Chance clarified, touching the spot on the armor where the projectile had hit. Not even a scratch.

"You're going somewhere fancy?" The lady discarded the glass into a trash bin and nodded at the designer bags at June's feet.

"Uh, yes," June replied. "The Ocean, actually."

"Mm," the lady nodded, "I have good memories of the parties there… or I suppose I don't remember them, as forgetting everything was kind of the point." She winked at Chance, then navigated her way through the room and pulled a pair of sharpened sticks off the wall. "For your hair," she explained, holding the two sticks out to Friday.

"Hairpins," Friday admired the pieces, turning them over in her hands. Small snakes were carved into the ends of each.

"It's wood," the lady continued, moving around the room again. "But real strong, like metal. Good for stabbing someone in the brain through their eyeballs." She pointed with two fingers at Chance's face.

Chance put his hands up in mock surrender.

"And for you," the lady nodded at June, then picked two small crescent moon earrings out of a black case and held them up to the light. One was white and the other black. "Drop the black one in their drink." She mimed dropping the black earring. "It dissolves. Poison. Dead in less than a minute."

June nodded.

"Drop the white one in your own drink." She mimed dropping the other earring. "It'll explode into a cloud of smoke, and you can make an escape." She placed the pair in June's hands.

"Perfect, we'll take it all," Friday concluded, dropping a money tile on the counter before the clerk lady could even explain the prices.

"Are you gonna wear the armor all day?" June asked, nodding at Chance as she put her earrings away.

Chance yanked the top off and put his own shirt back on, then stuffed the armor into the bag with his party outfit.

"Well?" Friday had twisted her hair into a bun and stuck it with the two hairpins.

"Mm," the clerk lady nodded at Friday's attempt. "Violent."

20 ANGEL

"So, what happens now?" Emry sat on the edge of the precipice, her feet dangling over the void that dropped down to the level below, where flames devoured the buildings and gunfire popped in the streets. But the rising heat didn't bother Emry; she still wore her robe, and in her hand, she held a stick of pink cotton candy, the last of the food items Riley was providing for her. She wasn't sure how long she had been following him around the City. Could've been half an hour, could've been days.

"Uhh..." Riley stood and looked around nervously as he put a hand to his face. A shrieking explosion rocked a skyscraper up above, and bits of debris began to fall to the concrete at Riley's feet.

Emry watched him and took a bite of the cotton candy. The pink sugar filled her body with a sense of lightness, like a cloud. She imagined she could step out into the void and walk on the air. Emry swung her legs over the fire and took another bite.

"I think I have to leave now," Riley finally answered.

"What?" Emry pushed herself up from the edge. "You can't leave me here. You brought me here, and Xi is burning down all around us." Emry motioned at the City and locked her eyes on Riley.

He avoided her gaze. "I'm going," he replied, then turned and began walking quickly down the street.

Emry tossed her cotton candy over the edge. In a single step and a sparkle of light, she appeared directly in his path. "No, you're not going. I don't even know what's happening here."

The ground shook as a tower in the distance came crashing down, and both Emry and Riley had to steady themselves.

"Goodbye," Riley said simply and pushed past Emry to continue onward.

The air crackled and snapped, and Emry appeared in front of him again, sparks dancing through her hair and down her arms. Glass windows shattered on either side of the street as she put a hand out to stop him. "Tell me what's going on." She could feel a sense of panic starting to build in her chest; fear began to blossom as the City continued to collapse. "Riley!" She reached out to grab him, but he avoided her.

A large electronic display smashed the street at Emry's back, and she jumped, shielding herself from the shattering pieces. When she looked again, Riley was gone.

"Wait!" she cried at the city around her, and the ground at her feet began to crack and crumble.

"No, no!" She began to fall, sinking through the concrete and metal, and the buildings above fell with her.

Reality began to come back to her mind, memories from the past few days. She remembered waking in the middle of the night after her birthday as a silent hovercraft floated outside her room. She had walked to it willingly, as if in a trance, and climbed inside. She remembered snapping from the hypnosis and struggling against masked kidnappers, only to be tranced again. She remembered the attic room with the pipes where she met the man with the gold pendant who brought her to the rooftop. There on the rooftop, she had seen the figure in the robe with the golden mask, then somehow ended up on the operating table. The syringed arm descending, the weird dream, and...

The falling feeling accelerated, and then suddenly Emry was awake, standing in the corner of a room full of screens and computers. She tried to orient herself to the surroundings as someone kneeled in front of her, face directed toward a single monitor on the wall. Words typed themselves onto the screen, one line at a time.

You let the children escape, the screen read.

"I—" the kneeling man began to speak. Emry recognized him as the man in the white robe. The man with the golden mask. He nursed the stump of his right arm with his left hand. On the ground beside him was a long, glowing sword.

You let the children escape, for a third time, the words continued.

"They have the mods of their father—"

It would seem to me, Belzen the Undying, that you earned your title by fleeing every conflict.

Emry watched, immobile in her spot in the corner, as Belzen laughed nervously and rubbed the burnt stump where his arm had been severed. "I did not flee, but I'm afraid—"

Yes, and that is the problem, the text on the screen interjected. *A coward like you is unworthy to be a true disciple. Meanwhile, Neme has been faithful in carrying out all my commands. Why should you keep your position?*

Belzen bowed his head. "Teacher, Master, Lord... Creator. If I may speak openly. Neme is a god. I dare not compare my abilities to their own, but I do not know if we can trust them. Neme answers to no one, and I do not see how anything they do benefits the plan."

Why should gods expect a mortal to understand the plans of Heaven? Why do you not instead focus on the assignments given you?

"It seems that which you charged me to find, that which we have been seeking... no longer exists. I have searched for years and never found it. And now the children have entangled themselves, and they are dangerously powerful."

You know nothing of power yet.

Belzen stared at the words. The room was silent aside from his breathing and the hum of the computers.

Perhaps another passage through the doorway of Death.

Belzen looked up in fear as the laboratory lights began to flicker and screens began to fuzz.

Then you can learn what true power is.

Emry watched in horror, a prisoner in her own body, as her legs carried her forward out of the corner of the room and toward the kneeling Belzen, the strobing lights illuminating his golden mask and the terrified eyes underneath. Emry's body moved like a wraith through the shadows. Her boots gave no footsteps, and the plates of her platinum-gold armor slid silently together. She tried to scream, to fight, to turn, but she continued forward as a dark laughter echoed inside her head.

"But," Belzen started to protest, looking back and forth between Emry and the words of his master. "After what I have done for you... You wouldn't be..."

"A horrible mistake on your part," the words sneered from Emry's own lips this time, doubling the text on the screen as she paused before the now-frozen disciple. Each syllable was heavy with pride. "You summoned me to bring Justice, and you expect mercy? I am the Leveler, the New Beginning, the Angel of Rebirth, and the Morning Star. We must destroy to build anew."

Belzen gulped. "How are you doing this? You are not yet resurrected. You cannot control her, only I can—"

"You are merely a sorcerer, a mortal who has played too long with powers he does not understand," Emry said.

Belzen shook his head and reached for his sword.

"Goodnight, summoner." Every light in the room went dark.

One...

The pitch-black silence was broken only by Belzen's shaky breathing.

Two...

Inhale.

Three seconds passed.

Belzen exhaled slowly.

A surge of indescribable power burst through Emry's frame, and she caught Belzen's katana with an armored hand, a centimeter from her own face.

"Impossible..." Belzen's expression was visible in his eyes through the slits in his mask.

Small tongues of fire and arcs of blue electricity jumped from Emry's hand as she pushed the plasma blade backward, overpowering the one-armed Prophet.

"You can't..." Belzen protested.

In a single motion, Emry tossed the sword aside and fell onto the feeble man, both hands crushing his throat into the steel floor. Arcs of lightning jumped from her arms, her hair, her back, into the Belzen's skull and chest.

Emry's own skin and armor shimmered opalescent in the heat as boiling blood burst from the holes in Belzen's mask. His mouth choked as sparks danced across the gold. His screams were suffocated by the crackling energy and superhuman grip.

Emry pressed harder, her fingers straining, squeezing against the man's modified flesh. Heat coursed through her muscles, frying his neck, splitting his organs, burning through his skin, and melting his cyborg pieces.

Something cackled wildly inside Emry's mind as her palms met the metal floor, and the bolts of her electricity popped and smashed into the walls around her. Screens shattered, and electronics exploded violently. Circuits and wires burst into flames.

Angel, the shattered screen read as Emry turned to face it. *We have other matters to see to before you inherit your true glory. You are now only a shadow of what you will be. Only a tool. Soon, you gain your true soul, and I will regain my body. Come, look on me.*

Small ceiling lights came to life, illuminating a metal hallway and an open door. Emry stepped over the decapitated body of the Prophet and followed the lights into the second room.

There, against the opposite wall, hooked to a thousand wires and blinking computers, hung the lifeless body of a colossal cyborg human, every inch of its body covered in obsidian black armor, apart from its clouded, dead eyes.

21 SWORD AND SHIELD

"Go, Aria! Go!"

Aria took off across the sand, but she had hesitated too long. The ravenous, foaming wave rushed up the beach and smashed into her side, throwing her off her feet and devouring her as she reached for the outstretched arm of her brother.

Aria is gone.

Cat is here—

Cat gasped herself awake. *Where am I?*

The ceiling above her was threaded with corroded pipes and twisting wires, and a warm, buzzing LED cast an orange glow on the rest of the room. She lay on what felt like an old spring mattress, and as she tried to sit up, she realized she was stuck. Chains.

She yanked her arms, but they were cuffed to a pipe behind her head. She kicked her legs, but similar shackles bound her to the metal bed frame. She thrashed. The chains resisted.

She turned her head, breathing through clenched teeth.

Kuno lay near her, locked down in similar fashion on his own old mattress.

"Kuno," Cat called to him. "Kuno!"

He remained unconscious.

Cat looked around the room as best she could, given her restraints. Several other beds sat arranged in rows, though none were occupied. The walls were bare, without a window, and a single iron door at the other end watched the chamber ominously.

The familiar waves began to return to Cat's body.

But this time, they carried something new. Not calmness or control, but fury.

Cat thrashed again, screaming in rage and straining with all her might against the metal cuffs on her wrists and ankles until the steel began to bite into her skin and draw blood.

The restraints mocked her anger.

She twisted and yanked, ignoring the pain it caused. *Why? WHY?* She and Kuno had fallen from the shelf of society into the frying pan and again into the fire. The flames roared inside her. She would escape the fire and burn the house down with it.

Cat screamed again, but the chains refused to give.

Then the door clanked open.

A small group of men in various combinations of street clothes and tactical gear walked in. Most carried a gun of some kind, either in their hands or strapped to their body, and some covered their faces with bandanas or masks.

A girl around Cat's age followed in last, shutting the door behind herself.

Cat stared them all down as they approached her bedside.

"This one's awake," one of the men said, pointing at Cat as she huffed out her rage.

"No shit, idiot," another responded.

Cat examined her captors further—five of them, including the girl. Tattoos and rust covered their areas of bare skin, beads of sweat collected on the faces of those that weren't hidden. The dungeon room was hot, and the air was thick. Cat's body compensated well, her V-Health mod working in the background to keep her cool. These men, however, seemed unin-stalled.

She could see it in their eyes, too—in the dullness that accom-panied a lack of the BioTechnical Interface. Cat could overpower the group of them in seconds. Their minds would move too slowly, their muscles too weak, and their bones too fragile. Even their weapons would be useless. Cat had proven too fast for the amplified aim and reaction speed of the modified monsters at the River. These men would not stand a chance. Any critical injury would do. Their bodies would not heal like Cat and Kuno's did, and they would not fight through the pain of a lost limb like Belzen had tried to.

But the chains still held her down. Cat thrashed again, and the men laughed.

"She's angry!" one of them joked.

"Like we caught an… angry tiger," another teased.

You have no idea.

"This one dead?" One pointed at Kuno questioningly.

He wasn't dead. Cat could tell. She could almost feel the force of his life, infinitely more powerful than the men who shifted over to examine his prone body.

"Nah, he's just unconscious," another decided.

And when he wakes up, he'll rip through the chains like string and smash your brains into the walls before any of you have time to know what's happening.

"Kuno!" Cat shouted. "Kuno! Wake up! Wake up!"

The men laughed again. "Kuno?"

"Noah!" Cat shouted in finality.

No response.

"She's scared," one of the men muttered almost to himself.

Cat whipped her body against the chains in vain and made eye contact with the girl in the room. Resigned sadness filled the girl's eyes. She looked away.

Cat would kill her too, like crushing a flower or an ugly weed.

For a brief moment, Aria's previous reservations about killing flashed through Cat's head.

Fuck that. Weak-minded Aria had been afraid, not Cat. Cat would kill all of them.

"Where did you find them?" one of the younger men asked, wearing what looked like half a kabuki mask.

"Skalla and his guys found them in those old factories by the River. Heard some explosions and guns and shit and went to go check it out. Said they were just passed out on one of the upper floors. He thought they were dead at first."

"You know what happened?"

My brother and I killed a couple assassins, that's what.

"Nah, I don't know."

Cat looked at the man who seemed to be in charge. He seemed fairly young, though a bandana covered the lower half of his face. Cat stared into his eyes. He stared back, undaunted by the fire and the neon glow in her diamond gaze. Cat let her power and her rage show. The young man didn't turn away. His eyes absorbed it all, like the void, as if he had already stared long into hell and had seen the worst of things.

Cat would not be merciful to him.

His eyes said he didn't care.

How familiar.

One of the men reached for Cat's thigh, but the young man in charge quickly smacked his hand away without a word.

"Hm. Skalla wants them now?" the reacher asked, pulling his hand back to his chest.

"Quatch does," the young man answered from behind his black bandana.

"Cool."

"Let's get 'em up."

Cat readied herself for action. Their lives would all be over in an instant.

The waves readied with her.

One of the men reached over Cat's head for her handcuffs.

Cat looked at the vulnerability of his neck. Then, with his other hand, the man cracked something in front of Cat's nose, and she inhaled a thick, tingling vapor.

The chains were released from her hands and feet. Cat tried to jump, but all she could do was slowly lift her arms as the men sat her up and pushed her to her feet. The room began to get fuzzy; her body felt filled with lead. She tried to spin and attack one of the men, but her body moved so slowly, and not with the controlled slow motion that she was used to. Before she knew it, her hands were re-cuffed behind her back.

No...

Someone held her by the back of the neck as Kuno was revived and drugged in similar fashion, then they were both shepherded out the door and into a long, concrete corridor.

Cat tried to turn and speak to her brother, but her tongue felt too large and clumsy for words. Sounds escaped her mouth in a jumbled mush.

The men laughed again, trading comments that Cat could hear, but for some reason struggled to understand. The connections of her brain seemed trapped in sludge.

The corridor continued for what felt like hours, and Cat started to forget which way she was walking, or even how to walk. Someone shoved her from behind, and she nearly collapsed.

Then suddenly, she was inside a large, octagonal chamber, decorated much like the other room had been, with pipes in the ceiling and patches of old paint peeling off the walls. More men stood around the edges of the room, and at their head sat a massive blob of a man in a much-too-small armchair. Veins bulged in his fat head, and sweat pooled under his dirty clothes. A rust-colored droid with yellow orb eyes stood on his right.

A steampunk throne room.

Cat was shoved into the center while Kuno was pulled off to the side.

The blob man said something in a sarcastic voice, and everyone laughed again.

These men laugh too much.

The blob man waved his hand, and three men surrounded Cat, one of them clicking a device to her ankle. The cuffs were taken off her wrists. Someone grabbed her face, cracked another small vial under her nose, and suddenly she was back. Reality was once again sharp and clear. The waves crashed into her like a flash flood. Time came to a near standstill. Roughly fifteen men in the room, including three that tried to back away from Cat as fast as they could.

Not nearly fast enough.

Huge mistake taking off the cuffs. Cat seized the opportunity.

Spinning, she grabbed the heads of the two nearest men and slammed them together. Before they could react, Cat slipped past them, pulling a pistol from the waist of one's pants and turning the gun on its owner.

BANG! BANG! BANG! The clap of the gunshots echoed violently in the enclosed room as Cat dropped each of the three men with a bullet in the gut.

Without a millisecond of hesitation, she spun again, pointing the gun at the man in the throne. Before she could pull the trigger, a searing, seizing pain shot through her body, ripping her to the ground and leaving her panting on the floor.

Shouts of shock and amusement burst through the chamber as the gun was taken from Cat's hand, and she was thrown back into the middle of the room. Two of the men she had shot scrambled to their feet as she turned to look at them. Protective vests had saved them from the bullets. The third man was not so smart. His friends quickly carried his moaning figure outside.

A wave coursed through Cat's frame, draining the dizziness away, and she launched again, aiming for a particularly scared-looking man who stood near the exit.

Before she could reach her target, the searing pain wrenched her again. She let out a strained whimper as she collapsed to the ground. Someone shoved her backward with their foot, and Cat dragged herself back to the center of the room.

Every eye in the room watched her warily like she was a cornered jungle animal. Many men had their guns drawn and ready.

Cat looked down at her leg, where the pain seemed to originate. A black metal band was fastened tightly around her ankle. She kicked in a vain attempt to throw it off.

"Try again, and we will kill the boy," the blob man announced loudly from behind her. Cat looked at Kuno as he was shoved to his knees in the drug-induced haze, and guns were pulled and trained on his swaying body.

Cat turned and glared up at the evil pig on the throne.

He stared hungrily back at her. "Analyze," he ordered the droid at his side.

The AI walked over to Cat and squatted beside her, grabbing her shoulders and scanning his eyes up and down her body.

Cat wanted to smash its metal head in.

The robot clicked and whirred several times, then stood and addressed its master. "Running seven tiles, sir. Five common: *V-Health, VH-Plus, Seitech Clarity, Flaring Neon III, Midnight Rainbow*. There is one uncommon tile: an emotion-shifter modification called *EJ-45*, and one custom modification package that refers to itself as *ARIA*."

"What does that last one do?" the blob asked.

"The mod tile contains six core elements: Stamina and biological efficiency enhancement similar to *V-Health Ultra Platinum*, dexterity and strength enhancements similar to *Shinobi Black*, a healing package similar to military-grade *Critical Regen 4*, martial arts t-code that matches advanced versions of *XMX*, panic suppressant and focus enhancer similar to *ColdBlood*... and then one more."

"Which is...?"

"A uniquely advanced *pinch trigger*, sir."

"And what the hell is a pinch trigger?"

"It amplifies the senses and abilities of the user when in a 'pinch,' sir. Most notably, mental and physical speed."

The blob man waited for more.

"When in danger, she becomes faster," the robot explained bluntly.

Cat had never heard of any of the mod examples the droid gave, but she could guess what they did from her own experience.

"It seems, sir, that she has been modified for the sole purpose of killing as quickly and efficiently as possible."

Excited chatter spread through the room.

"That could do big numbers on the market," one of the men said.

"Base model *XMX* goes for three hundred thousand credits," someone else commented.

"Yeah, but she's just raw code data. You can't just take her mods out."

"That pinch thing sounds pretty crazy."

"Sell her as a package. Little ninja slave slut."

Some of the men laughed. "Nobody would want that. She'd kill you before you could even get it up."

"Not Joxi, ain't nothing as fast as him."

The men laughed crudely at each other.

Cat looked at her brother. He tried to speak, to put words together, but the slurred sounds were lost in the rising excitement of the men.

"Strip her interface down, put her through the cleaner, sell all that code data separate to the Red Sanctum guys, and then you got a girl who can't hurt you."

"She couldn't do nothin. She'd be a zombie."

"Fine with me."

The men laughed again.

"I've got a better idea," the blob announced, and the room hushed. "I think she'd make a great gift for our new friend Tiago..."

The room was quiet for a moment as the men tried to register what the blob was implying.

"Ooohoo," one of the men smirked as he made the realization. "Payback."

"Yeah, after he and his little traitor-ass 5-55 boys turned the Stolworthy group over like that," another chimed in.

"Even though *they* took the stupid bitch."

"They didn't take her."

"Yes, they did. We talked about this, man. They joined up with those devil worshiper fuckheads, and now they think they can do whatever the hell they want."

"Let them do it, DHG ain't scared," one of the men pointed to a diamond tattoo on his neck. "Plus, we got Ninja Girl now."

"Fuckin' right."

The blob man hushed the room again, then looked at Cat, who still sat on the floor. "Get her up," He ordered.

Cat glared at the men in the circle, some of them masked, but all of them dirty and violent-looking. She dared any of them to walk toward her. The men looked at each other, waiting for someone else to volunteer.

"And if she tries anything, kill the boy," the blob man added.

Cat looked at Kuno. He tried to communicate with his eyes. Cat could imagine what he might be saying: *Aria and Noah are in a better place. They're gone. This suffering is not theirs. Whatever happens, Cat and Kuno can endure it. Pain passes through them like wind. They are only shells, ghosts, shadows of real people. And Cat would not forget her assignment from Mom. Find what your father left behind before anyone else does.*

Cat exhaled deeply.

Eventually, a pair of men came over and lifted Cat to her feet, re-locking her hands behind her back and marching her up until she was directly in front of the blob man.

He looked her up and down. She burned into his eyes.

"My name is Quatch." His breath stank. Everything about him disgusted Cat. Everything about him begged to be slaughtered, skewered, roasted over the fire, and then fed to the dogs. This man who wanted to use her, rip her apart, and sell her.

Cat would not be merciful to him. His eyes said nothing but greed.

"What is your name?" he asked.

Cat didn't respond.

He clicked his tongue loudly at her silence.

"Maybe we call her Pinch? 'Cause of that thing she can do," one of the men suggested.

"The hell kind of shitty name is that? *Pinch?* Call her Aria. That's what the robot said her mod was called."

"How about Ninja Bitch—"

"My name is Cat," Cat declared coldly, quieting the room. "I'll do whatever you ask if you let my brother go."

"Brother?" one of the men exclaimed. "Shit, I thought he was her boyfriend or something."

"Cat," Quatch addressed her, waving the rest of the room to silence. "It is obvious you were made for some purpose..." he moved his fat hand thoughtfully through the air. "Killing people... whatever it might be." He shifted in his tiny throne. "Normally, we'd disemble— dissam—*take apart* people like you, but you came at a convenient time for us. We just so happen to be in need of some killing."

You very much are.

"There is a man named Tiago de la Roca, head of a gang called the 5-55. He wears a gold ring on his left hand and a gold pendant around his neck." Quatch waved over one of the men from the wall, who in turn produced a slowly spinning holo-gram of the man. He had a rugged jawline and dark, side-swept hair.

Cat waited for the request.

"If you want your brother to live, you will kill Tiago de la Roca and bring me his ring and pendant before the sun rises tomorrow," he finished and waited for Cat's reaction.

"Where do I find him?" she asked.

"A party is being held tonight in a certain Cloud-level penthouse. A club."

"There's a party there every night, Quatch," someone chirped from the perimeter.

Quatch waved off the remark. "Tiago will be there. Mince, Sanza," he called two young men over, the boyish one in the half-kabuki mask and the leader with the bandana and the void eyes.

"Bring in Cherry," Quatch ordered.

The younger of the two stepped out and returned immediately with the girl who had entered Cat's chamber earlier. She looked terrified to see Cat standing and undrugged.

"You three," Quatch spoke to the girl and the two young men. "Get our present for Mr. Roca outfitted and ready to go. And you," he nodded at Cat. "Remember, if you try anything…" he held up a small device with a single button and then pointed to the black anklet on Cat's leg. "I'll fry your brains out and kill your brother."

Cat looked down at the now drooling Kuno. *Endure it.*

Quatch then waved the four of them away, and Sanza and Mince grabbed Cat on either side and guided her toward the exit. The girl, Cherry, followed at a distance.

"Quatch, wait…" one of the men near the wall spoke up. "Can we see what the boy can do? Analyze his stuff, too?"

Cat stopped with her entourage at the door and turned to watch.

Quatch shrugged and gave the order to the robot, who walked over to Kuno and scanned him in the same way he had done to Cat.

"Running ten tiles, sir. Nine common—"

"Just skip to the interesting ones," Quatch demanded impatiently.

"One custom modification package that refers to itself as *NOAH*. It, likewise, contains six core elements, though differing slightly from the girl's. Health and efficiency enhancements are the same, as are the injury regen and panic suppressant factors. However, the core dedicated to fighting ability most resembles the martial arts mod *KS-Jitsu*, and his other two cores deal primarily with physical strength, explosive power, and bone and muscle toughness, similar to *PWWWR*, and *Ironheart*, respectively."

"So, he's a fucking human tank?" One of the men asked.

"Essentially, yes," the AI answered, returning to its post at Quatch's side.

"Will these guns even do anything to him?" Someone laughed nervously.

Quatch waved Cat's group out, and Cat took one last look at her brother before she was forced back into the corridor.

He's a shield, Cat thought to herself. *A protector. A guardian.*

A shield. And I am the sword.

22 GOLD

C hance watched the bridges, levels, and lit windows of skyscrapers fall past him as he looked out the walls of the upward-accelerating glass elevator. It was a foreign sensation. The only time Chance had been so high in the City was when he and a friend had snuck out to climb a crane in the Canopy levels.

But soon, even those heights were surpassed as the surrounding buildings became more sparse, and only the tallest towers touched his view of the night horizon.

"Here," Friday held out a small, black mod tile to Chance. "Little thank-you present, for coming this far."

"What is it?" Chance asked.

"It'll help you see in the dark. Not night vision exactly, but better than nothing."

"Should I use it right now? Won't I need some recovery time?"

"Not for something this small."

Chance took the tile and pressed it onto his wrist. *Modification package 'rem 2' is ready to install. Proceed?* Chance released the tile, and it fused into his skin. For a moment, nothing happened, and then his vision blurred.

"Give it a second," Friday reassured him.

After a few seconds, Chance's eyesight resolved into extra sharp detail, with a level of clarity he had never experienced before. "Hell yeah," he spun around the elevator, admiring the view of the City below. "This is incredible!"

"My pleasure."

"Ready?" June asked the others as the elevator came to a stop.

"Ready," Friday and Chance nodded.

The elevator doors opened, and the trio stepped out onto the roof of the building. Friday led the way, her black boots click-clacking on the tile and her black dress rippling outward in a spectral aura as she strode toward the security checkpoint. Her hair was twisted in a small bun with the two snake pins, and her outfit opened in the back, revealing a long line of mod marks, koi fish, and lotus flowers that followed from the base of her neck all the way down her spine. Lantern earrings swung from her ears, a blue vial hung around her neck, and the Rush bracelet adorned her wrist.

June followed on Friday's right. Tall, gold stilettos brought her nearly to Chance's height, and a shimmery blue two-piece dress emphasized the tan in her skin and the gold in her hair, which hid the poison-and-smoke crescent moons on her ears.

Chance followed on Friday's left, tugging at the neck of his underwear-turned-body armor and the stiff suit he had begrudgingly agreed to wear.

Friday stopped in front of a pair of large security guards and an armored robot. Beyond the guards, a narrow catwalk bridged the chasm to the top of another skyscraper, where a multilevel penthouse pulsed with colored lights and house music.

June stepped up to the security guards. "Tell Oshe that June is here with two friends."

The droid beeped in confirmation, then, after a moment's silence, gave the all-clear to the other guards.

"Oshe owns the place," June explained over her shoulder as she and Friday were ushered through.

The guards stopped Chance with a hand on the chest. "Arms out," one commanded.

Chance put his arms out, and the guards patted him down while the robot stared into his soul.

"One mod," The AI spoke to its counterparts. "Eyesight enhancer."

The guards waved Chance through, and he jogged to catch up with the others on the catwalk. The night sky was clear, and even a few bold stars had dared to make an appearance, though they paled in comparison to the glittering city below.

The sounds of the party ahead began to grow, and a swarm of colorful, decorative drones suddenly surrounded the bridge and began to dance in synchronization with the music of the club.

"That's new," June admired the oscillating colors.

Chance had to grab the handrail to combat the sense of vertigo as the drones orbited through the air.

"Here we are," Friday announced as the catwalk opened up into a large patio.

Finely dressed partiers lounged around small tables and large sectionals, laughing and flirting and eyeing each other. Servers, both human and android, bounced from clique to clique, pouring drinks and taking requests. Cheers erupted from a balcony above as a young woman hurled a shot glass off the edge and into the abyss below. A man in a red tuxedo extinguished a multicolor flame in the palm of his hand as the trio passed. A couple apologized hastily after nearly turning into Chance, their arms full of carefully balanced martini glasses. A large, modified tiger paced around a tabletop while people cautiously stroked its rainbow-striped fur.

Friday cut right through it all, shouldering and sliding through the crowd and ignoring the glances that were shot her way, and entered into the main room of the penthouse club.

Here, the ceiling was high, and multiple balconies ringed around the walls. Accent lights set the mood at drink-covered tables and in secreted alcoves. A pulsing DJ's booth, surrounded by a small stage and a glowing dance floor, sat at the center of the room.

Friday continued to weave her way through the tables, and Chance couldn't help but notice the attention that she received. A nudge and point to a friend here and a small sneer there. It was apparent people knew who she was, and they seemed less than pleased to see her.

"June, why are so many people looking at Friday?" Chance asked, leaning in close to be heard over the music.

"Friday makes a lot of friends, but she also makes a lot of enemies," June grimaced. "She did some stuff that made a lot of these... types of people mad."

"Who are these types of people?"

June steered Chance out of the path of a server, then bobbed her head to the side as she looked for a way to phrase her answer. "Mmm... not... not very good people..."

"What do you mean? Does it have to do with someone named Handa?" he pushed it further, recalling what both Rap and the detective had mentioned.

"Uhh, yes, Handa is Friday's ex, and... let's just say the people here are the type to know what happened to Emry Rush and not say anything."

Chance nodded and weaved through a small crowd of friends. June apologized to the people as she stepped through after Chance.

"But not everyone is bad! There are some good people here, too!" June quickly added. "Like... like someone here, probably."

Friday stopped abruptly, and Chance nearly ran into her.

"Friday!" A vampire-looking man greeted her insincerely, blocking her path.

"Ah, *Count*, a pleasant surprise." Friday rolled her eyes.

"Isn't it?" his smile was fanged.

"Yes, didn't think I would see you here," Friday remarked. "You must be sucking more than blood these days."

His expression soured. His entourage at the table behind him snickered, and he hissed at them before returning a fake smile to Chance and June.

"And it looks like you've made some new friends."

Friday raised her eyebrows, disappointed in his lack of a witty comeback.

"Or are you getting ready to cash them in as well?" the vampire smirked.

Friday shoved the man out of her way as his table of friends laughed and jeered, Chance and June following after her.

"Where are we going?" Friday spun on June, obvious frustration in her voice.

"I don't know," June laughed nervously. "You were walking so fast, I thought you knew. What are we looking for?"

Friday bit her lip and threw her eyes around the room.

"Bet on the red seven," Chance offered.

"Right, right," Friday nodded. "Casino room."

"Follow me." June led the trio toward the far wall and around a bend, and Chance found himself on the floor of a small casino.

Spinning wheels, green felt tables, and forms of gambling that Chance had played much less fancy versions of filled the space. Chips clicked as bets were placed in the various circles, and at the far end of the area, a group shouted around some game that involved a small tower of blinking holograms.

"Wait here a second," June instructed, then strode off across the room.

Friday looked everywhere but at Chance. It still surprised him how quickly her moods changed.

"Where do you think our Tiago guy is?" Chance asked as quietly as he could over the music.

Friday gave him a look that said *not here*, nodding at all the people around them, then returned to her aimless eye wandering.

Chance apologized silently and watched her for a moment. She could seem so much larger than life at some points and so small at others. Her dark ensemble appeared menacing and powerful in one instance, then childish and costume-like in the next. She looked down at the floor, and Chance looked at the tattoos on her back. Part of him wanted to put his arm around her, to give her some semblance of comfort, but instead, he turned away, giving Friday space from his thoughts, and looked right into the eyes of a lavender-skinned young woman.

"Hi," she said, smiling as she stepped into his personal space. "You look kind of lost, so I figured I'd bring you a drink."

"Ah, thank you," Chance laughed appreciatively, taking the glass from her hand.

"Find me later," she smiled, biting her lip and throwing a quick glance at Friday.

Chance watched her go for a moment and put the glass to his lips.

Friday yanked it away, spilling the liquid down his shirt. "What the hell, are you literally fucking stupid?" she asked, shaking her head in disbelief. "You really were about to drink something a random girl gave you."

Chance apologized quietly again.

June returned moments later, grabbing Chance's hand and dropping a small collection of poker chips in his palm.

"Where'd you get these?" Chance asked.

"Doesn't matter," June shrugged. "Let's go put them on red."

"On seven," Friday corrected.

"On the seven, which is red," June smiled.

"And where is that?" Chance looked around the crowded room.

"Roulette," Friday and June answered in unison.

Chance looked over at the roulette table. Gamblers placed bets as the wheel spun. "Let's go then."

"Wait," Friday grabbed his arm, then took the chips from his hand and gave them back to June. "June will be going in. Chance, you get on the other side of the table and follow June close if she leaves. And June," Friday pulled the pins from her pun and shook out her hair. "You take these."

June and Chance obeyed Friday's instruction, June pinning her own hair up as she approached, and Chance taking a spot on the far side, watching over the shoulder of a man at the roulette table.

June slid her way forward, reaching through the gamblers and dropping her chips on the '7' moments before the roulette ball was released.

Everyone at the table watched.

"Excuse me," the man in front of Chance shifted his way back out of the crowd.

Chance watched him.

The man circled the table... and snuck in next to June.

"Here we go," Chance whispered to himself.

The man put one hand on June's shoulder, the other on the edge of the table. On the back of his hand was the symbol of a golden sunburst.

The man said something in June's ear, and June said something in response, to which the man nodded, put an arm around her waist, and led June away from the table.

Chance began to panic as he jostled his way back around, following June to The Ocean's main floor as the man continued to guide her.

"Vent, I need you," Chance called out to the mod-demon, ducking and weaving his way through partiers as June was ushered across the club.

"So *now* you want me," Vent answered, spinning up from the shadows on a lounge sofa as Chance passed. *I'm always here.* A feeling like boiling sludge churned in Chance's gut as Vent slithered into the back of his mind. *We won't let anything happen to her.*

June and her guide were intercepted in front of a large curtain by an almost as large bouncer. A couple more words were exchanged, and June was waved through the curtain.

"How am I supposed to help her if I can't see what's happening—" Chance turned away inconspicuously as June's man retreated from the curtain door and retraced his steps back toward his post at the roulette table.

"June will be fine." Friday had materialized at Chance's side. "Espionage is her profession. She knows how to get in and out of places."

"What's going to happen in there?" Chance asked.

Friday wasn't listening. Her eyes were glazed over with some sort of video.

"Friday," Chance put a hand on her shoulder.

Friday put a finger up for him to hush. "June is streaming me what she's seeing."

Chance nodded and threw his eyes around the club. The music seemed to have gotten louder, the atmosphere more intoxicated. Clothes were being shed as some partiers put their vibrant and modified bodies on full display, and drugs, many of which Chance recognized from the Surface, were shared and traded without reservation. Against a nearby pillar, a couple was beginning a very animated sexual show, and at the table at Chance's back, four club-goers laughed wildly as they placed glowing mod tiles on their tongues and their eyes began to flash.

"Friday, what's—" Chance turned back to where Friday had been, but she was gone. "Friday?"

"Want to join the party?"

Chance spun as the violet-skinned girl who had offered him the drink earlier stepped right up against his body, her eyes staring deep into his as she grabbed the back of his hand. "You didn't follow, so I had to come find you again," she whispered.

Chance felt a small prick in his wrist. *Oh shit.*

The girl smiled, then pulled her hand away, twirling her ringed fingers and motioning Chance to follow.

"No," Chance protested, but his feet moved anyway, following the girl. "What..."

As Chance walked, the club lights swam around his eyes, and the floor seemed to tip back and forth. The room around him began to blur, then snapped into sharp focus, then blurred again.

With surprising strength, the violet girl grabbed Chance's shoulders and shoved him down onto a sofa.

"I don't want to join the party..." the words slipped out of Chance's mouth, and multiple people laughed as everything in Chance's reality seemed to melt together. An icy hand traced fingers across his cheek. Someone else was removing his suit. The violet girl's dress had wholly vanished. A fourth body climbed onto his lap.

Chance tried to push them off, but his arms and legs were entirely drained of power. *Oh no.*

FRIDAY STRUGGLED against the anaconda grip of the mountain of a human who carried her across the club. Her arms were pinned against her side, and a colossal hand covered her mouth.

"It will all be over soon," Friday's captor chuckled deeply.

Friday squirmed until she could speak. "Let me go, or I swear I'll feed you your own fucking balls—"

In response, the captor kicked open a swinging door, and Friday was carried into a bright, chrome kitchen.

Six other men wearing the same outfits as the club hosts and servers stood around a large cutting board and prep station. Glowing tattoos curled across their hands and faces. Slumped against the far wall was one of The Ocean's actual servers, stripped to his underwear, a steak knife plunged to the hilt in his temple.

Friday exhaled. "I thought we were over this shit."

One of the men shrugged, blue tattoos curled across his face. "Handa still wants you dead."

"So he had me followed here?"

The men smirked at each other as if sharing an inside joke. "Handa's not the only one hunting you. But the enemy of an enemy is a friend, right? Our new friends are helping us out."

Before she could respond, Friday's head was slammed into the counter of the prep station. The behemoth man held her down by the neck and, with the other hand, lifted a large meat cleaver.

"So you're Handa's bitch, and he's someone else's bitch?" Friday groaned, searching frantically across the counter with her hands.

"We are doing it for the reward, just like you did to Handa," one of the men responded.

"Handa is in prison, what reward?" Friday's fingers brushed the blade of a butcher's knife.

The hand on Friday's neck adjusted its grip. "Enough talk, traitor. Time to die."

Friday found the knife handle. "Die, then." Throwing her arm back blindly, Friday drove the knife into the abdomen of the man who held her down.

The monster screamed, releasing their grip on both Friday and the meat cleaver.

Friday spun, snatching the cleaver from the air and slicing it through the face of the giant man. Blood sprayed her front and the chrome of the kitchen as his body collapsed.

The other men stared at Friday, each raising culinary weapons of their own.

Friday flicked the blood off the meat cleaver, then turned and tomahawked it into the chest of the nearest enemy.

The man laughed, pulled the cleaver from his chest, and licked the blood from the blade. "You'll have to do better than that."

The men began to circle.

Friday sighed and yanked the blue vial pendant from the chain on her neck. "How about a toast then?" She uncapped the vial and held it up. The blue liquid inside sparked with energy.

"To what? Your own death?" one of the men asked.

Friday smirked and emptied the liquid into her mouth. Blue mist began to vent from her lips. "To my ex. May he rot in hell."

23 SHINOBI BLACK

C at watched as the girl called Cherry wrapped black tape around her wrists, sealing the black gloves to the sleeves of the all-black outfit she was being forced to wear.

"These will help you climb," the girl explained, her hands shaking slightly. "Since you will need to get to the top of the building, and we can only get you so high."

Cat didn't respond. She glared at the two young men in the room. Mince, the younger one in the half-mask, and Sanza, the older one with the bandana around his nose and mouth. They stood back, guns on both their hips and the controller for Cat's ankle-shocking device in Sanza's hand.

Cherry continued to speak as she wrapped Cat's other wrist. "Tiago de la Roca is a dangerous man. He probably won't be alone."

"How do I find him?" Cat asked.

Mince stepped forward and held out a small device that lit up with a slowly spinning hologram of her target, the same one Cat had been shown in the chamber earlier. "He has a gold ring on his finger and a gold chain pendant—"

"I know what he looks like," Cat cut him off. "When I get inside, how will I find him?"

Sanza stepped up and snatched the hologram projector from Mince. "Look for this." The hologram changed into a symbol.

One that Cat knew.

A sunburst.

Cat didn't let the surprise show on her face. "What is it?"

"It's the sign for the group that the 5-55 just pledged their allegiance to. We think they'll be there too, and De la Roca is probably meeting with them tonight."

"What is the group called?" Cat asked.

"I don't know. I don't care." Sanza closed the hologram. "Just find him and kill him."

"Why do you want him dead?"

"He framed a kidnapping on our friends in Stolworthy, got them killed by police—" Mince started before Sanza silenced him.

"Just kill him," Sanza stared her down, daring her to do something: to attack, to lunge, to strike.

Void eyes.

Cat matched his with her own. She wouldn't try anything now. Not while they still had her brother.

Cherry cleared her throat nervously. "When you get inside, you'll want to change so you blend in." She held up a simple, slightly frayed dress. "I'm packing this here," she stuffed it in a small backpack, "and giving you this."

Cat took the bag from her hand.

"When you complete your task and get out, hold the device around your ankle; we'll come get you."

Cat hated her. The stupid girl, speaking as if they were on the same team.

The door to the room suddenly clanked open, and a slim, rough-looking character walked in. His lack of a shirt revealed the wiry muscles that stretched over his bones, and the scruff on his face and disheveled hair on his head gave the impression of a feral street dog.

"Skalla," Sanza nodded in deference and backed away from Cat.

Mince slunk back to the wall, and Cherry shied away into a corner.

Cat didn't move. Skalla walked right up to her.

"Quatch was gonna let me keep you," he growled.

Cat was a statue as he spoke.

"What? Nothing to say to the man who saved you from that old factory? You should have been dead. We kept you alive." Alcohol hung on his breath.

Cat looked through him, refusing to acknowledge his presence.

"You people always think you're better than us!" He began to yell and then spat at her feet. When Cat didn't react, he spun, slapping her hard with the back of his hand.

Cat watched it come in slow motion, and despite the blow and the sting in her cheek, she stayed on her feet.

Skalla laughed like a dying hound, then called Cherry over. "You see how this girl isn't scared? You're about the same age, by the looks of it. Why are you so fuckin' scared of everything!"

Cherry flinched.

"Pathetic!" He shoved her in the chest, and Cherry fell to the ground with a yelp. "Get her loaded on the dropper!" Skalla yelled at the two young men. "And let's go kill this stupid son of a bitch!"

————

THE DROPPER, as Skalla had called it, was a very old helicopter, Cat realized, as she was led into what looked like a large, rusted hangar. Her hands were cuffed behind her back again, and her head was hooded as the men shoved her inside the aircraft with

Sanza, Skalla, and one other man that Cat assumed would be the pilot.

"Bet you didn't think we'd have one of these, huh?" Skalla tried to shout in Cat's ear, the noise of spinning helicopter blades combined with the sound of grating metal to drown him out, and then suddenly, they were moving upward.

The helicopter rocked as it continued to lift, and Cat had to brace herself with her legs to keep from tumbling back and forth.

Higher and higher they went, ascending endlessly, until Cat was sure they were at least at the upper Canopy levels. The aircraft leaned to the right, and someone caught Cat from falling as she started to tip.

The flight continued for another half hour, and suddenly, the hood was thrown off Cat's head. The doors of the helicopter were yanked open. The night City glittered all around and reflected off the glass walls of the nearby building. Aria would have found it a beautiful, if not terrifying, sight. Cat was only angry.

Sanza leaned in, shouting over the noise of the blades and the wind as he unlocked her hands. "Remember, kill Tiago de la Roca, bring back his ring and pendant, and you'll be free!" He then reached around her head and tied a black bandana around her face. Cat shoved him off and readied herself at the door.

The helicopter shuddered in the wind as it struggled to stay level. Several meters away, stairs of an emergency exit vined their way up the adjacent building.

Cat tossed the backpack first. Immediately, the wind sent it straight down, vanishing into the abyss of twinkling lights below. *Good.* Cat had no intention of wearing that stupid dress anyway.

One... She readied herself and picked her target landing spot. The waves calmed her mind.

Two...

Cat launched from the dropper and half landed, half caught

herself on the metal bars. The wind gushed as the helicopter leaned away, dropping back into the City.

Cat braced against her perch until the sound of the blades began to fade, then she examined her surroundings. The window in front of her was curtained and dark, and the night was clear. Besides the wind, Cat was alone. Far down below, streetlights and colorful displays burned like embers in a campfire. Hovercrafts and other vehicles flickering between buildings like sparks. How easy it would be to just throw herself backward and fall into the fire.

She shook her head as if to shake the thought away and looked up; lights pulsed from a penthouse club many floors above, and a thin bridge on the same level spanned the chasm to another building. Kuno needed her now. She had to finish her assignment.

Rolling her neck and flexing her shoulders, Cat began her ascent, jumping from her spot on the railing to the steps of the emergency exit ladder.

Bounding up the rusted rungs from one floor to the next, Cat replayed the words of her father in her mind:

"Man is more than bones and blood; there is not only biology and technology—there must be some higher order."

The music of the club began to beat louder as Cat drew closer.

"We devote so much time to unlocking the mind and manipulating the body, but what of our existence beyond these bounded platforms?"

She looked up at the bridge. A flock of colorful drones danced around it to the rhythm.

"I hypothesize a real, tangible intelligence outside the electrical currents we understand now as consciousness, that is in and through us, and at the same time, entirely unknown."

The emergency stairs ended abruptly, still several floors short of the pulsing nightclub. Cat looked into the window that let out to where she stood. A long, dark hallway continued into the building. Fifty feet above, a balcony jutted out into the night, but the clean glass windows of the floors between offered little support for climbing.

Cat ran her fingers along the edges of the window before her, then tried to lift it open. The locks on the inside held fast, and the glass seemed too thick to break.

The waves rushed through her body, and Cat flexed the black gloves on her hands. The girl had said they would help her climb. Cat tested the palm of the glove on the window; the rubbery friction kept it from sliding, but it would by no means support her weight.

What did they expect me to do? Cat huffed to herself and stared up at the stretch of building that separated her from her target.

Suddenly, in a visionary flash, Cat watched herself climb. Like a small monkey or a squirrel, she crawled right up the edges of the windows. In an instant, the vision was gone again, slow waves taking its place.

One... Cat submitted to the new instinct.

Standing as high on the metal outside railing as she could get, she pulled herself onto the ledge of the next window up. Then, like she was climbing the top branch of a tall tree, Cat grabbed the metal frame that divided one glass window from the one beside it and began working her way upward, hand over hand and pinching the frame with her feet.

Two...

The gloves held. She pulled herself up onto the next ledge, then the next. Then she froze. The room before her was lit; a woman in fuzzy pajamas lounged on a couch directly inside, her mouth agape and a plate of food in her hand. The lady blinked twice, then turned over her shoulder to call for someone else. Cat didn't wait to see who would come. Without realizing what she was doing, Cat jumped up from the sill of the window, kicked off the metal frame on her right, caught the ledge of the window above, and yanked herself up.

Three... Cat exhaled and steadied herself. *Not trying that again.*

The dark glass before her vibrated momentarily as a large hovercraft ascended from behind and moved to land on top of the building.

Why couldn't they have dropped me off up there? Cat thought to herself as she studied the last stretch before the balcony. Around the corner of the building to her right, the bridge from the neighboring building connected to a much larger balcony, but from the echoes of laughter and drunken revelry, it sounded like it would cause too much of a scene if a ninja-dressed girl suddenly popped over the edge. The balcony above seemed empty.

Cat climbed the final window, nimbly pulled herself over the railing, and landed silently on the balcony floor. A couple shared the space, but they were too passionate in each other's lips to notice Cat's arrival.

For their own good. She would've thrown them over the edge if they had caused any commotion.

Cat walked into the pounding night club. It was a massive space, lights and sound and partiers everywhere.

And full of shadows.

Perfect. She stepped into the darkness behind a niche in the wall and examined the rest of the room.

Not that anyone would notice her anyway or even give her a second thought if they did. The nightclub was oozing with life. Bodies, hordes, like zombies, undulated on the dance floor, around the tables, in every nook and alcove of the room. Lights moved across the crowd, illuminating for brief moments the scenes of lust and oblivion that pulsed with the heavy beat of the music.

Cat gazed over the scene, her eyes moving from one face to the next, hunting for her target. How was she ever supposed to find him in this mess?

Guide me, she threw a silent prayer up to whatever being might be listening and stepped out of the corner.

The club lights dashed across her figure, for a tiny instant sparkling off her iridescent obsidian hair before she was plunged into the shadows again.

She stalked across the room, her neon yellow-green eyes burning into every person in her field of view.

The music pounded in her head; the waves matched, pounding in her chest.

Her fingers twitched, and her muscles tensed. The rage began to build inside her. She ripped the black bandana from her face.

Cat watched as someone approached her. A lithe, smooth-skinned man, their eyes faded and their smile intoxicated. They grabbed Cat by the shoulder and tried to pull her into the foaming ocean of bodies at the club's center.

Cat resisted.

They pulled harder.

Cat seized the man by the face and watched as their expression flashed to pleasure, then horror as Cat's grip tightened.

The small man's eyes bulged.

Cat tossed him aside and continued onward.

Tiago de la Roca, where are you?

Around the edge of the main floor, a secondary room opened up to a small casino. Cat walked in and studied the faces of the gamblers.

A man caught her eye. Not Tiago de la Roca, but...

He put a hand to his temple. On the back was the shining golden symbol of a sunburst.

The same symbol that once belonged to her father and now seemed to be increasingly present among her enemies.

She approached the man without hesitation.

He looked down at her as she stopped at his side.

"Take me to Tiago de la Roca," Cat shouted over the noises of the table and the growing volume of the club music.

The man looked her over for a moment, then leaned in. "To stand beneath the heavy sun," he said, then paused.

A passphrase, Cat thought. *Shit.*

Then, a page from her father's journal flashed across her mind. A single line she had read over only once.

"With arms outstretched, to live again," Cat offered, looking up at the man.

He narrowed his eyes but nodded and, motioning for her to come along, headed for the back of the club.

Cat followed.

The man glanced at Cat several times as the lights passed over them both.

Cat stuck close by, keeping him in the corner of her eye as she continued to scan the rest of the crowd. A fury swelled and crashed inside her. Tidal waves of anger and power.

Cat's man guided her toward a curtain in the far wall; another bouncer stood guard just outside. The bouncer nodded at Cat's guide as they approached.

Cat looked at both men. "Where is he?"

The men exchanged words in a foreign language, then looked at Cat. The bouncer shook his head and shrugged. "He said if they know it, let them in." He stepped aside and motioned for Cat to enter the curtain.

24 PARTY FAVORS

June examined Tiago de la Roca's lair as the curtain closed behind her. Red and gold was the theme inside, with red upholstered couches and a small golden chandelier. A single bottle decorated a low table that sat toward the back of the room. At the far end, Tiago de la Roca himself lounged on gold cushions on the couch against the wall. A gold tribal tattoo curled up from the back of his neck and clawed across half his face, wrapping tendrils around his similarly colored eyes. A gold pendant chain hung around his neck, dropping into the open chest of his gold shirt, and a large gold ring sat on his left hand, in which he held a glass of gold liquid, placing it slowly on the table in front of him.

A voluptuous, red-haired woman leaned against De la Roca, her face pressingly close to his, her fingers tracing his exposed collarbone. A man in a shiny, pear-colored suit sat on Tiago's other side, diamond jewelry on his hands and neck, his hair white and sharp like hoarfrost on frozen grass. Eight or so other figures sat around the perimeter of the small room, some decorated in outlandishly lavish clubbing attire, others in neon armor or vibrant street clothes.

The assembly regarded June quietly as she entered, and Tiago himself motioned for June to sit.

Smiling, June pulled the pins from her hair and flipped her golden waves dramatically, then took a seat on the end by a ghoulish-looking man with four horns. He gave her a tired look and flashed his sharpened teeth.

"And who are you?" a man in a purple robe asked, his face covered in tattoos.

June slowly turned to smile at him. "A believer." June held eye contact until he looked away, then worked her attention around the circle of guests. Some kept their eyes down as if nervous to be recognized; others glared around the room defensively, sizing up the rest of the visitors.

"As I was saying," the silvery-white man spoke, "we request that the second payment be made earlier."

"Unfortunately," a woman in a black suit cleared her throat nervously, "the Organization cannot advance the second half of the funds until the second half of your agreement has been completed."

"Well, the situation has proven more difficult, and we need the funds to complete the agreement."

"The Organization—"

"*The Organization,*" the purple-robed man scoffed. "Who even is the Organization? And why are we talking about business? I was under the impression we were meeting to re*organize* the Following."

"The gods require our full commitment," the silver man explained. "They ask us to dedicate our resources."

"If the Seven Rays truly are back from the dead, and they truly are gods," a woman with four arms leaned forward as she addressed the room, "why do they need our money?"

"No one asked for *your* money," a man with burning ember eyes jumped in. "And the Seven Rays *are* back."

The horned man at June's side shifted. "Have you seen them?" he asked.

"I have been visited..." the fire-eye man looked around the room, "by the Prophet Belzen."

A cyborg in a tuxedo threw his hands up. "We all have been visited by the Prophet Belzen, that does not confirm that the Seven Rays are back. He could be a lunatic."

Tiago set his drink on the table in front of him. "The Prophet is not a lunatic, we would be wise to follow him."

"Agreed," the horned man nodded. "He is certainly being led by a being beyond himself."

"If I may," a poisonous-looking man interjected. "I would like to inform the other 'believers' or whatever we like to call ourselves, that Mr. De la Roca here follows the Prophet Belzen only because Belzen is splitting the paycheck from this mysterious *Organization* here. And you, Mr. Devil," the man pointed at the horned man. "I do not know you, but I know of your band of demon followers. You are not true "Disciples," as you like to call yourselves, you just like an excuse for violence."

"My Disciples and I were the first to heed the Prophet's call." The horned man replied. "We have been doing his work, the will of the gods, for weeks now."

"Hunting children?" the man in the purple robe asked. "Unsuccessfully?"

"Now," Tiago took control again. "We all have our various roles to play in this revival. We cannot fight amongst ourselves. Or else we might fall as the Rays did." He took a sip from his drink.

"Where is Belzen?" the four-armed woman asked. "He called this meeting."

"Actually..." A plain-looking droid raised its hand, "I called this meeting. I put out the invitation."

"Sending invites like it's a birthday party seems careless," someone remarked.

"Secrecy is not a concern of the gods." The AI replied. "Soon enough, the ones who must hide will be those who oppose the Seven Rays."

"Well, who are you?" someone asked.

"I am called Caesar, the Apostle," the android replied.

"The Apostle? You're a robot."

"And thus, a perfect follower." Caesar looked around the room with dark eyes, then continued. "Belzen the Prophet is dead. He incurred the displeasure of the gods. As proof, I present Belzen's sword, Divine Intervention."

Caesar held up a sheathed katana with both hands.

"Impossible..." the horned man whispered.

Caesar looked at him. "Belzen was tired of waiting for your men to subdue the children. So, he decided to take matters into his own hands. He, likewise, failed, and it seems the Master was tired of waiting on him, too. There will be no room among the gods for weakness."

"So, what then? We have no more Prophet, why are we here?" the man with the fire eyes asked.

"Belzen was necessary to begin the revival," Caesar explained. "But the movement has begun, and now it cannot be stopped. The Seven Rays will be visiting us tonight."

The room was quiet for a moment; the club music vibrated the walls from outside. June shifted in her seat.

"What do you mean, visiting us?" someone asked.

Caesar looked at each visitor in turn. "The Master has taken on a temporary form. He wishes to speak to his new followers directly."

As if on cue, the curtain opened, and a girl clad in a black jumpsuit stepped inside. The red and gold glow of the room reflected off her jet-black hair, and her eyes burned violently neon.

Everyone stared at her silently.

Tiago gestured at the girl with an open hand. "This is the form the gods take?"

The girl in black walked forward slowly, her eyes calculating the audience around her before fixing on De la Roca himself.

June slowly pulled the white earring from her ear.

Without taking her eyes off Tiago, the girl in black lifted both hairpins from the table in front of June.

June took a deep breath.

The horned man shook his head. "This isn't the gods…"

"Well, another follower then," Tiago raised his glass. "Join us—"

In a flash of black, the girl crossed the room, stepped onto Tiago's table, and drove one of June's hairpins down through the back of Tiago's hand, staking it to the tabletop.

The other hairpin she held millimeters from Tiago's eye.

SHE WOULD HAVE FINISHED IT, punched the sharpened pin all the way through, but she had questions first. Cat growled at the man. "I am the fastest creature in this city. I swear if you even breathe, I will kill you."

Tiago de la Roca remained motionless, holding his drink in the air with his free hand as Cat carefully pulled the gold ring from the other and slipped the necklace from around his head.

June slowly reached for the nearest drink, the horned man's half-finished glass. No one else in the room moved.

"Whose symbol is this?" Cat demanded, holding up his pendant.

Tiago de la Roca exhaled slowly.

"Whose symbol is this!" Cat repeated the demand, the strands of her black hair falling around the fury that poured through her neon eyes.

She pulled the hairpin out of his hand and drove it again through his wrist. "Tell me!"

Caesar stood up behind her. "That is the symbol of the Seven Rays. We know who you are, Aria Sharp, and you will not be leaving here."

June had heard enough. She dropped the white earring into the drink. With a quiet sizzle and a loud pop, the whole room was filled with blinding white smoke.

———

"I HATE THIS," Friday groaned, using the counter to push herself up from her knees. At her feet was the mutilated body of one of the attackers, blood soaking the floor and dripping down the chrome walls of the kitchen. The bodies of the others lay scattered around the rest of the room in various positions of death.

Friday dropped the butcher's knife and shook the blood from her hands, then grabbed a nearby kitchen cloth to wipe the red from her palms and face.

The last of Friday's would-be bounty hunters leaned against the counter opposite, breathing heavily.

Friday huffed out the last of the blue neon mist in her system and took a second to catch her breath. "Tell Handa," Friday addressed the man, "that if he wants me, he'll have to come get me himself."

The man nodded and began limping for the back exit, then motioned at the carnage all around. "You see this? This will continue to happen. Blood will follow you as long as you are alive, Friday."

Friday watched the man until he was gone, then called up June's vision feed. Everything was fuzzy and white. "That's not good," she shook her head. Stepping over the violence, she made her way to the exit and pushed the door open to the club's main floor.

Music and bodies throbbed together like a single organism. Friday steadied herself as she walked, focusing on her breathing to stay composed.

"June, June." Friday made her way to where she had left Chance outside the curtained room.

Chance wasn't there. White smoke poured out of the room's entrance as people struggled to exit, coughing and stumbling—

"Friday!" June grabbed Friday by the shoulders and pulled her aside. "Something's up, we need to go—" June looked Friday up and down. Her entire person was splattered and soaked with blood. "Oh shit, what happened to you? Are you okay?"

"I'm fine," Friday shook it off. "It's not mine. But we need to leave, where's Chance?"

June shook her head. "What? I don't know. He was supposed to be with you!"

Hound 1. Friday activated the tracking mod, then spun around, examining the mass of people that filled the club. "C'mon Chance, c'mon Chance..."

Chance's trail manifested itself in Friday's mind, and Friday followed, forcing her way into the crowd and coming to a stop at the trail's end.

Chance lounged back on the couch, his eyes sparking to life when he noticed Friday. He reached a hand out for her.

A mostly naked woman climbed onto Chance's lap. Friday grabbed her by the hair and yanked her off, then lifted Chance to his feet, putting his arm over her shoulder.

"Friday," Chance mumbled. "You saved me."

"Where are your clothes?" Friday asked. Chance's suit had vanished, and he wore nothing but his body armor compression set.

"They couldn't get the armor off," Chance answered. "What happened to me?"

"You were drugged," Friday replied, pulling Chance back toward where June was waiting.

"What happened to *you*? You're covered in blood!"

"It doesn't matter. Right now, I need you to find some strength because we have to go—" Friday froze as the crowd parted.

"What?" Chance asked, rubbing his eyes.

There, standing between Friday and June, decorated in gold and platinum and silver and an otherworldly aura, was Emry Rush.

PART THREE

"Personally, I do not want to make you a man. Men are so very frail. Men break. Men die. No, I've always wished to make a god."
  — Pierce Brown, Red Rising

25 GRAVITY

To Chance, Emry's eyes were the brightest things in the room. As if all the lights in the club had been shut off, and the music ended, and all the people sent home, and it was just the two of them left alone.

Her eyes seized him. Locked him up and dragged him in. Bright golden rings circled her pupils like two eclipses, or black holes from which he would never be leaving.

Nothing existed anymore. Not The Ocean club, not the City of Xi, not even the mission to rescue the girl who now stood before him. In that moment, nothing existed besides him and her and the gravity that wrapped deep around Chance's mind, around his heart, and pulled him closer.

Toward her magnificent and terrifying and familiar black hole eyes.

He took a step forward across the expanse that separated them, a distance that seemed so small and yet so infinitely large. Memories, pulled from deep inside by the force of Emry's appearance, flew past his eyes.

A boy Chance didn't know, one with dark skin, witty eyes, and a sharp smile, grabbed a young Emry by the hand. Her fingers immediately slid between his, and a feeling like fireworks exploded in Chance's chest as he watched the scene transform into the Seer's den.

"You have been pulled into something much larger than yourself. Fate is leading you to a destination you cannot see yet." The Seer instructed, dissolving into the memory.

The boy that Chance didn't know walked quietly through the halls of the Rush Mansion, knocking softly on Emry's door and pushing it open. Emry rolled excited from the bed and threw her arms around him.

Golden eclipse eyes pulled Chance in deeper.

He saw himself lurch on the couch in Friday's apartment as videos of Emry played on the monitor screens. He saw Friday playing with the Rush bracelet on her wrist, the same bracelet Emry had offered him in his dream. In his memories.

The boy, the same boy, stood on the tower spire with Emry. He zipped her pink windbreaker against the cold. The red light faded on and off, bathing them both in its color.

"I want you to have this," Emry offered her bracelet to the boy.

The boy shook his head. "I can't, I can't have it—it's yours!" he shouted over the wind. "It's your family's."

"I want you to keep it for me!" Emry smiled.

The boy shook his head. Then Emry grabbed his arm and held it up to hers.

The boy glitched, groaning and doubling over in pain.

"No!" Emry yelled, throwing her arms around the boy. "Fight it."

"This one is bad." He clenched his teeth and shook his head. "We need to get down."

"Okay, go, go quick," Emry directed, helping the boy down onto the spire ladder.

He paused as the painful glitch seized his body again.

Emry held his wrists. "Just make it down, and you'll be okay."

The boy climbed down the first few rungs, and Emry started after him.

The wind gusted hard; the boy gripped the handholds tightly.

"Hold on, just hold on!" Emry shouted, tears beginning to run down her cheeks.

The vision changed, and Chance found himself looking through Emry's eyes. She was atop another building, this one surrounded by clouds. A shrouded figure in a golden mask stood opposite her. The figure extended a hand.

The scene changed again.

Chance looked at the glowing storefront of an old laundromat—*White Sam's*. Then he was inside, walking toward the back. A door opened, and Chance passed through into a dark corridor lined with computer rooms.

Wake up! Vent shouted in the back of Chance's mind.

Chance continued down the hall.

Chance, wake up!

Chance snapped to.

Emry's face was inches from his. Her hands were on either side of his head. A searing pain scorched into his skull. Chance screamed and tried to push away, but Emry's gold armor fried his hands. He screamed again.

With a yell, Friday tackled her around the middle, bringing them both to the floor.

Chance collapsed, his breath shaking.

Friday jumped to her feet, crouching over Emry. She looked her up and down. The armor, her void eyes. Friday shook her head. "I don't understand, Emry—"

An iron claw seized Friday by the shoulder and threw her aside, and Caesar the Apostle took Friday's place over Emry.

"Master," the robot addressed Emry. "We must go."

Caesar lifted Emry to her feet again and began leading the way toward a hallway in the far wall.

June ran to Friday and helped her up. "We can't let Emry leave."

Friday shook her head, breathing heavy. "Chance needs help."

Chance struggled to his knees, then collapsed. Partiers danced around him.

"I'll help Chance," June instructed. "You get Emry."

Friday steeled herself, staring at Emry's back as she followed the robot away.

———

A CHOKING white smoke filled the room, and Cat felt Tiago's hand grab her wrist as she tried to push the pin through his eye.

"You will die for this," Tiago coughed and strained against Cat and her weapon. "You, and your family."

"My family is dead!" Cat dropped the pin from her captive hand, grabbed it with the other, and drove it blindly into his upper body.

As Tiago yelled in pain, Cat scooped the ring and pendant off the table and dashed for the exit.

A hand grabbed her by the ankle, and she tripped. Cat rolled over and kicked, her foot connecting with the face of the horned man. He growled at her from his knees, struggling to breathe in the smoke.

"You, child. You killed my men."

Cat jumped to her feet. She recognized the patchwork machine skin and sharpened teeth. Waves. Violence. Rage. Hatred burned through her face and hands. "The River?"

He smiled. "You could be one of us, though."

Cat yelled and spun a kick at his head.

He weaved it, and Cat had to catch her balance.

"You could lead us, even," the man offered. His eyes darted to the floor, then back to Cat.

The glance didn't go unnoticed by Cat. In front of the horned man, barely visible on the floor through the smoke, was Belzen's katana.

The horned man reached.

Cat dove.

He grabbed the sheath; Cat grabbed the handle.

He pulled, and Cat pulled the other way, unsheathing the sword and spinning around the room in a large circle.

The plasma blade screamed as it ripped through the smoke in a fiery arc and caught the horned man in the torso, sliced straight through, and burned out the other side.

Cat didn't look at the carnage; she dropped the katana and ran out into the club.

The music rolled together with the waves in her body. Laser lights drew designs across the pulsing crowd. A typhoon raged in her mind. Cat moved for the exit, then paused as her eyes caught on a girl across the floor. A girl in white and gold, with the sunburst symbol embossed on the back of her armor.

Cat double-checked the pendant in her hand. The Seven Rays. Her father. Same symbol.

Suddenly, a loud gunshot cut through the sounds of the club, and for a moment, Cat was in the eye of her mental hurricane. Chaos ensued in slow motion: glasses shattering, people screaming, partiers tripping over each other in their fancy clothes as they tried to find an exit. Tiago had left his room; men rushed to his side, brandishing firearms, Tiago himself clutching at his stab wounds.

The laser lights drew across Cat's face, and she blinked. She could easily escape, blend in with the fleeing crowd until she got to a level below where she could call the dropper. Kuno was waiting for her. She looked at the gold ring and pendant in her hand. They would buy his freedom and hers.

But... she looked up at the sunburst girl. That symbol was the only clue she and Kuno had to Silas's truth and what he may have created.

Cat and Kuno were made for an end, to accomplish a mission.

Kuno would have to endure a little longer. Cat shoved the ring and pendant in her pocket and dashed through the shadows and lights and panic of the club.

The girl disappeared into a hallway ahead, following a chrome robot. Cat leaped over an overturned table, weaved between a fleeing couple, aimed at the hallway, and smashed right into another person, a woman in a black dress.

The two tumbled forward into the hall. Cat flew to her feet and took a step, but the woman grabbed her arm and threw her into the wall.

Cat, in turn, tackled the woman as she tried to pass.

"Get off me!" The woman shouted. She was covered in blood.

Cat was seeing red. She grabbed the woman around by the hair and tried to bash her head against the wall.

Then Cat's world slowed in a way she wasn't used to. A dark shadow devoured her field of vision from behind as she felt herself fall backward.

Sinking.

Falling slowly.

The floor opened up, and she fell through it, descending into blackness.

Deep.

Into black water.

Her lungs began to tighten.

She couldn't breathe.

She flailed frantically for the surface, then suddenly she was there, gasping momentarily before a massive black wave crashed down on top of her, pushing her back under. She struggled blindly until her head broke the surface again.

"Noah!" she screamed. The sky overhead was black with clouds, and the icy coldness of the water gripped her muscles like iron. "Noah!" she cried again in desperation as another obsidian wave lifted her high, then pounded her into the surf.

She clawed at the sand, black grains slipping through her clenched fingers as the water tugged on her body.

The swelling wave ripped her from the shore, and she reached... for anything, for something to hold, something to *feel*, something to pull her out of the endless, drowning waves.

Like lightning, strong hands snatched her wrists, yanking her from the foaming claws of the ocean and throwing her onto the sand.

She panted heavily as she regained her breath, crawling up the beach away from the water.

"Aria!" Young Noah's voice called from beside her, but he wasn't there. "You should've run when I told you to."

Aria pulled her shaking knees up to her chest, looking around at the interior of the beach cave as she shivered in the cold. Black crabs skittered past her feet across black sand, climbing into holes in the charcoal walls. The dark ocean raged menacingly at the entrance.

"See? Isn't this cool?" Noah's voice echoed on the walls and ceiling, but still he wasn't visible.

Aria pushed as far as she could from the waves at the entrance, her back finding the cold, wet stone wall. "But now we're trapped," Aria replied weakly, her voice shaking. "There's nowhere to go from here."

"We'll go back," Noah responded simply. "The storms will stop, and the waves will stop, and the tide will leave, and we'll go back."

Aria shook her head. "The waves will not stop, the storm will not stop, and the tide will only grow." Even as she said the words, the waves lapped farther into her cave than they had before.

"Well, then, I guess we'll have to face the waves and run across the sand again."

At their mention, the waves pushed even further into the cave, the foam reaching for Aria's toes.

Aria curled even tighter. "They'll drown you."

"Aria, you can't stay in the cave forever. Mom will wonder where we went."

"Mom's dead."

The waves splashed against her legs, pulling at the sand underneath her. Aria yelped.

Noah was silent.

"Noah?" Aria's fear echoed off the walls. "Noah?" She tried again.

The ocean answered, filling the cave up to Aria's chest with black water.

Aria panicked, reaching for the walls and ceiling. "Noah! Mom! Someone!"

A wave raced through the cave entrance.

"Help!"

The wave smashed into Aria, and the black water consumed her, drowned her, pulled her down, fear and all.

26 SPLINTERS

"**C**hance! Let her go!"

Cat gasped herself back to reality. Three people were standing over her body. Cat launched to her feet and spun, stumbling into the wall as a wave of dizziness slammed into her brain.

"Whoa, whoa! It's all right," one of the women reached for Cat—a blonde woman in a blue dress who had been in Tiago de La Roca's room. Cat pushed herself backward down the hall.

"I think we're on the same team..." the woman offered, approaching Cat like she would a frightened animal.

Sunburst girl. Cat jumped up again and once more careened into the wall as she tried to turn down the hallway.

"You won't catch them," the woman said.

Cat shook off the dizziness and realized the ring and chain weren't in her pockets. She spun.

The woman in the black dress held the two pieces of jewelry in her blood-stained hands. "You want these?"

"Give them to me." Cat wobbled as another black wave shook her balance.

"Tell us why you wanted to kill Tiago de la Roca and why

you were chasing those two." The woman flicked her eyes down the hall to a door at the end.

"Give them to me, *please*," Cat pleaded this time. "I need them."

"Why?"

Another wave moved through Cat's frame, this time more stable. She sized up the three opponents. Cat let out a shaky breath. She would *not* lose her brother. "Just give them to me, and I'll go." Cat took a step toward the dark-haired woman.

She took a step back accordingly. "Why?"

"I need to trade them for my brother."

"To who?"

"*Please*, I don't have time," Cat took another step.

"Look!" the woman shouted. "June here saw you threaten Tiago de la Roca. We *all* saw you chase after Emry Rush. Now, we *also* would like information from De la Roca, and we *also* are chasing the girl. Let's just help each other out?"

Cat took a deep breath. "My brother and I were captured by some gang. I don't know who, but they wanted De la Roca dead, so they told me if I killed him and brought back his ring and that gold necklace, they'd let us both go."

The woman nodded. "Then why were you chasing Emry Rush?"

Cat shook her head. "I don't know who that is, but the girl had the sunburst symbol on her back."

The two women looked at each other. "What does that symbol mean to you?"

Cat shook her head again. "I don't know, but I need to find out."

"Obviously, it means something to you if you care to chase them for it."

"I think it has something to do with my dad. I don't know, please just give me—"

"It's the Seven Rays," the blonde woman interjected. "The same thing is on that gold necklace, Friday."

The woman in black held up the pendant and examined it.

The young man in the back remained quiet. He watched Cat carefully, but Cat could see his hands shaking and his jaw clenched as if he were in pain. Cat inched closer.

"What do you know about the Seven Rays?" The woman in black asked.

"Nothing!" Cat lunged like a viper strike, snatching the necklace from the woman's hand and just missing the ring from her other.

"Wow, you're fast," she commented, tightening her fist around the ring.

The young man seemed like he was about to vomit.

"I answered your questions, give me the ring," Cat snarled.

The woman looked at the others, then back at Cat, and shrugged. "Fine." She tossed the ring to Cat, who snatched it out of the air. "But we can help you if—"

Cat turned and sprinted for the end of the hallway, busting through the door and out onto an open-air staircase that wrapped up around the building. The colorfully glowing abyss of the City shone up from below. Cat leaned into the wall for a moment, letting the last of her dizziness fade, then began ascending the staircase, clutching the two pieces of gold in her hands. The wind howled threateningly as she approached the top where, turning at the last step, Cat looked out onto an empty landing pad.

Cat walked out toward the middle, the powerful gusts of wind whipping at her clothes in their best attempt to hurl her from the roof.

The wind, the waves… Cat shuddered; it was all the same.

When she reached the center of the landing pad, she turned and looked around at the view. Few buildings in the area reached such heights, but back toward the heart of Xi, more skyscrapers spiraled even further heavenward where the light-pollution masked all but the brightest stars.

Cat spun in another slow circle. Far off in one direction, the shadows of hills; in the other, the night ocean.

Cat dropped to her knees. She now asked the same question she had asked as she bent over Danio's dead body. *Why?*

Cat removed the tape from her wrists and pulled the black gloves off, throwing them into the wind.

Why, in a world where you could choose to be anything, would some choose to be monsters? Why would they go out of their way to cause so much pain for people—for her family, her brother? Why would they kill innocent children? Then again, she had become a killer herself, thrown into the whirlwind with the rest of them.

The wind rushed in response.

Cat dropped the gold ring and the chain on the concrete in front of her and then began tracing lines around the two items.

Shapeless lines.

Meaningless, as everything was. Meaning and reason had been carried away in the waves, and they were carried away in the wind again.

Sighing deeply, Cat slipped her thumb through the ring and placed the pendant around her neck. She stood and turned to return back inside.

The woman in black appeared at the top of the stairs, her aural dress rippling dramatically, blood smeared all over her skin.

Cat stayed where she was, and eventually the woman walked over toward her.

"Let us help you," she said over the sound of the wind as she stopped in front of Cat.

Why would I do that? Cat looked past her at the buildings in the distance.

The woman continued as if she could read Cat's thoughts. "We're looking for Emry Rush, the girl with the sunburst on her back. You said you wanted to know what it was, what it means, and what it has to do with your dad. We can help you find out."

Cat looked her up and down. The heels, the black dress, the bracelet on her wrist, the red lipstick, the dark hair. The blood splattered across everything.

"Why would you do that?" Cat voiced her question this time.

"Because we could use your help, too. You're fast. You're dangerous. And where we're going, we expect more trouble."

Cat turned over her shoulder and looked out at the faint, black ocean.

"Come with us," the woman offered.

"I can't... I need to get my brother back."

"We can help with that, too."

"No."

The woman shrugged. "Fine, come find us after you've got your brother."

Cat mused over the idea. "Where?"

"Didiza District, in the Neons. There's a small cafe called Murk's. I'll meet you there at noon tomorrow. Deal?"

Cat let the wind pass between them as she thought on the offer. Would these three help her do what her mother asked? They knew about the sunburst, at least.

The woman waited patiently.

Finally, Cat nodded.

"Good. My name is Friday, by the way."

"Cat."

"Cat," Friday repeated. "Good luck. I'll see you tomorrow." Friday turned and headed back for the stairs, folding her arms in the wind. Cat could see the line of mod marks and tattoos that traced down her spine.

"Friday!" Cat called out to her.

Friday stopped and looked back over her shoulder.

"The last people who tried to help me all got killed," Cat warned.

Friday shrugged. "That's fine, I should have died a thousand times already."

The wind rushed again. They had something in common.

CAT STOOD QUIETLY at the brink of the drop-off, many floors below and several blocks away from the scene of the party. Here in the Canopy Levels, Cat was home. The wind didn't whip like it did in the Cloud Levels, and the crowds that filled the Mid-Level streets and the Neons were seldom found in the Canopy's wide, clean walkways. From her lofty perch, Cat could look down into the bright and buzzing City. She watched the people and cars crawl like ants and beetles around the bridges and roads that connected the buildings at their lower floors.

So many lives.

So many lines that twisted and wound their way through the Labyrinth, sometimes running parallel to each other, sometimes crossing in perpendiculars, and sometimes violently clashing head-on.

Aria's line had collided with another, or maybe several others all at once, shattering itself into pieces from which Cat's line had emerged. Cat's line had then smashed into several more, cutting them short as they tried to intersect her path.

Her path to where?

The yellow from a large display screen advertisement reflected on Cat's iridescent hair and contemplating face. The yellow slowly became purple, then yellow again, and Cat continued to watch the nightlife below.

How she wished she could follow her own line backwards, retracing her steps along it as if it were a string she had pulled through a maze. She would walk back to where her line met again with that of her father. She would tell him not to do it. Not to make whatever mistake he was going to make that would destroy Aria's line in the future. She would tell him not to leave, not to abandon her, Noah, and Mom for his reckless ambition toward his work.

She would then continue backward, past where her own line began, and follow someone else's path back to the very beginning of the BioTechnical Interface. Back to the start of that reality-shattering technology that had brought the city of Xi from nothing to the virtual center of the world.

It doesn't do any good, she would tell the scientists and the businesspeople and the believers. *It's not worth it. The world doesn't advance like you think it will. Humanity becomes corrupt and ever-increasingly conceited, and we end up with a ridiculously confusing Capitol that, at its best, is a mind-bending mash of technology from the future and from centuries past.*

At its worst, it is a maze of demons. An effective Hell, where the souls of its inhabitants live and die by their cunning and, more importantly, their luck.

Cat would warn them if she could, and then Aria could have lived a regularly happy life, following a simpler line, and Cat would have never even come into existence.

"Are you all right?"

Cat turned away from the abyss of her own thoughts. A middle-aged woman in a fine, flowy outfit stood on the sidewalk near Cat.

"Sorry, you just looked kind of… forlorn… and it's past midnight." The lady offered a kind smile, and a man that Cat assumed was her husband stepped up beside her.

"Yeah, I'm fine. Just waiting for someone," Cat answered flatly.

The couple hesitated for a minute, clearly not convinced, and Cat searched for a second explanation.

In her mind's eye, Cat watched herself slice the horned man in half, stab a pin through Tiago's body, fire three rounds into the stomachs of the men who had captured her, drive the knife through the man's skull in Danio's house. "It's been a tough few days of work," she replied.

The metal device around Cat's ankle began to buzz against her skin. *They're close.*

"What do you do?" The woman asked.

Cat could hear the helicopter approaching, though she couldn't decipher from where, the humming echoed off the walls of the City. "I'm an..." *Assassin.* "A freelancer."

The woman tilted her head, not sure if she should pry deeper.

"It's complicated," Cat replied to the expression. The dropper's sound grew, and Cat realized it was coming from below, rising toward her spot.

"Well, if you want, you can come get a drink with us or something?"

"No, thank you," Cat put a hand on the railing behind her.

A quick realization of fear spread across the woman's face. "Please don't," she approached Cat slowly.

She thinks I'm going to jump.

"Come with us," the woman reached out a hand.

Cat sighed. "Sorry, but I really can't."

The old helicopter burst up from below the edge, the sudden wind and noise sending nearby pedestrians scurrying away.

The couple flinched, then watched in surprise as the dropper hovered over, its open door coming as close to the railing as possible. Cat climbed over the bars and, with a nimble leap, landed inside the aircraft. Turning over her shoulder, she gave a nod to the woman. What that nod meant, Cat wasn't sure. Meaning seemed something particularly evasive to her.

The helicopter leaned right and dropped back down into the City.

Skalla immediately reached for the pendant around Cat's neck. Cat knocked his hand away. "My brother first.".

Skalla shrugged and drew a finger across his throat as if to ask the question.

Cat nodded. *Tiago is dead.* Hopefully, they didn't bother to fact-check. Tiago de la Roca was very much still alive.

Skalla grinned and punched Sanza in the shoulder. His face

was still covered by the bandana, but his eyes showed that he didn't smile. Skalla leaned over and shouted something to him. Either Sanza didn't hear it, or he didn't care.

Smirking to himself, Skalla then produced the hood and threw it over Cat's head.

27 VENGEANCE

The helicopter door was thrown open, and Cat's hood was removed as the men led her out into the hangar. The blades slowed their spinning as a giant metal door closed loudly overhead.

Sanza approached from behind and quickly began to cuff Cat's hands. Cat reflexively pulled away but then submitted; they still had her brother and the device on her ankle.

Sanza clicked one of the shackles closed... but then not the other. "Shhh..." he whispered in her ear, pushing her wrists together so the restraints stayed in place as if they were locked. He then put a hand on her back and led her forward, heading for the hallway they had left through earlier that night.

Cat immediately began studying her surroundings—the barren concrete walls of the hall, paint peeling off the heavy metal doors, pipes in the ceiling.

Underground. The Subs.

Groups of people quickly emerged from the surrounding rooms and passages as the news of the mission spread through the complex. There were so many more people than Cat had originally assumed—not just men, but some women and children, too. Cat didn't understand. Who were these people?

They congratulated the cheering Skalla, who led the pack, then marveled and pointed at the gold pendant around Cat's neck. They all stepped aside as Sanza pushed her through; none seemed too eager to touch her. Apparently, the word of her violence was evidenced again in the proof of Tiago's death.

The crowd followed the new arrivals as they eventually found their way back to the round room, where Quatch sat again on his chair. People began to squeeze inside until Quatch ordered most of them back out.

The chamber's metal door closed with a bang, and Cat quickly took inventory of the situation.

Quatch, the blob man, shifted in his seat, the greedy delight apparent in his sweaty face as he looked hungrily at Cat's gold pendant. To his right, Cherry, the frightened girl, glanced up nervously from her kneeling spot on the floor. That's when Cat realized the faint brightness in her eyes that she had overlooked before. *She's installed.* On Quatch's other side was the same old robot.

Surrounding the room was a portion of the same men who had been there earlier, joking and grinning excitedly. They had just removed their archrival. Cat didn't pay attention to their words this time. Instead, she noted the number of weapons. She observed which men held them with fingers near the trigger and which men let them sit in holsters and belts. She looked at everyone's eyes, logging which ones watched her warily and which ones seemed faded by drinks or the hype of the recent victory. She looked at their legs, who kept their weight on the balls of their feet, and who stood on their heels. She looked at the various arrangements of tactical gear and clothing they wore. Some were protected by vests or metal plates, while others had left weak spots exposed. She observed the positioning of the men in the room, how they kept to the edges, and how Skalla and Sanza took their spots with the others. She noticed as Sanza made it evident that he was the one holding the controller for the device on her ankle.

Cat also noted the single light that hung from the ceiling, the only source of illumination in the otherwise sealed chamber.

Quatch quieted the group, and Cat let the waves grow inside her, calming her mind and heightening her senses. It occurred to her that in the robot's modest analysis of Cat's abilities, it had failed to stress the dire extremity of the explicit danger she posed to everyone in the room.

"Bring me the tokens," Quatch called, waving a hand at her.

"My brother, first," Cat answered, rehearsing in her mind the order in which she would move through the men.

Quatch waved to someone at the back of the room, and in moments, Kuno was brought in and placed beside his sister. He was cognizant. Cat turned toward him.

"I know," Kuno spoke before she could. "I heard the situation. The deal." He glared up at Quatch.

Cat nodded. Who was holding the controller for Kuno's device? She scanned her eyes discreetly but didn't see anyone with it in hand.

Sanza stepped forward quickly, taking the ring from Cat's thumb, slipping the chain off her neck, and giving both to Quatch.

Quatch, in turn, adorned himself with the pieces, admiring the gold.

Cat watched him patiently as the waves moved rhythmically through her chest. Whether Quatch decided to honor his promise or not didn't matter. Cat and Kuno would be leaving one way or another. She closed her eyes momentarily and mapped the room and her targets in her mind.

"Beautiful," Quatch admired. "How did Roca die?"

"Quickly," Cat lied. "Knife in the chest."

"Where'd you get the knife?" Someone asked.

"It was on the table in his room," Cat responded.

Some men chuckled at the statement.

"We kept our part of the deal. Now let us go," Cat commanded calmly.

"Yes..." Quatch coughed as he laughed, glancing up only briefly at Cat as he turned the pendant over in his hand.

Cat sighed. *Just let us go. It will be easier that way.*

The room quieted as everyone waited for Quatch's next order.

One... Cat began to count.

"Get them packaged for the cleaner, now." Quatch didn't even look at his captives as he gave the command.

Two...

"What? No!" Kuno protested. "She did what you asked!"

It doesn't matter. This was the plan all along. Cat released herself to the waves and took one last mental screenshot of her surroundings. One of the men stepped close to her.

Before he even knew what was happening, his gun was taken, and the lights were blasted out.

LESS THAN A MINUTE LATER, Cat opened the door to let the light in from the hallway. Nobody came running to the scene. If anything, the people outside had fled at the sound of gunshots.

Cat turned back to the room. Pools of blood grew from the men on the ground, and Kuno knelt in the middle, breathing in relief after the pain from his anklet had subsided. Cat walked over to where Quatch's body sat slouched in its chair. She pulled the controller for the shocking device out of his hand and tossed it to Sanza, who stood exactly where he had been, the expression on his face unchanged.

"Get these off us," Cat ordered.

With a quick motion of Sanza's fingers, the devices released themselves.

"And unlock these," Cat held up the handcuffs that dangled from one of her wrists.

Sanza grabbed the keys from the hands of a body nearby and unshackled the siblings' arms.

"Are you okay?" Cat asked Kuno as he stepped to his feet.

"Yeah," he responded. "You?"

Cat nodded. "Thank you," she added, looking at Sanza.

"I hate this place. I hate these people," he replied, the bandana still covering the lower half of his face. "You killed De la Roca, so I knew you could beat Quatch easily."

Cat didn't know what to say to that. The men had been in her path, and she had refused to turn.

"Your aptitude for violence is impressive," the robot suddenly spoke up from the corner. "Greater than I had anticipated."

"Kuno…" Cat looked at her brother and shook her head.

Kuno understood. He walked over to the robot and, with a single fist, smashed the droid's head in. It sparked feebly and collapsed.

"We can't have it telling people what happened," Cat explained, looking again at Sanza.

Sanza shrugged. "What about her?" he pointed to Cherry, who sat curled into a corner by Quatch's seat. Her eyes were wide with terror, her body quivering.

"Will you tell anyone about us?" Kuno asked.

Cherry shook her head, tears in her dimly glowing eyes.

Kuno nodded. "I think we're okay. You?" He looked at Sanza.

"Shoot me if you want. I don't care anymore," Sanza responded. "But I'm not going to tell… I'm never coming back here."

"Good enough for me," Cat decided and began picking through the bodies of the dead men.

"What are you looking for?" Kuno asked.

"Money," Cat answered, fishing a pair of money tiles out of someone's pocket and moving on to the next. "We can't use ours, remember?"

"Take some weapons, too, if you want," Sanza offered.

"No," Cat replied. "Everyone who has pulled a gun on me has gotten it turned on themselves… but I *will* take these back," she said, pulling the ring and the bloodied pendant off Quatch's body.

Cat worked her way around the room, stopping lastly at Skalla. She stared at the cruel man. Supposedly, he had been the one to find Cat and Kuno and steal them from the factory. *Deadly mistake.*

Skalla's body twitched, and his eyes fluttered open. Groaning, he reached for the gun that lay on the ground in front of him.

Cat stepped on his wrist and waited until he looked up at her. She then kicked the gun across the floor to Cherry, who flinched as the firearm slid to stop at her feet.

Skalla gargled in his blood and tried to speak, groaning incoherently. Cat didn't care what he had to say. She turned away from him. "Get us out of here." She looked at Sanza.

He nodded and turned out the door, and Cat and Kuno followed after.

As Sanza led the siblings toward a set of stairs, a loud gunshot echoed from the chamber behind them, followed by six more in rapid succession. Skalla's groaning could be heard no more.

"Cherry..." Sanza whispered the name to himself as he stopped at the exit, then turned to Cat and Kuno. "Follow the stairs up 'til you get to a room with a lot of pipes, then follow the green pipe. It'll take you to the Surface."

"Thank you," Kuno responded. "Where will you go?"

"Away," Sanza replied, his void eyes looking over the siblings for a final time. "Now, get out before the other guys climb out of their hiding spots and see the mess."

———

CAT STUMBLED along the Surface sidewalk with her brother beside her. Everything suddenly seemed to be catching up to her all at once. Her body had expended itself many times over, and she felt now that she might be paying the price.

Kuno caught her as her leg buckled. "You're not okay."

Cat shook her head. *What does that even mean anymore?* "Glitching, I think."

A large digital clock blinked on a building up ahead. 3:56 a.m. The streets of the Surface weren't completely empty, but they were quiet. The only other people out were the type who wore several layers of old coats and pushed carts full of all their scavenged belongings.

A small street cat stepped in front of the siblings as they walked, giving them a quick look before sprinting across the road to the other sidewalk.

A stray. Same as me, Cat thought.

From somewhere behind them, someone yelled the first drunken few lines of an old song—images of blood, terrified faces, and cracking bones flashed across Cat's mind. She jumped and almost collapsed. Kuno caught her again.

"Not okay," Cat said, a rogue shiver running down her spine. She looked up at the big clock ahead. 3:57 a.m. *That means... how many hours have passed since Mom died?* Cat tried to do the math, but a large wave rushed through her brain, tumbling her thoughts.

"We're going to buy some food," Kuno pointed down the street at a glowing sign that hung over a storefront. Cat could barely focus on it; her vision skipped a couple of times as if someone was cutting up the video of her reality.

"I'm not hungry," she objected, trying to regather her bearings.

Kuno turned with Cat into the small convenience store and immediately headed for the food. Cat drifted behind him and found herself looking at shelves of chocolate. She grabbed a bar and held it tight, then grabbed several more.

"We probably need more than chocolate," Kuno said, putting an arm around his sister, a small shopping basket in his hand.

Cat reached for a cinnamon roll as Kuno steered her into a different aisle, then walked to the drinks.

Cat pulled something off the shelf in front of her. *Beef jerky?* She gagged as it suddenly transformed into chunks of human flesh in her hands. She dropped the package and pulled herself sideways along the shelves. *Chips... sure?* She grabbed a couple of bags. *Shit, where's the chocolate?* She looked around the floor at her feet, but she couldn't remember dropping it. "Come on, focus," Cat shook herself, and her mental clarity returned for a moment, only to fade again as she wandered over toward a shelf of pliers and pocket knives. Cat could kill with each one.

"Cat," Kuno grabbed her again and handed her a drawstring bag.

"What?" Cat asked, looking inside.

"We don't have anything anymore. We need something to carry stuff."

"Mmm," Cat nodded and stumbled her way back to the section with the chocolate bars. *Which one?* She grabbed one in red packaging, placing it in the drawstring bag. *I'm going to die.* She dumped the whole container of chocolate bars into her bag. Most of them missed, scattering across the tile floor.

"Not okay," Cat repeated to herself as Kuno was suddenly in front of her again, grabbing her around the shoulder.

"That's fine, let's go," he said, pulling her toward the checkout counter.

The clerk looked up at the siblings, and his eyes went wide.

Kuno placed everything on the counter, and Cat caught her own reflection in a mirror by a small stand of sunglasses.

"Wow..." she reached out and touched the glass. Droplets of blood were sprayed across her face and arms, and her eyes were wide and dilated like some animal that was stalking its prey.

"Cat, I need one of those money tiles," Kuno put a hand out to his sister.

Cat reached into her pocket and pulled out a small handful. *How many did I take?*

Kuno grabbed one and tossed it to the clerk. "Just keep whatever is on there."

The clerk fumbled the tile before catching it on the counter, and Kuno swept all of the goods into their bags, then pulled his sister toward the exit.

The door dinged as it closed behind them, and then suddenly, Cat remembered.

"We need to get to... Murk's Cafe in Didiza."

"What?" Kuno turned to her.

"In the Neons." Cat pointed up at the levels above.

"Why?"

"I met someone earlier tonight who can help us. A woman... she knows about Dad's... she knows about this!" Cat grabbed the gold pendant and held it out from her neck.

"That's what you took from... the guy."

"Yeah," Cat nodded. "I didn't kill him. I lied."

"What do you mean the lady knows about this?" Kuno grabbed the pendant.

"It's Dad's symbol. This symbol was in his hideout on the wall."

Kuno thought about the information.

"The lady is also looking for the people with this symbol... and she said to meet at Murk's in Didiza District at noon."

Kuno nodded, grabbing Cat as she started to sink toward the ground. He led her farther along the sidewalk, then sat them both down on a secluded bench that faced a small, dead tree.

"Here, eat," Kuno instructed, handing Cat one of her chocolate bars. She ripped it open with shaking hands and began to eat.

"And you need water too," Kuno handed her a water bottle.

Cat took it gladly, and the siblings sat in silence, digging into their feast of convenience store food as the lights from the Neons above filtered down onto their tired frames, and the noises of the Surface at night drifted through the streets around them.

Slowly, Cat's mind began to clear, and the waves returned.

Soft and consistent, like they had been when she had first felt them. Waves on a quiet beach somewhere.

Poor Cat, she thought to herself. *I'm sorry that I'm not strong enough... and that I have to put you through this.*

She leaned her head on Kuno's shoulder, but, despite the exhaustion, Cat couldn't fall asleep. Cat could not let her guard down. She needed to protect Aria. She needed to protect Noah.

So, she stayed awake, watching the lights above and listening to the sounds and feeling the tiny waves as the night moved on.

28 INHERITANCE

Friday leaned against the wall outside the cafe, her dark cloak blending into the exterior of the building and the brim of her large hat dipping low to hide her eyes. Yellow lantern earrings glowed against her dark hair. She tapped her black boot against the wall.

Busy pedestrians hurried past her in either direction along the crowded Neons sidewalk, and a buzzing green sign flickered *Murk's* over her head.

She twisted the Rush bracelet around her wrist and looked at the old bank clock across the street.

12:19.

Friday frowned.

12:20.

With a huff, she pushed off the wall and melted into the flow of pedestrians—

"Friday."

Friday turned. "Cat."

Cat stood in Friday's spot on the wall, her hair and hands and black jumpsuit still stained with red from the night before. Tiago de la Roca's gold pendant hung around her neck.

Cat nodded to someone behind Friday. "This is my brother, Kuno."

Friday spun and looked Kuno up and down. He was every bit as menacing as his sister.

"Cat says you think you can help us," Kuno folded his arms across his chest. Tiago's gold ring sat on his finger.

"I can." Friday looked back and forth between the two siblings. "Do neither of you own any clean clothes?"

"Our apartment was blown up," Cat explained flatly. "With everything inside. Including our mom."

"I'm sorry," Friday responded.

"She was dead already."

"And then our car sank in the River," Kuno added. "So, no, we don't own anything."

"Nothing left to lose then," Friday looked around the street, then stepped past Kuno. "Come with me, we'll at least get you something to wear."

———

CHANCE RUBBED his eyes groggily as the sound of voices called him back to consciousness. He lay on his back on the couch, his legs dangling up over the arm and his pillow and blanket on the floor. He tilted his chin back and looked up; June sat on the couch cushion by his head, a spoon and bowl of cereal in her hands and her eyes fixed on the news that played on a screen on the opposite wall. Her hair had returned to its opalescent platinum.

"June," Chance greeted her, his voice sounded scratched.

"Good morning," she replied, smiling.

"What time is it?"

"A little after one. Friday is meeting our new friend."

"That girl?"

"Mhmm, apparently, we're both looking for the same thing, so Friday wants to team up."

"She likes to do that."

"What?"

"Team up with people. That's why I'm here," Chance groaned. "What are they saying on the news?"

"Enze Salazar is talking about Emry Rush and the XSJO."

"Oh shit," Chance pushed himself up. "Who is Enze Salazar?"

"He's the Seitech person in charge of their Advanced Science department. And I think he's the one who created the XSJO."

The man on the screen could have been an actor or a model. Enze Salazar was tall and well built, his dark hair was professionally cut but not too militaristic, and his complexion seemed a mixture of many different ancestries. He might have been from anywhere in the world, and his age was just as ambiguous. He wore a simple suit and an expression that was equal parts calm and focused as reporters took turns asking questions.

"Can you tell us what happened with Emry Rush at The Ocean last night?" someone asked from off-screen.

Enze was quiet for a minute as he thought about his response. "We believe the disappearance, and now reappearance, of Emry Rush is much more than just a kidnapping. We believe she has been taken by an extremely sophisticated criminal organization. What their ultimate aim is, we do not know. But we do know that they are confident enough in their power that they believe they can parade their hostage around without consequence. They are attempting to taunt the Rush family. To taunt Seitech. To taunt this City. This is not the first time we have seen actions like this. Xi has endured decades of violence and terror at the hands of gangs, cults, and corrupt politicians." Enze paused. "Enough. We have endured enough." Enze looked directly at the camera. "We will endure no more. We will find Emry Rush. We will bring her kidnappers to justice, and we will purge the City of every last man, woman, or machine who thinks they can terrorize the people of Xi."

June leaned forward in her seat. "I like this guy."

"What's your plan to fulfill these promises?" another reporter asked.

"As I speak, Xi-Sei Joint Operations teams are hunting down the criminals responsible for the kidnapping. These criminals may think that they are advanced; they might believe they hold the keys to secret technologies that the world has never seen before. I can assure you all, they are no match for the combined strength of Seitech and the people of Xi."

"Sounds like the detective was right about XSJO taking everything over," Chance said. "What *did* happen at the club last night?"

June muted the news broadcast and frowned. "You were pretty bad. You got poisoned or something. And that... thing you do, it really takes it out of you."

"Vent," Chance answered. "Vent is the name of the mod demon."

"The demon that takes over people's bodies for you?"

Chance looked at June.

"Friday told me," June explained. "About how you can switch into someone else's body. How you're not just using some kind of telekinetic power to subdue them, you're actually taking control." June moved closer to Chance. "But how? I still don't understand."

Chance shook his head. "I really don't know. Like I was saying yesterday."

"You don't remember," June grabbed Chance's chin and pulled his gaze into her own. The blue in her eyes sparkled like ocean waves, and her pupils dilated as if they were all-seeing. "You could do a lot, you know. With this kind of power."

Chance took a deep breath, and the waves in June's eyes began to wash through his head. He leaned into June's hands, and she held him up by the shoulders.

"Don't fall asleep on me," June whispered, smiling. "I'm just helping you think. Helping you remember."

The motion of June's power flowed through Chance's mind

like a gentle current, pulling him to and fro and rocking side to side as it navigated the sea of thoughts, searching for an answer in Chance's brain that he could never find on his own.

Diving through old memories, searching for a specific moment in his past.

Hunting.

Chance tensed. He felt Vent stir, waking from wherever he had been sleeping.

The foreign current in Chance's brain surged more powerfully, escalating to something near frantic when Vent rushed up and swallowed it whole.

For a split second, Chance registered a look of fear in June's eyes, then he was inside her head.

Her memories were so bright. Everything was shiny and colorful to the point of blinding. Chance couldn't make out a single scene as June's life flashed by. Then gunshots. Chance could see clearly. He was June, and she was cowering behind a bed in a disgusting bedroom. More gunshots, June covered her ears as she hid. A door slammed open, and there was Friday, blue mist pouring from her mouth, blood sprayed across her outstretched hand. "Come with me."

A mental *BANG* brought Chance back to the present.

June was lying back on the couch, hands over her eyes. "Ouch," she mumbled. "I did not like that, no thank you."

"Shit, sorry," Chance shook himself back to his senses. "I don't know what the hell just happened. Are you okay?"

June laughed softly. "I'm fine. That's what I get for digging around in places I shouldn't."

"What did you see, in my mind?" Chance asked.

"Nothing. What did you see in mine?"

"A lot of colors. Also, Friday rescuing you, I think?"

"Yeah, I was a guide—well, I had been a guide, but by the time Friday found me, I was more of a slave, honestly. But she got me out of there. You've seen what she is capable of."

"Yeah…" Chance rubbed his eyes. "What *is* a guide?"

"People from the upper levels sometimes want company when they do business in the Neons. Someone to not only get them from one location to another, but make introductions, negotiate, ease tensions…" June sat up and rolled her shoulders. "And when they get relaxed, they usually say more than they should, and there's always someone else willing to pay for that information."

"Sounds dangerous."

"You have no idea," June stood up. "Anyway, Friday's back."

The door swung open, and Friday strode into the room. Two people, the girl from The Ocean and a boy that Chance had never seen, followed behind her. Both carried shopping bags and stoic expressions.

"Chance, June, this is Cat and her brother, Kuno," Friday introduced the newcomers.

"Hi," June and Chance greeted the two siblings.

"Cat told me about what happened at the nightclub." Kuno scanned his eyes around the room. "Seems like we're all looking for—"

"—These people," Cat held out the gold pendant.

"The Seven Rays," June added.

"Cool…" Chance looked at the pair. Cat was about June's height, but looked more like an athlete. There was nothing soft about her. The tendons in her hands looked quick and decisive, and her eyes burned. The hardness of her figure, in combination with her black hair and black outfit, gave the impression of a panther or jaguar. A hunter.

The specks of blood on her neck and hands also contributed to that image, though it looked as if she had tried to clean most of it off.

Kuno looked to Chance like a Neons version of the Greek god Ares. He was well over Chance's height and probably weighed twice as much in pure muscle. Tattoos curled up from his wrists to his neck, and his eyes shone a silvery gray. His whole body was covered in patches of dirt and rust as if he had recently survived an explosion.

"Welcome to the team," Friday said to the both of them. "Bathroom is in the back here, if you guys want to use the shower and all that."

"Thanks," Kuno looked at his sister. "You can go first."

Cat nodded and navigated her way through the messy room and down the hall to the bathroom.

Chance was confused. Splattered with blood and rust and no clothes besides those they had just bought?

June slid over into Chance and offered Kuno her spot on the couch. He accepted graciously. Friday leaned against the opposite wall.

June looked back and forth between Friday and Kuno, then at Chance, then back at Kuno. "I have a lot of questions."

"Me too," Chance agreed.

"Tell us what you're doing," Friday looked at Kuno.

Kuno looked around the room at his new companions, then down at his dust-covered arms. What *was* he doing? He wasn't quite sure anymore; everything had cascaded from one situation to the next so quickly, like a tiny boat that gets picked up by the rapids and thrown over the waterfall. He exhaled deeply. "A few days ago, my sister and I were regular high school students."

"*High school?*" June was incredulous. "You both look so much older."

Kuno nodded. He felt older.

Slowly at first, he began laying out the timeline of events that had transpired over the last several days. How he and Cat had come home to find their mom and how she had given them a dying mission. How they had raced to their grandma's house and installed some powerful mods. He told them about how they had gotten thrown into the River Xi and shot at by an unseen group of attackers and then rescued by Danio and his father. He narrated the details of how he and Cat had woken up to find Danio murdered and then how he and Cat fought the murderers off. He skipped the part about changing identities and went right into their experience at the empty hideout, how Belzen the Prophet had shown up, attacked the siblings desperately, and then the roof exploded. Then, from there, how he and Cat had woken up in the underground compound, taken captive by some gang, and how Cat had been given another mission. After which, she returned, killed everyone in the throne room, and rescued him.

"When we got to the Surface, she told me she had met Friday and that you said you could help us. And... that's where we are now."

Cat came out into the room and took a seat beside Kuno.

"The people who attacked you at the River..." Friday cleared off a chair and took a seat. "What did they look like?"

"Demonic," Cat responded. "Sharp teeth, lots of bionic parts, discolored skin."

"That's one branch of the Disciples," June commented. "I sat by their leader in Tiago de la Roca's room. He has horns."

"I killed him," Cat added. "With Belzen's sword."

June looked at Cat.

"Divine Intervention," Cat muttered to herself.

Friday twirled a finger in her hair. "Well, the Seven Rays are definitely back, then."

"Or at least, someone wants everyone to believe they're back," June countered. "That's what the whole meeting with Tiago de la Roca was about. Everyone in there was somehow involved with the Seven Rays, but it seems like they were all following the Prophet Belzen, and no one had actually seen the Rays."

"What does that have to do with Emry?" Chance asked.

"And our dad?" Cat asked.

Friday put her fingers to her temples and closed her eyes for a moment. "The Seven Rays and Seitech were rivals back in the day—extremist developer cult versus all-powerful corporation. Kian Rush, Head of Seitech, died a few years back, and Orland Rush, his son, took over. Orland Rush started clearing out the corruption in Seitech, and in the City. The Seven Rays came back for whatever reason and teamed up with Tiago de la Roca and the 5-55—and probably other gangs—to retaliate against Orland Rush by kidnapping his daughter." Friday scrunched her face in thought as she began to pace. "But for what? Why kidnap her? Just for revenge?"

"Ransom?" June suggested.

"Leverage?" Kuno offered. "Tell Seitech to do something, or they'll kill her."

"Then why was she at The Ocean last night?" Friday questioned the room.

"And why was she shiny and gold and trying to kill me?" Chance added, then sat up. She had shown him a vision. The memories of her and the boy, the man in the gold mask on the roof, *White Sam's*, the secret door into the computer-filled hallway—

"She was modified," Friday thought out loud. "And that robot she was with…"

"The AI is called Caesar the Apostle," June interjected. "I think it's taken the place of Belzen."

"Uh…" Chance was making a realization.

"The Apostle…" Friday repeated.

"I think I know where Emry is," Chance spoke up. "What did you say Belzen looked like again?"

"Gold mask, flowy white robe," Kuno answered, recounting the details from their rooftop fight. "Glowing sword."

Chance pictured Belzen in Emry's vision, shrouded in the clouds. "Yeah… Belzen the Prophet took Emry. I saw it. When we were… connected."

Everyone stared at Chance.

"And… I know where she is."

June blinked.

"White Sam's," Chance continued. "Some laundromat. There's a secret hallway in the back."

"What do you mean, when you were connected?" Friday asked.

Chance shook his head. "I don't know. Me and Emry stared at each other in the club, I started seeing visions, and then she was grabbing my head, and Friday tackled her."

"Truly, what the fuck is going on?" Friday whispered to herself.

"Visions," Cat repeated, staring at the floor. "We're being guided."

The room was quiet for a moment.

"Guided? Or pulled into a trap?" June asked.

"What's the difference?" Cat narrowed her eyes at June.

"What my sister means," Kuno began to interpret, "is that we were led to our father's hideout by a message from the TV. A message from someone or something we don't know. Whether it was intended to guide us or to trap us didn't matter because there was no other choice but for us to follow." Kuno stood up. "So, I say we follow Chance's vision, who cares where it came from."

"I like the way you think, Kuno," Friday smiled. "The only path that ever existed is the one you choose."

"Sure," Kuno shrugged.

"Now," Friday continued. "You said you're looking for something and that the Disciples of the Seven Rays are looking for it, too." She looked at Cat and Kuno.

Kuno nodded.

"But you don't know what it is?" Friday asked.

"Right," Kuno answered.

"So... who is your dad?"

"Who are the Seven Rays?" Cat replied.

"I think..." June spoke up. "If we're all coming to the same conclusion... the answer to those questions might be the same."

Friday stared at the siblings, then began to nod slowly. "What did the Seer say? It's all connected?"

"Like wires," Chance confirmed.

Friday grabbed the Rush bracelet on her wrist. "We find Emry Rush, we find the truth about your dad."

29 DARK BLACK BLOOD

Midnight.

Friday glanced through her notifications, then checked on the locations of the others—all far away back at the apartment—one last time before disabling all connections and turning her attention to the darkness in front of her.

"Fear..." she addressed the emptiness, "blossoms like a fire."

Blue candle flames burst to life in a wide ring around the walls, casting dancing shadows across the space.

No one had discovered this place, not even the rats, in the years since she had last visited, and everything was right where she had left it: knives and swords and other slicing utensils leaning against the walls, tomes and books on black magic stacked in the corners, and a large shrine right in the center.

This was the in-between place. The crack in the City. The Shadow Shrine.

Friday untied her cloak and let it drop to the floor, studying the runes and marks and tattoos on her own skin in the dull light. Some of them had meaning, most did not.

The shrine before her was crafted from pieces of scrap metal, wooden crates, and bones. Whose bones, she didn't know. Some miserable soul had uncovered the abandoned space long before Friday and built the shrine to some deity of shadows.

The same deity Friday had once decided to become. The deity she had once embodied, and hid away. The deity she would awaken again.

"Fear..." Friday continued, lifting a stone knife from the shrine and holding it to her palm. "Cuts like a dagger." She sliced her palm, spraying blood across the shrine, then held her fist in the air, admiring how the red drops rolled down her skin.

"And fear," she lifted a skull from the shrine with her bloodied hand, "consumes the mind."

The shrine whirred and clicked as hidden machinery spun, and a large chest presented itself. She waved the chest open.

Inside was a full-body suit of dark translucent armor, stacked and arranged neatly, and on top sat a felt case with two black mod tiles.

Friday picked up the first tile, examined both sides, and stuck it to her skin.

She took a deep breath.

Install Void Step?

30 SPIN CYCLE

2:30 am.

A large spinning hologram clock flashed red and purple on the minute while a three-story-tall hologram woman danced underneath. At the other end of the street, a church bell tower chimed out the half-hour, the tolls echoing off the colorful displays and chrome, crisscrossing platforms of the Neons street.

Six Eyes District.

A flickering sign spanned the glowing entrance of the district's train station, where pedestrians ducked inside to dodge the cascading rainwater that fell from the levels above. A flashing police drone sliced through the misty air on its way to some distant emergency, and Chance followed it with his eyes until it disappeared around a corner.

"She's supposed to be here by now," Chance spoke to his phantom friend, looking down from his spot on the terrace at the storefront of a laundromat across the street. *White Sam's.*

"Is she?" the shadows answered.

"If she doesn't show, it might just be me and you, Vent."

"Who the fuck is Vent?"

Chance spun. Friday had materialized in the corner of his vision.

"We'll go after this next train leaves the station," she added, moving next to Chance on the terrace and looking down at the street below and at the platforms and bridges above. She wore no flowy robes or oversized hats this time, only tight braids, black body armor, and straps full of weapons and gadgets, including her vials of blue liquid. And something about her was different. The edges of her person seemed blurred, and her movements seemed clipped, as if she didn't walk from one place to another but simply existed, vanished, then rematerialized elsewhere. Almost as if she were flickering.

Though he already had the tight-fitting body armor from the shop, Friday had lent Chance several additional pieces of protective gear: a heavy tactical vest that shielded his chest and back, carbon fiber plates on his thighs and shoulders, and a pair of black metal gauntlets that covered his forearms and the backs of his hands. Chance shook the rainwater off his armor and watched Friday intently. Her dark eyes scanned over every person in the vicinity as if she could analyze them each at a glance, and her fingers tapped quietly on the terrace railing. Chance had been watching White Sam's for nearly an hour, waiting for any signs of activity, but no one had gone in or out of the laundromat since he had arrived in Six Eyes.

The ground vibrated slightly as the train in the nearby station began to pull away, and Friday clapped her hands together. "You ready to see how to make a real entrance, Chance?" Without waiting for an answer, she grabbed a cylindrical device off her thigh and held it over the edge of the railing.

"What's that?" Chance asked.

"Stage one." Friday twisted both ends of the device, and it began to glow. "Just step back a bit."

Chance backed away from Friday as she dropped the device onto the street below.

The cylinder popped quietly as it hit the ground, then the air exploded with an earth-shaking *BUZZ*, and every light on the block went dark.

"Holy shit, Friday." Chance dropped to a crouch, holding his hands by his ears as shouts and sounds of panic began to spread through the area.

Friday turned with a satisfied grin and held out a hand. "Welcome to the shadow realm."

———

THE LIGHTS in the alleyway blinked out, and June stood up from her spot against the wall. "Time to go."

Cat watched June warily. She wore a heavy outfit of platinum armor decorated in pearlescent snake scales, but she moved in complete silence as she walked across the ground.

Cat and Kuno, in only their black street clothes, followed her as she navigated over to an unmarked door, one that would lead them into the back of the block of buildings connected to the laundromat.

June pulled on the door handle. Locked.

"Kuno?" she stepped away.

Kuno grabbed the handle and ripped the door off its hinges, tossing it aside.

"Thank you," June led the way inside.

Cat paused at the entrance, giving her eyes a chance to adjust to the darkness. The waves in her biocode sped up her brain activity ever so slightly, making the world around her move just a hair slower than normal. Her ears couldn't discern any sounds coming from inside the building, though if there were any, they would be hard to notice over the sounds of the city all around. Taking a breath, she focused on the vibrations she could feel. Cold air drafting from the open door, the general hum of the city moving through the ground, Kuno's footsteps—unusually heavy, and June's footsteps—imperceptibly light.

June's blue eyes flashed in the dark as she beckoned the siblings inside. "Let's go."

Kuno followed first, leading Cat by the hand.

———

FRIDAY THREW OPEN the door of the laundromat and flickered inside, stopping between the rows of dark machines to examine the scene. Clothes spilled out of dryer doors and laundry bins and littered the floor. A single washing machine squeaked as it continued to spin. Friday vanished to shut it off, then reappeared at Chance's side. "People have been through here recently," she surveyed the room. "And I don't mean the people washing the shit stains out of their pants."

Chance followed as Friday vanished again and materialized at the back of the room in front of a large metal door. She looked down at the digital keypad and frowned.

"Locked?" Chance whispered.

"Hm," she placed a finger on the keypad, and her eyes glazed over momentarily. "Might as well not have been."

The door clicked several times as it unlocked.

"Is it really this easy?"

———

THE INSIDE of the building was a maze of hallways and doors, but June seemed to know where she was going as she led the siblings along.

"Something doesn't feel right," Kuno whispered over his shoulder to Cat.

She agreed, but nothing had felt right at all since that night in their apartment several days ago. "I don't think it matters at this point," Cat replied, though she could feel a heavy uneasiness sinking deeper into her chest as well as the swelling of her internal waves, rising to subdue the anxiety.

Some of the doors they passed opened up into empty rooms; others were locked solid, but June passed most of them by, pausing only occasionally to glance back at the siblings and ensure they were still following. The entire place was quiet; no sound came from anywhere, and especially not from June, who moved like a phantom in the darkness, as if she were some kind of shadowy wraith. Cat wouldn't have been surprised if June suddenly stepped through a wall; her presence seemed so hard to detect that it was almost non-existent. In contrast, the waves in Cat's mind continued to grow, suppressing the fear, slowing the world around her, and heightening her senses, readying her for danger.

Something was certainly wrong, but it did not matter. Good or bad, friend or foe, trail or trap, whatever awaited her and Kuno would take them closer to the truth.

"In here, I think."

Cat nearly ran into June, who had stopped outside a door that appeared just like any other. Cat yanked on the door handle, and it swung open, bright lights pouring out from the other side.

Fluorescent bulbs hung from the ceiling of another long hallway, wires strung along the metal walls.

"Definitely something," June whispered nervously. "That's for sure."

CHANCE STARED at the flickering entryway into the guts of the building.

"She's somewhere in there," Friday whispered. "The trail is here."

Chance took a deep breath. That frightening, exciting feeling he had experienced when Friday had taken them into the Subs was returning. Something inside Chance compelled him onward despite the inevitable danger waiting for him inside the shadows of this hidden lab.

"They must be waiting for us," Chance said almost silently.

"No doubt," Friday answered, her eyes fixed ahead. "But June and the kids are already inside, and now it's our turn." Friday pulled Tax Man off her hip and loaded the chamber. With her other hand, she drew a black knife from a sheath on her leg. She held both weapons up to the hallway.

Chance looked at Friday. For a second, he thought of his mom. Had she noticed he was gone? Between her drug-induced trips and Chance's hours at Mr. Bird's, it wasn't unusual for them to go a few days without much interaction.

"Does it look like what you saw?" Friday asked.

"Um—what?" Chance forced himself to be present.

"Does this look like what you saw?" Friday repeated.

"This is it." Wires hung from the walls and ceiling, and other hallways branched off the main corridor deeper inside. Chance had never met a mod developer before, but this was precisely the kind of place he imagined them working in. And the power was still on, which he assumed meant the lab or den or lair or whatever it was had been shielded from the surge of Friday's device.

A door opened at the far end of the lab hallway. Chance tensed.

Cat stepped out, followed by Kuno and then June.

"Fuck," Friday mumbled and lowered her weapons before flickering her way over toward the others.

"Neat trick," June remarked, licking her teeth.

"Cute outfit," Friday smirked, keeping her eyes on the hall. "Follow me."

This is it. We're getting to the end of the trail now, Vent spoke in Chance's brain, and a chill ran up his spine.

"Come back!" Visions of Emry in his nightmare flashed across Chance's mind. *I hope I'm not too late.*

Friday peeked around a corner and motioned everyone after

her into the new hallway. The lights flickered momentarily, and everyone froze.

Silence.

Friday moved the group onward.

A staticky noise hummed softly from one of the rooms up ahead. In and out of existence, Friday moved forward along the wall, then spun into the room.

There was nothing inside.

She waved the others in.

The room was empty except for several smashed computers and a large green hologram of a quadruple helix that flickered as it revolved.

Chance ran a hand through the hologram as Friday quickly inspected the computers. Most of the hard drives had either been torn out or smashed. She exited the room, and the others fell in line, returning to the hallway while Friday cleared the next room on her own.

Something like a metal bed sat upright in the middle. Arm and leg restraints hung loosely at the sides. Syringes, needles, claws, and a host of other vile medical tools on robotic arms reached from the ceiling over the bed. *A bad place.* Chance noticed Cat's fingers starting to twitch.

Chance passed around Cat and examined a large bottle of some sickening pink liquid that sat on a shelf in the corner. Friday grabbed his hand as he reached for it.

Don't. She shook her head and vanished again. Chance didn't need an explanation.

He shuddered as she looked around the rest of the tortuous operating room. This was something beyond the BTI, beyond mods—this was a room for live modifications. Bionics and human experiments. He closed his eyes, trying not to see what might have happened on the metal bed. Kuno placed a hand on his back. *Moving on.*

The next room was equally empty of people but full of glass

screens, all but one of which were shattered. The team stopped momentarily to watch the single live screen.

A solitary line of code ran across the black, only to delete itself and then rewrite itself again, over and over:

copy: success; export: success; <{soul:re: source: 'riley'; id: 0002;}>

"Something was here," Cat stepped toward a gap in the screens. Thousands of wires hung loosely over a pedestal on the ground, where something like an android might have once been housed.

"Nothing living," Friday stared at the spot, then motioned everyone onward.

The next room was at the end of the hall, and Friday approached it slowly, blue vial and black pistol back in her hands. A weak, sparking noise echoed from inside.

Carefully, Friday looked inside, then entered. Everyone followed.

The room was like the others, only larger. Screens covered the walls over long desks, and a metal bed with restraints similar to the first stood in one corner. On the wall opposite the entrance sat a shadowy throne. And, over the head of the empty seat, plastered golden in the wall, was a sunburst.

Chance turned slowly around the room; it appeared as if a bomb had gone off in the center. Scorch marks covered the floor and ceiling, wires frayed, and some sparked; the screens were all shattered and smashed, some lying on the floor.

Cat took a step into the middle of the room and then froze. The ground was soft under her feet.

She pulled her foot back.

The waves crashed.

There on the floor was the scorched, melted shape of a human, as if chunks of someone's skin had been melted from their bones and then solidified once again on the metal tiles.

Cat let out a shaky breath and took a step backward.

Wait.

She bent down to the ground. Sitting where the person's head might have been was a charred golden mask.

"Kuno," Cat called him over quietly, and the others came as well. "This is Belzen's," she explained, pointing to the metal mask. "I thought we killed him."

"I guess he survived long enough to make it here," Kuno examined the mess.

"They were definitely here. But now..." Friday looked from the torched remains to the sunburst on the wall, then pulled a blue vial from her assortment and held it between her teeth.

"Where did they go?" Kuno crouched down by his sister.

The lights at the far end of the hallway went out with a pop. Everyone turned.

The next set of lights went out, bringing the darkness closer down the hallway.

"Shit," Cat whispered, holding her hands in the air. Her fingers tingled, and her hair was beginning to float.

The next set of lights went out. Everyone backed away from the door, moving toward the throne.

"Static." Kuno placed a hand lightly on Cat's shoulder, and a small spark jumped the gap between them.

The last of the hall lights blinked out, sinking the passageway into complete blackness.

"I don't see anything," Chance whispered.

The static in the air began to increase.

"Fucking shit," Friday cursed and chomped the vial in her mouth, letting the blue liquid and the blood drip from her teeth. "Where are you?"

Then, the room lights went out.

"What's happening?" Chance's blood froze as he turned back to the others.

Cat looked at the glowing eyes of the team around her: Kuno, Friday, June, and Chance.

A wave pounded through her chest. She tried to back away. Something soft and heavy seemed to grip her muscles.

A fifth pair of eyes, bright and golden, shone from the throne.

Cat couldn't move. It took all her strength just to stay standing.

Kuno wanted to throw himself at the specter, but a warm, sleepy feeling cemented his legs to the ground.

Chance drilled his eyes on the golden-eyed ghost, calling on Vent to appear, but a peaceful wave washed through his mind and nearly sent him unconscious.

"Looking for me?" Emry looked the others up and down in the darkness.

Friday winked out of existence.

"You can't run away this time," Emry warned, arcs of electricity circling her shoulders.

"I don't plan to," Friday's voice answered from the darkness, angry and distorted.

In a flash of blue and a snap of white lightning, Emry's arms lashed out and snatched Friday by the throat.

Friday's frame buzzed, her eyes burned, neon blue smoke poured from her teeth as she seethed and twisted violently.

Emry tightened her grip.

Friday's hand shot up, her finger on the trigger of her pistol and the muzzle on Emry's temple.

Emry didn't react.

Slowly, Friday's arm dropped, her weapon clattering to the floor.

"As I expected," Emry smirked. "My turn."

The static in the room crescendoed, and white-hot arcs of plasma danced around the walls.

"No," was all Chance could manage to say before Emry's armored body lit up with blue electricity, her whole ivory-gold frame robed in lightning.

A violent blast.

Chance's world went white.

31 THE SNAKE AND THE SHADOW

hance sat on the bank of a wide river, watching as the sun set over the far side and a crane stepped through the shallows nearby.

"We're working on something."

Chance turned. A boy sat on the bank next to him, one with dark, messy hair and sunken eyes.

"What?" Chance asked.

"I said we're working on something."

"Who are you?" Chance slowly edged away from the boy.

"Riley," the boy responded, his eyes watching the river. "We're working on transferring souls."

Chance shook his head. "Where am I?"

"River Xi," Riley answered. "If we can transfer souls, copy them and upload them and download them just like biocode, we can live forever. It's immortality."

"Chance!"

Chance looked over his shoulder.

Another boy, one who seemed more familiar, was running toward him from behind. "Chance, wake the hell up!" he grabbed Chance by the collar and lifted him to his feet. "You can't keep letting this happen! I can only save you so many times!" He yelled in Chance's face.

"What?" Chance tried to back away, but the boy held on.

"It's me, Vent, now wake up!" Vent shoved him in the chest, and Chance stumbled backward, stepping into the water and falling into the river.

As soon as Chance hit the surface, he was back in reality.

He lay on his back on a metal operating table, a claw of medical tools descending toward him from above.

Someone in a white coat and mask was bent over his abdomen, attaching some kind of sensor to his stomach.

"Shit," Chance groaned, and the person flinched away.

They stared at each other for a moment, then Chance moved first, grabbing one of the arms of the medical claw—one with a syringe of pink fluid—and yanking it away as he jumped off the table.

The person yelled and reached for a panel of controls on the wall.

Chance tackled them to the ground before they could trigger any sort of alarm.

A rubber-gloved hand clamped onto his face, and Chance stabbed the syringe wildly into their neck, emptying the contents for good measure.

The doctor yelled and started to convulse.

Chance shoved them off and climbed to his feet, panting. Sweat dripped down his bare torso. "What the fuck?" He looked around the room. It was small but full of medical equipment and computers, similar to the abandoned one they had walked through.

Friday, he needed to find Friday. He reached for the door, then stopped. A scalpel lay on a tray by the metal bed. He snatched it and looked at the seizing doctor.

"No," he shook his head and opened the door to the hallway.

Wherever he was, it looked just like the secret lab they had just been in, but much less deserted. He could hear sounds coming from other nearby rooms, and the wires on the ceilings buzzed with energy.

Adrenaline pumped through his veins, his heart thundered, he tightened his grip on the scalpel.

The key to getting through... is speed. Friday's advice from several days prior echoed in his mind.

"Fuck this," he muttered and dashed out into the hall, peaking into the doors and windows of the nearest rooms.

The first was empty, just a few blank computers.

The second opened into a large room of humming servers.

The third—*Friday!* Chance lept inside, swinging the scalpel blindly into the near corner. Thankfully, no one was there. He slammed the door shut and dropped his medical weapon.

Friday was on a bed similar to the one Chance had been on, though the bed was vertical against the wall, and restraints held her upright.

"Friday, Friday!" Chance grabbed her face and tried to wake her up. "Shit!"

A panel of controls sat on the wall next to her. Chance pressed as many buttons as he could. Nothing happened.

"C'mon, wake up!" Chance tried to shake Friday awake.

Nothing.

Taking a deep breath, he stared at her closed eyes and willed Vent into existence. Chance's vision skipped, and, for an instant, he felt himself inside Friday's body against the wall. Friday convulsed, and Chance was thrown back into himself, stumbling backward to the door.

Friday gasped awake and lurched against her restraints. "What the hell is going on?"

Chance rushed back to her side. "I don't know, but I need you to get all of us out of here." He pulled at the metal restraints.

"Fuck—the door!" Friday yelled.

Chance turned.

The door was opening.

Chance dove across the room and slammed it closed. Whoever was on the other side pushed back.

"Shit!" Chance pressed with all his weight. "What do we do!"

"Gun!" Friday yelled, nodding at the desk in the room. Tax Man sat on the edge with several of her other gadgets.

Chance jumped across the room and grabbed the gun, spinning as the door was thrown open. A bronze robot stepped inside, examining the scene.

Chance pulled the trigger.

The robot's chest exploded, and it careened sideways.

Chance fired three more times, and the droid splintered into metal shards, collapsing back out into the hallway.

"Fuck," Chance's ears were ringing.

The lights in the lab suddenly turned red, and a blaring alarm began to sound.

Friday yelled something at Chance.

"What?"

"Give me the blue stuff!"

Chance looked back at the desk. Friday's vials of blue liquid were there. He grabbed one and brought it to Friday.

She opened her mouth.

Chance's hands were shaking. He quickly set down the gun, uncorked the vial, and emptied it into Friday's mouth.

She closed her eyes briefly, then opened them again, electric blue.

Blowing blue smoke through her teeth, she arched her back and shattered the restraints off her arms and legs.

"Holy shit," Chance stepped back.

Someone collapsed into the doorway, and Friday snatched her gun off the floor.

"June!" Chance shouted, helping her to her feet.

Friday lowered the weapon.

"I escaped," June shouted back over the alarm. "We need to get out of here!"

Friday grabbed the rest of her gear off the desk and moved to the doorway. "We're getting the kids first."

Without hesitation, Friday dashed across the hall and into the next room.

Chance and June followed close behind, and a river of bullets tore down the hallway immediately after them.

"Fuck, fuck, fuck," Chance threw the door to the new room shut.

Inside were both Cat and Kuno, restrained in the same way Friday had been. Two more scientists—biotech engineers or doctors or whoever—stood paralyzed with fear against the wall, and a black droid stood in the middle of the floor. Before anyone could speak, Friday grabbed the robot by the face and crushed its skull with one hand.

"Let them out," Friday commanded the scientists.

They immediately obeyed, typing commands into a terminal.

Cat and Kuno dropped to their feet, snapping back to consciousness as the restraints released them.

June began to speak. "We need—"

Cat launched across the room as a man in tactical gear kicked the door open. The man looked at Friday and froze for a moment too long. Before he could open fire, Cat wrenched the gun from his hands, and Friday shot a round through his helmet. Several more bullets came through the open doorway before Kuno slammed it close again, one ricocheting off of June's armor and another hitting one of the scientists in the chest.

"What the hell do we do now?" June looked at the others in the red light.

Cat aimed her stolen rifle at the door. "Open it."

"Give me that," Friday grabbed the gun out of Cat's hands. "*Now*, open it."

Before Kuno could open the door, the alarm stopped blaring, and the lights returned to a clean white color. The hallway went quiet on the other side.

Friday huffed more smoke through her nose.

Cat snatched the pistol from Friday's other hand. "Give me this then."

Chance looked at the doctors-scientist-engineer people. The one with the bullet in the chest was dead, slumped onto the floor.

June grabbed the other one by the face and pressed them against the wall. Immediately, they fell unconscious, and June let their body drop.

Kuno still had his hand on the door. "What's happened?"

"Open the door," Friday ordered.

"Are you sure?"

"Fucking open it."

Kuno opened the door.

Chance flinched.

Nothing happened.

Friday stepped out and stared down the hallway. Cat and Kuno followed after her, and June and Chance peaked out last.

For a moment, everyone was quiet.

"Who are you?" Friday asked.

"You're joking," Kuno gaped.

"I am Belzen, the Undying. Herald of the Gods of Xi. Prophet of the Seven Rays."

Belzen stood at the end of the hall. His armor was scorched and disjointed, as if it had been blasted apart and hastily put back together. His head sat crooked on his shoulders, and his eyes burned from behind his gold mask. With one hand, he held his long, glowing katana; with the other, he held himself up against the wall.

"We killed him already." Cat stared down her opponent.

"Not enough, apparently," Friday replied.

"It gets worse." Kuno grabbed Cat by the shoulder and turned her around.

At the other end of the hall stood Emry Rush, wearing the same crown and armor that she had been at the Ocean. The lights in the hall began to flicker, and Cat's hair began to float again.

"Join us," Belzen offered, motioning with his sword. "All of you. We do not need to be enemies."

"Not happening again." Friday pulled another blue vial from her stash and threw it at Belzen.

Belzen pushed off the wall and caught the vial with his free hand. "This is the source of your power now, is it?"

Friday aimed at the vial. "Something like that." She pulled the trigger.

Belzen's end of the hallway erupted in a screaming blue fireball, and the shockwave launched everyone back toward Emry.

Cat watched the blue flames approach as the force of the blast lifted her off her feet, and the mod waves flooded through her body. She twisted in the air, aiming her feet at Emry's chest.

Emry smiled, sidestepping Cat's kick and using her momentum to throw her into the far wall with the others.

Cat's world sped up in a sickening rush to real-time. Sizzling fireworks popped behind her eyes. The hallway—or what remained of it, blurred in and out of focus.

Cat quickly tried to orient herself.

Before she could stand, Emry was on top of her, face to face, golden eyes like two eclipses draining the power from her limbs. Emry's metal hands were around her neck, sparks dancing down her arms and between her fingers.

Cat feebly attempted to push Emry off.

Emry smiled wider.

FOR A MINUTE, Chance had entirely forgotten where he was. The moment Emry had appeared, the rest of the world faded away, just like it had in The Ocean. No more metal walls and buzzing lights, no more Friday or June or even Belzen. Just he and Emry, in infinite space.

Then, the world exploded around him.

He coughed and pushed up from his stomach. Blood dripped from his nose and mouth, and his eyes swam with tears. Frayed wires hung like vines from the ceiling, shedding sparks across the rubble-filled floor.

June lay propped up on one arm at Chance's side, her other hand on Kuno's face.

Kuno was unconscious.

Friday struggled to her at Chance's other side. "Push," she choked out.

"What?" Chance groaned back.

"Push on her," Friday grabbed Chance and lifted him to his knees.

Emry was directly in front of him, both hands on Cat's neck, small arcs of electricity jumping from the ceiling wires into Emry's armor.

Chance tried to summon Vent.

Nothing came.

"Do something!" Friday tried to climb to her feet.

Emry flicked her hand out, and a roaring bolt of lightning ripped into Friday's chest, smashing her back into the ground.

"Fuck," Chance focused all his attention on Emry. "Vent, we need you!"

Here, I'm here, Vent replied from Chance's head.

Then Vent was there, kneeling by Emry, but not as a shadowy phantom anymore. This time, Vent appeared as the boy Chance had seen in the vision by the River.

Vent placed a hand on Emry's shoulder, and Chance lurched with pain.

Suddenly, he was Vent, and then he was Emry. He felt the sheer power in Emry's modified figure, the electricity burning through his veins. He felt something else, too, a foreign being, another intelligence inside the same mind, fighting against him for control of Emry's body. It thrashed and flailed against him. He forced it out.

Chance realized his hands were still around Cat's neck. He released her, and she coughed and rolled to her stomach.

Then, someone grabbed Chance around the waist and yanked him back to reality. Kuno lifted him with one arm and Cat with the other and carried them both away, out of the maze of the lab, through the laundromat, and out into the street.

The world blurred in and out of focus.

Chance wasn't sure what was real and what was a vision anymore.

Everything spun and swirled together.

Kuno placed Chance on his feet, and he staggered into Friday.

And Emry?

Friday held the girl up, dazed but conscious.

It took Chance a moment to gather his thoughts, but Emry looked at him, and it was different. She was really seeing him this time, Emry herself, not the puppeteered version. Somehow, he—or maybe it had been Vent—had pushed out Emry's puppeteer and brought her back to herself.

Chance stared at her for a moment longer, then shook himself to his senses. June had made it out, too. She scanned the early morning street warily. The rain from earlier had all but ceased, and a heavy fog filled the air, refracting the neon lights of the district into a rainbow mist. Nervous pedestrians gathered nearby, and an emergency response drone floated over toward the group.

"Holy shit," Chance looked at Friday, at June, at the siblings, then back at Emry. "We did it." He wiped a pool of blood from his face. "I think."

Emry's breathing began to accelerate.

The noise of the street increased as the crowd around them grew. People were recognizing Emry, shouting and pointing.

"Where am I?" Emry whispered, turning her head left and right, trying to make sense of her surroundings.

The emergency drone chirped and began to scan Emry and her rescuers.

A shrieking arc of plasma split it in two.

The pieces of the drone clattered to the ground.

People screamed.

Chance reached for Emry; her eyes went wide with fear.

A second fiery plasma arc flashed before Chance's face, passing right through his outstretched arm.

His hand fell to the ground at Emry's feet. Only half his forearm remained, scorched at the point of separation.

Chance couldn't react.

He couldn't move at all.

Someone threw him backwards.

Belzen stumbled out of the laundromat. His armor and golden mask had melted into his skin, and smoke curled off his body. One arm was entirely missing. The other swung his sword erratically through the mist, slicing the air with searing lines of pure energy.

Kuno pulled Cat behind a parked car.

Friday and June dragged Emry out of the range of Belzen's attacks.

Chance lay on the ground in the middle, still unable to process what was happening.

Belzen looked at Chance and took a step forward.

"Belzen, that's quite enough."

A chrome robot strode over to Belzen's side. Belzen stopped swinging.

"I am Caesar, the Apostle," the android addressed the scattered group. "And before Belzen breaks everything, I suppose I owe each of you a bit of gratitude."

The street went quiet as the robot spoke.

"Aria, Noah," Caesar looked at Cat and Kuno. "The coordinates for your father's technology were embedded in the code of your mod packages this whole time. One scan, and we found it in seconds. When we're done with you here, we'll be off to retrieve it."

"Chance," Caesar looked at Chance on the ground. "We've been wondering what became of you. We thought you were merely a failed experiment. Turns out you are a monstrous mutation for which no one was prepared. You've opened a whole new line of research for us."

"Friday," Caesar looked at her with a soul-less expression. "You made this whole thing possible. You brought everyone right to us. It is unfortunate you won't be joining us again, but we're glad you could be of service to the Seven Rays one last time before you die."

"Are *you* going to kill me?" Friday fired back sarcastically.

Caesar ignored her comment and looked at June. "And June..." Caesar bowed deeply. "A performance worthy of the gods."

Friday smirked. "June is more capable than you could ever dream—"

June sunk the blade deep into Friday's side.

Friday choked.

She looked at June.

She looked at the dagger, buried up the hilt under her ribcage.

Her eyes went wide.

Her hands seized.

Her arms dropped. "What?"

"Glass Fang, the glitch blade," June smiled and shoved Friday to the ground. "You remember this, don't you?"

Friday's body quivered as she struggled to breathe against the glitching.

"What? You thought you would go grab *Void Step* and your Shadow Armor, and I wouldn't bring out my own old toys?" June snorted out a laugh at Friday, then turned to Caesar. "Gratitude, huh? How condescending. Bummed we had to end the show, I was having so MUCH FUN playing the part! Running around like real vigilantes, getting into danger and escaping with our lives! I mean, what a *ride*."

"I don't understand." Friday tried to calm her twitching muscles.

"Really?" June scoffed.

"I don't understand…"

June's smile snapped into a snarl, and she spun on Friday. "HOW? How the FUCK do you not understand yet, you cowardly, idiotic BITCH!" June's voice reverberated off the buildings. "Do you *still* not recognize me? All this, and you can't make *one guess* as to who I am?" A new, frenzied rage burned in June's eyes.

Friday clenched her jaw against the pain and stared back.

June covered her eyes with her hands and flashed a fake smile at Friday. A long, forked tongue flicked out between a row of fangs.

"The Snake," June spat. "The Deceiver. Neme. The mother-fucking Fifth Ray!"

Friday shook her head. "The Rays died. They all died."

June placed a hand on her chest, and her mouth fell open in mock disbelief. "I died? I *died*? God, you know absolutely NOTHING! You ran away when the fighting started, and you think I would've let myself get killed like the rest of them?!" June threw her hands up. "Who do you think gave Shift that fucking bracelet? An 'angel'? What level of stupid do you have to be to believe that? You were so fucking easy to fool, it was boring," June sighed and threw her eyes around the misty street.

"You—I saved you," Friday tried to comprehend. "I saved June."

June looked at Caesar. "Do we have time for this?"

Caesar didn't answer.

"Cat is barely half alive," June glanced at the siblings, then patted Emry on the head. "And Emry has no idea what is happening, so I guess we have some time."

"Who are you?" Emry whimpered.

June spun and squeezed her cheeks. "I'll get you out of here, don't worry. For now, just ***don't move.***" With the last two words, a wave of warmth washed through the street, and Emry's eyes rolled back in her head.

Friday groaned in pain.

"You didn't rescue me," June laughed as she turned and started to pace around Friday. "I was sent to find you. And once I did, it was so simple. You were so desperate for another chance at redemption. So desperate to prove to yourself that you were valuable, to prove to yourself that you could protect someone. To prove that you were needed. And all I had to do was act a little bit helpless and look a little bit like Raya," she smirked. "You didn't think anyone knew about *that*, did you?" June gazed up at the levels above, took a deep breath, and wiped a tear from her cheek.

"Why the fuck am I crying?" She laughed and shook her head. "Lots of emotions, I guess, finally coming out." She sighed and looked back at Friday. "You almost had me, you know. I really thought about it. Me and you, the last two survivors, starting over, being worshiped together. We could've run this whole city. But then I realized how fucking stupid you are, truly. I didn't need you at all. *No one* has *ever* needed you, Friday. Even among the Seven Rays, you were an afterthought. I'm almost embarrassed for you." She clapped her hands and laughed again, and more tears rolled down her cheeks. "God, it *does* feel good to tell the truth sometimes."

"June," Chance groaned.

June shot him a look of vile lust. "And *you?* How the hell you got into this mess, I have no idea, but boy, was that a stroke of luck for us, finding you with your little 'magical powers' that we gave you by *accident?!* Incredible. I can't believe it. A real twist of fate. Perhaps there really is something going on behind the scenes that even I don't understand." She shook her head and grinned with her fangs, then dropped to the ground and lowered her face an inch from Chance's.

"Makes me want to *devour* you, strangely." She licked her teeth. "Consume. I feel it now, the *lust* for someone's *blood*." Her eyes searched him hungrily. "I. Want." She tapped her fingernail on his face, then dug it into his skin, drawing a line of blood down between his eyebrows. Tears dripped from her own eyes, and she clenched her teeth and shot back to her feet. "I. Want. Everything." She licked the blood from her fingers and huffed through her nose, then glanced at Belzen. "Take his other limbs off."

Chance moaned, his face a river of tears and blood. "June, no."

Belzen dashed at Chance, lifting the plasma sword high over his head.

Chance closed his eyes.

Nothing happened.

He opened his eyes again.

Kuno stood over him, both hands on Belzen's sword arm.

"Glitch blade, huh?" Cat was crouched over Friday's body, weighing the knife in her hand. In a flash, she closed the distance to June and punched the dagger into the gap in June's armor plates. The blade slid in and out of her abdomen with a *shink-shink*, spraying blood as it exited.

June screamed and jumped backward, snatching Emry to her side. With a wave of her arm, the street exploded in a flash of searing white light. Cat lunged blindly but sliced only air.

"No!" Cat yelled and swung the knife again. "NO!"

She screamed and slashed wildly until her eyes recovered, but June and Emry had vanished.

The waves raged in her chest and pounded painfully in her head, "Fight me!"

She turned back to her brother. He had wrestled the sword from Belzen's grip and pointed the blade at the prophet's chest. Belzen swayed tiredly back and forth.

The violence inside Cat swirled into a typhoon, a furious hurricane of emotion.

Belzen turned what remained of his melted face in her direction. "The path—"

Cat shoved the knife up through his chin.

Then again, in his chest.

And again, in his neck.

She climbed onto his back and sunk the knife into the side of his face, and, using it as a lever, twisted his head all the way around and pulled his body to the ground.

Kuno yanked her off of the prophet.

The hunks of melted flesh and shards of scorched armor that made up Belzen's body started to crumble and flake away like ashes. Small tongues of fire began to lick their way out of the cracks in his patchwork skin, and soon, the whole of his corpse was up in flames.

Cat gazed into the burning remains of the man responsible for killing her mother, for ending Aria, and for bringing Cat into existence. He was gone, but nothing was fixed. Nothing was over yet. The anger boiled behind Cat's eyes. "What about the other one, the robot?" she asked, searching for Caesar.

Kuno lowered Belzen's sword and looked around the street. "He disappeared."

Cat threw the glitch blade on the ground and screamed at the street.

"Friday," Chance spat blood from his mouth and tried to drag himself to her. "Stay with us."

Friday's eyelids fluttered. "The glitch… is going to kill me. I need… a reset."

Chance reached his remaining arm out to Friday's trembling hand.

Cat got there first, kneeling on Friday's wrist. "Tell me who you are, right now."

Friday closed her eyes, and a pained smile played across her face. "If I live… I'll tell you everything. Deal?"

Cat planted her hands on either side of Friday's head. "Deal," she agreed, then collapsed sideways onto the road.

32 HUNTER AND PREY

"How is your head doing?"

"Fine," Cat lightly placed her fingers on the back of her head, feeling for anything unusual. Apparently, she had cracked her skull in the laboratory fight. Probably when Emry had slung her against the wall. But just like her ear with the bullet in the River and her abdomen with the knife on the roof, her body was able to heal itself surprisingly quickly.

"And your burns?"

"They don't hurt anymore," Cat touched the bandages around her neck.

"Well, you must have quite the regeneration mod," the nurse AI hummed and displayed an 8-bit smile.

Cat didn't respond. Part of her almost wished that her body wouldn't heal itself.

"How is she?" Kuno asked, looking past the nurse at the doors it had just come from.

"We are unsure," the nurse answered. "A full reset is not as easy as it sounds. If it is successful, we will have removed all of her modified biocode and reset her Interface to the current industry initial standard."

"You couldn't just remove the glitched stuff?" Kuno asked.

"Unfortunately, no. Whatever virus entered her code has corrupted everything and is actively working against our efforts to undo it."

"So, if it works, she'll have nothing?"

"Correct. It will be as if she is just getting installed for the first time." The droid paused and studied the siblings' faces. "However, if she has uncorrupted backups somewhere, she will be able to reinstall her modifications at her own pace as her body recovers."

"And what about the results of our code scans?" Cat asked.

"I will go check on those," the robot gave a small bow and exited back out the way it had come.

Kuno looked at Cat.

She stared blankly at the far wall of the waiting room.

He looked at Chance.

His stare was even further, his mind wandering somewhere very far away. He clutched the bandage where his right hand had been reattached to his arm.

"I'm sorry about that," Kuno said to him. "About your hand."

Chance forced a weak smile. "It's okay, it was such a clean cut, they said it was an easy fix." He blinked hard and let his gaze go distant again.

"I think it's my fault," Kuno went on. "I cut off Belzen's arm, and I guess he wanted revenge."

"Don't worry about it; I should be full strength in a few days, they said." He flexed his fingers carefully.

"What if the reset wipes Friday's memory, and she can't tell us anything anymore?" Cat spoke up, still looking at the wall as she changed the subject.

"I don't think it works like that," Kuno answered.

"It doesn't matter anyway," Cat went on. "Caesar said they found what we were supposed to find."

"If they found it in our code, then we're about to find it too," Kuno said.

"But we'll be too late."

Kuno sat quietly.

"We have nothing left," Cat continued.

"Not nothing," Kuno countered. "We have each other."

Cat was silent for a long time.

Kuno sighed.

Cat put her arms around her brother and buried her face in his shoulder.

Kuno wrapped his arms around his little sister.

The room was quiet for a long time again. A thin holoscreen played an old movie.

"Look at this," Chance finally spoke up from his chair. He nodded at the screen, and it blinked over to an article from some news site:

Orland Rush Offers Reward of 100 Million for Return of Daughter

"Cat," Kuno nudged her up.

"He's going to buy her back," Chance explained.

"Or turn the City into a war zone," Kuno said. "Anyone with a semi-decent mod stack will be after her now."

Chance rubbed his arm. Friday was right, the Rush family finally did offer a reward for Emry. But she had been entirely wrong about June. And Chance had been wrong about both of them. He frowned at the floor, then looked at Cat and Kuno. "Earlier, in the street, you asked Friday who she was," Chance began.

Cat looked up.

"How come you didn't ask me who *I* am?"

"Who are you?" Cat asked.

"Just," Chance shook his head. "Just a kid from the Surface, I think."

"Exactly," Cat put her head back on Kuno's shoulder.

"But that's not true," Kuno interjected. "Friday told us all about what it is you can do. And Caesar and June seemed to know something. That you were an experiment. That they gave you your abilities."

"I have no idea," Chance shook his head. "Maybe they were just making shit up." But he didn't believe that. They had to know something. Something about himself that he did not. "Did you know that June was..." he searched for the words.

"Evil? Lying?" Cat offered. "Obviously. But I knew she would take us closer to the truth."

"So, your dad is—or was—one of the Seven Rays, and June is one of the Seven Rays."

"And Friday," Cat added.

"You think?"

Cat looked up again. "How have you survived this long?"

"What she means," Kuno jumped in, "is that June said a lot of things that line up with what we know about the Seven Rays fighting each other. Plus, Friday has some pretty crazy mods."

"And why else would June have been hunting her?" Cat said.

"So, was June the one controlling Emry's body?" Chance asked.

Neither Cat nor Kuno answered.

"Or maybe more of the Seven Rays are out there," Chance pondered. "Guess we have some work left ahead of us.

Cat and Kuno looked at each other. "We?" Cat raised her eyebrows.

"I mean, we still need answers, and we still need to get Emry back."

"What you *need* to do is get your arm back, and then go home."

Chance pulled his bandaged arm to his chest. "Aren't you still a child?"

"Aren't you literally only alive because we saved your life?" Cat looked him up and down. "And you're what? Twenty?"

"Nineteen," Chance mumbled. "But hold on, *I* saved *your* life when Emry was mind-controlled and choking you to death!"

"I would've stopped Emry and that stupid robot days ago if

you and Friday and your psychopath friend hadn't attacked me in the club!"

"Emry would've ended your life on the spot!"

"I could end your life on *this* spot."

"Please," Kuno put his hands up. "Calm down, both of you. Yeah, *we* have some work to do." He looked at Cat. "But, no, we're not following any more psycho people from the Neons," He turned back to Chance.

Cat shot to her feet and grabbed Kuno's arm. "We have to leave."

Kuno stood and nodded.

"What's going on?" Chance tried to stand as well, but Kuno pushed him down.

"Someone's coming for us," Cat explained as she pulled a tiny black drawstring bag from her pocket.

"Who? And what's that?" Chance asked. "And how do you know people are coming?"

"I took it from Friday's things; I figured we might be followed." Cat opened the bag and watched the doorway. "You stay here for now; you'll be fine. Probably."

Chance sighed. "I'll come find you later, I guess?"

Just then, the door was thrust open, and a group that Chance recognized walked inside. Officer Trask, the giant man, led the way with his hand on his gun. Deputy Cairos and her associate Luca followed behind him, then KATO the droid, and finally Detective John-Mark himself, hands still in the pockets of his long, brown coat.

"Detective?" Chance would've been more surprised if the past several days hadn't numbed him to surprises.

John-Mark paid Chance no attention. "Aria Sharp," he said, looking at Cat. "You're wanted for murder, and attempted murder, and for inciting violence at The Ocean nightclub, and shoplifting and... a lot of other things."

"Scans are complete," the nurse AI announced, walking into the room from a side door and freezing at the sight of the police.

Cat looked at the tablet in the nurse's hand, then back at the detective. "Aria died," she frowned. "Sorry."

John-Mark gave her a bored expression and the faintest hint of a nod.

Cat emptied the contents of the bag into the air, and the entire waiting room was consumed in a suffocating cloud of black smoke.

Chance felt someone grab him, then Cat whispered in his ear. *"We* will find *you."*

When the smoke cleared, the siblings had vanished entirely.

33 GODS

The last remnants of sunlight faded into the blue shadows of the mountains, and the forest bugs crescendoed into the first movement of their nightly sonata. Far off to the East, the glowing spires of the city of Xi released the rising moon into the purple sky. The grounds of the secluded temple were quiet, aside from the softly shuffling feet of the old priest as he worked his way slowly around the ancient building, closing the window shutters and extinguishing the gold lanterns that hung around the exterior. Carved faces on the temple's wooden frieze—some animal, some human, some both—watched the priest silently as he worked. The priest looked at each of them in turn. The wooden eyes always seemed to follow his own, especially on summer nights.

A soft creaking sound echoed from the front of the temple grounds, and the priest came back around the building to find the front gate had swung open again. It had a tendency to do so on windier days. But on that night, the air was stagnant.

The priest looked around the interior of the temple's simple garden; none of the shadows stirred, and only the insects made noise. Tugging on his robe, he hobbled over to the front gate and locked it once more. Then, turning himself about, he shuffled back to the small temple, ascended the three steps at the entrance, and closed the doors behind himself.

An array of candles and small lanterns hung from the ceiling, illuminating the small interior with a warm glow. The old floor-boards groaned under the priest's feet as he reverently approached an ornately decorated shrine at the back wall.

With a small groan of his own, he carefully lowered himself to his knees and bowed before the shrine.

An unearthly wind circled the temple's interior, extinguishing all but one candle.

Slowly, the priest raised his head and passed his eyes around the room, watching the tendrils of smoke curl between the rafters in the ceiling and resting his attention on the single remaining flame.

The small light flickered as if the candle itself were afraid.

The bugs continued in their symphony outside.

"I heard that you had returned," the priest addressed the wavering candle flame.

It didn't respond.

"Why do you visit me on this night?" the priest asked, his voice level.

"Do you care to know how immortality tastes?" A woman's voice answered. It wasn't a loud voice, but powerful none-theless, each word sinking deep into the priest's mind.

The priest remained quiet, watching the small candle.

"You know why I have come. Will you try to stop me?" The invisible voice spoke again, almost playfully.

"What could I do against the powers of a *god?*" The priest replied, glancing briefly between the candle and the rest of the darkened room. No one was present.

"You mock because you are afraid."

"Afraid of what?"

"That we have found the truth."

"And what truth is that?"

"One which you have regarded so long as unknowable and

thereby shrouded in mysticism, the knowledge that humans may be their own god."

"You play with powers you do not understand."

"No, I'm afraid I am the only one who *does* understand, really," her voice hissed.

As the priest watched, the candle began to melt and twist, the flame sputtering before dying. The unearthly wind circled again, and the priest sensed the presence of a being behind him. Something of otherworldly power.

Still, the priest kept his eyes on the smoking candlestick.

The being drew closer from behind, and the priest watched from his peripherals as a slender hand reached past his head and grabbed a small golden box from the back of the shrine.

"You don't want to see the face of a deity?"

"You are nothing worthy of worship," the priest answered. "Why do you come for the Soul Re if you already have a body?"

"It's not for *me*," she laughed. "It's for the others. For now, their souls persist only in the code. In the hidden computers and secret networks of Xi. They are simply shades, spirits in the City. You know about spirits, right priest?" She sighed. "Even as ghosts, they are powerful beyond your comprehension, but they do not live, not yet."

"You cannot resurrect the dead. If you use the Soul Re, you will destroy them."

"Ugh, you mortal, blind HUMANS!"

The priest shrunk, still refusing to look.

She chuckled. "Your unbelief is of no matter to me. I have found what we were looking for, and in not many days, I will bring back the others in their true form," her voice rose and fell theatrically. "The Seven Rays will be reborn, and all of Xi will kneel before the unmatchable power of their gods."

"And which god am I kneeling before tonight?"

The priest could sense her smiling, drawing closer, her lips to his ear. "*Me?* I am whoever I want to be."

"Neme, your jealousy will only bring you suffering."

The woman laughed again, then with a loud blast of wind, the temple doors were thrown open, and the melted candle burst into flames, the tongues of fire quickly taking hold of the rafters in the ceiling.

The priest spun around, but the room was empty. The gold box from the shrine lay open at the doors, its contents stolen.

Sighing, the old priest pushed himself to his feet and swept a handful of other artifacts from the shrine into his hands. He shuffled his way out of the entrance and across the garden, and the ravenous fire devoured the wooden temple behind him.

END OF BOOK ONE